About th

Alexandra Turney grew up in Lon
at the University of Oxford. Her l
inspired her to move to Rome, wl. ... ...vu ....ve ~v..v. vile
works as an English teacher and freelance writer. *In Exile* is her first
novel.

@ALJTurney

IN EXILE

IN EXILE

ALEXANDRA TURNEY

Unbound Digital

This edition first published in 2019

Unbound

6th Floor Mutual House, 70 Conduit Street, London W1S 2GF

www.unbound.com

ISBN (eBook): 978-1-78965-007-5
ISBN (Paperback): 978-1-78965-006-8

Design by Mecob

Printed and bound in Great Britain by Clays Ltd, Elcograf S.p.A.

For my parents

Dear Reader,

The book you are holding came about in a rather different way to most others. It was funded directly by readers through a new website: Unbound.

Unbound is the creation of three writers. We started the company because we believed there had to be a better deal for both writers and readers. On the Unbound website, authors share the ideas for the books they want to write directly with readers. If enough of you support the book by pledging for it in advance, we produce a beautifully bound special subscribers' edition and distribute a regular edition and e-book wherever books are sold, in shops and online.

This new way of publishing is actually a very old idea (Samuel Johnson funded his dictionary this way). We're just using the internet to build each writer a network of patrons. Here, at the back of this book, you'll find the names of all the people who made it happen.

Publishing in this way means readers are no longer just passive consumers of the books they buy, and authors are free to write the books they really want. They get a much fairer return too – half the profits their books generate, rather than a tiny percentage of the cover price.

If you're not yet a subscriber, we hope that you'll want to join our publishing revolution and have your name listed in one of our books in the future. To get you started, here is a £5 discount on your first pledge. Just visit unbound.com, make your pledge and type TURNEY19 in the promo code box when you check out.

Thank you for your support,

Dan, Justin and John
Founders, Unbound

Super Patrons

Anonymous, in honour of Erica Buist
Kat A
Zoe Alderton
Hannah Bond
Tara Isabella Burton
Tom Chalmers
Pamela Cresci
Jeremy Dimmick
Alice Driver
Nicola Erskine-Tulloch
Carl Farrugia
Yvette Fautsch Macías
Steve Fenton
V.V. Glass
Barbara Herbin
Elizabeth Herbin
John Herbin
Helen Izard
Richard Jones
Joanna Kerry
Simon Lewis
Claire Montagu
Kwaku Osei-Afrifa
Valentina Pettoruto
Valeriano Pettoruto
Mark Phillips
Hannah Rome-Hall
Imogen Rome-Hall
Phoebe Rome-Hall
Suzanne Rome-Hall
Myra Sefton
Michael Switzer

Alexander Tessarolo
Dean Turney
Elizabeth Turney
Harry Turney
Pippa Turney
Kate & Mike Turney/Lakin
Giovanni Vergineo

Part I

The [Church] by no means declared the ancient gods to be myths, inventions of falsehood and error, as did the philosophers, but held them to be evil spirits, who, through the victory of Christ, had been hurled from the summit of their power, and now dragged along their miserable existences in the obscurity of dismantled temples or in enchanted groves, and by their diabolic arts, through lust and beauty, particularly through dancing and singing, lured to apostasy unsteadfast Christians who had lost their way in the forest...

—Heinrich Heine

I

A white pyramid. When he opened his eyes he could see nothing but bright stone, splitting the sky in two. For a while he lay in the grass, watching it through half-closed lids. The world was too bright, too real.

If he closed his eyes, he could almost pretend that he wasn't there, but his breaths betrayed him. He was alive. There was no smoke this time, no hand coming to grab him from the flames, but he was alive.

When the pain of his headache had softened a little, he tried to sit up so he could look around. Behind him, the grass was scattered with white tombstones. If he crawled towards them, he could reach the shade of the umbrella pines. Despite the early hour it was already hot. His naked skin was a deep gold, and he was in no danger of burning, yet the intensity of the sunlight was too much for him. He dragged himself into the shade, flinching at the sensation of the rough grass on his skin. He couldn't bear to touch anything. He had been away too long.

Later it would dawn on him how unfair it was, how desperately unfair that he should be awake again for no reason. The others were long dead, yet here he was again. Why him? Why now? Why here? Wherever *here* was...

As his eyes adjusted to the light, he was still too dazed to think clearly. He drew his knees up to his chest and tried to remember, but everything was blank. No, not blank – just dim and distant, as if glimpsed through a dark cloud. The past could not help or release him, so it was better not to dwell on it. The first thing was to find out where he was. In a sense it didn't really matter, but it would help him decide what to do next.

On his hands and knees among the tombstones – the columns, angels and mysterious doorways – he searched until he found a clue. At last, here were words he could read. Above the wildflowers, between the name of the dead and the date, there was the name of a city.

He remained crouched in front of the tombstone, whispering the city's name to himself. So he was here again. It had been a long time – four or five hundred years – but a century and a second were more or less the same to him.

The birdsong was joined by another sound, a distant roar that gradually grew louder. He saw the rider emerge from behind the pyramid in a haze of noise and shining metal, and then disappear at the cemetery wall. The world was so old, he thought, and yet so new. *As am I.*

He stood up, using one of the columns for support. He didn't know where to go, but he couldn't stay here, naked among the dead. Wherever he went, there was always someone who would try to lock him up, often for the most irrational reasons. If he got caught this time, he wasn't sure he had the energy to escape.

With the sun in his eyes, he took his first steps in the city that had once loved him.

II

The water had gone cold at least half an hour ago, but Grace didn't care. She lay immersed up to her neck, entranced by the image of the king being pulled down from the tree, and the women, his own mother among them, tearing his body apart while the god watched. Even as she turned the pages she felt as though her eyes were closed, dreaming the most extraordinary dream. She could hear the king's screams and see the women running, leaping, covered in blood and ivy. It was just like a dream, only much more beautiful.

It was actually her homework, one of the many books on Miss Seymour's lengthy summer reading list. Grace had mostly ignored the stack of books on her desk, but on a whim, attracted by the lively, dancing figures on the cover, she had picked up *The Bacchae*. Now she was so close to the end that she could not bear to put it down, even with the icy water and Barbara hammering on the door.

'You've been in there for ages.'

'I'll be out in a minute.'

The mother carried her son's head triumphantly through the streets of the city, thinking she had killed a lion. It was only when she looked at the blue sky that her mind cleared, and she realised what she'd done.

Horrible, thought Grace, eagerly turning the page. It was the most horrible thing she'd ever read. Then came the lamentation, the god returning to announce the family's exile, black-eyed and imperious. Grace was transfixed until the very end, when the perfunctory Chorus broke the spell.

> *Gods manifest themselves in many forms,*
> *Bring many matters to surprising ends;*
> *The things we thought would happen do not happen;*
> *The unexpected God makes possible:*
> *And that is what has happened here today.*

She sighed and flung the book over the side of the bath, where it fell on the floor beside her towel. It was too soon to make sense of it, to know what it meant or what the message was, but perhaps it wouldn't matter even if she never knew. She didn't really want to understand. The imagery was enough. It had given her a vision of another world, a vision of mystery and violence unlike anything she had ever known.

It was infinitely better than Shakespeare. Everything ought to be translated into modern English. If only everything could be simplified, she might stand a chance in her exams.

Barbara was knocking on the door again.

'One minute!'

'You said that fifteen minutes ago.'

'There's no clock in here. How am I supposed to know?'

Reluctantly, she dragged herself out of the bath and reached for her towel.

She stood naked in front of the mirror in her bedroom, counting mosquito bites. Fifteen. One for each year of her life. She ran her finger over one of the marks on her arm and remembered how she'd been driven mad by them when she first arrived. Now she accepted them almost as a fact of life.

Similarly, she could now regard her reflection with a level of detachment. She was no longer overwhelmed with self-loathing at the sight of her body. Her breasts, as Caroline had pointed out, were something of a consolation. The worst thing was to be utterly flat-chested, like Esther McDonald.

Grace turned to look at herself in profile, and then suddenly felt embarrassed. She got dressed and painted her nails with the red polish Caroline had stolen. She only ever painted her nails when she was bored, and she always did a bad job of it. As she waited for them to dry, she paced up and down her room and wondered what had become of the summer. Just like last year, she had made grand plans – draw every day, lose weight, have some kind of holiday romance – and they never happened.

The truth was that she was simply too lazy. All she did was lie in bed beside the electric fan, imagining what it would be like to be the kind of person who actually did things.

Perhaps her plans were too ambitious. When she felt like it, she would start with her room, which was messy even by her own standards. There were clothes strewn everywhere, half-finished drawings on the floor, records out of their sleeves, dying flowers turning their water green, and former crushes coming unstuck from the walls. She had cut them out and placed them there so lovingly, and now she couldn't even bear to look at them.

She lay in her unmade bed, still blowing on her nails out of habit, and picked up an old magazine she found tangled in the sheets. An article on the clothes boys hate failed to hold her attention, and she discarded the magazine with a sigh. After *The Bacchae*, it was just too banal.

Then she remembered the postcards. She had already practically committed them to memory, but she would read them again. Thinking of her friends' holidays always gave her a small pang of jealousy. It seemed that everyone she knew had left the city for the summer – it was the only sensible thing to do – and yet her mother had insisted on staying.

'You can amuse yourself here.'

This was patently untrue, as Grace had pointed out repeatedly. It was impossible to amuse oneself alone in such oppressive heat. Without her daily ritual of two-hour baths, she probably wouldn't have survived the summer at all.

But now, at last, it was nearly September. Caroline and Sara would be back soon. Grace picked up the first postcard; the front depicted a lake and mountains of conventional beauty, and the back was covered in dense handwriting. There was barely space for the address.

Dear Grace,

It's lovely here – so nice to escape, though there isn't an awful lot to do. I've mainly been reading and swimming. M says the water's meant to be particularly good for you or something. I've made a couple of friends, some Americans from one of the states beginning with 'O', but obviously it's not the same. I miss you and Caro lots, and also Charlie. It's hardly worth going on holiday if you have to leave your dog behind. The hotel has a sweet

7

cat, though if you try to talk to it in English it runs away. The food is dreadful. I hope you're well and not dying of heat. Wish you were here. M&D say no promises but maybe you can come with us next time. Wouldn't that be wonderful? I'm writing this on 1 August but bet I'll see you again before it arrives, typical. No more space so lots of love, Sara

The other postcard was a picture of one of the Buckingham Palace guards, and was comparatively concise.

Darling Grace,

England is heaven as always. Wish I could stay here forever and ever and have you with me. Is it beastly there? I bet it is. Stuff yourself with ice cream for me.

xxxxxxxxx

P.S. Just finished The Bacchae. *Have you read it yet? I swear the Greeks were just as bad as the Romans.*

Grace re-read the postscript several times; it made her impatient for Caroline's return. She needed to discuss the play with someone, even if they didn't feel as strongly about it as she did.

She opened the shutters, upsetting some pigeons, and was momentarily blinded by the sunlight. It would be horrendously hot outside, maybe forty degrees, but she suddenly had the mad desire to go for a walk. Why not? There were hours to kill before supper, and being out in the heat might transport her back to that feverish world of gods and maenads. Everything in the play happened outside. That was where life took place, after all – if you stayed indoors, nothing ever changed.

The lift was out of order, as usual, so she took the stairs, listening to the familiar sounds of TVs, children and pianos. On the ground floor Grace held the front door open for an old lady with a face like a raisin, sinking to the ground under the weight of her bags of shopping. The old lady muttered something that was too long to be a simple expression of thanks, but Grace was used to not understanding most of what was said to her. When the door – twice her height and as thick and impenetrable as the entrance to a medieval fortress – had shut behind her, she put on her sunglasses and stepped out into the fierce light.

Most intelligent beings stayed inside at this time of day. There were only idiotic tourists, fanning themselves with maps in the church shade, and seagulls screaming over the ruins.

'Stupid, stupid, stupid,' Grace muttered to herself as she crossed the cobblestones, skin prickling with the heat. Her family lay asleep in shuttered darkness in the cool breeze of the fans, while she walked in the white heat of two o'clock. It made no sense. She walked from boredom, that was all. She had spent all summer hiding in her bedroom, and now she had a restless, irrational urge to walk.

She gave the columns she loved only a momentary glance – they were too white, too bright to look at now – and then lingered at the edge of the square, shielding her eyes from the dazzling wedding cake of a monument and waiting for a break in the traffic.

They were always in such a hurry, these mad, lawless drivers. Despite the rosaries dangling from their mirrors, if Christ himself attempted to cross the road, they probably wouldn't stop for him. But at last a nun appeared, and with a sandalled foot on the faded white lines brought the flow of traffic to a halt. Grace followed her, and reflected that the art of road-crossing was only a matter of confidence. Caroline never had any problems, after all.

On the other side she slipped into the divine shade of a narrow street. She had set out with some vague notions of destinations – the path by the river, or any square that had a bench and a fountain – but now all she wanted was the shade of the backstreets. These were the streets where she always got lost, thwarted by dead ends. The mental compass that usually served her so well inevitably broke down, so east became west and churches moved mysteriously.

She stopped to drink from a fountain and then, because there was no one to see her, splashed water down the front of her dress. She already felt disgustingly sweaty. She walked on, past shrines and barred windows, through alleys smelling of rotten fruit and something even more unpleasant, beneath flags and herbs on precarious window ledges. A tiny emerald lizard sparkled on the pavement and then vanished into a crack. On a nearby cobblestone Grace spotted a small golden coin and impulsively picked it up. It was almost value-less, but it felt light and cool between her fingers.

Standing in these lovely, lonely streets it was almost possible to believe that you were alone in the city. Grace traced the carved initials on a church wall with her finger and wondered if H. N. had ever felt like her. Probably not. There were moments when she felt utterly unique, the first, the only one to walk down a particular street. Only the street name spoiled the illusion.

And the man. At first she didn't see him, sitting so still and half obscured in shadow. He might have been a statue, slumped beside his pedestal. He wore a tattered black shirt, and his feet were bare. Grace continued walk-ing, watching him out of the corner of her eye. The homeless always made her nervous. If you had nothing, she reasoned, you had nothing to lose. She had visions of men attacking her, demanding money. This one didn't look desperate, but he was young, and for some reason that made her feel more nervous and guilty than usual. She took the golden coin from her pocket and dropped it at his feet.

'You can keep your money.'

Grace turned around, startled. He had rejected her money and addressed her in English. This had never happened before.

'Don't you need it?'

'No.'

They stared at each other. Grace saw that his brown eyes were almost black, and felt a sudden chill come over her. She usually found dark eyes beautiful, but his were hollow, shallow – she didn't know what, but something wasn't right. His golden skin had a kind of pal-lor, and his lips were pale and dry. He must be ill. An alcoholic, she guessed wildly.

'Don't you need anything?' Grace asked, preparing to make her escape as soon as she had done her charitable duty.

'I want lots of things,' said the man in his peculiar, lilting voice. 'But I have everything I need.'

'Sorry for bothering you.'

Grace knew that she could walk away, but something in the man's stare held her. It was not the carnal stare of the men on buses, but rather a penetrating gaze that looked right through her body and saw what lay beyond. She could not remember ever having felt so afraid and uncomfortable in the presence of a man, yet she could not leave – not while so many questions threatened to spill from her lips.

'Where are you from?'

'Everywhere,' he said, as if the answer were obvious.

'Where do you live?'

'Nowhere.'

'What do you mean?'

'You wouldn't believe me.'

Grace blushed, suddenly aware that her conversation with the stranger had gone on for too long. She turned to leave.

'Wait.'

He was not smiling – there was such a hard, mirthless quality about his lips that a smile was unimaginable – but a certain dark amusement flickered in his eyes.

'Watch.'

Grace watched. The man ran his finger over a crack in the pavement. A second later, a white liquid bubbled up from the gap and streamed across the stone where the rejected coin lay.

'What is it?' asked Grace, eyes widening in wonder.

'Milk.'

'I don't believe you.'

'If you don't believe me, maybe your tongue will convince you.'

Grace made a grimace of disgust. But even as the street ran with rivulets of milk, the stranger was performing another miracle. He brushed an idle fingertip over the wall that he leaned against, and then held up his finger for Grace to see. The nail glistened with a sticky, golden substance.

'Ugh,' said Grace. 'Before you suggest, I'm not tasting it.'

'That's a pity,' said the man, sucking his finger. 'Honey is delicious. And perfectly natural.'

You're un*natural.* Grace shuddered and quickly walked away before he could trick her again. As she turned the corner she thought she heard him laugh, but it was such a strange and savage sound that it was more likely a dog's bark.

III

Grace was silent at supper. She twirled her fork round and round, watching the pasta slide off. Mauro was giving her a disapproving look from the other side of the table – he hated to see food go to waste – but no one else seemed to have noticed her lack of appetite. Henry was rolling a toy car back and forth across the table, while Barbara and their mother were having one of their usual differences of opinion over something that didn't really matter anyway. Olive oil was high in calories, or it wasn't, but at any rate it was good for you, everyone knew that, even if pasta tasted better with butter, though of course Mauro would never agree. They could keep at it for hours.

Tonight everything had a faint air of unreality. In the candlelight Mauro looked more grotesque than usual, and Grace could almost picture him as a satyr. The bulbous nose, the beard, the narrow, glinting eyes hinting at indescribable lecheries... perhaps that was what had attracted her mother in the first place.

God, what a repulsive thought. Grace raised her eyes to the ceiling and imagined vines, vast tendrils creeping up the walls...

She felt paws scrabbling at her legs – Pippin the dachshund, begging for leftovers. When she was sure no one was looking, she dropped some pasta on the floor. It was gone in a second; Pippin wolfed it down and then licked her toes. Grace giggled and tried to kick him away, but once he got a taste he was unstoppable.

'Are you feeding him again?' asked Grace's mother. 'You really shouldn't.'

'It just fell off my fork.'

'We might go to the sea on Saturday,' said Mauro. 'That would be nice, no? All five of us.'

'Hurrah!' Henry immediately lost interest in the car. 'The beach!'

'I'd rather not,' said Grace.

'Why not?' asked her mother. 'You've been complaining all summer about how you want to get away.'

'Beaches are boring. Anyway, Caroline's back on Saturday. It's our great reunion.'

'Caroline can wait,' said Barbara.

'I can't.'

'Caroline could come with us,' said Mauro.

Grace thought that the sight of her stepfather in swimming trunks was one she'd rather not inflict on her friends. But her mother was always telling her off for being rude to Mauro, and as she could think of nothing polite to say, she merely shrugged. While the others discussed details of the beach trip, Grace imagined her meeting with Caroline, and how she would describe the encounter that had haunted her all day.

He's got black eyes.

He looks savage, evil, ugly.

No, not ugly. Handsome but in a horrible way.

Hair like black grapes.

He stares and stares and never smiles.

He's like something from another world.

Grace grasped for other similes and then gave up. She probably wouldn't tell her, anyway. Caroline would only laugh, as she laughed at everything.

Forgetting Caroline and her laughter, Grace touched a crack in the dining table and remembered the milk and honey. The magic was only really dawning on her now, hours later in the candlelight. It was just like something out of a book.

Then the thought struck her, and she couldn't wait another moment. Ignoring Mauro's protests, she left her pasta to go even colder and hurried to her room.

In her excitement it took her a few minutes to find the right page, but at last she found the lines:

> *The earth flows with milk, flows with wine,*
> *Flows with the nectar of bees.*

In stark black and white they seemed like proof. Proof of what? It was absurd to make a connection between a homeless stranger and a god, but then, she had witnessed something without a rational explanation.

It kept her awake that night – the image of the honey running down the wall, and the stranger's cruel lips. She hadn't seen his teeth, but she was sure they were sharp and white and savage. Like an animal, like a god. She dreamed that her room was overgrown with ivy, and someone grinned at her in the dark.

She awoke in the grey light of dawn, with the pigeons cooing in the courtyard, and felt the familiar ache in her stomach. In her dazed, half-asleep state she told herself that everything was hormonal. The milk, honey and ivy were all part of a mad dream, and they would pass in time.

Despite her half-hearted plan to forget him, Grace returned to the street where they'd met. She told herself that it was only because she happened to be in the neighbourhood; what she really wanted to do was get some ice cream from the shop on the main road. Why not slip into the side street for a moment, just to see? But there were no signs of him, or the coin. Perhaps he'd taken it after all. She searched the face of every man she passed in the Ghetto, and the statues too, just in case he'd been transformed. Even on ordinary trips to the neighbourhood shops with her mother, she found herself hoping that he would emerge from one of the aisles and give her a look, just one look, to prove she had not dreamed it after all.

Those evil eyes, swallowed up by the city. She would never see him again, and it was probably just as well. A silly, childish fantasy, and besides, dreaming of him was a distraction from the pile of untouched books on her desk. She had not yet found inspiration for her essay on *The Bacchae*.

On Saturday her family went to the beach without her, and Grace had her long-awaited reunion with Caroline.

'Oh, I missed you so much,' said Caroline, hugging her.

'I bet you didn't really. You were probably having too much fun in London.'

'It was fun, but it would have been infinitely better with you. Did you get my postcard?'

'Yes. I got one from Sara too.'

'She's not back till next week, is she? I bet she's already done all her homework. It's sickening.' Caroline sighed and collapsed on Grace's bed, where Pippin was dozing. 'I haven't even started thinking about mine. I read *The Bacchae*, but then I looked at the essay Miss Seymour gave us. Something about Euripides' intentions. Honestly, I haven't the faintest idea. It's not like it matters, anyway.'

'What did you think of the play?' asked Grace, trying not to sound too interested.

'Mad and unbelievable – not like life at all. Anyway, please let's not talk about school. I want to hear all about you.'

Grace abandoned all hopes of a literary discussion, and became even more resolved not to tell Caroline about the stranger.

Grace and Caroline told each other nearly everything. Their very first conversation had been a mutual confession of sorts. On her first day at school, desperately homesick for England, Grace had noticed a girl resembling a choirboy, with bright blue eyes and blonde hair, which, like her skirt, was deemed unacceptably short. For a few weeks Grace had not dared to talk to her, and she had allied herself with the quiet, bookish girls instead, believing that these were the sorts of friends her mother would approve of. But one day there had been nowhere else to sit at lunch, and they were forced to share a bench. Grace panicked – she could think of nothing to talk about. But then Caroline sighed deeply and exclaimed, 'God, don't you hate it here?'

Their friendship was born out of a mutual hatred of their school and adopted country, but over the terms it blossomed into something deeper. They were not like the other girls, with their week-long friendships, bitching and backstabbing; they were far above all that. Theirs was a relationship that had excluded everyone else, until the arrival of Sara a year ago.

'You ought to spend more time with Sara,' Grace's mother had said. 'To be just with Caroline all the time… well, it isn't healthy.'

Grace thought of her mother's words as she looked at Caroline, lying in her bed and carefully defacing a magazine with a biro. Her mother had forgotten what it was like to be fifteen. Without Caroline, she'd probably have killed herself, and besides, it was ridiculous to talk of friendships being 'healthy' or otherwise.

Caroline soon lost interest in the magazine and started to rummage through Grace's record collection.

'You've got all the same records as Jeremy,' said Caroline, 'only his don't look like they've been used as Frisbees.'

'Did you see Jeremy?' asked Grace.

'Yes, a few times. We had dinner with his family and went to the theatre and – oh, let's listen to this.'

'It's horribly scratched.'

'I don't care. Anyway, Jeremy is as beautiful as ever, but I think I'm becoming disillusioned.'

Jeremy was the teenage son of a friend of Caroline's mother, and for the past few years he had been the highlight of her summers in London.

'Don't say that, Caro. He's meant to be the love of your life, remember?'

'Maybe when he's older. He's practically a child.'

'The same age as you.'

'But it's different with boys. I'm not sure they even realise girls exist. What a waste.'

The record skipped again, ruining another chorus. Grace lifted the needle and tried to find a record that wasn't damaged. Caroline, staring wistfully at the ceiling, seemed oblivious to the change.

'I've been thinking about it a lot recently. It *is* a terrible waste – all the energy of loving someone who barely notices you. Just think of all the crushes, all the unrequited love in the world, throughout history. It all amounts to nothing. Someone ought to do something about it.'

'Like what?'

'I don't know. I'm not being entirely serious, but you must know what I mean. Remember when you liked *him*.' Caroline touched the ripped face of one of Grace's former idols, taped to a chest of drawers.

'I never liked him all that much. I was only thirteen.'

'You liked him enough to cut him out of a magazine at any rate, and there are plenty of girls in the world who are obsessed. It's mad. The time and energy of all that pointless devotion.'

'Don't depress yourself by thinking about it.'

'Well, better to think about *it* than *him*. I'm very nearly over him.'

'Just wait till next summer.'

'I can't possibly think that far ahead. Anyway, enough about Jeremy. Are you in love yet?'

'No.'

'No tall, dark, handsome strangers?'

'Only strangers. I got groped on a bus again. He pretended it was accidental – pushed against me in the crowd – but it absolutely wasn't.'

'Ugh. Honestly, this country...'

For a moment Grace was tempted to tell Caroline about the man she had met in the street, but then the record ended. In the silence that followed she felt too self-conscious to share her secret. It would sound absurd, like something she'd made up to compensate for the boredom of her summer and her lack of a Jeremy.

Instead they talked of other girls at school and their shared dread of seeing them again in less than two weeks, until Caroline finally dragged herself off the bed and announced that she had to go.

'I'll see you tomorrow,' said Grace.

'And the day after.'

'And the day after that.'

'And so on until school starts and we're well and truly stuck together, along with Frances Murphy and other similarly tragic people. Twelve days!'

The prospect of returning to school still didn't quite seem real to Grace. This was probably why she found it so difficult to start her homework. The stupefying heat and the monotony of the past weeks now felt eternal, as if this was how life was and would be forever.

Even her excitement about Caroline's return had faded a little. It was hard to think of anything else when you were haunted. One sleepless night she got out of bed, cleared some space in the chaos of her desk, and began to draw. She was desperately tired, but there was something soothing about the movement of the pencil, sketching the jawline and creating a mesmeric pattern of curls. But when she came to the eyes she stopped. She remembered their dark vitality with a kind of fearful reluctance, but she could not begin to recreate them. She drew the outlines and then stopped, leaving them blank. It was nearly four o'clock, and surely sleep could not be far away. She turned off the light and left her unfinished portrait staring from the page with his white, empty eyes, as vacant as a marble god's.

IV

Sara returned, dusty shops opened their shutters once more, and the city slowly awoke from its summer stupor. Grace wrote a few paragraphs of her essays and then abandoned them, but she knew she couldn't procrastinate for much longer. When Mauro offered to help her with her maths homework she thanked him and said that she'd consider it, instead of flatly rejecting him as she would have done in usual circumstances. She watched the days disappear from her calendar and realised that she was running out of time.

After meeting Sara and Caroline for ice cream in the centre she resolved to go home and at least think about her translation. But as she waited for a bus that would probably never come, staring at a cloudless blue sky and rocking back and forth on her feet, she was taken by a random impulse to go to the river. She found herself longing for the sight of green water, the raging torrent that suddenly calmed and became almost motionless.

She could not look at the river without imagining the thousands of bodies that had plunged into it over the centuries. The water had always had a curious, deadly stillness in certain parts. There were no boats, and the branches of the trees were filled with rags and tattered plastic, the remnants of winter floods. The river was so far below, so quiet, that at times it hardly seemed part of the city at all. It was merely a ghostly, pale green stream drifting towards the sea.

Concrete paths ran alongside the water's edge, but they were mostly deserted, apart from the occasional cyclist and the homeless. The river was not a place to linger. Grace gazed at the water, tranquil and empty as always, and then looked along the length of the riverbank. There were no pedestrians, only a solitary sleeper basking in the softening rays of the late afternoon. Shielding her eyes from the sun, Grace stared at the man and tried to decide if the resemblance was just wishful thinking.

Against her better judgement, she descended the stone steps and left the shade of the trees and the noise of the traffic behind her. She kept her eyes fixed on the figure below, afraid that if she blinked, he would vanish. Of course she would not talk to him; she only wanted to see.

He was dressed in a loose white shirt and trousers, face tilted up towards the sun. As she crept towards him she became convinced that it was the same man, and she felt a shiver of fear despite the heat. Thank God he was asleep, and she could walk past without ever seeing—

'You again.' He hadn't even opened his eyes. 'It was just a matter of time before we found each other. I know you're afraid, but...'

There was no end to the sentence. He opened his eyes and looked at her.

'Sit down.'

They were utterly alone. Grace looked helplessly at the trees belonging to the world above, and then lowered her gaze. She was afraid to look him in the eye, but after a few seconds, her curiosity got the best of her. His eyes were not brown, as she had first thought, but black – two dark, bottomless pits – and now they were inviting her, drawing her towards him as if they were the only living souls in the entire city. She sat beside him.

'Grace.'

'Yes?' Somehow it was no surprise that he already knew her name.

'Tell me, Grace. Do you believe in gods?'

'God?'

'Well, if you can believe in one, surely you have sufficient imagination for belief in another.'

'I don't know what I believe,' said Grace, trying to avoid his gaze. 'I'm only fifteen. I think it's too young to know what you believe.'

'Belief has nothing to do with knowledge. You know a man cannot draw honey from a stone, yet I gave you no choice but to believe it.'

'Seeing is believing, I guess.' Grace turned towards him, expecting a mocking smile. But his face was utterly expressionless. There was not even the slightest trace of humanity in his eyes. Grace willed herself not to be afraid.

'I read *The Bacchae*,' she said.

'Ah.'

'The Lydian is Dionysus. God as man.'

'We're made in each other's image. For thousands of years… hundreds of thousands. I lose count.'

'You're a god,' she said, hearing the tremor in her voice.

'Yes.'

'Dionysus.'

'Yes.'

Grace took a deep breath and forced herself to stare at the water. A piece of driftwood was being carried slowly downriver, and it calmed her to look at something so small, so ordinary. But even without looking at him, she was acutely aware of his presence – it was as though he disrupted the atmosphere.

'Have I frightened you?'

'I was already frightened.'

'I'm not going to hurt you, Grace. I have neither the desire nor the power.'

'What do you mean?'

'No one in this city has believed in me for two thousand years. I'm unknown and unloved. And I'm very, very ill.' He sighed, and the sound chilled her blood. 'Give me your hand.'

No one had held her hand since she was a small child, and the touch of those fingers, cold like marble, gave her a queer sensation, as if she had been violated in some way. When he let go, she noticed that his palms were smooth and unlined.

'Well,' said Grace, repressing a shiver. 'I don't think I can help you.'

'Oh, but you can. I've always been loved by women, so to have one in this city who knows my name…'

'I'm not a woman, I'm fifteen.'

'It's the same to me. Anyway, I won't keep you. I can see you're dying to get away.'

Grace stood up, scarcely able to believe her good luck at being released unscathed, and only briefly touched.

'But promise me, Grace,' the god called after her, 'that you won't go to church.'

When she looked back he was sleeping again, or pretending to be. She felt that she had been tricked, somehow – taken advantage of. But then she had gone down to the river of her own volition, just as she had chosen to give him the coin. Hadn't she?

Another week of troubled dreams. Grace could not bear to look at her drawing again, but she couldn't bring herself to throw it away either, so she compromised by hiding it in one of her neglected books. She avoided going out in case she encountered him, and as a consequence of this tedious confinement in her bedroom she finally made some progress with her homework. Only the *Bacchae* essay remained unwritten. She flicked through the pages of the play and bit the end of her pen, then stared at the title of the essay until it made no sense:

> '*I don't despise religion. I'm a mortal man.*' *What does* The Bacchae *tell us about the playwright's religious beliefs?*

Grace hardly knew what her own beliefs were, let alone those of a dead Greek.

The weekend before school started, Grace went to Caroline's flat for a sleepover. When she arrived she was greeted by Caroline's mother, who rarely bothered to make eye contact with Grace, or indeed with anyone. Their conversations were always short and mildly awkward. As soon as Grace could escape without seeming rude, she went straight to Caroline's bedroom. Grace had visited so many times, she could have found her way with her eyes closed, even in a flat as enormous as Caroline's.

Caroline's bedroom came as a surprise to anyone who had already met and formed an impression of her. No one would have expected this short-haired, sharp-tongued girl to sleep beneath pink sheets, in a room decorated with floral wallpaper and filled with the remnants of her childhood. Beloved dolls and teddy bears were propped up on every surface. If you rummaged through her drawers – as Grace had once done – you would find her stolen treasures, which included make-up, her mother's romance novels, and a bracelet that Grace thought she had lost at school. Grace had slipped the bracelet into her pocket, and she and Caroline never spoke of it.

Sara had been invited to the sleepover too. She sat on the bed, reminiscing about her European travels in a dreamy monologue while she dusted Caroline's eyelids with blue powder.

'Even though I was bored – hold still, Caroline – I wouldn't mind going back next year. I didn't tell you about the boy, did I? In the hotel I made friends with an invalid of about our age – I think he was a consumptive – from Hungary. We're going to write to each other.'

'You only like boys who are dying or dead,' said Caroline.

'That's not true. Anyway, I don't *like* him like him, though he did have beautiful hands.'

Sara spoke about everything in a mild, faraway tone of voice. When she had arrived a year ago, the daughter of an Australian diplomat who had already lived in seven different countries, she found it difficult to make friends. Her tastes were eccentric, her clothes not quite right, and she cried too easily. She had spent her lunchtimes alone until Caroline suddenly and quite randomly took a liking to her. At first Grace thought it may have been pity, but then Caroline was not the kind of person to take pity on anyone.

Perhaps it was the fact that Sara was so much less talkative. She never demanded an equal role in the conversation, and she certainly never expected to be made the centre of attention. She was a good listener, too; she had a gift for making it seem as though she were listening to every word, even when she was lost in her daydreams. She was also incapable of spite, which was a rare quality in a teenage girl.

Caroline had a large collection of make-up, comprising eyeshadow that her parents had given her and lipstick she had shoplifted, 'more for the thrill than anything else'. When they could think of nothing else to do at sleepovers they went through the old routine of putting make-up on each other. Grace grew tired of it sometimes. She sank into the pillows, watching Caroline's makeover and feeling the familiar boredom, tinged with envy. They were both so much prettier than her.

And yet, *she* was the one who had caught the attention of a god. True, it was easier to feel smug about it out of his presence, when she wasn't shaking with fear, but at least she had a secret the others could never rival. She caught a glimpse of her lipsticked, glittering reflection in the mirror and smiled. She barely recognised herself.

'Shall I do your nails, Caroline?' Sara was rummaging through the enormous make-up bag, scattering bottles and brushes across the bed.

'No thanks, I've had enough. It's still early, though. What shall we do? Daddy will complain if we play music. Oh, I know – truth or dare.'

'We already know all of each other's secrets,' said Sara.

'You don't know all of mine.'

'Stop pretending to be mysterious, Grace. All right then, just dares.'

The dares began with Caroline being dared to run up and down the stairs of the condominium in only her underwear – on the second floor she panicked and raced back upstairs – and climaxed with Grace being dared to open and drink one of Caroline's father's bottles of wine. As none of them could work out how to use the corkscrew, however, this was the end of the game.

'It's three o'clock,' said Caroline. 'I suppose we might as well go to sleep.'

With the lights out they carried on talking until questions and answers became further and further apart. The silences expanded, and quiet breaths made Grace suspect that she was the only one still awake.

'Are you awake?' she whispered.

No reply. She looked at Caroline's silhouette and sighed. It was a convention of sleepovers that you didn't actually sleep, yet she was alone again, in the dark, her head full of gods. If she was still awake in an hour perhaps she would wake one of them up out of the selfish desire for company. The hands of the clock were just about visible in the dark; she forced herself to watch the clock instead of Caroline.

Twenty minutes later and the boredom was killing her. But she had been bored even before – make-up was boring, Sara's holiday stories were boring, and even the sight of Caroline running down the stairs in her underwear was boring. She was being unfair on them, she knew, but it was impossible to be entertained by a sleepover when you had caught a glimpse of another world. Now she knew how those Narnia children had felt when they came out of the wardrobe at the end – disappointed, but above all bored.

She waited another few minutes and then climbed into the bed beside Caroline.

'Caro, wake up.'

'Ugh.' Caroline sighed her familiar leave-me-alone sigh.

'I can't sleep. Let's play truth or dare.'

'Again? But we ran out of truths. And dares.'

'I've thought of one.'

'What?'

'I dare you… to go down to the river.'

'Now? Are you out of your mind? I'm not going to get raped and murdered for a dare.'

'It's not that dangerous. I've been there before.'

'Not at night, I bet. And even if I went, how would you know?'

'I could come with you.'

'If we both do it, that defeats the purpose of the dare. Forget it.' Caroline rolled over and turned her back to Grace. 'And get out of my bed, please. It's too hot to share.'

Grace returned to her mattress on the floor and glanced at the clock. Five minutes past four. It had been worth a try. And if she were to go on her own?

Are you out of your mind?

If Caroline thought it was dangerous, then Grace must be mad to even consider it. As her mother had once said in anger, in response to a game gone badly wrong, 'There's daring, and then there's stupidity. Go and get my first-aid kit.'

V

The halls were disgustingly familiar. If she had caught a whiff of that sour, chemical smell anywhere in the world she would have recognised it at once. School. She felt enveloped by a great wave of dreariness as soon as she walked through the door, into the permanently chilly hallway of grey walls and lockers and the portrait of the Queen that watched over them. The painting was meant to inspire patriotic feelings, but it just made Grace feel depressed and homesick.

She avoided the eyes of every girl she walked past; she knew all their names, had shared desks or played netball with them, but the thought of saying 'Hello' was too much. She felt like a new girl all over again. She felt slightly sick.

Caroline's head emerged from behind a locker door.

'Hello. You look cheerful.'

'I can't stand it, Caro.'

'Cheer up. We've only got three more years.'

Caroline looked Grace up and down and then pulled her by the arm into the nearest toilet.

'What are you doing?'

'Your skirt's too long.'

They stood by the sinks while Caroline made the necessary adjustments.

'Honestly, I don't think it matters. The uniform's frightful either way, and I'd rather not get in trouble with Miss Humphries on the first day.'

'You don't want to look like a frump.'

Caroline measured the space between Grace's knee and the edge of her skirt.

'That's better. Above the knee but not scandalously so.'

An American girl walked into the toilets and gave Grace's skirt a disapproving look.

'Miss Humphries won't like that.'

'Americans are such prudes,' Caroline muttered. 'Come on, let's go.'

Grace's first lesson was English. Caroline and Sara were in different classes, so Grace was forced to sit next to a Swiss girl with whom she had barely exchanged a sentence. There would be no opportunities for whispering or passing notes, so she would have to retreat into daydreams instead.

Grace was average in History, Geography, French, Classics and Biology, and below average in Maths, Chemistry, Physics and PE. She was slightly above average in Art, and also English, where she occasionally felt under pressure to concentrate, as this was the only academic subject she was remotely good at. She would certainly rather read a poem than struggle with equations.

Yet the question that lingered at the back of her mind during every lesson was 'What's the *point*?' Even if she could write a coherent paragraph on Dryden or understand algebra, was this preparing her for life? Grace only had the faintest idea of what 'life' was, but she felt sure that nothing she did at school would be of the slightest use after she turned eighteen. Most of them probably wouldn't have jobs, anyway. They'd get married and have babies, and you didn't need to be clever for that.

A job or a husband? Grace couldn't decide which was worse. The future she envisioned certainly didn't involve a job – being an artist wasn't a job but a vocation. A vocation that would hopefully give her enough money to live comfortably in London. Just as she was picturing her fully furnished imaginary flat, her thoughts were interrupted by the realisation that the Swiss girl had finished speaking, and it was her turn to read.

> *Though one were strong as seven,*
> *He too with death shall dwell,*
> *Nor wake with wings in heaven,*
> *Nor weep for pains in hell;*
> *Though one were fair as roses,*
> *His beauty clouds and closes;*
> *And well though love reposes,*
> *In the end it is not well.*

The words were beautiful but meant nothing to her. At least she was sitting by the window. The worst thing was to be stuck in the middle of the classroom with nothing to look at but the head of the girl in front of you or, worse, the blackboard. Here Grace had a square of blue sky and red rooftops, and the curved trunk of an umbrella pine.

Grace was generally unmoved by nature, but she loved the umbrella pines. They were as ubiquitous as pigeons but retained a certain aura of exoticism and elegance. If they were human they'd be dancers. She watched the branches sway and forgot about poetry and even Dionysus. But later in the lesson she looked again and saw Pentheus in the branches, wearing a dress, unaware that death was near. He had been punished for rejecting a god. It was only a story, of course, but in light of her own encounters, the thought made her uneasy.

At the end of the lesson, Grace was asked to stay behind.

'It's as if you're on another planet, Grace.'

'Sorry, Miss.'

'Perhaps being by the window is a distraction? I'll move you next lesson.'

'No, please – it's so hot. I'll fall asleep if I'm not by the window.'

'You might contribute more to the lesson asleep than awake. Well, try harder next time. And Grace?'

'Yes?'

'Please unroll your skirt.'

Grace blushed and did as she was told.

The day dragged on. She forced herself to be a little more attentive in Chemistry when they were using the Bunsen burners, and in French she had no choice but to try hard, as otherwise she would look like an idiot compared to Caroline, who was excellent at languages. Their French teacher had once said to Grace, 'You're not a natural linguist, are you?' and ever since, Grace had been determined to prove her wrong, knowing all the while that she was right.

At the end of the day Grace could feel her hair sticking to the back of her neck, and her skirt chafing at her waist. It was horrible being back at school in thirty-degree heat. She went to her locker to meet Caroline and Sara, enjoying the perpetual chill of the hallway.

'A hundred days till Christmas,' said Caroline.

The three girls walked out into the street together, and almost at once, Sara nudged Caroline.

'Look, it's your admirer.'

A young man stood by his motorbike on the other side of the street, watching the girls come out. His expression was so comically serious that you could almost believe that he was being paid to do it, and that he'd been threatened with a fine if he smiled. When he noticed Caroline, however, it was clear that she was the only girl who held any interest for him.

'Creep,' said Caroline. They walked down the street, conscious of his eyes following her.

'I don't know, Caro.' Sara turned to look at him. 'He *is* quite good-looking.'

'In a boring, conventional way, yes. But he probably smells of oil and garlic, and I reckon he plucks his eyebrows too. Give me an Englishman any day.'

Grace – who would have done anything for an admirer, no matter how oily – secretly thought that Caroline was being ungrateful. It seemed to Grace that having one man find you attractive meant that you could, in theory, have anyone you liked. Until that happened you were invisible and sexless, living in Caroline's shadow.

That evening Grace ignored her homework and had a long bath instead, lying in cold water and pretending not to hear Barbara's protests at the bathroom door. If only her entire life could be spent in the bath or else asleep, with no responsibilities. *I was born in the wrong body*, thought Grace, watching the water fall from her fingertips. *I should have been an animal.* It was a much happier existence, really. She would trade places with Pippin in an instant.

After her bath she felt too tired even to read. She paced around her bedroom, looking through boxes of old magazines and notebooks, trying to find something that would hold her interest. Drawing was always a possibility, but that unfinished portrait was blocking her; she didn't feel like she could start anything else while the eyes were still empty.

She suddenly became aware that the lights were on and the shutters were still open. The neighbours on the other side of the courtyard would be able to see her wandering around in her nightdress. Part of her secretly liked the idea of being spied on – only if it was the young man with the aquiline nose who lived opposite – but she didn't want to be seen in this particular nightdress, which was one of Barbara's hand-me-downs.

As she pulled the shutter she looked down into the courtyard and saw someone leaning against the wall. The courtyard was usually deserted, empty but for a few withered palm trees.

Hoping she was at least half hidden by the shutters, she stared at the stranger. He was dressed in black, and his face was lost in the shadow. In the few seconds while his back was turned, she was able to tell herself that it was probably one of the neighbours, or someone else's visitor. Then he moved into the lamplight, and she could no longer pretend.

It was him. Of course it was him. He knew where she lived, and now, like Caroline's admirer, he would be waiting for her.

Grace quickly closed the shutters before he noticed her, until she realised that there was no point in hiding from a god. He had passed through locked doors to enter a private courtyard. He could probably climb into her room if he wanted.

Despite the cool night air, she could feel herself sweating. She wiped her forehead and then got into bed, staring blankly at the opposite wall while she waited for an idea. It was an awful situation. For an ordinary stranger lurking in your courtyard you could call the police, but there was nothing ordinary about him. She would have to deal with it herself, yet the thought of speaking to him again filled her with dread.

Time passed – ten minutes or an hour – and then, without making a conscious decision, Grace was putting on her shoes and a dressing gown. Someone might see her, but it hardly seemed to matter. Her mother and Mauro would be sleeping, and who cared about the neighbours? She slipped the key into her pocket and shut the front door behind her.

She met no one on the stairs, and heard nothing except for the blare of a TV – incomprehensible words and laughter. Perhaps he would have tired of waiting, and in two minutes she would be going back upstairs, listening to the same TV. Everything back to normal.

The courtyard was dimly lit, casting strange shadows of the palm leaves on the walls. It had been neglected for years and the flagstones were coming loose. Grace almost tripped, and grabbed on to a trunk.

'At last.'

He was standing by the far wall, in exactly the same position. His voice and face expressed nothing, so she could hardly tell if he was pleased to see her or not.

'What do you want?'

'I should have thought it obvious.'

'No, it isn't. I wish you'd leave me alone.'

'We need each other, Grace.'

'I can't help you,' she said, trying to sound more assertive than she felt. 'Really, I can't.'

'Grace.'

'I can't. I have to go.' She was almost pleading with him now. She should never have come down.

'If you leave now you won't sleep, I promise you. Let's talk.'

'About what?'

'Ah, you're curious, aren't you?'

'No. I mean… yes, but—'

'One conversation. That's all I ask.'

He had trapped her, somehow. She couldn't argue with him, and she couldn't even get away from him. Some instinct – the same sub-conscious instinct that made her avoid certain men in the street – told her that if she left, he would follow her. Perhaps it would be safer to give in and see what he wanted.

'All right, we can talk. But not here.'

'No. I think your bedroom would be best.'

A thousand thoughts raced through Grace's mind. Newspaper headlines, rape, a film she'd seen, murder, Barbara's room next door…

'Take your time,' said Dionysus. 'We have all night.'

He looked ludicrously out of place in her bedroom, sitting on a chair covered with her discarded clothes. Nothing in the room seemed to interest him except for a photograph of Caroline and Sara stuck to the pinboard. As they talked he stared at Grace for disconcerting lengths of time, and then glanced at the photograph. Again, Grace found herself wondering uneasily about his intentions. He was a man as well as a god.

'You're the only person I've spoken to in this city,' said Dionysus. 'Did you know that?'

'I still don't understand why.'

'Neither do I. To be quite honest with you, I don't know why I'm here. Alive. Something's wrong.'

'What do you mean?'

'The other gods are dead and gone, yet here I am. Alive in a century where I've been forgotten. I've always had believers in the past. I was never this alone. I had companions, lovers…'

He closed his eyes. Grace, sitting awkwardly on the edge of the bed, crossed and then uncrossed her legs.

'It's degrading,' he said. 'I can't continue like this. Walking aimlessly and thinking, always alone, while the world worships a mere man.'

'Jesus?'

'A man,' said Dionysus, the word dripping with contempt. 'It's unbelievable. You might as well worship the person who sweeps the streets.'

'It does seem unfortunate that you've been, well, reincarnated in a Catholic country.'

'I just don't understand it. I woke up beneath a white pyramid. At first I barely knew who I was. But it's happened before.'

'What do you mean?'

'Rebirth. One time it was a beach, an island – some far-flung corner of the world. I remember the moment I woke up on the sand, with the tribe peering down at me. I didn't have to say a word. They recognised my divinity at once – venerated me. Within a matter of hours they were drinking, praying, sacrificing their animals. All as it's supposed to be. But here…'

Grace tried to visualise the scene – a newborn Dionysus being found by some savage tribe on a remote island. For some reason the image made her feel dizzy, even slightly sick. She forced herself to take a deep breath.

'I don't understand,' she said slowly. 'How can a god die and be born again? And how is it possible that you don't understand, or don't remember? Aren't you supposed to be omniscient or something?'

'I don't have time for a philosophical discussion, Grace. All I want to know is if you're with me.'

'With you?'

'You do believe in me, don't you?'

'I don't really have a choice.'

He looked relieved, and leaned back in the chair. There were dark shadows under his eyes, as if he hadn't slept for days. Did gods need to sleep? It might seem impertinent to ask.

Grace's fear was slowly dissipating, and turning into a kind of tentative pity. It must be terrible, living when you were supposed to be dead. A vampiric existence. But he wanted her belief, not her blood. It wasn't so much to ask.

'I'm not asking as a favour, Grace. I can help you too.'

'How?'

'By relieving your infinite boredom and showing you things you've never even dreamed of.'

Once again he turned to the photograph behind him.

'Are these your friends?'

'Yes.'

'Catholics?'

'Sara is.'

'That's a pity.'

'Next you'll be asking to meet them. Is that it?'

'Clever girl.'

She had been starting to like him, and now she suddenly felt repulsed again.

'It's late,' said Grace.

He was still staring at the photograph and didn't seem to have heard her. Then he turned his head, and his shadow was caught in the lamplight – a sudden silhouette of ivy leaves. But when she looked again, it was only his shadow. No leaves, just the dark curls of his hair.

Dionysus saw her discomfort and smiled.

'Well, then. Until we meet again…'

Even after he'd gone, Grace did not feel entirely safe. Without saying 'Yes' she had somehow formed an agreement with him, and now there was no escape. He might be in the courtyard every night from now on, or waiting outside her school. How much of it was her fault?

She pressed her face into the pillow and waited for sleep.

VI

'Are you all right?'

'You've been odd all week.'

They were huddled together in a shady corner of the playground. Grace pulled at the hem of her skirt, deliberately avoiding Caroline's eye in case she accidentally told her everything. Of course it had been Sara who noticed first – caring, sensitive Sara. Caroline was generally oblivious to people's feelings, but once she sensed that something was wrong she became morbidly curious.

'It's nothing, really.'

'You know you can tell us anything, Grace.'

'It's nothing. Or maybe it's just my period or something. I don't know.'

'Liar,' said Caroline. 'Your period was last week.'

'How do you know?'

'So was mine. We're so in sync.'

'Well, even if it isn't that, does there have to be a reason? Maybe it's a phase or a hormonal thing.'

'Ah, so you admit something *is* wrong.'

'Not wrong – different. I can't explain it.'

'You don't have to,' said Sara. 'If you can't talk to us you can always try praying. No, don't laugh, Caro. It helps. I know you don't really believe, but try it.'

'I've already tried,' said Grace.

'I prayed for a whole year that we would go back to England,' said Caroline. '*Nothing.*'

'I don't mean that kind of prayer.'

'What's the use of praying if you can't get exactly what you want?'

Caroline and Sara began one of their habitual arguments about religion, and Grace tuned out. The truth was that she *did* want to talk. She had never liked keeping secrets, and this one was too immense to be dealt with alone. It was like the early days of her parents' break-up, when no one was supposed to know. She had managed to keep it a secret for an entire day before telling Isabel, who had then told Mary, who had subsequently told the rest of the class. She probably should have waited before telling Isabel, but she had needed someone else to help her make sense of it, or even just to offer an opinion.

Her mother's affair had been within the realms of normality, at least. Even if Grace had resisted the urge to share the secret, she probably would have been able to imagine her friends' responses and comfort herself with these hypothetical conversations. But a situation like this... She could just about imagine herself making the revelation to Sara, or even to Caroline, but when it was time for them to respond, the scene faded to black. There was nothing you could say to a story like that.

When she was stressed, anxious, or sometimes simply bored, Grace liked to retreat to the future. It was always the same scene. Although she could never see herself clearly, all the other details were there – the small but tidy London flat, filled with her drawings. Future Grace was an artist, somehow making enough money from her pictures to rent or – why not? – buy a flat in a fashionable part of London. She was not alone because she had her dachshunds, all of whom were Pippin's descendants. (Never mind the fact that he was neutered.) She spent her days drawing, walking the dogs, and having Caroline over for sleepovers. Of course Caroline would be in London too, and live nearby. They would see each other all the time. Grace would be beautiful and rich and fulfilled in every area of her life.

The future was her safe place. It never failed to calm her, at least for a little while. She found herself going there more regularly during certain periods of her life, and this was one of them. Yet to her frustration, the same thing kept happening, again and again. She would be in the bath, or at the dinner table, or staring at the back of someone's head during a lesson, quite immersed in her future, when she suddenly lost her grip on it. The pictures on the wall were all transformed into her unfinished portrait of the god, and her chorus of dachshunds started barking, not like dogs but like Dionysus laughing.

As the daydream vanished, she sank deeper into the bath, or the chair, and let out an exasperated sigh. She didn't mind if he took over her present, but taking over her future was a step too far. She had once read that the only way to rob a secret of its power was to say it out loud.

If that's what it takes, thought Grace. He was leaving her with no choice.

After school on Friday, Grace and Sara went out for ice cream. They sat on the low wall outside, enjoying the softening heat of the late afternoon and the ice cream melting on their tongues. For a moment their conversation was suspended as they tried to stop their ice creams from dripping all over their uniforms, but when the situation was under control, Grace gave in to her impulse.

'Sara, you know our conversation the other day? Something *is* the matter.'

'What is it?'

'I'll try to explain. Just promise you'll try to believe me.'

'Of course.'

Grace recounted her meeting with the stranger in the Ghetto, her subsequent realisation and the encounter in the courtyard. Sara listened in silence, paying no attention to the rivulets of ice cream trickling through her fingers.

'Well?' Halfway through her narrative Grace had started to feel self-conscious, knowing how absurd it all sounded. Sara would think her mad.

'It's…' Sara seemed to be struggling to find the right words. 'Very, very strange.'

'But you do believe me, don't you? I couldn't make it up.'

'You'd have no reason to. I mean, Katie Upton in the fourth form makes things up all the time, but she's crazy.'

'And I'm not.'

'I know.' Sara began to lick her fingers slowly; the pensive expression remained.

'What do you think I should do?'

'I don't know. I'm hardly in a position to give you advice on something like that. But then, who is?'

'Exactly.'

'Do you think he's dangerous?'

'Potentially. But why would he want to hurt me? He keeps saying he needs me.'

'Be careful, though.'

'You mean I shouldn't see him? I don't know if I have a choice.'

'Maybe you should tell someone. An adult, I mean.'

'Who? My parents? The police? "Help, I'm being followed by a Greek god."'

'I really don't know what you should do. But I'll think about it.'

'Thank you.'

Grace reached out for Sara's sticky hand and held it.

'And another thing – please don't tell Caro just yet.'

On Saturday Grace slept in late, and then spent the day pacing restlessly around the flat, occasionally leaning out of the window to see if there was any sign of him. By the afternoon the strain of constant dread – a strange new emotion – was becoming intolerable. She resisted the urge to look out of the window, and sat down to watch TV with Barbara instead.

The only time she ever felt close to her sister was when they were watching TV together, usually in silence. When someone made the mistake of trying to use another electrical appliance while the TV was on, the inevitable result was a brief power cut. This meant that whenever the TV was on, all other activity in the flat seemed to stop. It was like another member of the family, demanding everyone's attention.

Barbara was particularly attached to it. She would sprawl across the sofa, watching programme after programme as she worked her way through packets of gum.

Today it was a music programme. The sisters watched every performance without comment, except for the occasional 'I like her dress' or 'He's miming, you can tell'. Grace was not really giving it her full attention, but she idly translated the odd word in order to make sense of the lyrics.

> *If burning* (?)
> *The city*

To you
To you
(words drowned out by screaming audience)

'Dreamy,' said Barbara.

Grace was trying to decipher the next verse when her mother walked in.

'Caroline's on the phone for you.'

'Oh, all right.'

She went into the hallway and picked up the receiver.

'Hello?'

'What's all this rot about Dionysus?'

The question was so unexpected that Grace was rendered speechless.

'Sara told me, and of course she told me not to tell you. But I know. You've got to tell me everything or I'm going to start fearing for your sanity.'

'Not on the phone.'

'No. Let's go for a walk.'

'Now?'

'Meet me by the fountain in ten minutes.'

'I've got homework to do.'

'It's five o'clock on a Saturday.'

'Fine. I'll be there.'

Grace looked into the courtyard one more time just to make sure. He wasn't there. If he had the power to read her mind, perhaps he already knew that Sara and Caroline had been made aware of his existence. That would cheer him up.

When she reached the fountain, she found Caroline waiting for her. She sat on the steps with her legs spread wide apart, like a man, restlessly searching the faces of the people passing through the square.

'You got here quickly,' said Grace.

'I thought it was rather urgent. Daddy gave me a lift.'

Caroline stood up and took her by the arm.

'I'm really quite worried about you, you know.'

'You needn't be. I know it sounds mad, but...'

'Grace, it's the maddest thing I've ever heard. How can it possibly be true?'

They walked down Grace's favourite street, a shady, cobbled hill with some crumbling Roman columns rising up at the end, all the more beautiful for being so unexpected.

'If you met him you would understand. He looks almost human, but he isn't. And the thing with the honey – did Sara tell you? Well, how do you explain that?'

'He could be some sort of seedy magician. A drunk. You said he's living on the street?'

'I don't know where he lives. He just *appears.*'

'All right. So let's say he is who he says he is. Why would he choose you?'

'What do you mean?'

'It's like all the people who believe they're the reincarnation of Napoleon or Cleopatra. A nice coincidence. What makes you so special?'

'He didn't choose me. I just happened to be there when he needed someone. And he said something about me being a girl.'

'Ugh, he's obviously a pervert then. A drunken, sex-obsessed magician. He ought to be in prison.'

Sometimes it was difficult to tell how serious Caroline was being, as her default position seemed to be hyperbolic contempt for everyone and everything.

'You can think what you like, Caro,' said Grace. 'But I know what I saw. I know what I feel.'

'RIP Grace's sanity.'

'Very funny.'

They turned into a wide road lined with ruins on both sides. Vines and little white flowers sprouted through the cracks in ancient walls, and shattered faces gazed sightlessly from columns and archways. At the end loomed that familiar monster of a ruin, its countless windows filled by the blue sky. The road never failed to make Grace feel insignificant, and even a little alienated. Caroline suddenly decided that it was too hot to link arms, and they walked silently, separately. A man tried to sell them a parasol and they ignored him.

'It's like living in the strangest dream,' said Grace, 'or perhaps a nightmare. I'm frightened but I want to see him again, so I don't know.'

'Introduce us.'

'Why? You don't believe in him.'

'I might if I met him.'

'I can't just summon him. It's not like I can call him up.'

'So he doesn't have a house or a telephone. I don't think it was very wise of you to befriend him.'

'I know this is all just a big joke to you, but I wish you would take it seriously. You never take anything seriously though, do you?'

'Don't be cross. You have to admit, it *is* funny. A homeless magician.'

'It isn't funny at all. You would understand if—'

'If I met him, right. If it matters that much to you, find a way of introducing us.'

'I told you,' said Grace, exasperated, 'I don't know how. He just… *appears*.'

'Well, the next time he just… *appears*, call me. Or take a picture. That's the next best thing.'

'You've still got my camera.'

'So I'll give it back. Stop making excuses.'

'I'm not making excuses. Please, can we just drop it for now?'

'For now. But I'm not going to forget about this, you know.'

'I know.'

'You've made me curious. I want to see some of his tricks.'

'Caro, enough.' If the conversation continued, she would snap. Caroline could be maddening sometimes.

'Fine,' said Caroline, in a way that made it clear it was not fine at all. She was no longer playful, but on the verge of sulking.

'Come on, let's get a drink. Or get into the shade, at least.'

They pushed through the crowds in the shadow of the ruin. Grace glanced at another parasol-seller and for a second her heart froze. She looked again and felt relieved and disappointed at once. It wasn't him. She told herself that it was probably just as well; Caroline would dismiss it as another convenient coincidence.

VII

Miss Seymour's classroom was a small, airless room with a narrow window revealing nothing but the colour of the sky. Sometimes it felt like being in prison; on other days it was the top of a tower in a fairytale. It depended on Grace's mood.

The room contained six chairs, a blackboard, and a poster of a red-figure amphora. This was the only decoration in the room, so Grace had memorised every detail of the vase. Maenads in transparent dresses wielding enormous sticks, a wrist encircled by a snake, vine leaves cascading from the neck of the vase. A bearded Dionysus danced on a geometric floor, draped in a leopard skin, lascivious eyes gazing at the woman beside him.

The previous year Grace had written several essays about Greek vases, trying to sound enthusiastic about a beauty she could not see. They were too flat, too cartoonish. Art needed passion and drama to interest her, and she could not find it in a vase, where all the figures were eternally static. A single line of Homer or Ovid contained more interest than a thousand black-and-red pots.

Today, however, she looked at the poster with renewed interest. Caroline noticed her staring.

'Does he have a beard?'

'What?' Grace snapped out of her trance. 'No, he doesn't.'

'Who are you talking about?' asked Frances Murphy.

'No one,' said Grace. It would be so easy for Caroline – and so like her – to tease, or even to humiliate her by revealing her secret. But Caroline hated Frances as much as Grace did, so hopefully she would deem her unworthy of knowing. Caroline would never do anything that might give Frances satisfaction.

There were five of them in the class: Grace, Caroline, Frances Murphy, Jessica Collins, and Genevieve Latour. Frances was insufferable, Jessica dull, and Genevieve silent. Grace and Caroline usually ignored the others and pretended they were alone, squashed together in their corner by the poster. In the summer it was unbearably hot, and the smell of Caroline's sweat became so familiar to Grace that it was almost like a permanent feature of the room. A warm, musty smell; because it was Caroline, it wasn't particularly unpleasant.

As they waited for Miss Seymour to arrive, they fanned themselves with the pages of their homework. Genevieve opened her mouth as though she were about to say something, then closed it again. Grace counted the spots on Frances's forehead and felt better about herself at once. Having bad skin was infinitely worse than being plain. Or was it? Frances might grow out of her acne, whereas Grace would stay the same forever. You couldn't change your eyes or your mouth, or whatever it was that made some girls beautiful and others ugly.

Grace wasn't ugly, but she knew that she had one of those bland, forgettable faces. She was often confused with other girls, and even teachers less distracted than Miss Seymour sometimes got her name wrong. But she couldn't be entirely plain and unremarkable if Dionysus had chosen her. Even if looks were not the most important consideration, she knew that beautiful people were more conscious of other people's attractiveness, or lack of it. He would not waste his time on a girl like Frances, for example. If Grace were being generous, Frances was a five, which meant that Grace was at least a six and a half. Caroline was an eight, and she knew it. Dionysus was N/A, because you couldn't rank gods using the same criteria as humans. The only man she could think of comparing him with was Caroline's admirer – undeniably good-looking – but that was absurd.

She tried to recall the exact details of Dionysus's face, to analyse him like a figure on a vase. It was surprisingly difficult to picture him, as the image that kept coming to mind was more of a mask, an interpretation of his face rather than the real thing. How was it possible to have spent so much time looking at him, thinking and dreaming about him, and not be able to recall precisely what he looked like?

Grace was still meditating on the mystery of the god's facial features when Miss Seymour walked in.

'Sorry I'm late, girls. I wish I had a good reason, but the truth is that I was talking to Mrs Rodgers in the corridor and I simply lost track of time. Forgive me.'

As a sixty-something spinster and possible lesbian with dyed red hair, Miss Seymour was a popular target of schoolgirl spite, possessing nicknames ranging from 'the Stick', on account of her extreme thinness, to 'Carrot-Head'. Caroline was vicious about nearly all her teachers, but Miss Seymour was exempt from criticism. For reasons known only to Caroline, eccentricities that would have been contemptible in others were admirable in a Classics teacher.

'Besides,' said Caroline, 'if you're going to give her a nickname, it might as well be something related to Sappho. A missed opportunity. Honestly, this school is full of absolute dunces.'

Grace did not hold Miss Seymour in such high esteem, but she liked her more than the other teachers. She had very nearly become a professor at Oxford, and you could tell that she was superior. Her sharp mind and dry wit were incongruously paired with frequent forgetfulness – she often struggled to remember her students' names – and a tendency to stare vacantly into space for long periods of time. It was possible that she was deep in thought, but there was no evidence for this. Grace believed that her own lapses of attention went unnoticed by the teacher, and that they had similarly scattered minds.

'Yes, but don't delude yourself,' said Caroline, after Grace made this comparison. '*You're* not exactly Oxford material.'

Miss Seymour turned to the blackboard and wrote a sentence in ornate, cursive script. Her handwriting was almost indecipherable, but after a year or so you got used to it.

Gods should not be like mortals in vindictiveness.

'Cadmus says it,' said Frances.
'Very good. When?'
'At the end of the play.'
'Be more specific.'
'Page 243.'
Miss Seymour sighed heavily.
'Dionysus has just told Cadmus his fate, and talked about the dangers of insulting the gods,' said Caroline.
'Exactly. The god has had his revenge. But is it right?'
'I don't know if he deserved it,' said Frances. 'Pentheus did.'
'Cadmus sinned too.' Caroline was not content unless she was con-

tradicting Frances. 'Anyway, it's a tragedy. Of course it was going to end terribly for everyone. It's not a question of deserving it.'

'Should the gods be vindictive?' asked Miss Seymour. 'That is the question.'

'Vindictive like mortals?' said Caroline. 'I don't see why not. The Greek gods were basically human anyway.'

'No,' said Grace, 'they're not.'

Miss Seymour turned to Grace.

'Would you care to elaborate?'

'No.'

Grace blushed and pretended to read the page in front of her so she didn't have to participate in the discussion. She had nothing to contribute, anyway. The play that had thrilled her at the end of the summer now seemed stale and lifeless compared to subsequent events. Analysing a two-thousand-year-old text seemed especially pointless now that the character had become infinitely more real than its author.

For the rest of the lesson she remained as silent as Genevieve, a girl so chronically shy that even saying 'Yes' or 'No' was an ordeal. Not speaking made you look stupid, but saying the wrong thing made you look stupid too, or worse – mad. Grace no longer cared what Miss Seymour thought of her. Caroline and Frances could show off all they liked, while Grace slumped deeper and deeper into her chair, eyes glazed over as she thought of other things.

Nothing seemed entirely real. Miss Seymour herself, pale and thin, might be a ghost. Grace imagined reaching through the teacher's body to touch the blackboard on the other side, which was now covered with scrawled hieroglyphics relating to theatrical conventions in 500 BC.

It was only at the end of the lesson that Grace woke up. Miss Seymour's words suddenly came through to her, as clear and urgent as a foghorn on a silent sea.

'But returning to the original question – the vindictiveness of the gods – perhaps we should stop searching for a moral message. It isn't a matter of punishment at all. Pentheus denies reality, repressing an instinct, the wild and savage part of himself. It's the *repression* of something natural that causes tragedy. When we deny ourselves we are doomed.'

Miss Seymour was not looking at them, but at some random point on the far wall. So much of what she said was not aimed at her students at all, but was spoken aloud for her own benefit.

Grace stopped chewing on the end of her pen and let the last word reverberate in her mind. *Doomed.* She glanced down at the corner of her notebook and saw that Caroline had decorated it with swirling lines and three words: *Well, well, well.*

'What?' Grace mouthed at her.

Caroline shook her head and smiled.

'That concludes the lesson for today, girls,' said Miss Seymour. 'Remember, your translations are due next Monday. Please use a dictionary if you are in doubt. It will make the experience easier for both of us.'

In the stairwell Caroline murmured, 'That got your attention, didn't it? It's practically an order to see him again or else risk being doomed and dismembered.'

'I wish you wouldn't say things like that,' said Grace, sounding genuinely anguished. 'And especially not at school.'

'You're perfectly safe. If I don't believe you, no one else will.'

'Sara believes me.'

'Sort of. Anyway, she already believes in God with a capital "G", so she's obviously susceptible to these sorts of things.'

'Drop it, Caro. I don't want to talk about it.'

She quickly walked ahead, and began a conversation with Jessica about the translation, before Caroline could say anything else on the subject of Dionysus and his non-existence.

When she arrived home she heard the familiar blare of the television – Barbara watching a soap – and Henry's voice chattering away in a high-pitched monologue. His bedroom door was ajar, and Grace could see him sitting on the floor, rearranging his cars and talking to himself.

'No, silly. Not like that. It goes here – *vroom.*'

'Who are you talking to, Henry?'

'Max,' said Henry, without looking up.

'Is Max the cat or the rabbit?'

'The rabbit.'

Grace lingered in the doorway, but after a few seconds she realised that her presence was making him self-conscious. She closed the door and went to her own room.

When she was Henry's age she had had lots of imaginary friends. She had recently found the diary she had kept as a seven-year-old, a beautiful book bound in green leather that was completely wasted on a child. The entry for 7 September read: 'Today Emily said Snowy the barn owl doesn't exist. I don't know why I bother to believe in *her* imaginary friends.'

The owl had been entirely the product of her imagination, but the god? She hardly knew what to think. It was tempting to confide in Henry, who trusted her absolutely, and who would never question the existence of anyone or anything. If Father Christmas could deliver presents both to their house in England and their flat here, despite the absence of a chimney in their current home, then why shouldn't a god visit his sister?

But it was too risky, of course. Henry was not very good at keeping secrets, and if he let it slip to their mother, Grace would probably find herself in a psychiatrist's office by the end of the week. Madness ran in the family, after all. Grace's aunt had lost her mind, and even her mother was not entirely sane. Leaving her husband and running off to a foreign country to be with someone as charmless as Mauro was not an indication of a sound mind.

No matter how mad it sounded, Grace wanted to see the god again. Even if it were only a glimpse of his shadow in the courtyard, it would be better than nothing. She asked herself *why* she wanted to see him, and couldn't find an answer. Was it because she needed to prove to herself that she wasn't imagining things? That was only a part of it – her feelings were much more complicated than that. It was an indefinable, bittersweet longing, like a reluctant crush or perverse nostalgia for a sensation that ought to be forgotten. When she thought about it for too long she felt faint and breathless.

Standing at her bedroom window, she saw that the courtyard was empty. Even craning her neck to see the far side of the courtyard, it was clear that there was no one there. Only the stones and the dying palm trees.

'What have you done to me?' she whispered. She waited for a second, and then reluctantly closed the shutters and got into bed.

Grace often prayed in a vague, weak-willed way to a god she didn't believe in. She had done this for years, more as a superstitious habit than anything else, whenever she wanted something.

O God, please make Mummy buy me those shoes for Christmas.
Please don't let Mrs Farthing realise I cheated.
Please make it rain tomorrow.
Please make Mauro go away.
Please may I pass the French test.
Please make Caroline nicer.

Her prayers were granted so rarely and randomly that she learned to pray without any real expectations. She found the ritual comforting nonetheless. Saying the words was all she could do; the rest was up to fate.

Now she understood that what she had lacked was faith. She hadn't believed, and she hadn't wanted anything badly enough. That had all changed.

Before she went to sleep she lit a candle and kneeled down beside her bed.

Dionysus, please come back.
Come back, come back, come back.

VIII

At the weekend, when she had nothing better to do – and she rarely did – Grace followed her mother around the local market. The fact that her mother was able to converse so fluently with the stall-owners was a mystery to Grace. How was she able to speak the language when she had never studied it, and only spoke to Mauro in English? The only way Grace could get what she wanted was if she pointed and mimed. In the market she stood beside her mother feeling mute and stupid, glowering at the vegetables while her mother shared a joke with the man weighing the tomatoes.

'Have you nearly finished?' asked Grace.

'Yes, that's it now. Let's go and get a coffee.'

There was a tiny bar around the corner which was always in a state of chaos – a confused attempt at a queue, and people crammed together at the bar shouting their orders, which always sounded disproportionately long and complicated for something that was basically just a cup of coffee. They drained their cups in a single swallow and were replaced a second later by the next customers, pushing their way to the front and waving their receipts.

Grace found the experience a bit of an ordeal, and without her mother she would never have attempted to order. But her mother always managed to join the scrum without becoming flustered, and two minutes later she would emerge from the crowd and bring two cups of coffee to one of the tables at the back of the bar.

'Thanks, Mummy.'

She didn't like coffee that much, but drinking it made her feel grown-up. Besides, if she couldn't speak their language, the least she could do was drink their coffee, the drink that seemed to be of such fundamental importance to everyone who lived here.

'You never drank coffee when we lived in England,' said Grace.

'No, but it's so much better here. And that reminds me – are you going back for Christmas? You need to decide soon.'

'I don't know.'

'Barbara will probably go. Henry wants to stay here. It's up to you. I know your father would like to see you.'

'Daddy doesn't care.'

'Darling, how can you say that?'

'He never writes.'

'Well, neither do you. It works both ways, you know. You can't expect him to write you letters all the time if you can't be bothered to reply.'

'It's not a question of being bothered. Are you saying I'm lazy?'

'That's not what I meant.'

'Anyway.' Grace drained the dregs of her coffee and grimaced. 'I don't think I will go. There are too many things I need to do here.'

'Very well. But I don't want you to complain about feeling home-sick in January.'

Grace didn't reply. She could not possibly put her feelings about England and her father into words. There was also no way of explaining that part of her reluctance to leave came from her stubborn desire to see the god again. Two weeks in England, and then what? By the time she came back he might have disappeared forever. It had been nearly two weeks since she'd last seen him – an eternity.

She began to tear the sachet of sugar into shreds.

'No one understands me.'

'Everyone thinks like that when they're fifteen. You'll grow out of it.'

'No, I mean it. Absolutely no one.'

'Barbara said the same thing at your age. One day Henry will say it too.'

Suddenly, Grace felt like crying. She tore up the remains of the packet and scattered them across the table.

'Can we go home now?'

'If you want.'

Grace didn't really care where she was, but she couldn't stand her mother's company any longer. She was always so maddeningly calm about everything. In the first few weeks after the move, when Grace had been suffering from every aspect of the change – the heat, the food, the mosquitoes – she had longed for her mother to acknowledge that things were difficult. But even in the hardest moments, like the power cut, or the day when they'd found the 'cockroach grave-yard' in the back of one of the kitchen cupboards, her mother never cried or got angry, or even admitted that there was a problem. She only repeated her mantra of 'It's all right'. They hadn't slept for a week and they were being massacred by mosquitoes, but 'It's all right, it's all right'. The only way to provoke a stronger reaction from her was to do something spiteful or violent, neither of which came naturally to Grace.

Maybe it was better to have a mother who got angry. Caroline had been hit by her mother once. Grace could remember Caroline's tears, the torrent of bad words. Grace couldn't imagine thinking of her own mother as a 'bitch', let alone saying the word out loud, but perhaps being able to do so was liberating in a way. If you stopped trying to believe your parents loved you, you were free.

Back in her room, she searched through all her drawers until she found some blank writing paper that wasn't crumpled. She sat at her desk, biting the end of her pen, and then wrote the letter, without pausing to think.

Dear Daddy,

How are you? I'm all right. Sorry for not writing before, but I've been terribly busy with homework and school and everything. I got an A for my Tennyson essay, thought you'd be pleased. This year in Classics we're studying The Bacchae, *it's great. How is Mog? I'm not coming for Christmas but I probably will for Easter.*

Lots of love,

Grace

She stuck the letter in an envelope and carefully copied out the address from her address book. She didn't know it by heart because it had not been her home when she lived in England. All the same, the very English 'Harrow-on-the-Hill' gave her a slight pang.

When Barbara saw the envelope in the hall she said, 'It only took you, what, four months?'

But Grace would not be made to feel guilty. She had done her duty.

Another week passed. School happened in its usual, predictable way – failed science tests, hours staring out of the window, Caroline's young man waiting in the street – and every night, she prayed. One day after school she had the urge to go into a Catholic church and pray for Dionysus's return, so she did. She lit a candle in front of a statue of John the Baptist and prayed again. Afterwards she smiled to herself and wondered which god would send a thunderbolt to punish her heresy.

There were no thunderbolts – no signs at all. Grace was reluctantly becoming resigned to the fact that a door had closed. The god had vanished, the excitement was over, and she would have to get used to being an ordinary teenage girl once more. To compensate for the disappointment, she began to cross off the days on her calendar, counting down to Christmas even though she was not remotely excited about it. The only thing to look forward to was the end of term.

That weekend she and Sara went round to Caroline's flat for another sleepover. The three of them sat on Caroline's enormous bed, eating sweets and watching a film they only vaguely understood.

The bedroom window was at the same level as the street lamp, which filled the room with a golden light. The shutters and the window were rarely closed, so the light, the night air, the moths and the mosquitoes all came flooding into the room.

'We might as well be outside,' said Grace, scratching her leg.

'You can close the windows if you like.' For some reason Caroline seemed to be immune to insects – yet another example, Grace thought, of Caroline's unfair privilege and luck.

'I don't understand this film,' said Sara. 'I mean, even if it was in English and we'd started watching from the beginning, I still don't think it'd make any sense.'

'The albino is obviously the baddie,' said Caroline.

'And the cowboy? What's he trying to do?'

'Something to do with a bank and a girl with golden hair. I'm not sure.'

'Why are we even watching this?' asked Grace.

'You're right, westerns are boring.' Caroline turned off the TV. 'What shall we do instead?'

'I'm quite tired,' said Sara.

'Don't be dull, it's not even midnight. I know – Grace. Entertain us with your stories. Better than any film.'

'I don't know what you mean.'

'Dionysus. Is he still lurking in your courtyard?'

'I haven't seen him since.'

'Grace,' said Sara, 'are you sure – I mean *really* sure – that it happened?'

'Yes, of course. I couldn't imagine something like that, and I'd have no reason to invent it.'

'It just seems strange. Assuming it's true, why would he make all that effort to see you and then disappear?'

'I don't know. I think about it all the time, but I have no idea.'

'Perhaps it's a test,' said Caroline. 'He's testing your faith.'

'He knows I believe in him. I can't *not* believe, after everything that's happened.'

'It might sound odd,' said Sara, 'but have you tried praying to him?'

'Yes.' Grace felt embarrassed to admit it.

'Out loud?' asked Caroline.

'No, I've never prayed out loud. I feel too self-conscious.'

'That's a rubbish excuse. Also, the Ancient Greeks definitely did their praying out loud. Miss Seymour said something about it once. They made offerings too.'

'We're not Ancient Greeks.'

'So? For someone who supposedly believes in a Greek god, you haven't done much to express your faith.'

'And what would you suggest?'

Grace regretted the question the moment she asked it. Whatever Caroline came up with, it would probably be stupid and humiliating.

'I know what we can do,' said Caroline brightly, as though she'd only just thought of it.

She searched through a pile of books on her desk until she found the one she was looking for. Grace recognised it at once – they had the same edition of *The Bacchae*.

'Here,' said Caroline, giving the book to Grace. 'Find a bit with the Chorus.'

Grace turned the pages while Caroline arranged a circle of candles on the floor.

'You can't be serious, Caro,' said Sara, looking at the candles with wide-eyed alarm.

'Don't worry, we're summoning Dionysus, not the devil.'

Grace raised her eyes from the book.

'I know you're just making fun of me, but what if—'

'What if indeed.'

In certain lights, there was something demonic about Caroline's smile. She was still grinning as she lit the final candle.

'I suppose it'd be better if we had an animal to sacrifice or something, but I'm not killing Bella.'

'They didn't kill animals for everything,' said Grace.

'No, but it would probably help. What else? Cut ourselves? Get drunk? Oh, cheer up, Sara. Nothing's going to happen. It's just a bit of fun.'

'Maybe to you it is, but—'

'Oh, come on,' said Caroline impatiently. 'Don't be such a spoilsport.'

'Fine,' said Grace, 'I'll do it. But you have to promise not to laugh.'

'Cross my heart.'

Grace gripped the book tightly, trying to ignore the racing of her heart. Nothing would happen. She took a deep breath, looked down at the page again, and began to read.

> *O Thebes, old nurse that cradled Semele,*
> *Be ivy-garlanded, burst into flower*
> *With wreaths of lush bright-berried bryony,*
> *Bring sprays of fir, green branches torn from oaks,*
> *Fill soul and flesh with Bacchus' mystic power;*
> *Fringe and bedeck your dappled fawnskin cloaks*

With woolly tufts and locks of purest white.
There's a brute wildness in the fennel-wands –
Reverence it well.

Caroline bit her lip to stop herself from laughing.

Soon the whole land will dance
When the god with ecstatic shout
Leads his companies out
To the mountain's mounting height
Swarming with riotous bands
Of Theban women leaving
Their spinning and their weaving
Stung with the maddening trance
Of Dionysus!

Grace raised her eyes, and there he was. Standing in the circle of candles, his eyes shining. Caroline had put her hand over Sara's mouth to stop her from screaming.

'You'll wake up my parents,' Caroline whispered. They were both stunned – terrified, even if Caroline would never admit it. They held on to each other, trembling violently.

'I told you,' said Grace. She felt neither shock nor triumph, only a strange kind of chill spreading through her.

He was taller than she remembered, or perhaps it was only the low ceiling. He was gaunt too, and if he were only a man you would think him close to death. But despite the hollows beneath his cheekbones and the pallor of his skin, there was a trace of a new vitality, something about his expression and the way he stood. At that moment he might have led an army into battle. *An army of three*, thought Grace. *He knows he has us now.*

'I'd waited long enough,' said Dionysus.

'I prayed to you every day. Why didn't you come?'

'I was busy.'

'That can't be true.'

'Are you calling me a liar? A nice way to speak to a god. Aren't you going to introduce me to your friends?'

Grace turned to Caroline and Sara, who were huddled together on the bed.

'Caroline. Sara. And this is… well, you know.'

If she hadn't been feeling so tense, she would have laughed at the absurdity of it all. Grace looked at the god, then her friends, then the god again, waiting for someone to say something.

'Now what?'

'A drink,' said Dionysus. He kneeled down and held out his cupped hands. They were filled with wine; the slightest movement could stain Caroline's rug forever.

'No glasses?' said Grace.

'I can go to the kitchen,' murmured Sara, who was still pale with shock, and anxious to get away.

'Babies.'

Caroline was making a superhuman effort to regain her self-control, having suddenly and inexplicably decided that she wanted to be a part of this new experience, whatever it was. If she couldn't be the first, she had to be the one who went the furthest. She climbed down from the bed and kneeled in front of Dionysus. She looked him straight in the eye, repressed a shudder, and then drank the wine out of his hands, like a cat with a bowl of milk.

'You're disgusting, Caro,' said Grace, a little enviously.

'She's more adventurous than you.' Dionysus licked his palms clean. '*You* wouldn't even try a drop of honey.'

Caroline leaned back against the bed, smiling. Sara stroked her hair with trembling fingers, fighting the impulse to escape.

'Are you all right?'

'Oh my God. It's the divinest thing. I can't even begin to describe it.'

'Are you drunk?' asked Grace. 'Already?'

'I have the power to do *that* at least.' Dionysus looked at Grace, and then at Sara, who was still shaking. 'Next time, it's your turn.'

'Why not now?' Grace couldn't help but feel a little jealous, seeing Caroline's smile. 'I'm not afraid.'

'You are afraid – not that it matters, but you are. And besides, I have to spare my energy. I can't waste wine on non-believers.'

'But I believe in you more than Caroline does,' said Grace indignantly. 'That's not fair.'

Dionysus ignored her and reached out to touch Sara, who flinched.

'And as for you, you'll get a taste when you stop going to church. No more Christ. Do you understand?'

Sara nodded, her eyes wide.

'The communion wine is nothing compared to what I can give you. And while it's not flowing freely yet, it will. Just wait and see.'

He stroked her shoulder, as though she were some timid little animal that needed reassurance, and she shrank away from him, closer to Caroline.

The girls watched him step back into the circle of candles; he stood there with his eyes closed and breathed deeply. This was where he belonged.

When Dionysus opened his eyes, he was looking straight at Grace. She was sure of it – that dark gaze was intended for her, and her only. She wanted to believe that the look was an apology for favouring Caroline, or a promise that the next time they met, they would be alone. But the truth was that she had no idea what it meant. It was like staring at the letters of an ancient language, trying to imagine what the words meant – if you thought you understood, you were deluding yourself.

She turned to look at Caroline and Sara, and saw that they were staring too, eyes fixed on the god. But before she could turn back, to meet his gaze once more, the candles were out and the god was gone.

IX

Sleep was out of the question. They stayed up all night, talking till their throats went dry, going over the details again and again. Caroline's drunkenness, which Grace suspected was exaggerated, wore off after a while, and they were able to have a serious conversation.

'When he told me not to go to church,' said Sara, who still looked pale and anxious, 'was that a threat?'

Grace hesitated.

'Not exactly. But to be on the safe side…'

'I can't change everything just like that.'

'You can't say no to a god,' said Caroline. 'Terrible things happen.'

'Like what?' asked Sara.

'You turn into a tree, get your skin flayed off. That kind of thing.'

'Don't scare her,' said Grace. 'Anyway, we're not going to say no to him, are we?'

'For another taste of that wine…' Caroline smiled. 'I'd do anything.'

'All right, stop going on about it.'

'How do we see him again? Do we have to do this candle ritual every time?'

'How should I know? It's the first time I've done it. It's like I keep telling you – he would appear in the street, or in the courtyard. He comes when he wants to.'

All of a sudden Grace was supposed to be the expert, to know his thoughts and intentions, when she was in the dark just as they were. It was like suddenly being appointed tour guide of a vast, wild country she'd never been to, and expected to know all the answers.

Dionysus rarely gave her answers. The next time he appeared, he appeared to Grace alone. During that enchanted part of the evening that Mauro called 'the blue hour' – the moment after sunset when the sky melted into a deep, luminous blue and everything seemed to shine – Grace saw the god in the street. Every encounter startled her;

whether she tried to summon him or not, it always felt unnerving and unexpected, as though it were the first time.

'Grace.'

She nearly jumped out of her skin. She hadn't noticed him, standing in a dark corner beneath cascading vines. There was no one else there, and no noise apart from the gurgle of the drinking fountain. It was one of those picturesque yet pointless streets that was only used by tourists looking for water or a photo opportunity, or by locals looking for somewhere to dump their rubbish.

'I didn't see you,' said Grace, taking a few tentative steps towards him. 'What are you doing here?'

'Passing time.'

She didn't know why he had chosen to come to her alone, when he could have just as easily visited the three of them together. Was he waiting for Sara to overcome her fear? Or was it part of a game, to make them wait, to make them want him? He had done the same thing to her, after all.

Grace was never sure how she was supposed to talk to him. It was hard having a conversation with someone whose questions were rhetorical rather than personal, and whose answers, when he gave them, seemed to invite no response. Whenever she tried to turn the conversation into a 'chat', daring to talk to him as though he were just another person, he acted as though he hadn't heard her.

'You must find me boring,' said Grace, with a nervous smile. 'I don't know what to say sometimes.'

'Then don't say anything,' said Dionysus.

They had been standing by the fountain for what felt like an eternity to Grace. She was trying to summon up the courage to ask about the wine – to ask for the taste that she felt she was entitled to by now. But what if he was still too weak? Or perhaps her faith was not enough, and she needed to do more, somehow, before she would be granted a sip. Did he really think that Caroline was more deserving than she was?

'There's your answer,' he said. She glanced down at the fountain and saw that the water had turned to wine. It was gushing out, spraying their feet and creating dark rivers between the gaps in the cobble-stones.

Grace quickly kneeled down and took a gulp. As soon as she swallowed, she was drunk, or at least what she imagined drunkenness felt like. She had never been drunk before. But if this was what it was, she understood why people did it all the time – a glorious light-headedness and warmth spreading through her. She tasted purple fruit, spices and... blood? That was the closest thing; there was a metallic tinge in the aftertaste that was somehow familiar.

She was about to lean in for another gulp when she realised, disappointed, that it was water again.

'That's it?'

'For now.'

'I didn't even ask you,' said Grace uneasily, as it suddenly dawned on her. 'Not out loud.'

She would have to be careful with her thoughts when she was in his presence. Watch her words, watch her thoughts... she would never be able to relax. Perhaps that was the real reason why his followers drank – to endure his company without anxiety or fear.

'Don't tell the others,' said Dionysus. 'When it's time...'

She didn't know what he meant – not tell them about the wine, or the mind-reading, or the fact that he had appeared to her alone? She would try to keep it all a secret nonetheless, if for no other reason than to prove to herself that she could.

'When it's time,' Grace repeated.

More than a week had passed since the sleepover, and Caroline was obsessed. Every moment between lessons – and sometimes, dangerously, during lessons – was spent in an ecstatic whisper, reliving the appearance in her bedroom and analysing it from every angle. She spoke rapturously of the wine: how it was truly divine, how she would sell her soul to taste it again.

'You shouldn't joke like that,' said Sara.

'What makes you think I'm joking?'

When Caroline wasn't reminiscing about the sleepover, she was constantly asking questions. When would he come back? Why hadn't he come back? How could they make him come back? Grace, who had said nothing of her private encounter, answered with a vague statement about how it was bound to happen sooner or later. 'When it's time,' he had said, and she trusted him. In the meantime she just had to persuade Caroline to be patient.

The endless discussion made Grace uncomfortable, especially when it took place in public places like classrooms and corridors, where anyone might overhear. The toilets struck her as particularly dangerous, as it would be easy to talk normally, thinking you were alone, only to find that a cubicle wasn't empty after all, and then what? Her imagination reliably failed her whenever she tried to picture the consequences.

One conversation made her especially uneasy. The three of them were going down the stairs together, on the way to PE. They had been talking of other things when Sara said, as if thinking aloud, 'I want to tell someone about it.'

Caroline and Grace exchanged glances.

'Tell *who*?' asked Caroline.

'I was thinking of telling my mother.'

'Of all the idiotic things… why would you tell her?'

'I'm not used to keeping secrets. I usually tell my mother everything and… it feels like an awful weight.'

Caroline waited until some sixth-formers had passed them on the stairs, and then she grabbed hold of Sara's arm.

'You mustn't, under any circumstances, tell *anyone*. Especially not your mother. You know what would happen, don't you?'

'It wouldn't necessarily be a bad thing, other people knowing.'

'All right, let's say you tell your mother. Then what? Most likely, she thinks you're mad. She makes you see a psychiatrist, takes you out of school, stops you from seeing us. Or, she thinks *he's* mad, and she panics and gets the police involved. Whether they catch him or not, that's the end for us. He goes to prison or flees the city, never to trust a girl again. Either way, no more wine.'

'Is that all you care about, Caro?' asked Grace.

'If you'd tasted it, you would understand. Anyway, do you promise not to tell, Sara?'

'Yes. Please let go of my arm. It hurts.'

'If you tell anyone we'll never forgive you. Never ever *ever*.'

Grace was used to hearing Caroline making threats, but never with such passion. It was as though everything before had been a mere rehearsal. From now on, it was real.

In the changing room Grace noticed the bruise on Sara's arm. No one mentioned it. At one point during the netball game Sara seemed to refuse to pass the ball to Caroline, but it was difficult to tell if this was an intentional slight, as none of them were any good at sports. At the end of the day, they hugged goodbye as normal. It wasn't the first time that something similar had happened – Caroline unleashed her temper, Sara sulked, and then they made up wordlessly. Every falling out began and ended just as abruptly.

During the short walk home Grace forgot about school and indulged in daydreams instead – alone with Dionysus in an empty city, every fountain flowing with wine. *The Eternal City belongs to the eternal*, said the god, wading waist-deep through blood-red pools. Marble stallions reared up, nostrils flaring and eyes rolling, and Grace clambered over the boulders, wine raining down...

A sudden explosion of car horns broke the spell, forcing her to wake up and focus on crossing the road, but the image had been beautiful while it lasted. She would return to it later, in the bath. Maybe she would even try to sketch it. She might not be able to draw the god, but she could at least try to capture the world that came with him.

In the evening, Grace had a phone call from Caroline.

'We need to talk about Sara.'

'Why?'

'I'm worried about what she might do,' said Caroline.

'You're always the one who tells *me* not to worry.'

'I know, but I feel like she could do something unpredictable.'

'She never does anything unpredictable.'

'And I never worried – until now. There's a first time for everything.'

Grace sighed.

'You shouldn't have called,' she said, watching Barbara pass through the hallway. 'I can hardly talk about it here. Unlike you, I don't have a phone in my bedroom.'

'Of course you can talk. You just have to be careful about what you say. So, how can we keep her quiet?'

'Keep her quiet? God, Caro. You make it sound like we've killed someone and she's about to confess.'

'It's at least as serious as that. Maybe more.'

'Well, I don't think she would tell anyone. Apart from anything else, she's probably scared of what you'd do to her.'

'Ha ha.'

'I mean it. At the moment she's just feeling scared and over-whelmed because it's new. That's how I felt a month ago. She'll calm down.'

'Grace!' Mauro was calling from the kitchen in his abominable accent, giving her name an extra syllable.

'I've got to go, Caro.'

'No, wait. I have a theory and I want to know what you think.'

'A theory? Sounds fancy.'

'An idea, whatever. I think Sara is more likely to tell someone while she feels detached, like she's not really part of it. At the moment it probably seems like a crazy dream.'

'It still feels like that to me.'

'Anyway, we need to get her more involved. Get them alone together, maybe, get her drunk.'

'What are you suggesting?'

'She needs to be part of it. It doesn't matter how, but until she's properly involved and racked with guilt I think she's a risk.'

'I don't think so. I think people are more likely to talk if they're feeling guilty. Besides, Catholics have that whole confession thing.'

'Grace!' Mauro bellowed.

'Coming!' Grace shouted back. Then, turning back to the receiver, 'We'll talk tomorrow, okay?'

'If you sin deeply enough, you'll never dare to confess,' said Caroline. She hung up.

X

The following days brought grey skies and the threat of rain. It seemed unnatural here, somehow. Grace looked above the pyramid, searching for a spot of blue. Dionysus sat beside her on the bench, wearing a long grey coat and scarf. His arms were folded, and he was staring at the white marble of the pyramid as if it held the answer to one of life's great mysteries.

'Are you cold?' asked Grace.

'Freezing.'

'It's not that cold really. Only when you compare it to the summer. In England I'm sure it's much worse.'

It comforted her to compare the weather with England and appreciate one small advantage of living abroad. Dionysus stared at her blankly, as if to say, 'Why should I care about England?' Grace wasn't sure if he wanted to talk or remain silent. It could be difficult to tell. She glanced shyly at him, sideways. He was sitting at the opposite end of the bench, pressed into the corner, and she was acutely aware of the distance.

'It's a beautiful place,' said Grace tentatively. 'I've been here before, with Sara. She used to be obsessed with a couple of poets who are buried here, and she wanted to bring them flowers. They died young.'

'I've looked at some of the graves. Mostly foreigners. And you're right, lots of them died young. Lucky.'

'Lucky? Eighteen-year-olds who died of tuberculosis?'

'Well, I wouldn't trade places with them. But at least there's a kind of sense in it. You live, you die, your body rots. That's it. Whereas I...'

He trailed off. Grace followed his gaze to the tip of the pyramid.

'Was that the first thing you saw when you woke up?'

Dionysus nodded.

'There must have been a moment before the pyramid. I can't have suddenly changed from non-existence to lying on the grass in a cemetery. But when I try to follow the chain of memories back, my mind goes dark. Everything fades too quickly, and I can't put things in order. The smell of smoke, Ariadne's lips. Which came first?'

'Does it matter?'

'At the moment I'm as stupid as an infant, but with the powers of a god. I'd say that makes me rather dangerous, wouldn't you? To myself as well as others.'

'You mean you need some kind of understanding.'

'Exactly.'

How was she supposed to help him understand when she understood nothing? It made her anxious when their conversations took this turn – as though she was being pressured into promising something. She had nothing to offer him but her belief.

'I really don't think I can help you,' said Grace.

'But you must, you must.' His voice hardened as he tried to disguise his desperation. 'You and Caroline and Sara. You don't know how powerful you are.'

'I don't know what you mean.'

'You will.'

Dionysus shivered and clenched his fists in his coat pockets – a small, human gesture that was somehow calming.

'If you're too cold sitting here,' said Grace, 'we can move.'

'No, I like it here. It calms me.'

'It's very peaceful.'

'Only us and the dead.'

Grace wondered if in some sense Dionysus was also dead, which would make her the only living soul in the cemetery. She looked at him curiously for a moment, and then quickly lowered her gaze. Despite their growing intimacy, he still horrified her sometimes.

'You're afraid of me,' said Dionysus.

'No, I'm not.'

'Yes, you are. I can sense it. It's only natural. Even my lovers were afraid – my mortal lovers. Ariadne trembled perpetually.'

'You're shivering too. I could believe that you're afraid of me.'

'Except that would be ridiculous.'

Grace suddenly remembered Pippin's existence. He was sitting on the ground, as far away from the god as the lead would allow, and trembling from head to tail.

'Come here, Pippin.'

Pippin ignored her and strained even further on the lead as if in protest; next time she would leave the dog at home.

'You should go,' said Dionysus.

'Why?'

'If you're afraid, then your poor dog is petrified.'

'I wonder why. What's the matter, Pippin?'

Pippin would not even turn to look at her.

'Do you have that effect on all animals?' Grace asked.

'Some are more sensitive than others.'

Grace stood up, and Pippin immediately started straining on the lead, pulling her away.

'I suppose I should probably go home. My mother will be wondering where I am.'

'Next time, don't bring him. Bring *them*.'

She left him sitting alone among the dead, and walked away to rejoin the world of the living.

At Caroline's insistence, Sara read *The Bacchae*. She did not study Classics and the play was entirely new to her. When she returned the heavily annotated copy she had borrowed from Caroline, she seemed even more confused and anxious. When she was upset a line appeared on her forehead, and it seemed to be an almost permanent feature these days.

'So the message of the play,' said Sara, 'is that you have to worship the gods or be punished?'

'It sounds awfully reductive when you put it like that,' said Caroline. 'But essentially, yes. Love him or be torn to pieces.'

'But *The Bacchae* is just a play, isn't it? Euripides' Dionysus is a character. He's not the same as our Dionysus.'

'Still, I wouldn't take any chances.'

At last, for reasons known only to himself, Dionysus decided that it was time. For their next meeting with the god they received instructions – through a handwritten note that appeared in Grace's bedroom – to be in front of a certain church at ten o'clock on Friday night. The letters were difficult to decipher and written in a peculiar, purplish ink, but the paper seemed to have been ripped from one of Grace's own notebooks. Once the initial excitement had faded slightly, Grace was unsettled by the idea of him prowling around in her room when she wasn't there – or worse, when she was sleeping – and rifling through her possessions.

'But what does he want from us?' asked Sara. She held the note between a pinched thumb and forefinger, unsure whether to treat the piece of paper as a precious relic or a potentially toxic substance.

'We'll just have to go and find out,' said Caroline. 'We can tell our parents that we're at a sleepover at someone else's house – me at yours, Grace at mine, you at Grace's – and that gives us all night.'

All night. The thought was enough to make Grace shiver with anticipation, but deep down she shared Sara's fears – more than she would admit to herself or Caroline. Before he had appeared at random. Once they had summoned him, and now he was summoning them. She looked at the note again, written in handwriting that was at once beautiful and nearly illegible. He had given no reason for the meeting. He was not begging or threatening, but simply telling her to be at the church at ten o'clock. And she would be there, of course. The days of believing she could ignore him were long gone. Ignoring him would be like denying the existence of an oncoming bus as you stepped into the road. He was inevitable and highly dangerous if neglected. Like Caroline, she chose to believe that Euripides was right about this.

As she put on her coat and scarf, preparing to go out on Friday evening, she reflected that acting out of fear was not the ideal way to live one's life. But even before him, hadn't most of her choices been made out of fear? She studied for fear of failing; she did and didn't do certain things for fear of Caroline. That was life for most people, she suspected. All she could hope was that her feelings for Dionysus – an uneasy mix of fear and pity – would one day be transformed into the rapturous love of the Chorus.

She was the first to arrive at the church. She was always the first to arrive anywhere. Standing in the shadows, arms folded to keep herself warm, she hoped she did not look too suspicious to anyone who was passing by.

This was a quiet part of the city. Lonely by day, lonelier by night. The church was only a few streets away from the place where she had first met him and watched him make honey ooze from sun-baked walls. As she waited, her eyes moved restlessly from the moon to the dark windows of the surrounding buildings – grand, crumbling edifices with barred windows, which resembled palaces or prisons, depending on your mood. No one lived there now. This square had always been strangely deserted, and whenever she passed the church during the day, it was invariably closed. This aura of neglect was particularly peculiar considering that the chaotic heart of the city was just a five-minute walk to the east.

He must have chosen the square for its silence, thought Grace. Not for its church. He must hate churches. She could still recall the contempt in his voice when he'd spoken of Jesus.

In the next few minutes a priest and an old lady appeared and then disappeared at the opposite edges of the square. It was so poorly lit that when someone turned a corner, they seemed to be swallowed whole by the darkness.

At last the recognisable shapes of Sara and Caroline materialised on the far side of the square.

'You're late,' said Grace.

'No, you're early.' A moment later the bells of another church began to chime ten.

'See?' said Caroline. 'We're exactly on time. Anyway, where is he?'

Her voice sounded shaky; although she had sneered at Sara for being afraid, she was just as nervous now. Or perhaps it was just the cold. She was also wearing more make-up than usual; Grace smiled to herself, wondering if Caroline's eyelashes were supposed to impress the god.

'It's so cold,' said Sara, her voice barely more than a whisper. 'I hope we're going inside, wherever we're going.'

'This way.'

They turned round in unison and saw that familiar, mask-like face half hidden in the shadows behind them. Grace felt tremulous and disorientated, as though the ground beneath her had suddenly turned to water. Sara held tightly on to Caroline's arm – a lifebelt in uncharted waters.

'How long have you been waiting?' asked Grace, not quite daring to look the god directly in the eye.

'Centuries,' said Dionysus. 'Come on.'

He was standing in front of a low door in a wall, which Grace had not noticed before. It looked as though it had been locked for decades, but as soon as he touched it, it swung open soundlessly. They followed him into a narrow courtyard, filled with broken chairs and dying plants, and then through another door.

Logically, there was nowhere else they could be, but Grace was still astonished to find herself standing in the middle of the church, beneath blazing candles and the fading eyes of the saints.

'My home,' said Dionysus.

'You live *here*?' Caroline sounded incredulous.

'It's warm, it's dry. Comparatively, anyway. I used to rest beneath a sort of archway not far from here, but apparently I wasn't the only one attempting to live there. The smell was appalling.'

Here, instead, Grace could still breathe in the lingering incense from the evening's service. Despite having no inclination towards Catholicism, she had often thought that the smell of incense alone might be enough to make her go to mass.

'I didn't think this church was used any more,' she said.

'It is, sometimes. But at night it's mine.' He stood behind the altar, his face inscrutable.

'Unbelievable.' Sara was shivering in the pews. Grace sat beside her and put an arm around her.

'I know it's cold even in here,' said Dionysus, deliberately misinterpreting Sara's shivers. 'But I have something that will warm you up.'

He sat on the carpet at the front of the church, framed by vases of lilies and rows of candlesticks, seven feet high. Caroline came forward eagerly to join him, and Grace led the trembling Sara by the hand. For a split second an image flashed into her mind – someone leading a lamb to be sacrificed.

She let go of Sara's hand and sat cross-legged on the floor. Looking up at him, she thought how strange it was that every time they met, it felt like the first time. He was a stranger once more. It was partly because she had no idea how he passed his time when they were apart – whether he was orchestrating bacchanals in faraway hills or lying in the gutter and dreaming of the past, it was a total mystery to her. The one time she had tried to ask, instead of appeasing her with one of his short, enigmatic answers, he hadn't even responded but had simply stared into the middle distance. He turned into a statue when it suited him.

He also seemed to change between each encounter, something so subtle that it was almost imperceptible. It was only after the shock of his reappearance had faded that she could tentatively begin to define it as a change of light. He did not shine, but somehow lent a peculiar brilliance to the surrounding atmosphere. The dark spaces around his body crackled; the ground beneath him glowed.

It was not something she had noticed at all during their first meeting; possibly it had not even existed then. Now, however, he seemed to grow steadily brighter, which could only mean that he was becoming stronger.

He was staring at her, eyes gleaming in the candlelight, and she suddenly became convinced that he was reading her thoughts. She lowered her eyes to the carpet.

'It is time for your education,' said Dionysus. 'At the moment all of you are only half alive.'

Grace certainly didn't *feel* half alive. She was wide awake, and her heart was pounding as though she had drunk ten cups of coffee. She glanced at her friends and saw that they were also looking at Dionysus with wide-eyed solemnity. Grace had never seen Caroline look so attentive and serious about anything before.

'The first thing you must understand is the importance of wine. Why do we drink? To escape?'

'Yes,' said Caroline.

'No. We drink to experience the moment fully, in its greatest intensity. You don't flee from the fire, but fling yourself into the heart of it.'

'Then you burn,' said Grace.

'That's half the pleasure.' Dionysus took four silver cups from the altar and filled them with wine like blood: a deep, seductive red.

'We can't drink from those.' Sara was aghast. 'I'd never forgive myself if...'

Dionysus's stare prevented her from finishing the sentence.

'Jesus doesn't care, because he's a dead man. God doesn't care, because he doesn't exist. The priest would care if he knew, but he'll never know. So you would only be making yourself feel guilty for no reason. Guilt is an absolutely useless emotion.'

The girls accepted the cups that were offered to them, though Sara still looked unhappy.

'To me,' said Dionysus.

They raised their cups and drank.

The moment it touched Grace's lips, she had a flash of Caroline's ecstasy, and of the wine gushing from the fountain in the street. But as the taste deepened, her mind cleared, fogged, cleared again. It was so rich that it made the memory of every other taste turn to ashes, so deep that to drink it was to bathe in it. She felt a delicious warmth spreading through her body. The others must have felt it too, as coats and jumpers were soon discarded, and they lay on the church floor in a state of utter bliss, moving only to sip from their cups, which were filled again and again.

She was aware of Dionysus speaking, but she could not distinguish the words. They were merely honeyed sounds that dissolved in the air, while Caroline's laughter rose up like bubbles. Then the god disappeared – she could no longer see his face, and for a moment she was afraid. She raised her eyes to the church ceiling to look for him, only to realise that he was still beside them, or even inside them. She couldn't say exactly where he was, but the more she drank, the more she was filled with the beautiful certainty of his presence. He had transcended his body and was with them in a higher form. She could feel his light, his warmth. Every time she swallowed it was like a dazzling kiss, turning everything gold.

There were words and music she would never be able to recall. The last thing she saw was the wine from her overturned cup dyeing the carpet a deeper red, and then darkness.

He had gone. When she woke up, he had gone. Her first feeling was of a sorrow so deep, an abandonment so wretched, that she could have wept. The church was filled with the grey light of morning, and as she looked around all she could see were the mournful eyes of Christ on the cross high above her.

Everything ached. If it were only her head, it wouldn't be so bad, but it was *everything*. A dull pain throbbing through her limbs and torso, like a punishment or warning. Pain was the body's way of telling you not to do something again. But what had she done?

She would think about it later, once the ache had subsided and she was able to sit up. She couldn't move now, not with this strange weight on her thighs. It was like a stone. She was struck by a wild, hysterical thought: they had tried to bury her alive.

Grace finally managed to raise her head and see Caroline's messy blonde hair. In the absence of a pillow, she had settled on Grace's legs.

She was not alone, thank God. The relief flooded through her. Just the weight of Caroline's head was enough to calm her, to remind her to breathe. While she had Caroline she could breathe. Everything would be all right.

Then she looked at her watch, and her newfound sense of tranquillity vanished in an instant. 7.35! That was practically eight. Was there such a thing as morning mass? Or would there be a cleaner? The prospect of being discovered was so horribly real that it immediately eclipsed all other fears.

'Caro, wake up.' She was trying so hard not to panic, but she could hear the anxiety in her voice. 'We have to wake up.'

She shook Caroline until she was finally able to rouse her from that mysterious state of sleep or unconsciousness. Caroline awoke with a smile on her wine-stained lips.

'God, what a night. Could you ever have dreamed—'

'We can talk later. We have to get out of here quickly, before someone finds us.'

'Where is he?'

'Who?'

'*Him.*'

'How should I know?' It was difficult to think, and Grace was as frustrated by her own slowness of mind as by Caroline's inability to wake up and comprehend the danger of their situation.

'I want him,' said Caroline, her blue eyes disturbingly vacant.

'What about Sara? Where's Sara?'

Grace disentangled herself from Caroline and held on to the edge of a pew for support as she stood up. She limped down the aisle, trying to ignore all those unanswerable questions – *Why does my whole body ache? What happened?* – as she concentrated on the figure of Sara, slumped over in a pew in the middle of the church.

'Sara. *Sara.*'

Sara didn't respond. Grace pushed the hair away from her face and was alarmed to see that she was several shades paler than usual.

'She looks like a corpse.' Caroline had followed Grace down the aisle, having rapidly sobered up.

'Help me, Caro. What can we do?'

'We have to wake her up.'

Caroline turned around and looked thoughtfully at the floor. Grace assumed that she was trying to think of an answer until Caroline asked, 'What happened to all the snakes?'

'What snakes?'

'The ones from last night. They were there, and there, and at one point I felt one—'

'Caro,' Grace pleaded, 'please can we save this for later? We need to get her out of here.'

'I'm thinking.'

Caroline walked towards the font and filled her cupped hands with holy water. A moment later Sara was awake and spluttering. Another moment, and she was in tears.

'It's so cold,' she said, wiping her eyes. 'I want to go home.'

'Here's your coat and scarf. We're going now.'

They left the church and emerged in the empty square. There were no priests or other passers-by to fear. The sky was grey, and it was even colder than in the church. The girls linked arms; they were craving each other's warmth, and needed to hold on to each other just to stay upright. Sara was particularly unsteady, tottering over the cobbles while supported on either side by Caroline and Grace. She had stopped crying, but she looked around with wide, frightened eyes, as though she didn't recognise her surroundings. Above them a pair of seagulls whirled and screamed, and the bleak music of the church bells drifted across the city.

'Coffee,' said Caroline decisively. 'That's what we need.'

In the square with the turtle fountain they found a small bar where a couple of dustmen were shouting at each other to be heard above the noise of the coffee machine, and a mother was trying to soothe her wailing child. The din and the smell of coffee clearly appealed to Caroline, who dragged them inside before either of them could protest.

Once they were squashed together at a table at the back, drinking tiny cups of bitter coffee, Grace was forced to admit that Caroline had been right. When she reached the dregs she savoured the bitterness on her tongue, a reminder that the madness of last night was over. Then she felt the rush of her heart as the coffee kicked in, and she realised that waking up would mean reliving everything she could remember about last night. It was not like some schoolbook she could leave to gather dust on a shelf, in sight but out of mind.

'I wonder,' said Caroline, 'if anyone's ever been that drunk before.'

Grace reached for a glass of water, eager to get rid of the awful aftertaste.

'Of course,' she said between gulps. 'You always want to be the first at everything.'

'I *feel* like the first.' Caroline rubbed her eyes, and her fingertips became smudged with the remnants of yesterday's make-up. 'I must look a mess.'

'We all do. But I'm starting to feel better.'

'And what about you? How do you feel?' Caroline turned to Sara, who was mechanically stirring her coffee. She was still pale, but she had lost the deathly tinge.

'Hideous,' said Sara, with the ghost of a smile. 'Also kind of wonderful.'

'I know what you mean. It's the strangest sensation... like being hollowed out and filled with something, a kind of possession. It's like I don't belong to myself any more, or the world. I'm above it.'

'That's exactly it.'

'I suppose we'd better try to pull ourselves together.'

'What about our parents?' Grace asked suddenly.

Caroline and Sara looked at her as if she had just uttered the name of an old, long-forgotten friend who had no relevance to the conversation.

'What about them?' asked Caroline.

'Where do they think we are?'

'We said we were having a sleepover, didn't we?'

'Did we? I don't remember anything.'

'Neither do I. Only the snakes.'

'I don't remember any snakes.' Grace frowned. 'What about you, Sara?'

'Yes,' said Sara. She looked troubled, but spoke in a calm, matter-of-fact tone of voice, as though she were recounting an incident that had happened to someone else, or something she had read about in the news. 'They were everywhere, all over us. Long, green snakes with yellow eyes. At one point one of them talked to me.'

Caroline spluttered over her coffee.

'It talked to you? Don't be ridiculous.'

'Why is it any more ridiculous than anything else that happened?' asked Sara.

'All right, what did it say then?'

'It wasn't in English. But it said *something*.'

'Yeah, right.'

'I don't remember the snakes,' said Grace. 'I really don't remember anything at all. I thought it would come back to me when I woke up, but my mind's blank.'

It wasn't fair that Caroline and Sara had been left with a memory, while she had nothing. All she had was a headache, a stomach ache, and the worrying sense that she was not merely forgetting, but was actually repressing what had happened. She couldn't shake the feeling that some part of her mind was trying to protect her. Not just from the snakes, which seemed like a colourful but insignificant detail, but from… what? Only he could tell her, and she knew already that he wouldn't.

'Maybe you need another coffee,' said Caroline.

'I'm not sure that's a good idea. I already feel a bit jittery.'

'I don't feel jittery enough. Sara?'

Sara shook her head and took a deep, tremulous breath. 'Excuse me.'

She got up, crossed the room and locked herself in the toilet. Even the existing din – the shouting and the wailing and the explosive hiss of the coffee machine – was not enough to drown her out entirely.

XI

Grace stood in the kitchen, staring at a bottle of red wine on the kitchen counter. It belonged to Mauro, and it was the only one she could find that had already been opened. She uncorked it and poured a modest amount into a glass – not too much, just in case Mauro noticed. She held it to the light, turning the glass so the liquid swirled, and tried to discern a difference. Then she took a cautious sip and let it linger for a moment before swallowing.

Of course it was the same drink. Wine was wine. It was silly to expect it to have some immediate effect, and yet she was disappointed when nothing happened. She supposed she would have to drink at least a bottle to come close to the sensations of Friday night, and even then, it probably wouldn't be the same without his presence.

She was still contemplating this mystery as Barbara walked into the kitchen.

'What are you doing with Mauro's wine?'

'Drinking it,' said Grace, who could think of no other answer.

'I wouldn't, if I were you. You know what he's like.'

Mauro was famously bad at sharing. Grace nodded and put the cork back in the bottle, glad not to have been questioned further. She had friends with sisters who were always asking questions, and rummaging through their wardrobes and drawers when they were denied answers. Grace was lucky to have a sister who never even pretended to show the slightest interest in anything she did.

In this respect Barbara had taken after their mother, whose lack of interest extended to other people in general. In the past Grace had sometimes felt uninteresting and unlovable as a result, but now she could see the advantages of their indifference. It was useful when you had secrets.

It was around this time that Grace had a whim, which later transformed into something rather more serious. She had a small set of decorative shelves with tiny drawers, made of wood and hand-painted with green and pink flowers. It had been a gift from a relative – she couldn't remember who – and she had once used it for displaying ornaments and storing jewellery. Now she had the urge to dust it off and put it to a different use.

If her mother ever explored the depths of Grace's wardrobe, she would discover little shelves lined with candles and an old perfume bottle filled with Chianti. Dried flowers and ivy leaves were entwined around the handles of the drawers, and in the centre was a white figure cut out from a postcard. Dionysus held his thyrsus, an expression of divine indifference on his pale face.

Grace had already prepared an explanation, in case her mother found the shrine.

'It's for school.'

Art project or Classics homework. It would be easy to explain if it were found at the bottom of the wardrobe; less easy if someone walked in on Grace worshipping, candles burning.

To an outsider it would seem absurd, but for Grace it was a necessity. The terrible isolation she had felt on first waking in the church was perhaps her most vivid memory from the whole experience. She had feared his presence, but now she dreaded his absence even more. This amateurish little shrine helped her to feel closer to him.

She didn't mention it to Caroline. Caroline would only laugh, or reveal that she had made a bigger and better one first, and that she worshipped twice a day. But nearly every aspect of this new part of her life was discussed with Caroline, especially at weekends. Out in the city, away from the gossips at school, they could talk freely.

'I don't think I've ever felt this excited about anything in my life.'

They were sitting together in a grotty carriage on the metro, sometimes practically shouting in each other's ears to be heard above the roar of the train. Grace couldn't understand how a mere train could make so much noise. From the shuddering of the carriage and the ominous screeches inside the dark tunnel, she sometimes wondered if the driver had a death wish. She envisioned derailings and explosions while Caroline talked in her ear.

'And it's like he chose us. We're special.'

'When it was only me,' said Grace, 'you said that there couldn't be anything special or significant about it.'

'Did I? I don't remember saying that. Anyway, everything's different now. Our secret.'

She grinned and pulled a lock of Grace's hair affectionately. Grace pretended to find it irritating, but she secretly rather liked it. She liked Caroline's teasing, and she loved Caroline when she was like this – bright-eyed and smiling and full of excitement for the future. When her disdain for other people was not so obvious, Caroline could be extremely endearing. She was softer today, somehow.

'I wonder when we'll see him again.'

'Soon, I think. I bet he's just as impatient as we are.'

'He could come at any time. I suppose that's—'

A young gypsy entered the carriage and started attempting to play the accordion. Caroline abandoned her sentence, and the conversation was put on hold, as they could not hope to compete with the din of the train *and* the accordion.

Caroline wanted to go shopping, so they went to the usual places in the centre, looking at shoes they couldn't afford and spending hours looking at themselves and each other in changing-room mirrors.

'It looks quite good on you,' said Caroline, 'but it'd look better on me.'

'Fine,' said Grace, unbuttoning the dress. It was not as though she could buy it anyway. She was used to these shopping trips, which mainly involved watching Caroline spend all her pocket money. Grace could never work out if she was deprived or Caroline was spoilt.

She leaned against the wall of the booth and watched Caroline change into the dress, pale pink with a ribbon around the waist.

'Isn't it strange to be doing something so normal again?'

'I know what you mean,' said Caroline. 'Back to reality. Well, I suppose we can't be drunk all the time.'

'Not just that. I mean, right now it's just like before. Before we met him.'

'But it isn't really. We know he's there – somewhere. We know he'll come back to us.'

'It just seems hard, having to carry on with normal life when we know that an alternative exists.'

Together with Sara, they had spent an entire lunch hour imagining the alternative – living as maenads in the eternal summer of the dappled woods, drinking wine all the time and never having to go to school. As blissful as it sounded, they all agreed that they weren't quite ready yet.

'I don't know,' said Caroline. 'I rather like leading a double life. Besides, I wouldn't give up shopping, not even for a god.'

Caroline turned around to admire herself in the mirror. Grace noticed that it did look better on Caroline after all, but of course she would never say it.

'I think I'll get this one. Then shall we go? I need a drink.'

On the way to the till, Caroline discreetly slipped a silk scarf into her bag. When they were out of the shop Grace said, 'I thought you were going to give that up?'

'What?'

'Stealing.'

'God, keep your voice down.' For a moment Caroline looked embarrassed, but when she next spoke, it was with the tone of indifference she used whenever she was trying to hide her guilt.

'I don't see why it matters. What we did last week was far worse, and if I don't regret that, I'm not going to feel bad about taking something small here and there.'

'I guess there's a kind of logic in that.'

They walked on in silence until they reached the cafe.

Hot chocolate seemed like the most innocent drink in the world after the previous weekend's excess. Grace took slow sips and watched Caroline put on her stolen scarf and admire herself in the mirror.

'It does suit me, doesn't it?'

'So would the crown jewels, probably. Would you steal those?'

'I don't know why you're being so judgemental all of a sudden. Anyway, I was going to ask you if you'd spoken to Sara.'

'About what?'

'About this crisis she seems to be having.'

'You can't really blame her, can you? It must be awfully strange, spending your whole life believing in one thing only to be confronted with… well, the opposite.'

'I had a chat with her on Thursday.'

'When?'

'After school. I invited her over.'

'You didn't invite me.'

'We don't have to be together all the time, Grace. I am allowed to spend time with other people, you know.'

Grace knew that Caroline and Sara often did things without her, and it hurt. Of course it was always Caroline who instigated it, and she did the same thing with Grace sometimes, deliberately excluding Sara. When Grace had complained about this to her mother, her mother had replied, without looking up from her book, 'It's a power thing, darling. She likes to have you both under her control.'

Grace's mother was always portraying Caroline as some kind of tyrant, and Grace was reluctant to believe this was true – not for Caroline's sake, but because of what it implied about her own character.

'What did Sara say?' asked Grace.

'Not much. I think I did most of the talking.'

'I'm sure you did.'

'She seems a lot calmer now, strangely. I thought she would be even more upset, after everything that's happened. But it seems to have had the opposite effect. Now she's sort of resigned to it. She can't deny that he exists, or that she's part of it.'

'So she's not going to tell anyone.'

'I don't think so. I mean, maybe one day she'll break down and tell her priest, but then he could hardly go and talk about it with someone else, could he? They're meant to keep everyone's secrets.'

'I don't know. I think if you confess that you've killed someone or something like that, the priest would have to tell the police.'

'Really? That doesn't seem fair. I thought it was just supposed to be between you and God.'

'I'm not sure. You'll have to ask Sara.'

'No, I don't want to give her ideas.'

Caroline sighed and poured some sugar into her hot chocolate.

'I don't know how you can drink it like that.'

'Well, too much sugar is the least of my vices at the moment.' She licked her lips. 'You know, my admirer wasn't there on Friday. I wonder where he was.'

'Maybe he's found another girl to stalk.'

'I hope not. It's not that I like him, because I don't, but I've become sort of used to him.'

'You should talk to him one day and see what he wants.'

'I know what he wants. All men are the same.'

Caroline was never very convincing when she spoke with the air of a woman of the world, but nonetheless, Grace suspected she was right.

When Grace went home that evening, she found Dionysus waiting for her in her bedroom. She managed to stop herself from screaming, and instead gasped a barely audible 'Oh my God.' It was not the first time she had found him here, but it still felt like a violation, some kind of nasty trick.

'You gave me such a fright,' she said breathlessly, slamming the door shut.

Dionysus was lying on her bed, completely at ease; it might have been his own.

'I found your shrine. Pretty little thing.'

'Did you notice when I prayed?'

Grace was still standing with her back pressed to the door, as if keeping her distance from a large and dangerous animal whose cage she had fallen into.

'Of course. I feel it every time.' He rearranged the pillows to make himself more comfortable. 'Come and sit next to me so we don't have to shout at each other. You don't want your mother to hear, do you?'

'Or my sister. She's right next door.'

'Well, then come over here and whisper.'

Grace sat on the bed, drawing her knees up to her chest. She still found it hard to look at him directly, so as they spoke she would give him short, sidelong glances, seeing his lips, then the curve of his jaw, then the arch of an eyebrow that almost made him look human.

'How do you feel a prayer?'

'It's difficult to explain,' he said slowly. 'Imagine you have another part to your body, like an invisible limb. With every prayer you feel it growing harder, stronger, until you believe that you could stroke the face of the sun without being burned. It's the most beautiful sensation.'

Grace frowned as she tried to imagine this.

'But it can't be like that now, with only a few of us believing in you.'

'No, I'm much weaker now. It won't ever be exactly the same. It won't be a chariot drawn by leopards and thousands chanting my name, but it will be something – a little of my old glory recaptured. I can't have been born just to wander the streets and dream of the past.'

'Is that what you do when you're not with us?'

'Most of the time. I couldn't tell you exactly. All I know is that I've spent too many hours trying to recollect the past in the hope of making sense of the present. Wasted nights thinking of my father, my leopards, my lovers. Nostalgia is like guilt – another emotion serving no purpose.'

'So it's better not to think of it at all.'

'Dwelling on it is the dangerous thing. When I first woke up in the cemetery I was frightened by how little I could remember, but it's all flooding back to me now.'

Their conversation continued late into the night, and as Grace grew used to his presence and the absurdity of him being in her bed, the distance between them narrowed, so that their bodies were almost touching. It was surreal to recall how remote and imposing he had seemed when talking to them in the church; now, lying side by side and talking in low voices, Grace felt as though she were talking to an older, more experienced friend, whom she loved and envied in equal measure.

She had curled up next to Caroline like this many times before, and comparing the experiences made her aware of a subtle but significant difference.

'You don't smell of anything,' she remarked.

'Why, should I?'

'Most people do.'

'I'm not "people", let alone most of them.'

'I was just thinking of Caroline, who has this particular smell. I can't really describe it. And generally with people there's always this faint scent of *something*, whether it's soap or sweat or something they've eaten.'

'According to my father I had the smell of smoke and singed flesh for weeks after I was born. But that's it.'

'What about in India? Euripides talks about you coming to Thebes from India, all perfumed.'

'Oh, well, if Euripides says it…'

'But you did go to India, didn't you?'

'I've been everywhere, Grace. It makes my head ache just to think of it.'

'Please tell me about India.'

His lips twitched and he closed his eyes.

'I remember dust and snakes, a dance that lasted from sunrise to sunrise, a girl with eyes like fire winding flowers through my hair…'

The memories, real or imagined, were whispered into her ear in that peculiar accent, like a man who has taught himself to speak every language beautifully without ever feeling the words. There was something soporific about his voice, which became lower and lower until the words turned into dreams chasing each other through Grace's bewildered mind.

XII

'Grace, can I have a word?'

Miss Seymour looked up from her books and peered down at Grace through her glasses. Grace had already seen the exclamations scrawled across her essay in red ink, so she knew what the 'word' was about.

'I'll wait for you outside,' said Caroline.

Grace stood by Miss Seymour's desk in the inelegant, slouching way that most of her teachers reprimanded her for. Miss Seymour, however, was indifferent to posture and only cared about scholarship.

'I can see that *The Bacchae* is a play you feel quite strongly about.'

'Mmm,' said Grace.

Miss Seymour picked up the essay and glanced at the comments she'd written; presumably they were intelligible to her, if not to Grace.

'I've never known you to write anything quite so forceful. It makes a change from all the essays last year where you seemed reluctant to express an opinion on anything at all.'

'So I've improved?'

'Well, er…' Miss Seymour hesitated, and then turned back to the first page. 'I would draw your attention to the title.'

'The use of stichomythia and other dramatic devices.'

'You did write about stichomythia somewhere in the introduction, I believe. But the rest of your essay bears no relation to the question.'

'You mean I digressed.'

'Quite. And some of the views you express near the end surprised me. Here you seem to imply that Pentheus's punishment wasn't harsh enough.'

'It could have been worse. That's all I'm saying.'

'Worse than having your own mother tear your body to pieces?'

Grace bit her lip and did not answer.

'Please try a more objective approach next time.'

'Yes, Miss.'

'And remember that they are only characters. We mustn't treat them like real people.'

'Of course.'

'I won't keep you any longer. Off to lunch.'

Caroline was waiting at the top of the stairs.

'What did you get?' asked Grace.

'"Odysseus". I got a "Penelope" a couple of weeks ago, but it's mostly been "Odysseuses" this term.'

Miss Seymour had developed her own idiosyncratic system. Instead of assigning grades or marks out of ten, she wrote the name of a character from the *Odyssey* at the bottom of the page. 'Odysseus' was the best you could hope for, while a less important character such as 'Nestor' or 'Nausicaa' signified that there was room for improvement.

'I don't know how you always do so well.'

'Why, what did she give you?'

'Eurydamas.'

'Ouch.'

'I don't even know who that is.'

'I think he's one of the suitors. Anyway, better luck next time.'

They found Sara waiting for them near the entrance to the dining hall. The three of them always sat together for lunch, as eating alone was a kind of social suicide. Once, when Sara had been ill and Caroline mysteriously absent, Grace had missed lunch rather than enter the dining hall on her own.

It was a cold and dreary room, with no windows and nothing on the walls. The food was unpleasant but mostly edible. There used to be a teacher patrolling the room and ensuring that the younger girls finished everything on their plates, but this practice ended after a first-form girl choked – perhaps on purpose – on a chunk of unwanted meat and had to be taken to hospital.

Today it was vegetable soup and rock-hard potatoes. Caroline, the fussiest of the three, pulled a face.

'How was RE?' asked Grace.

'All right,' said Sara, trying to cut into the potatoes. 'A lot on transubstantiation.'

'That reminds me,' said Caroline, 'are you still going to church?'

'On Sundays? Yes, I always go on Sundays.'

'But isn't it odd? Doesn't it feel wrong now?'

The bacchanals had become a weekly event – a Friday ritual. It took them the entire weekend to fully recover, but while Caroline and Grace were still comatose in their bedrooms, Sara forced herself to get up early on Sunday mornings and go to mass with her parents.

'I can't really explain how it feels. It's different.'

'It's not like you can believe in both.'

'I know.' Sara looked uncomfortable.

'So it's a bit hypocritical, don't you think?'

'Drop it, Caro,' said Grace. 'Besides, her parents might get suspicious if she stops going.'

Sara nodded.

'They'd be really upset.'

'And what about *his* feelings?'

'Caro—'

'Go on. Who's more important?'

Before Sara could answer, they became aware of the hunched figure of Genevieve putting her tray next to theirs. The pained expression on her face seemed to be her way of apologising for the inconvenience. Grace looked over her shoulder and saw that there was nowhere else for Genevieve to sit.

Caroline didn't acknowledge Genevieve's presence, but began talking at length about a new film at the cinema. She had described the entire plot by the time Grace finally felt guilty enough to stop ignoring Genevieve.

'What have you got next, Genevieve?'

Genevieve looked startled. Her hand froze, fork suspended halfway between the plate and her mouth.

'Maths,' she whispered. Then her fork continued its journey, and Grace was left struggling to think of another question.

'Is that with Mrs Harvey?'

'No.'

'Miss Davis?'

'Yes.'

Caroline rolled her eyes, her usual expression of boredom and impatience. Grace continued to attempt a conversation with Genevieve for a few more minutes before giving up. Genevieve finished her lunch, picked up her tray, and hurried off as quickly as she could.

'Why do you bother?' asked Caroline.

'It's nice when someone tries to include you, isn't it?'

'You're thinking of how you would feel in her position, but you're not like her.'

'You mean Genevieve doesn't want to be talked to?'

'Conversations are clearly torture for her. It's a waste of time.'

'I don't know,' said Sara. 'I feel sorry for her.'

'Of all the people in the world to feel sorry for... Anyway, now that she's gone we can talk.'

'About?'

'You know what. Friday.'

It was all Caroline thought about. She frequently declared that the church bacchanals were the highlight of her existence, 'the only thing that makes life worth living'. She counted down the days until Friday, when 'sleepover' was code for the ritual of lying to their parents, meeting in the centre for something to eat – drinking on an empty stomach was dangerous, as they had learned the hard way – and then spending the night in the church. During the comedown the following morning, and for the whole of the next week at school, Caroline would reminisce, analyse, and then fantasise about what pleasures awaited them next time. 'I feel like sooner or later, I'm going to transcend my body altogether. I don't know what it means, exactly, but it's a beautiful idea.'

Grace loved the bacchanals too, but she didn't have the same urge to discuss them endlessly. Sometimes she even found herself getting irritated with Caroline; for all her boasts, for all her rapture, she still didn't really get it. She didn't know Dionysus, for a start – not like Grace knew him. Unless Caroline was also having private meetings with Dionysus, which she very much doubted – Caroline would never be able to keep such a thing to herself – Grace was the only one who had spent hours in conversation with the god. She was beginning to understand that the bacchanals, no matter how glorious they were,

were a means to an end. It was not just about getting drunk. There was a higher purpose. Perhaps Sara, who had always been more spiritually inclined, understood better. But then who knew what Sara really thought? And as long as she continued to go to church with her parents, she could never be a proper devotee of Dionysus.

Grace supposed that she was the only true believer, the only one who knew and loved the god. It was a shaky kind of knowledge, and a cautious, fearful kind of love, but it still made her superior to the others. Sometimes this thought made her feel proud, or even powerful, but there were also times when it made her feel like she was standing alone on a cliff high above thrashing waves, her insides turning to water.

When she was alone, she thought about him almost constantly. She wanted to be able to remember everything he'd said and done, but the memories of the bacchanals were so vague and fleeting that trying to capture them was a futile exercise. Drawing, which was her usual form of creative expression, turned out to be useless. One Saturday morning she had sat at her desk, exhausted beyond words, and only managed to sketch the outline of his body before she gave up and threw the paper in the bin. It was impossible to draw something that she couldn't even visualise in her own mind.

Then she tried words, writing down everything she could remember in her tiniest, most illegible handwriting.

> *Candles brighter than the sun, C always laughing, music but I don't know where it's coming from, lighter than air, bodiless even, more alive than I've ever been, the cup flowing over, snakes in C's hair, the whites of her eyes, S vibrating, D behind, above, glowing glowing glowing*

She paused, suddenly remembering one of the mornings after: Sara holding her hair back while she vomited. That had been a horrible moment, not only because she hated being sick more than anything else, but also because it brought her back to earth. During that moment she could have been anyone – any sweaty, hungover person regretting the amount they had drunk the night before. She didn't want to think that her experiences with the god bore the slightest resemblance to the prosaic kind of drunkenness that happened to other people.

When he next appeared, sitting on the steps of the fountain, she told him what had happened.

'Are you blaming me?'

'No, no, of course not.' Blame was reserved for friends and family, not gods. If studying Classics had taught her anything, it was that blaming a god for your problems never ended well.

'I'm sorry you suffered, but the body is a treacherous thing.'

He was right. Even though Grace's family remained oblivious to her secret life, she could not disguise her sleeplessness. Looking in the bathroom mirror, she noticed that the dark shadows under her eyes were becoming a permanent feature.

'Really, Grace,' said her mother, 'you must start going to bed earlier. What do you *do* all night?'

'Study.'

'Then why aren't you getting better marks?'

'I got good marks from Signora Battistini.'

'Who's she?'

'My Art teacher.'

'That doesn't count. I mean the academic subjects.'

Grace searched her memory for a vaguely complimentary comment from one of her other teachers.

'I'm doing excellently in Classics.'

'Well, that may be true. I couldn't understand a word of your report.'

'Miss Seymour says I have an admirable appreciation of Greek tragedy.'

'Liking something isn't the same as being good at it.'

'That's the problem with school. All teachers care about is how good you are at something. As if that's all that matters.'

'What's more important?'

'Lots of things. Pleasure, for example.'

Grace's mother laughed.

'This country is turning you into a hedonist. It does have that effect on people. Mauro, *amore*, please can you pass the wine?'

Part II

The golden age had indeed come back for a while: – golden was it, or gilded only, after all?

—Walter Pater

I

There was a hill in the heart of the city, with silent streets lined by walls and umbrella pines. At any time of day it was eerily quiet, as there were no shops or restaurants, and only the occasional car. The signs of life one found in other neighbourhoods – children playing, the smell of cooking, laundry hanging from the windows – were missing. Instead there were only churches, embassies, and empty villas with overgrown gardens. You were more likely to encounter one of the black cats that prowled in front of the church than another person.

In the summer the shady streets provided a welcome respite from the heat, but now, in winter, Grace yearned for a ray of sunlight. She shivered and held Dionysus's arm tighter.

Sometimes she tried to imagine how they looked to other people. Friends? Lovers? Or did they even see him at all? She might look mad, talking to herself as she slowly walked up the road that led to the top of the hill.

'Why are we here?' she asked. He rarely suggested going anywhere, preferring to meet her in the church or her bedroom.

'For old times' sake,' he said.

'I thought you were going to stop thinking about the past.'

'I try, but it has a way of creeping up on you.'

They passed a fountain, water gushing from a bearded head, and entered the garden. The gravel crunched beneath their feet and for a moment Grace was distracted, something that happened so rarely when she was with him. She saw the orange trees, the elegant symmetry of the pines, and the great white dome rising up at the end of the avenue like a mirage.

'It's so beautiful,' she said. 'I can't believe I've never been here before.'

She let go of his arm and walked to the edge of the garden, leaning over the wall to take in as much of the view as she could. The domes and ruins were golden in the winter light, the city basking beneath a blue sky. The din of the traffic faded to a quiet murmur, until the air was pierced by a solitary siren. From up here the green river hardly seemed to move at all.

'I can see why you brought me here.'

'We didn't come for the view.'

Dionysus stood beside her, unmoved by the spectacle of the city below. While she was still admiring the view, searching for buildings she recognised, he moved away impatiently. After a while she reluctantly joined him on a marble bench beneath the pines, wondering why he had not chosen a spot in the sun.

'So what do you remember?'

'A few fragments. This used to be a sacred place, but a long time ago...'

He trailed off and turned to look behind him.

'What is it?'

'I can't remember exactly where. The women used to worship me, in the earliest days of my presence in this city. They had so much passion, and they gave themselves completely. Body and soul. It was a beautiful time.'

'What were they like?'

'Wild. Mothers, daughters, wives, virgins, all losing their minds by the firelight. It was more secluded then, a kind of clearing in the woods. And there was hardly anything on the hill except for a palace and some shrines here and there.'

'Do you wish you could go back?'

'There's no point in wishing. I may be a god, but I can't turn back time.'

'You could make it happen again.'

'Ah, yes, with the three of you. One day, perhaps.'

'Why not now?' Grace was suddenly overcome with jealousy. These faceless, nameless women from the past had been there first, and loved him so fiercely that he remembered even now.

'It isn't quite the wilderness that it used to be.'

'Somewhere else, then. In the country.'

'One day, one day.'

She couldn't understand his reluctance. It hurt, being denied the opportunity to express her devotion.

'You know we'd do anything for you.'

'I don't think you would. Not yet.'

Grace sighed.

'How's your fifth limb?'

'What? Oh, that. Feeling the effects of your devotion, of course. But I think it would be better if Sara stopped going to church.'

'Caroline's always trying to talk her out of it. Do you want me to say something to her?'

'No, she will realise on her own, sooner or later. Such confusion can't last forever.'

He noticed that Grace was rubbing her hands together to keep them warm, and enclosed her left hand in his own.

'You're warm!' Grace exclaimed. She remembered the first time he'd touched her, the shock of the cold.

'Warm-blooded – almost human.'

'What happens when you get even stronger? Will I get burned if I touch you?'

'It's a possibility,' he said.

They sat there for some time, holding hands and staring at the trees – one imagining, the other trying to remember.

Before they left, Dionysus reached into the branches of an orange tree and took two pieces of fruit. He offered one to Grace.

'Thanks, but I'm not really hungry.'

'You should take it. If you don't, it will only go to waste.'

He pointed at the fruit that had fallen on the grass and was slowly rotting. Grace began to peel the orange he had given her, and together they left a trail of orange flakes across the grass.

Grace never told Caroline or Sara about these walks, these private moments with the god. Sometimes she was tempted to tell Sara, but then she remembered how Sara had told Caroline about Dionysus in the first place, despite promising not to. While Sara seemed kinder and more sensitive, ultimately she was no more trustworthy than any other girl in school. Everyone let you down sooner or later.

One afternoon Sara invited Grace over, which she never normally did without asking Caroline. Grace thought it strange, but of course she accepted, having nothing else to do. It was the end of the Christmas holidays, and Dionysus had disappeared again.

'How was the skiing?' asked Grace. She didn't have the slightest interest in skiing, having never done it herself, but she felt she ought to fake an interest in Sara's holiday.

'Oh, it was all right. I'm still not very good at it. But it felt like the longest week.'

'What do you mean?'

'I missed him.'

Grace looked up from the magazine she had been flicking through.

'We don't normally see him more than once a week anyway.'

'I know, I tried telling myself that. But it was no use – I thought about him all the time. He just seemed so far away. Whereas here, even if he's not right beside me, I know he's near.'

'I know what you mean. That's one of the reasons I stayed here instead of going to England for Christmas.'

'Didn't your father mind?'

'No. I mean, probably not. He has Mog. Anyway, Barbara went.'

'Oh. Well, you were lucky, getting to stay. I had a pretty miserable week. Even my parents noticed – they kept asking me what was wrong.'

'You didn't tell them?'

'Of course not. You and Caroline can stop worrying. I've lost the urge to blab.'

'You get used to keeping secrets after a while.'

'Exactly. Anyway, I was feeling so miserable by the end of the week that I went down to the cellar in the chateau at night and stole a bottle of wine.'

'I'm sure he'd approve.'

'I didn't do it for his approval. I did it because I needed to do it. I can't explain.'

'So did you drink it all?'

'Nearly all of it. I was awfully sick. I was worse than that time with you, after the church. I couldn't go skiing the next day. I had to pretend I was ill.'

'Impressive.'

'I felt pretty stupid. I thought it would make me happy, or bring me closer to him or something.'

'Do you think your parents suspected?'

'They could never even dream of it. They think I'm a saint, remember.'

'You were until recently.'

Sara smiled weakly. She was becoming quite good at looking martyred, as if she rehearsed her facial expressions in private beforehand.

'Anyway, enough about me. What about your Christmas?'

'Uneventful,' said Grace. 'Henry didn't get one of the presents he wanted and cried. Mauro ate too much and complained of a stomach ache for days.'

'Get any good presents?'

'The usual. Chocolate, bath stuff, some nice perfume. I don't know if it's got anything to do with what's happened, or if it's just a consequence of getting older, but Christmas isn't as exciting as it used to be.'

'You mean a bag of chocolate coins can't compare to a bacchanal.'

'Yeah.'

Christmas already seemed like a long time ago, and Grace didn't feel like discussing it. Then she noticed the picture of St Anthony next to Sara's mirror and remembered what she wanted to ask.

'Are you still going to church then?'

'That's kind of what I wanted to talk to you about.'

'Without Caro, right?'

'Yes. She's so against it that we can't have a reasonable conversation. It's not that you understand – I don't think you do – but at least you're nicer.'

Nicer. This was Grace's value as a friend. Caroline was prettier, funnier, more intelligent and more interesting, but Grace was nicer.

Grace looked around the room, which more or less resembled her own in its chaos of books and clothes that were rarely restored to their rightful places. The main difference in Sara's room was the prominence of the family photos and an excessive number of framed pictures of her dog. Then there were the hints of Catholicism. There was a picture of the Virgin Mary in a small silver frame on the bedside table, and a rosary curled up like a snake on an old book.

'My parents have noticed that something's changed,' said Sara. 'If I stop going to church I'm admitting that there's a problem, aren't I? They'll want to talk about it.'

'They can't make you talk, if you don't want to.'

'It still puts me in an awkward position.'

'You're already in a pretty awkward position though.'

'I know, but I really don't know what to do.'

'Be vague. Say you're having doubts, and leave it at that.'

'That's the worst thing I could do. They'll make me talk to my priest.'

'So?'

'Lying to my parents is one thing, but lying to my priest...'

Grace made a scornful noise.

'You're just like Caroline,' said Sara.

'Sorry, but I don't know what you want me to say.'

'I'm not expecting any answers.' Sara sank deep into the pillows and sighed. 'It's like... I don't even know how to describe it. All your life you believe the sky is blue. Everyone tells you it's blue, and you can see it with your own eyes. Then, one day, someone tells you that it's actually green. In fact, it's always been green. At first you can't believe it, but then you start to catch glimpses. Everyone else still thinks it's blue, and sometimes you see blue skies too. But there are brief moments when it's different, and so it can never really be the same again. One of the colours must be an illusion, so you don't know what to believe in any more.'

Grace said nothing. She was staring out of the window, where the sky above the neighbouring roof terrace was a bright, pure blue.

'It's not a very good analogy,' said Sara. 'I told you I couldn't explain it.'

'It doesn't matter what the colour of the sky is. It isn't a question of some abstract truth. If Christ was the son of God, or if he wasn't, who cares?'

'*I* care.' Sara sounded a little shocked. 'And so do millions of other people.'

'Yes, but what difference does it make to your life? It's just a random thought at the back of your mind. It's not like it actually affects you in any way.'

'Whereas Dionysus—'

'Is changing us. Giving us something. You can't deny that.'

'I know. It's terrific fun. But is it right?'

'Again, who cares?'

Sara laughed disbelievingly.

'Have you absolutely no morals?'

'No,' said Grace, 'I haven't.'

She was only half listening to Sara, distracted by the coil of the rosary.

'You don't know what it's like to be raised with the fear of Hell. The concept of sin. It's not something you can simply forget about, give up for something more fun. It's with you all the time, like it's part of your own body. Caroline doesn't get it, so of course you wouldn't either. How can I—'

For a second Grace's vision clouded over, and all she could see was the weary god, shivering in the shade of the orange garden. With a short, violent movement, she pulled the rosary apart. The beads scattered across the wooden floor and rolled beneath the bed.

She stood up, taking no notice of Sara's expression of hurt and confusion.

'I've decided for you.'

It hadn't been the nicest thing to do, but it was the *right* thing, she was sure of that. It was what he would have wanted. She left without another word, and walked out into the winter sunshine, where the god would be waiting for her.

II

The board was filled with numbers. Every inch of its surface was covered with squiggles and lines and baffling equations, as if it was supposed to make sense. Looking at the chalk symbols gave her a headache, so she looked down at the sheet instead.

$$kx^2+6x+k=0$$

Ancient Greek was incomprehensible sometimes, but at least there was some kind of reward for solving it. Ten minutes' concentration revealed a god or a wine-dark sea. Algebra, on the other hand, gave you nothing, only a headache.

Mr McCulloch was sitting at his desk at the front of the classroom, oblivious to her struggle. He had once told them that Maths was beautiful. At the time Grace had thought it a strange thing to say, but now it seemed so devoid of truth that it was almost offensive. A picture could be beautiful, a poem or a person or even a tree, but never algebra. Perhaps Mr McCulloch had been here too long and picked up the foreign habit of overusing 'beautiful', when an adjective like 'nice' was more appropriate. Not that algebra could ever be 'nice' either.

She looked at the equation again.

$$kx^2+6x+k=0$$

And then she glanced at the desk of the girl to next to her. Georgia was much better at Maths, but she was too far away to copy. They sat at tiny, rickety, individual desks, arranged in the classroom like an unnaturally ordered archipelago. Caroline and Sara were even further away, the other side of the laminate sea.

$$kx^2+6x+k=0$$

The numbers swam before her eyes. She raised her head. Mr McCulloch was absorbed in the textbook, so she coughed. He got up and walked stiffly over to her desk.

'What is it?'

'Please may I go to the toilet?'

'You should have gone during the break. Wait until lunch.'

'But it's my time of the month, sir.'

Mr McCulloch changed colour.

'All right then. Quickly.'

Grace crossed the classroom at a leisurely pace and walked down the empty corridor towards the toilets. Everyone else was in lessons, and the room was silent except for the perpetual trickle of the cisterns. She found a cubicle that looked reasonably clean, locked the door, lowered the seat, and sat down.

She had come here to escape from algebra, but there was more to it than that. Her headache and her desperate boredom were a symptom of some more serious malaise.

'Who cares?' she had said to Sara. The same question could be asked about Maths, or about school more generally. It was the question for every second that was not spent with him, under his influence. Before it had all felt pointless, but now she *knew* it was pointless, and it was much harder to endure.

Grace had never enjoyed going to school, but these days having to turn up and pretend to care was not only boring, but also unbelievably draining. More than that – 'enervating'. A word she had found in a novel, which made her think of her nerves disintegrating, one by one, and her blood drying up until she was just a pale, lifeless body. School was sucking the life out of her.

One of her friends in England, Isabel, had once had a mania for horses. Horses were Isabel's sole interest in life, and the fact that she didn't have one of her own made the interest grow into an all-consuming obsession. At this time Isabel had been Grace's only friend, so Grace's mother had advised her to tolerate Isabel's obsession and listen politely. If she could do this it would make Grace very grown-up, not to mention popular. According to Grace's mother, adults had to pretend to be interested in dull things all the time; that was how one got on in life.

So Grace had tried. She tried very hard, smiling and nodding while Isabel rambled on about gymkhanas and rosettes and her favourite breeds. Isabel considered Grace her best friend in the whole world. But during this time Grace became extremely tired. It was like an extraordinary weight, dragging her down, making her want to sleep for thousands of years.

Now, several years later, Grace was experiencing a similar sensation. One shouldn't feel this world-weary at fifteen, but it was the inevitable result of leading a double life, where one existence was thrilling and the other so dull and meaningless that it made her want to weep.

She sat there for some time, not thinking about anything in particular but staring vacantly at the door of the cubicle. Then, while she was counting the hexagonal lines on the floor, she heard the door open on the far side of the room, near the sinks. She quickly drew up her legs so the cubicle looked empty.

'Grace? Grace, are you here?'

It was Caroline. Grace's feet slowly returned to the floor.

'Are you all right?'

'I'm fine,' said Grace. 'Go away.'

'Have you got an upset stomach or something?'

'No.'

'That's what everyone'll think. You've been gone for about twenty minutes.'

'So what?'

'Grace, open the door.'

Reluctantly, Grace unlocked the door and then sat down again.

'What's the matter?' Caroline stood in the doorway with her arms folded. 'I know you don't like Maths. Neither do I, but I don't hide in the toilets.'

'It's not about Maths.'

'What, then?'

Grace's silence seemed to provide the answer. Caroline let out a little sigh of exasperation.

'Look, you've got to get a grip. I know you and Sara are both finding it difficult, but you need to keep it together, or people will start to get suspicious.'

'They'd never guess the truth in a million years.'

'No, but we don't want them to start prying.'

'I guess you're right.'

'Of course I am. It doesn't matter if you're hopeless at Maths, but they have to think you're trying, at least. Try to be normal.'

Grace went to the sinks and washed her hands out of habit.

'Right,' she said, looking at her reflection. 'Normal.'

The weeks were only tolerable because of Friday evenings, the light at the end of the tunnel. This was the night when they all claimed to be staying at each other's houses, and although their parents were confused by their daughters insisting on the necessity of a weekly sleepover, they didn't ask too many questions. Sara's parents were more concerned about her sudden refusal to come to church on Sunday mornings, and it would have been no consolation to discover that she attended a different kind of service on Friday nights.

'I feel much stronger now,' said Dionysus, eyes shining in the dark. The wine rained from his palms, and all guilt disappeared in a cloud of divine drunkenness.

Although they had a kind of routine, their evenings were never quite the same. Sometimes the god was late, and the three of them would stand shivering outside the church until he materialised out of the dark air an hour later, with no explanation. One time they awoke cold and disorientated hours before dawn and, with no desire to stay in the church, they lingered on the streets. At one point a dark, bearded man appeared out of nowhere and started chattering at them, his face ghastly in the lamplight. A warning bell was ringing, a siren wailing somewhere in the depths of their drunken fog. Even though she didn't know the language, somehow Grace understood. *He thinks we're prostitutes.* The realisation made her nauseous with fear.

'No, no, no,' they said, shaking their heads and hoping that the gesture, if not the word, was universal.

They walked briskly away, glancing over their shoulders now and then to make sure he wasn't following them. When they reached the vast, silent square, with its white monument rising up like an elaborate tombstone, they huddled together on the marble steps and waited for their hearts to return to normal.

'I think,' said Sara, 'we might be a little out of our depth.'

Moments like this were undeniably bleak, but Grace was willing to withstand the waiting, the cold, and the occasional threat. From Monday to Friday she was sick with impatience, and after Friday nights she was invariably a wreck for the rest of the weekend. But those few hours of ecstasy made everything worthwhile.

His elusiveness still frustrated her. Though it was ridiculous to expect reliability from a god, she was always pained by his random disappearances. It was like being led into the heart of a wild, enchanted forest and then being abruptly abandoned, left to find one's own way back. He never gave an explanation, and she would never dare to ask for one.

So she was grateful when she awoke one night and found herself deep in Caroline's arms. They were clinging to each other on the church floor, and in her first moments of consciousness Grace could still sense the remnants of the vision – the scent of the grove, the solid presence of the bull beside her. Then she opened her eyes and there was only Caroline, arms wrapped tightly around her. It felt good to be so close to another person when the room was cold and your god had vanished once again.

It was also the most intimate Grace had ever been with anyone. She had never been held this closely before, so close she imagined she could feel the other heartbeat. She smiled, feeling the warmth spread through her body until the darkness descended.

III

The next afternoon, shivering in her bedroom and suffering from the usual headache, Grace found herself craving fresh air. She had grown used to spending her Saturdays curled up in bed with the shutters closed, drifting in and out of sleep. She always felt incredibly weary, incapable of moving or even thinking.

But that day she was cold and restless and, knowing that outside it would be warmer than her bedroom, which turned into an ice cave in the winter, she resolved to go for a walk. She called up Caroline and Sara, who took some persuading but eventually agreed to join her.

'I feel a wreck,' said Caroline, yawning. They were walking slowly up the hill where Grace had wandered with Dionysus, talking of past rituals. She didn't know where he was, and in her aching, sleep-deprived state, she could do nothing but wearily accept his disappearance.

She raised her eyes and saw a walled garden full of lemon trees. Plants grew between the cracks in the wall, and she imagined it as another one of his tricks, coaxing the vines and the honey from the stones. There were cracks in the road, too – they were everywhere in this decaying city – and she wished he would fill them all with flowers, trees...

'Are you all right, Grace?'

'Yes. I was just thinking.'

'What did you want to show us?'

She led them to the garden with the spectacular view, taking them to the edge without saying a word. Caroline looked underwhelmed.

'I think I've been here before.'

'But it's beautiful, isn't it?'

'I suppose so.' Caroline rested her elbows on the low wall and sighed. 'Sorry, I feel too ill to really appreciate anything today.'

'It's marvellous,' said Sara. 'Maybe the best view of the city.'

Grace watched the seagulls circling an ancient tower in the distance. It had lost a little of its magic on second viewing, without the

god at her side, but it was certainly preferable to staring at her bedroom walls. She breathed in deeply and felt almost alive.

'Look,' said Sara. 'You can see the hills on the other side. I wonder
why they look blue. Something to do with the light?'

Caroline grunted, a noise that was meant to indicate her total lack
of interest in the colour of the hills, and then walked away to find a
bench in the sunshine. After Grace and Sara had tired of admiring the
view, they crossed the garden to join her.

She had her eyes closed, face turned towards the sun. With her
golden hair and the hint of a smile on her lips, she almost resembled
one of Botticelli's angels. Almost, because Grace knew her too well.
Caroline only looked innocent in the sunshine, with her eyes closed.

'I'm longing for spring,' said Caroline. 'Aren't you?'

'It's all right outside, but I'm freezing at home.'

'My bed's right next to the radiator,' said Sara, 'so I just press myself
against it and try not to move at all. Anyway, cheer up. It'll start getting warmer soon.'

'Not soon enough. I want it to be warm *now*. No, not warm – hot.
Thirty-five degrees and humid.'

'You always complain in the summer, Caro.'

'I know. It's always the way, isn't it? You're never satisfied with
what you have.'

'You mean *you're* never satisfied.'

'Fine. Anyway, I've been thinking about the weather a lot, and it's
not just because I'm cold. I was thinking about the bacchanals.'

'You shouldn't use that word,' said Sara, glancing anxiously over
her shoulder. 'Someone might hear.'

'I don't think that old lady and her dog over there can hear, and
even if they could, they wouldn't give a damn.'

'But still, just to be on the safe side...'

'I don't want to be cautious,' said Caroline irritably. 'I want to talk
about it now. It's not like we're at school.'

'Go on,' said Grace. 'What were you saying?'

'All right, our *gatherings*, if that word makes you less nervous –
they're always in the church, always inside. I think it might be
restricting us.'

'What do you mean?'

'Even if he's there, it's still a church. A building. A *Catholic* building, even worse. It would be a lot more liberating if we were outside.'

'Where?'

'It would have to be somewhere fairly secluded, of course. We could hardly do it in the streets.'

'He told me that they used to do it here,' said Grace.

Caroline and Sara turned to look at her.

'When did he say that?'

'It was... oh, I can't remember. He just mentioned this hill, this garden. Women used to worship him here.'

'Just imagine it,' said Caro, gazing at the branches of the pines, 'in the summer...'

They were silent for a moment, envisioning their predecessors and then themselves, running across the orange-strewn grass. Of course there wouldn't be oranges in the summer. They were one of the few compensations for the cold weather.

Grace walked towards a tree and picked one of the oranges, remembering how Dionysus had done it before, turning it over in his pale hands. She returned to the bench and peeled it.

'Yuck,' said Caroline.

'Why "yuck"?'

'I don't know. Maybe it's just my general nausea. It doesn't look very appetising.'

They watched Grace bite into the first piece and then promptly spit several seeds into the grass.

'That really was disgusting, Grace.'

'Sorry, what should I have done? Swallowed them?' Grace wiped her mouth and threw the orange on the ground. 'Well, I've had better.'

Caroline waited until a group of tourists had walked past, and then said, 'We could do it here anyway.'

'Do what?'

'A bacchanal.'

'They'd lock us up,' said Sara. 'It's a *park*.'

'I don't mean *now*, obviously. We would have to wait until night.

Break in. Actually, we wouldn't even have to break in. I bet he could just open the gate for us. And then...'

'And then what?'

'I don't know. But it would be something. We can't just sit here and wait for things to happen.'

'We're his followers,' said Grace. 'That means following his lead.'

'Not being passive sheep, though.'

'Caro,' said Sara softly, 'Grace is right. It's not up to us.'

'That's what you think,' Caroline retorted. 'You think it's all about following and obeying because you've been brainwashed by the Church. "The Lord is my shepherd" and all that nonsense. They tell you you're sheep, and you believe it.'

Sara was so used to being insulted for her Catholicism that the jibe didn't register. She hesitated for a moment and then said, 'But it's the same for all religions, isn't it? You've got to have patience and humility, and wait for your god to come to you, to give you a sign – whatever. You can't just do whatever you feel like.'

'You don't think he'd like it if we showed some initiative?'

Grace and Sara exchanged glances.

'No,' they said.

Caroline frowned but said nothing. Grace was relieved that she had let it go for the time being; secretly, she thought Caroline might be right, but the idea of a bacchanal in a public park on a winter night was just too frightening. It was beyond reckless. If Caroline was right, Sara was right too – they would get locked up. Grace would consider taking the risk only if Dionysus asked her – begged her – and not for one of Caroline's whims.

They left the garden and followed the red wall until they came to a turning. A cobbled path wound towards the river, lined on both sides by high walls and a wilderness of long grass and hanging vines. It might have remained untouched for centuries.

'It looks like something from a painting,' said Sara. 'Let's go down there.'

Caroline shook her head.

'I wouldn't if I were you.'

'Why not?'

'It's full of perverts.'

'What on earth are you talking about, Caro?'

Grace peered through the iron gate, which was half open, and was overcome with curiosity, the desire to see whatever lay round the corner. She pulled impatiently on Caroline's arm.

'No, I'm serious,' said Caroline. 'I came here when I was about twelve, with my mother. I remember it was raining heavily. The path was deserted, but about halfway down this young man suddenly overtook us and then just stopped in the middle of the path and began fiddling with the front of his trousers. I had no idea what was happening and it never occurred to me to be frightened, but my mother grabbed me and marched us back up the hill, back to a normal street with cars and people.'

'How gruesome,' said Sara.

'I know. That's when I first learned how disgusting men are. And my mother made me promise I would never go down that path again.'

Caroline seemed to have a hundred stories like this. Surely they couldn't all be true? But now, with the spectre of the man lurking in the bushes, the path had suddenly lost its charm.

'Come on,' said Caroline. 'I've thought of something else to show you.'

She led them in the opposite direction, past the garden and the church where the black cats prowled. At the end of the road was an empty square surrounded by walls. In the middle of one of the walls was a large set of iron doors, turning green with age. They were probably designed to keep nuns locked up, thought Grace. Someone had built a wall around the convent hundreds of years ago and then locked the doors. They had never been opened since. Somewhere behind those ancient doors were ancient nuns, haunting the cobwebbed corridors of their convent prison...

A tap on her shoulder interrupted the ghost story.

'Look through the keyhole,' said Caroline.

'Why?'

'That would spoil it. Go on.'

Grace bent down and pressed her face to the keyhole. She saw the great white dome of the basilica, floating, with an avenue of parallel pine trees in between, gracefully arched to create a tunnel of branches. Nothing but the trees between her eye and the dome. On the surface of the dome itself she thought she could see trees, or perhaps they were only shadows. The keyhole created a double illusion, bringing the dome into focus and drawing it closer, while also heightening the sense of distance through some kind of magic. The unexpected beauty and symmetry of the view transformed the basilica into something as remote and unreal as a fairytale.

'Stop hogging the keyhole. Let Sara have a look.'

Grace reluctantly pulled herself away and waited while Sara became glued to the keyhole in silent awe. She was tempted to have another look, but she changed her mind when she saw a young girl with a spaniel puppy waiting. After Sara had moved, the girl had a brief look, and then picked up her puppy and held it to the keyhole.

'*Guarda*,' said the girl.

Look.

'This city's full of secrets,' said Caroline.

The keyhole was a humble little secret, but in the absence of the greater one, small pleasures would have to suffice. Yet when Grace finally succumbed to sleep, buried beneath her duvet later that afternoon, it was not the keyhole that she dreamed of.

Grace decided to make an appearance at dinner, even though she wasn't hungry in the slightest. When she walked into the dining room everyone turned to look at her. Usually when she arrived late to the table – which was almost always – she was ignored. There was something ominous about the way they were all staring at her, spoons suspended mid-way between bowl and mouth. Henry's face was red, as if he'd been crying.

'What is it?'

'Have you seen him?' asked Barbara.

'Who?' Grace panicked.

'Pippin.'

'Oh…' She relaxed at once. 'Not in the last few hours, no. But I was out, and then I had a nap. Why?'

'He's gone missing.'

Henry started crying noisily into his soup.

'What do you mean, missing?'

'None of us have seen him all day,' said Barbara. 'No one really noticed until midday, when Mauro was about to take him out for a walk. That means the last time anyone saw him was last night.'

'But where could he be? It's not like he could have left the apartment.'

'He must have done,' said Grace's mother. 'He's not here. We've checked absolutely everywhere.'

Their apartment was on the fourth floor, and the only way out was through the front door or the kitchen doors that led to the private terrace.

'He's not on the terrace somewhere? Are you sure?'

'We've searched the building, Grace. If he were here, we would have found him.'

'A bad man stole him,' said Henry tearfully.

'What bad man?' asked Grace.

'Henry thinks someone kidnapped Pippin,' said Grace's mother. 'Of course it's not possible. And anyway, why would they? What possible motive could they have? He must have simply slipped out through the front door without anyone noticing.'

'I'm going to make posters,' said Barbara, 'and put them all over the neighbourhood. Will you help me translate them, Mauro?'

'Of course.'

'We ought to have a photo…'

Grace tuned out of the conversation as she began to sip her lukewarm soup. *A bad man.* Henry was just speculating, of course. He couldn't be referring to *him*, because he didn't know *he* existed. And besides, why on earth would Dionysus want to take her dog?

After dinner she went to her room and started drawing to take her mind off it – silly doodles, the kind of thing she drew at the edges of her notebook during lessons – but she soon found herself drawing Pippin instead. They had once had a family joke that Pippin was Grace's muse; for a period when Grace was about twelve years old, he'd been the subject of almost all her portraits, or at least lurking in the background somewhere.

It came to her so easily – his pompous little body and his pricked-up, curious ears, always listening. She could draw him endlessly, filling a whole page with Pippins that wriggled and trotted and rolled, his lopsided tongue lolling out of his mouth.

Barbara knocked at her door.

'We're going out to look for him. Are you coming?'

Grace hesitated.

'Where are you going?'

'Just around the neighbourhood. If he's wandered out, which is what Mummy thinks, then he can't have gone far.'

'I don't know…' It was cold outside, and Grace was tired.

'Grace, he's your dog.'

'Not just mine.'

'How can you be so heartless?' Barbara sounded almost angry.

'It's not that. It's just that…' Grace struggled to justify herself. 'I'm not feeling great. And if the rest of you are looking for him, I don't see that it makes much of a difference whether I come or not.'

'They call it a search party for a reason, you know. Not a search person.'

'If you don't find him I'll go out tomorrow morning. Promise.'

'Suit yourself.'

Barbara closed the door loudly behind her – not loud enough to be called a slam, but just loud enough to show her irritation. Grace looked at the drawing and suddenly became aware of a lump in her throat. She was upset, but not as upset as she should be.

It'll be fine, she told herself. Pippin had to come back; he had to come to London with her one day, after all, and then live a very long time. Some things were destined, and as you couldn't change destiny, there was no use in worrying about it.

When she heard the front door close, she went to her wardrobe and uncovered the shrine, which she kept hidden beneath piles of old jumpers that were too small for her. She arranged the candles in a semi-circle and lit a match with shaking fingers.

Just in case.

IV

It was already dark when they came out of school. They had stayed later than usual, to attend a talk given by the mother of a classmate, ostensibly on the subject of 'your future'.

'If my future is anything like that, I'd rather not have a future at all,' said Caroline. 'I don't know why they got her to give a talk. They should have asked Matilda's mother instead. I heard she used to be a dancer, and not one of the respectable ones either.'

As they stood talking outside the school gates, Grace noticed a familiar figure standing on the other side of the street.

'Look who's here.'

Caroline's admirer was standing next to his motorbike, attempting to light a cigarette without much success.

'He hasn't been here in ages,' said Caroline. 'And usually we come out of school much earlier. Do you think he's been waiting all this time?'

'It must be love.'

Caroline stared across the street, and then handed her books to Sara.

'Can you take these?'

'Why?'

'I'm going to talk to him.'

'Caro—'

They watched Caroline cross the street and begin a conversation with the young man as if it were the most natural thing in the world. They weren't close enough to hear anything, and even though the man's face was visible in the lamplight, his expression was completely blank.

Grace was cold, and she hoped the conversation wouldn't last too long. But after only a few minutes she no longer needed to wait – Caroline was getting on the back of the motorbike.

'What's she doing?' asked Sara.

'It's pretty obvious, isn't it?'

'Don't you think we should stop her?'

They watched the motorbike reverse, and then speed down the cobbled street.

'Too late,' said Grace.

'She's not even wearing a helmet.'

'What's more dangerous, the bike or the man?'

'I really don't know. I just don't have a good feeling about it.'

'Well, there's nothing we can do.'

They went home. Grace tried to do her English homework but found it difficult to concentrate. She kept thinking of Caroline – Caroline on the motorbike, Caroline lying in the road, Caroline alternately encouraging and fending off the advances of the serious young man. She thought about it all through dinner, barely noticing what she was eating, and afterwards she called Sara.

'Have you heard anything?'

'No, of course not. She'd call you first, anyway.'

'That's not true,' said Grace, although she knew Sara was right.

'And Pippin?'

'Nothing yet. Barbara's making posters.'

'Do you think we ought to do something? About Caroline, I mean.'

'Like what?'

'Tell her parents. Or the police.'

'You're obsessed with telling parents, Sara. Why can't we just keep it between ourselves?'

'I'm worried about her, that's all. She doesn't even know him.'

'He might be all right.'

'He might not.'

'We've all done more reckless things.'

Yet Grace was still thinking about it when she went to bed. As she pulled the sheets up to her neck she hoped that Caroline was also tucked up in her own bed. If she was honest with herself, it was not entirely from concern about Caroline's welfare. She hated the thought that Caroline might be having some kind of adventure which she was not part of.

Grace had never been on a stranger's motorbike. She was not sure that she particularly wanted to, but she was still resentful about Caroline being granted this exciting new experience, while she had spent the evening making a half-hearted attempt at her homework.

Caroline was at school the next day, which meant she hadn't been raped or murdered. They found her getting her books from her locker, and immediately began to bombard her with questions.

'Where were you?'

'What happened?'

'Why didn't you call us?'

Caroline smiled the superior smile of one who has a story to tell, and who takes pleasure in withholding it.

'I'll tell you at lunch,' she said. 'It's a long story.'

During lunchtime they found an empty classroom where the radiator had been left on. They huddled together on the floor while Caroline told her story. Grace suspected she had been planning how to tell it all morning.

'The motorbike was pretty nerve-racking. Exhilarating in a way, but I don't think he's the safest driver. It was difficult to talk, what with the wind and the noise of the engine, so I just clung on to him and concentrated on not falling off.

'We went east, to that basilica with all the statues of the saints lined up on the roof. When we stopped I suggested that we go and have a drink or something. He said he didn't have money for a drink, which struck me as a strange thing to say. He wanted to go and sit on a bench in front of the basilica, so we did, even though it was really cold and I'd rather have been inside with a coffee.

'We'd been sitting there for about ten minutes, talking about various things—'

'In English?' asked Sara.

'Yes, his English was very good. Anyway, we'd been talking, when he suddenly just leaned forward and kissed me.'

'What was it like?' Grace didn't want to show too much interest, but she couldn't hide her curiosity.

'It was nice, I suppose. I don't know, I can't compare it to anything else. It was just so unexpected. It's not like he'd been saying all these romantic things or holding my hand or anything. We were just talking about normal things, and then before I even realise what's happening, his tongue's down my throat.'

'You don't make it sound very romantic,' said Sara.

'It wasn't. It wasn't at all. Being kissed in front of a basilica in the moonlight ought to be romantic, but...'

'What happened next?'

'He suggested going back to his flat.'

'And you said...?'

'"Yes."'

'Oh Caro, you *didn't*.'

'I did. Don't look so judgemental.'

'What were you thinking?' asked Grace.

'I wasn't thinking. I suppose that's why I did it.'

'So you actually went to his flat?'

'Yes. He lives right out in the suburbs, to the east. Practically at the end of the metro line. He was driving so fast, at one point I was convinced we were going to crash.'

'Oh my God.'

'But we didn't. We arrived, went up the stairs... The flat was almost empty. He said he'd just moved in, which was why there was no furniture. Except in the bedroom.'

'That's convenient,' said Grace.

'I know. Well, I sort of went along with it. I didn't know what else to do.'

'What *did* you do?'

'I'm not going into all the sordid details.'

'Go on. You can't look so smug and not tell us anything.'

'You didn't do it, did you?' asked Sara. She looked very serious, as if they were discussing a matter of life and death.

'It?'

'*It.*'

Grace demonstrated with her fingers. Caroline laughed.

'No, but almost. He was very persistent. You know, I'd say "No", and then I'd feel him trying again and again. The whole experience was so surreal. He didn't say much. Except at one point...' She blushed, then put on an accent. "'I'm arriving." I didn't have the heart to correct him.'

'I can't believe you went along with it,' said Grace.

'You're just jealous.'

'Really, I'm not.'

'That's what a jealous person would say.'

'What happened next?' asked Sara.

'Well, after a point I felt like I should leave. So I told him I was going, and he said he'd walk me to the metro. As soon as the light of the metro sign came into view, he did the kiss on each cheek thing, said goodbye, and left. Which is weird, right? After all that, the generic cheek-kiss. I don't know what to think.'

The classroom door suddenly opened and Grace jumped, banging her head against the radiator. It was a teacher.

'What are you doing in here? You know you're supposed to be outside after lunch.'

'But it's like Antarctica outside,' said Caroline.

'If your skirts were a little longer, maybe you wouldn't feel the cold so much.'

Grace was sure that Caroline was biting her tongue to stop herself from answering back. The girls sullenly left the classroom and faced the cold of the playground.

Although the experience had been unromantic and rather anti-climactic, Grace felt insidious little pangs of jealousy whenever she thought of what Caroline had done. Surely any experience was better than no experience. She imagined herself remaining unkissed, untouched, while Caroline was pounced on by an array of young men.

When this particular young man did not appear outside the school that week, Caroline was prepared to be philosophical.

'I've been thinking about it. I'm sure that kiss on the cheek was him making up his mind, there and then, that he wasn't going to see me again.'

'But why?' asked Sara. 'He obviously liked you.'

Caroline shrugged.

'Anyway, I don't care.'

On Friday night, waiting for the god on the church steps, she mentioned it again.

'Even if we had done it, you know, I think it would have been a disappointment. I always thought it was the most thrilling thing you could do, but now I'm not so sure.'

'What do you mean?'

'Our nights here, with him – they've given me a glimpse of something else. Haven't you felt it? There's so much more to life.'

She inspected the backs of her hands, which were chapped and red.

'Oh, my poor hands. This cold is killing me. I wish he'd come.'

He came, of course. He would make them wait – without apology or explanation – but sooner or later, he would emerge from the shadows in the piazza. The moment he arrived, everything else was forgotten. One glass of wine and the walls of the church were disappearing, turning to trees, while vines descended from the ceiling, twisting through the starry sky, and they were overcome by the dark wave. Under his influence they entered a world without thought – everything was pure sensation. There was nothing within the realm of ordinary human experience that could compare. Why seek out the normal, fleeting pleasures that anyone could experience when there was the possibility of losing yourself absolutely?

Grace often thought of what Caroline had said about there being 'so much more'. She couldn't imagine what Caroline meant, as to her the nights in the church were still so beautiful and strange. To be completely overwhelmed by wine and filled with ecstasy – what could be greater than that? Divine drunkenness was enough, and whatever Caroline dreamed of was probably more than Grace could cope with right now. She was only just beginning to get used to their rituals, to accept it as a permanent feature of her life.

But as her mother had once told her, it was dangerous to get too settled, too attached to certain habits.

'Change is the one constant of life,' Grace's mother had said, while Grace wept at the airport in London.

V

Something had happened. She sensed it the moment she walked through the door. Dumping her school bag on the floor, she walked instinctively towards the kitchen, aware of the anxious flutter of her heartbeat. It was too quiet – the awful, strained kind of hush that came in the aftermath of tragedies or revelations. Flashbacks to her aunt's suicide attempt, and the day her father had discovered her mother's affair.

'We mustn't tell him.'

'No, of course not. Not the details, anyway.'

'It's just too awful.'

Grace could overhear a hushed conversation between her mother and sister. She was tempted to eavesdrop from behind the door, just in case it was something she wasn't supposed to know, but she was feeling slightly sick with anxiety. It was better to make her presence known and find out everything at once.

'What's happened? Is it Pippin?'

Grace's mother dabbed at her nose with a tissue.

'I'm afraid so, darling. Come and sit down.'

'You can have my seat,' said Barbara. 'I don't want to hear it again.'

Pippin was dead. Grace had prepared herself for this possibility, and seeing her mother and sister whispering in the kitchen, she knew that the worst had happened. This was the nature of things, Grace told herself, as her mother offered her a tissue. Dogs died no matter how much you loved them. *Be strong. Don't cry.*

'The porter found him on the roof terrace,' said Grace's mother. 'I'm sorry to have to tell you this, but...'

Roof terrace? Reeling from the discovery that Pippin had been close all along, she didn't immediately feel the blow from the next words.

Broken neck. God knows who.

'I don't understand,' said Grace.

'Neither do we. Some sick person... I don't know. The police said they would talk to the neighbours, but I doubt anything will come of it. It's probably better not to ask why, or how. Let's not torture ourselves further. Try to focus on the fact that Pippin had a long and happy life until…'

'Until someone broke his neck?'

'Shh. Keep your voice down. Henry's in the other room and I don't want him to know.'

'You're going to lie to him?'

'We haven't decided exactly what we're going to tell him. We only found out this afternoon, Grace. Give us time.'

'Poor Pippin,' said Grace, picturing the small, lifeless body of her dachshund lying on the roof. He had been there all along, right above them, and none of them had known, or even thought to look.

'He was such a darling, wasn't he? The sweetest of dogs. If there's a heaven for people then there's got to be one for dogs, too, given that they're so much nicer than us. That should give us some comfort.'

That night Grace woke up in bed with the terrifying sensation that she was not alone. She lay very still, breathing hard and trying to convince herself that everything was normal. It had taken her ages to get to sleep, as she couldn't get the image out of her head. The thoughts went round and round in an endless cycle – his broken little body in black and white, like the photo of a crime scene in a newspaper, then the question (*Why aren't you crying?*), then his body, then the question again. On and on and on. When she first woke up, confused and afraid, she was sure that it was just the aftermath of an awful dream.

Yet the longer she lay there, the more vividly she could feel his presence. She dared herself to turn around.

She had forgotten to close the shutters, and the moonlight fell upon the sleeping face of Dionysus. In the daylight she craved his company, but now she could hardly stand to look at him.

Even before he woke up she was sure he was drunk. She could smell it on his breath. When he finally awoke and opened his mouth to speak, she saw that his teeth were black.

'You'll never guess what's happened.'

'What are you *doing* here?' she hissed.

'I was sleeping, but before that—'

'You frightened me half to death.'

'You don't understand. I had no choice.'

His words, usually so clipped and precise, were slurring into one another.

'You're drunk, aren't you?'

'Outrageous. Dionysus, god of wine, drunk. No one will believe you.'

'For God's sake, be quiet. Barbara will hear.'

'Then she can join us, and there shall be five.'

'Don't you mean four? Who's the fifth?'

Dionysus waved his hand impatiently, suggesting that it was of no consequence.

'Why are you here?'

'I had to flee. They know.'

'Who?'

'The priests.' Dionysus licked his lips, where a trace of wine remained. 'It's not safe. We can never go back again.'

'But you can't stay here.'

Grace was becoming increasingly frantic.

'Just for one night. It's so cold outside.'

'But—'

'Shh. Go to sleep.'

His eyes, which had been half closed during this conversation, now shut completely. Grace bit back the words, realising it was impossible to argue with him in such a state, and then turned over so she was facing the wall.

Go to sleep. But it wasn't that easy. You couldn't sleep when you felt as though you were sharing a bed with a wild animal. The bed was not that wide, and even though they were not touching, she became convinced that she could feel him pressing against her. She had a greater chance of getting up and completing a sheet of algebra problems than falling asleep.

When she awoke, or rather arose from her trance the next morning, he was gone. The sheets on the other side of the bed were smooth.

At breakfast she surprised her mother by asking for coffee.

'You never usually have coffee at breakfast.'

'I need it this morning.'

'Didn't you sleep well?' Barbara looked up from her cereal. 'I thought I heard you talking in your sleep.'

Grace was too tired to judge whether it was safer to admit it or deny it.

'Oh, was I?'

'Remember when we shared a room? You used to make the most awful noises in your sleep, like you were possessed or something.'

Grace sipped her coffee and said nothing.

132

VI

Caroline was appalled.

'That's it? It's over?'

'He says it's too dangerous,' said Grace. 'He needs to find somewhere else.'

'But where?' asked Sara.

'Sara, you weren't even happy about it being in a church in the first place.'

'I know, but that's better than nothing. I can't stand the thought of not doing it any more.'

'It'll be all right,' said Grace. 'He'll find somewhere.'

'But when?' asked Caroline. 'We need to talk to him. Where is he?'

Grace hadn't told them the full story of her last visitation. In her mind it was nightmarishly connected with the death of Pippin, and she couldn't bear to relive the moment.

'Maybe it's another test of our faith,' Sara suggested. 'If we want him enough, he'll come.'

'Or we could start looking for him now.'

'You're so impatient, Caro.'

'Your hands are trembling,' said Sara.

'You're imagining it,' said Caroline, 'or it's just the cold. Anyway, shall we go?'

At Grace's suggestion they went to the Ghetto, which was both the location of the church and the place where she had first met him. They walked down every narrow street, searching the faces of all the people they passed in case he was disguised.

'But why would he be in disguise?' asked Sara.

'You never know.'

In this obsessive, highly strung state, everyone seemed to resemble him. A young priest, a gypsy girl and the naked boys of the turtle fountain all acquired some familiar trace – something that turned their heads.

They almost walked right past him. An archway had been carved out beneath an old building, and among the parked motorbikes and rubbish bins was a man, barefoot. Some instinct made Grace turn around.

'It's him.'

She crouched down and was about to touch him, to rest her hand on his shoulder or make some other little human gesture, when he looked up. Her hand froze mid-air. His eyes were narrow and heavy-lidded, and he looked almost malevolent in the gloom of the archway.

Caroline and Sara were used to seeing him in a more dignified state, and were shocked to see the god lying in the street, like the tramp Grace had once mistaken him for.

'Why are you here?'

'If you'd been a little more hospitable, I wouldn't be here,' said Dionysus.

'What?'

'He means me, Caro,' said Grace. She gave the god a nervous smile; he remained expressionless. 'Never mind. We were worried about you.'

'How touching.'

Grace and Caroline were both crouched beside him, while Sara kept her distance. She reminded Grace of a visitor at the zoo, warily peering into an enclosure, not quite sure what she was looking at.

'Is it true?' asked Sara timidly. 'We can't go to the church any more?'

'Yes.'

'Then what are we going to do?'

Caroline's voice was oddly high-pitched, like a child about to burst into tears.

'Don't fret. I'll find somewhere.'

He sounded indescribably weary. Grace was beginning to feel guilty for having reacted so badly to his appearance in her bedroom. He had needed her, yet she had tried to cast him out. She hoped he didn't remember their conversation, and that if he did, he wasn't angry. He didn't *seem* angry, but maybe that was just because he was tired and weak.

She suddenly became aware of how close she was; hoping that it wasn't too noticeable, she slowly drew back and went to join Sara at a safe distance. If he ever wanted to harm her, of course, a couple of metres wouldn't make any difference, but she felt more comfortable with a space between them. Even if she had been the one to approach him, it always felt like the other way round, as if he had silently crept up on her. She never noticed until it was too late and he was breathing over her shoulder.

'You're not really living here, are you?' asked Grace, noticing some bags of rubbish piled up in the corner. She found it incomprehensible that he should have chosen this squalid street when he could have gone to a park, a rooftop terrace, or even back to the river. A cynical part of her wondered whether he enjoyed suffering.

'I don't live anywhere,' said Dionysus. 'I've never had a home, Grace. Only temples and shrines, and there aren't any of those left. I should take the synagogue next. That might be amusing.'

'You're not serious.'

'No.'

'I can't tell when you're joking, because you never smile.'

His lips twitched, as if to contradict her.

'But until you find somewhere,' said Caroline, 'what are we meant to do?'

'What do you mean?'

'I'll die without wine.'

She said it so sincerely that Dionysus laughed, a bark that echoed.

'Dear Caroline, you should know by now that you'll never want for wine.'

He lifted his hands and showed them the red liquid blooming in the centre of his palms like a stigmatic's wound, oozing from his fingertips.

'See?'

Before leaving, Grace and Caroline both invited him to come and stay – Grace awkwardly, Caroline practically begging. Somehow Grace was not surprised when he declined both offers.

'No,' he said simply. He gave no reason, but in one syllable managed to convey a total lack of interest in the idea. *He's impossible*, thought Grace. First he had turned up drunk and uninvited in the middle of the night, then he had made her feel guilty for not being more welcoming, and now he was rejecting her offer. What did he want?

'Finding a place to sleep is the least of my problems.' He was gazing at his hands, holding them up to the thin sliver of sunlight that had trespassed the gloom of the archway.

'You need a temple,' said Caroline. 'We can help you find somewhere.'

'No, you can't. Leave it to me.'

He closed his eyes, and they understood, with conflicting emotions of guilt and relief, that for the moment he had no use for them.

Caroline was not easily pacified. All that week at school she seemed unusually agitated. She had forgotten her old admirer completely – the night at his flat and his subsequent disappearance were no longer topics of conversation. All she thought about was Dionysus and finding a replacement for the church.

'If only it were spring,' she said, 'then it wouldn't matter. We could go outside, do it in the woods and the fields. Damn the cold. And the rain – God, it's even worse than England.'

'It'll be all right,' said Grace. 'We've just got to wait and have faith in him. He'll find somewhere – he's got to.'

Part of Grace was impatient too, but when it came to the bacchanals she knew she had to trust him. Although she was never treacherous enough to say it out loud, she knew that his apparent indifference masked desperation. Caroline was blinded by her fervour and Sara was too timid, always holding back; only Grace understood how much he needed them.

The message was delivered in the most unexpected way. Grace was in the middle of writing an essay in a History lesson, struggling to recall the little she knew about Tudor politics, when some words appeared in the margin.

Nine tonight – the turtles

The handwriting was unmistakeable. She felt goosebumps appear on her arms, and quickly pulled down her sleeves as if to hide her secret from the girl sharing her desk. The other girl was still hunched over her paper, writing at a frantic speed, and Grace told herself that there was no logical reason why she would have noticed anything. They were only a few words scrawled at the side of the page – it was not as though the god had entered the classroom in a halo of light and started talking to her.

She looked up and saw that Caroline was staring at her. Sara, who was sitting a couple of rows forward, had turned round to look at Caroline. So they had all received the message. Grace tried to convince herself that she was not disappointed about not being the only one. When she glanced down at the page, the words were gone, but they might as well have been tattooed on her skin. She could think of nothing else.

'Well?' said Caroline, as soon as they were out of the classroom.

'I don't think I can come,' said Sara unhappily. 'My parents have got some friends coming over for dinner, and I said I'd be there.'

'Who's more important? Their friends or your friends? Dio—'

'*Careful,*' said Grace.

'All right, *he* won't be very happy if you choose them over us.'

'But it's Wednesday,' said Sara. 'What excuse can I give for being out late on a Wednesday?'

'The cinema?' Grace suggested.

'I never go to the cinema.'

'Tell them it's a film about something you're studying, a school trip of some sort. Or *you* think of something. I don't know.'

'But you have to be there,' said Caroline. 'I'll never forgive you if you're not. Neither will he.'

When Grace arrived at the turtle fountain at ten minutes to nine, Caroline was already there. She was pacing back and forth, hands deep in the pockets of a black coat that was several sizes too big for her.

'That's not yours, is it?' Grace pulled on Caroline's sleeve.

'No, it's my father's. It's warmer than anything I own.'

'It makes your head look tiny.'

'Thanks. I don't care how I look, anyway.'

'I never thought I'd hear that from you.'

Caroline shrugged impatiently and peered around the edge of the fountain to see if the god had appeared.

'It's not even nine,' said Grace. 'Sara isn't here yet?'

'No. She'd better come.'

'Why do you care so much? Why does it matter?'

'It matters to me because it matters to him. I'd have thought you would understand.'

'Isn't that her?'

Someone was walking briskly down the narrow street that led to the square. The lamplight revealed Sara, flushed and out of breath.

'I thought I was going to be late,' she said.

'What did you tell your parents in the end?'

'I said I was going to the cinema. They're expecting me back by 11pm, so I've got to keep an eye on the time.'

'What a bore,' said Caroline.

'Well, what about *your* parents? Where do they think you are?'

'They don't know I'm out. Even if they notice, they'll probably be more concerned about my father's missing coat.'

While they were talking, Dionysus emerged from behind the fountain. As he appeared between the black bodies of the smiling statues, Grace had a sudden vision of the past, the god in his former glory followed by a procession of grinning satyrs. There were no satyrs now, no wild animals or maenads beating drums. His triumphant arrival had been replaced with something much more subdued – stalking through the shadows with no sound but the indifferent trickle of the fountain.

'Good evening,' he said. 'I have something to show you.'

'Is it—'

'Wait and see.'

He led them into a dimly lit alley and pushed open an iron gate. Grace noticed the rows of names next to the buzzers, lit up in gold, and couldn't decide if it made her feel safer or more uncomfortable to know that they were entering a block of flats where people lived. She had imagined an empty building somewhere secret. As they climbed the dark staircase, she heard faint voices, and she was suddenly afraid that someone would appear on the stairs and confront them.

On the top floor, Dionysus walked ahead of them down the hallway, brushing his fingers against the doors on both sides.

'People here,' he murmured, 'and here, and here, but here...'

For a moment he paused, stroking the door. Then his fingers slipped to the knocker, a lion's head, and within a second the door was open.

'No key?' said Sara.

'Not necessary.'

They heard footsteps at the far end of the hallway, and quickly stepped into the room. Dionysus shut the door behind them.

It was a large, bare room, with a tiled floor and paint peeling off the walls. There was no furniture. Some shallow candles flickered on the ground, their weak light struggling to reach the high ceiling, where dim flowers appeared and then retreated into darkness.

'In the absence of a temple,' said Dionysus, 'this will have to do.'

He sat cross-legged on the floor and filled four glasses with wine. Shivering, the girls joined him and eagerly reached for the glasses. Caroline drained hers almost immediately.

'Careful, Caro.' Sara looked alarmed. Caroline smiled and closed her eyes.

'I feel much better now. The warmth...'

'Quite right,' said Dionysus. 'Why hold back?'

He refilled Caroline's empty glass, and then drank from his own. Some of it spilled, and Grace watched a drop of wine trickle down his neck. In the dark of the room it looked almost exactly like blood.

Grace looked towards the window, visible only as a black space in the wall. There were no lights beyond the glass.

'Are there any windows overlooking this one?' she asked.

'Ah, you're worried about being seen,' said Dionysus.

'Not just for my sake – for yours too.'

'I think we're quite safe here. Safer than before. No priests. No longer surrounded by that man...'

'What man?' asked Sara.

'He means Jesus,' said Grace. 'Yes, I suppose you're right. Here you could create your own temple, if you wanted to.'

Caroline, who had finished her second glass, stood up and began pacing around the room like a caged animal.

'What's the matter, Caro?'

'It's all very well finding another place, but it's still a room.'

'What do you mean?'

'We're inside. I want to be out there.'

She went to the window and opened it.

'It looks like there's some kind of garden. I can see an orange tree.'

'It must be a shared garden,' said Grace. 'Hardly a place for a bacchanal.'

'I didn't mean that garden in particular. I mean outside, in nature. Just like the places I see when… you know.'

'Close the window,' said Sara. 'You're letting in the cold.'

'You must be patient, Caroline. Soon it will be spring.' Dionysus filled her glass again. 'Come away from the window and have some more wine.'

'You really shouldn't.' Grace had noticed that Caroline was not walking entirely steadily. 'You're already drunk, and we've got school tomorrow.'

She waited for Dionysus to reproach her, but the god merely sat there in silence, swirling the wine in his glass.

'I ought to go soon,' said Sara. 'I told my parents I wouldn't be back too late.'

'Just tell them you had to wait for a bus,' said Caroline, sitting down again. 'It's perfectly plausible.'

She took two deep gulps of the wine. Grace and Sara exchanged nervous glances.

'We've got to go,' said Grace, without much conviction. Caroline ignored her, while Dionysus seemed to take pleasure in watching the glass become empty. Grace suddenly became aware of how powerless she was. Caroline never listened to her anyway, and by trying to persuade her to leave now, there was the risk of angering the god. Gods were vindictive when you defied them, and sometimes for no reason at all. Grace had a sudden flash of the ending of *The Bacchae*, and then, out of nowhere, Pippin.

Stop it, she told herself. She was getting hysterical over nothing. The only real danger was Caroline overdoing it.

'Caro.' She was close to pleading now.

'Just let me finish,' said Caroline irritably.

'If your parents see you like this they'll know.'

'You and Sara, always trying to make me think about reality. You're so boring.'

'You could stay, you know.' Dionysus turned towards them. At this angle his face was hidden in shadows, and Grace tried to ignore her treacherous fear.

'Thank you, but not tonight. We – we'll come again on Friday. I promise.'

'Cross our hearts and hope to die,' said Caroline.

'Friday, then.' Dionysus took one of the glasses he had filled for them, and drained it in a single gulp. 'You know where to find me. It's the bell with no name.'

VII

The room was filled with light. For the first time she saw the flowers distinctly: twisted vines and faded petals blooming across the ceiling. At first she was content just to lie there on the cold stone, and follow the patterns to the corners of the room, but then she felt the need of warmth – someone else's body.

Caroline was curled up beneath her heavy black coat. Grace moved closer to cover herself with the coat, and discovered that it was big enough for both of them.

'Morning,' said Caroline, her eyes still closed. Dionysus had gone, vanished into the cold air. Even though there was no one to disturb them here, no priests to stumble on the aftermath of their worship, the god would not stay. The window was open; Grace imagined him floating out, his body transformed into a mystical cloud, and then disappearing into the branches of the orange tree.

'Isn't it nice,' said Grace, shuffling closer to Caroline, 'being able to stay? No need to pull ourselves together and rush out as soon as it's morning.'

'Mmm.'

'Are you awake?'

'Sort of. I don't want to open my eyes, because then it might all go.'

'What?'

'The trees and the bull. The men. They're not men exactly, but...'

She let out a sigh, which turned into a yawn, and covered her face with the coat.

'Caro?'

Caroline didn't reply. For a moment Grace was envious, watching her friend retreat deeper into a dream, where she couldn't follow. Grace remembered nothing she had seen that night. She only felt it, the golden cloud still overhanging and the pleasurable aching of her limbs. If only she could still see what Caroline was seeing.

The trick was to drift, not to wake up immediately but to linger in the space in between. She closed her eyes tightly but saw only darkness. When she opened them again and saw Caroline's face, half hidden by the coat, she was overcome by the desire to wake her.

Caroline's bare arm was right next to hers. She gave her a short, sharp pinch.

'Ow.' Caroline raised her head, eyes open. 'What did you do that for?'

'I didn't want to be alone.'

'You could have given me five more minutes. Something divine was about to happen.'

Grace felt fingernails digging into her wrist.

'Stop it, Caro.'

'You started it.'

Grace pinched her again, and within seconds they were clawing at each other beneath the coat, alternately yelping with pain and giggling.

'It isn't fair,' said Grace. 'Your nails are sharper than mine. Look what you've done to my arm.'

'Serves you right.'

Caroline pulled Grace's arm over her body, not as an affectionate gesture but to cover herself and stay warm.

'Just think of the summer. We'll be waking up in the grass, underneath a warm sun. Bliss.'

'This is nice too.'

'I don't want "nice". I want...' Caroline paused and raised her eyes to the ceiling, 'Maybe – I can't even put it into words. There's so much I want.'

'Greedy.'

'I prefer "aspirational".'

'Fine, what's your aspiration right now, then?'

'A bath. My kingdom for a bath.'

Caroline disentangled herself from Grace and stood up unsteadily.

'Looks like Sara's already gone. Traitor.'

'It's already ten o'clock,' said Grace.

'Breakfast time. Breakfast, then a bath. Come on.' She helped Grace to stand up, and they left the room, bruised arms linked together. They both felt gloriously light-headed and light-limbed. Not quite bodiless, but hovering on the edge of transcendence. The colours of the city – the pinks and oranges of the buildings, the pure blue of the sky – pulsed and blurred into each other, and when Caroline hugged her goodbye, Grace felt, just for a moment, that they were the same person.

The coffee at the bar didn't bring her back down to earth, and neither did the walk home. It was only when she was standing in front of the door that she realised, with a growing knot of anxiety in her stomach, what she'd done. She could only hope and pray that no one was at home.

'*Eccola!*' Mauro's voice boomed from another room. 'You see? I told you.'

Grace glanced at her reflection in the hallway mirror and hoped that nothing about her appearance would give the secret away. Or did she smell? Of wine, sweat, or something more sinister? She resisted the urge to start sniffing at her clothes as her mother appeared in the hallway.

'Where the *hell* have you been?'

'I – I...' Grace was not clear-headed enough to think of an excuse.

'We've been worried sick. We were *this* close to calling the police.'

'But... didn't I tell you I was going out?'

'You most certainly did not.'

It was true. She had been stupid. All it would have taken was a vague reference to a sleepover as she walked out of the door, and she would have been fine. Instead she'd rushed off without giving her mother a second thought.

'I'm sorry, I thought I told you. I was at... I was at...'

Think. If she mentioned Caroline or Sara she was done for. Her mother would have called their parents last night. She would know she was lying.

'Genevieve,' she said finally. 'I was at Genevieve's house.'

'Who on earth is Genevieve? I've never heard of the girl.'

'She's in my class. She's new. She had a sleepover last night, and I guess I forgot to tell you. Sorry.'

'You didn't think to call?'

'I forgot and I was distracted. I'm sorry, I've been feeling a bit muddled lately. Ever since Pippin...'

'You've got some nerve, blaming this on poor Pippin.'

'Girls, girls,' said Mauro. 'Be calm. I make you a coffee.'

'I'm all right, thanks. I've already had one. I think I'll go and have a bath.'

'Yes, do.' Grace's mother was looking at her strangely. Then she turned to Mauro. 'I'll have a coffee, darling. You know how little I slept last night.'

Grace knew that she ought to feel guilty, but she was too overwhelmed with relief to feel anything else. This wouldn't be the last confrontation with her mother, but this time, at least, she had got away with it.

Lying in the bath, she replayed the conversation in her head. *You've got some nerve, blaming this on poor Pippin.* That had stung. Although she had used it as an excuse, in a way it was true. She hadn't been thinking straight. She hadn't really given herself time to grieve, to think about what had happened.

Caroline and Sara didn't know the truth. She had only told them that Pippin was dead, leaving them to assume that it was from natural causes, or something sad but mundane like being hit by a car. The truth – that he'd been deliberately killed – was too awful to think about. She didn't want to think about who, or why, or how. Whenever the thought came, she would shut her eyes so tightly that she briefly gave herself a headache. That was the only way to repress that insidious shiver of fear. She would never know, and she would certainly never ask.

All the same... poor Pippin. She shut her eyes and slipped under the water.

The room in the Ghetto gave Grace another excuse to neglect her homework and avoid her family. She no longer had to wait for him to appear in the street or send her messages through margins. Now she knew where to find him.

She would often go there straight after school, alone, walking briskly down the streets she knew by heart until she reached the nameless buzzer. She became such a frequent visitor that an old man she had bumped into a couple of times on the stairs began to greet her. She stammered over her response, fearing that if they kept meeting he would ask her questions about her reasons for being in the building.

She never felt safe until she was behind the closed door of that bare room, waiting for her heart to stop racing. Dionysus lay on some cushions on the floor – his sole concession to comfort – and watched her wordlessly. Grace had been there so many times, both alone and with her friends, yet whenever she first entered she felt inexplicably timid and guilty, as if she were trespassing.

'Sit down,' said Dionysus, with a vague gesture towards the cushions beside him. He had a skill for making a command sound like an invitation.

'Have you been here all day?'

'Yes.'

'For someone without a home, you seem to spend a lot of time in the same place.'

'Too cold. I'm not leaving this room until the sun comes out. But that still doesn't mean I live here. There is a difference between living in a room and merely existing in it.'

'You could make it more comfortable with a little furniture,' Grace suggested.

'Excellent idea. Some little tables and cabinets, a bit of lace and pictures of the Pope.'

'That's not what I meant.'

'I have absolutely no need of furniture. Unless you were thinking of your own comfort…'

'Of course not,' said Grace quickly. 'I don't need anything here except you.'

'You mean my wine.'

'No, I mean you. Though I don't know how to make the distinction sometimes, when we're drinking.'

'Oh, you can have wine without me, just as the sun continues to shine in the absence of Apollo.'

He sometimes mentioned the other gods, in a strange tone that was at once mocking and mournful. The past made him bitter, and despite her burning curiosity and the thousands of questions at the tip of her tongue, Grace tried to change the subject whenever it came up.

'They say it's going to start getting warmer this week,' she said. 'Practically spring.'

'Good. There's somewhere I want to take you when the nights are warm.'

'Where?'

'Guess.'

'How can I possibly guess?'

'Very well, don't guess. You will enjoy it more when we finally get there. Out in the open.'

'That's what Caroline dreams of.'

'That's how it's meant to be, you know. The city can stifle you, make you old. Nothing could be more unnatural than this. Listen.'

Grace held her breath and listened, but she could hear nothing but a distant police siren.

'What is it?' she whispered after several seconds had passed.

'Can't you hear it?'

'What?'

'The women next door are arguing. The man below is watching the football on TV – it's all he ever does. Downstairs someone has pressed the buzzer for the third time. Dogs are barking, children shrieking. A police car is following an ambulance. A plane just passed over us. Then there are the birds and the church bells and a million other incessant noises.'

'I hadn't realised you were so sensitive.'

'If I really paid attention I could probably hear a child being conceived on the other side of the city. It's terrible.'

'If it bothers you that much, you could always leave.'

'And go where? To the forest, where I can live in silence and form a solitary little religion, worshipping myself?'

'I don't understand.'

'Don't humiliate me by making me say it.'

Grace was still confused. She looked into the depths of those strangely vacant eyes and waited for an answer. Caroline wouldn't have had to wait. She would have known instinctively what he meant, and what to say to comfort him. Grace could only sit there tongue-tied, hardly daring to move in case she accidentally brushed against him. She was always so painfully conscious of his presence, his arms and feet bare despite the cold, his head lowered as if it were an effort to hold it up.

'I wish I knew what you wanted from me,' she said. The words sounded more self-pitying than she had intended and she blushed slightly, imagining that he would think her pathetic.

Instead he raised his head to look at her, and said, 'You're enough. I only asked for your belief, and you gave it to me. There's nothing more you can do for me until I become stronger.'

'But I don't want to be "enough". I want to be—'

Dionysus shook his head and turned away.

'I don't remember if you were always this dissatisfied, or if you only became like this after you met me.'

It was probably Caroline's fault, Grace reflected. Caroline was perpetually dissatisfied with everything, and it was inevitable that Grace would acquire the same habit, spending so much time with her.

'It's hard, having to wait.'

'If I've waited this long,' said Dionysus, staring out of the window, 'you should be capable of waiting just a little while longer. And then there will be plenty to do, don't you fear.'

Sunday was Grace's sixteenth birthday. Her presents were conventional and mostly underwhelming. Her mother and Mauro gave her clothes and jewellery, Barbara a set of bath oils and shampoo ('You ought to treat yourself to a nice, long bath for once'), and Henry a puzzle, which he offered to help her with. When she opened the present from her father – clumsily wrapped and clearly bashed around in the post – his thoughtfulness upset her to the point that she almost wished he hadn't given her anything. It was the drawing set they'd seen in the art shop on the Charing Cross Road, the one with the pencils that real artists used.

'You must write him a thank-you letter,' said Grace's mother.

'Of course,' said Grace, blinking rapidly and hoping that no one had noticed. 'Maybe I can call him later.'

'Yes, a quick call.'

Grace spent the rest of the day, and then the rest of the week, in an inexplicably foul mood. Over the last few years, birthdays had started to have this effect on her; perhaps it was the anti-climax.

The pleasure of the puzzle only lasted an hour, and then she was bored again. When she was younger Grace had been content to spend hours doing nothing in her room, idly cutting up magazines and barely paying attention to the record on her turntable. Long afternoons in the summer with the shutters closed and the radio on. Now she found it difficult to understand how she had spent so many hours in this way without dying of boredom. She could only guess that when she was thirteen there had been absolutely nothing to look forward to, no hopes or dreams. Her thirteen-year-old self could not have imagined how strange and beautiful and overwhelming life could be.

One evening she sat on the sofa, only half watching the TV. Part of her mind was already anticipating Friday night, and she began to squirm with boredom and impatience.

'Stop fidgeting,' said Barbara, still staring at the screen.

'This is boring. Can't we change the channel?'

'You used to like these kinds of programmes.'

'It's boring.'

'Fine.'

On the next channel a man in a suit and glasses was saying something about politics. It was totally incomprehensible, but Grace would have groaned just as loudly even if it had been in English.

'Go and do something else then,' said Barbara. 'Go and... I don't know. I have no idea what you do in your free time.'

'Just normal things.'

'You're out all the time. I never see you any more.'

'So?'

'Nothing. It was just an observation. You get angry when you think we're ignoring you and then you get angry when we show interest in your life.'

'That's not true.'

'You'll grow out of it.'

Barbara changed channels again, and returned to watching the soap that neither of them understood.

'Boring, boring, boring.' Grace got up and went to the window. It was still raining heavily, and the lamplight revealed the gutters being transformed into dark rivers. Even with the torrential rain and the threat of thunder in the air, she was tempted to go to him. She imagined him sitting there, surrounded by candles, staring at the bare wall. If only she could slip into the downpour unnoticed and keep him company.

Mauro walked into the living room, wearing the dressing gown that struggled to cover his stomach.

'It's late,' he said. 'You should be in bed.'

'I'm not a child,' Grace retorted.

'Technically you are,' said Barbara.

Grace glared at both of them, and then went to her room without another word. It was dreadful to think that she had at least a couple more years of being watched and told what to do. She was only just sixteen, but what they didn't understand was that she felt centuries older. Examining her face in the bathroom mirror before she went to bed, she noticed that some strands of hair had turned white. That had to be proof of something. Instinctively she reached for the tweezers and pulled them out, one by one.

VIII

Daisies covered the graves in the cemetery, and the sun grew warm again. As the Easter holidays approached, Grace discarded her gloves, then her scarf, and finally her coat. It had been an unnaturally bitter winter, but the spring was their reward. She raised her eyes to the sky, which was empty but for a single soft cloud, and felt a shiver of anticipation.

Sara was taken from the city against her will to spend the entire holiday in France.

'I can't stand it,' she said, as she hugged Grace and Caroline goodbye outside the school gates on the last day of term.

'You'll survive,' said Caroline.

'Easy for you to say. You're not going anywhere.'

'I have to go to England, remember,' said Grace. She kept trying to forget about this obligation, but it loomed on the horizon like a darkening cloud.

'You're only going for a week though. Before that you've got two whole weeks, and you can do whatever you want. I feel like I'm going to miss out on everything.'

'We'll try not to have too much fun without you,' said Caroline.

As soon as Sara had left, Grace and Caroline plotted together, trying to make excuses that would let them spend as much time with the god as possible.

'I wish we could just leave home,' said Caroline. 'Run away in the night and then live with him forever. If only we were grown-ups.'

'Even if we were, we couldn't do that.'

'Why not?'

Grace glanced at Caroline's fingers and noticed the almost imperceptible tremble.

'Patience, Caro.'

They limited their visits to two or three times a week, to prevent their parents from becoming too suspicious. As Caroline incessantly pointed out, it was really just Grace's parents who they needed to worry about. Caroline had been chastised for an inexplicable stain on

153

her father's coat, but neither of her parents had questioned the frequency of the sleepovers.

The room in the Ghetto was a little less bleak now that the nights were getting warmer and lighter. The window was left permanently open, allowing the ivy to creep inside and spread itself across the wall, like the arms of a sea creature. This detail struck Grace as being particularly magical, and she never tired of gazing at it as she slipped deeper and deeper into drunkenness.

One night she was counting the leaves as the walls began to dissolve, when she was suddenly pulled out of her trance. Caroline's voice boomed and echoed, while Dionysus's words ran beneath like the murmur of a stream. Grace tried to listen, but she kept losing the shapes of the words until Caroline was leaning over her, flushed and bright-eyed.

'Come on, we're going.'

'Going where?'

'Out. While we can still walk.'

Caroline giggled, and pulled Grace to her feet. Dionysus said nothing but opened the door for them.

'We have to follow you,' said Caroline. 'Lead the way.'

For a moment he stood motionless in the doorway – a vision, a statue. Grace could hardly believe he had ever breathed. She grasped at his shirt and marvelled to see it fold beneath her fingers, not like marble at all. Then he was moving, striding down the dark hallway. His footsteps made no noise. Grace and Caroline staggered behind him, arm in arm, struggling to keep up.

The streets were deserted, except for the seagulls pecking at the rubbish, and the occasional stray cat. They passed the turtle fountain and held on to each other in silence, suddenly conscious of their vulnerability. Then Caroline began to whisper, but it sounded like another language.

The god was leading them to the river. He walked ahead with such slow solemnity that he might have been leading a funeral procession. He only looked back once, when they reached the bridge.

'Where are you taking us?' asked Grace.

He gestured towards the island, which rose out of the river like a vast shipwreck. Its mast was a bell-tower, its deck a maze of flowering rooftops. The land narrowed at both ends, where the torrents raged.

Grace and Caroline descended hand in hand to the loneliest part of the city. It was not the wilderness Caroline longed for, but it was the closest thing. Far below the lights and the windows, they could almost believe they were alone in the universe.

'It's only us,' Caroline whispered. The god's body was nowhere to be seen, but Grace felt strangely at peace. Even if they could not see him, he was still with them, watching. She was feeling drunker by the second; the wine was in her blood, her heart, dripping from Caroline's lips.

She was completely overwhelmed. She looked up and saw the stars; she looked down and saw Caroline. All the blood rushed to her head and she was kissing her, lips pressed together for a dizzying split second. And then another, longer. Caroline did nothing, but let it happen until she could no longer hold herself upright. She sank down on the ground, her head only inches from the river, and the memory of the kiss was lost in the depths of some mysterious dream, where Grace could never follow.

Grace sat at the furthest edge, staring into the dark water, and waited.

She was awoken by the sun streaming through her bedroom window. Her head was killing her and her throat was a desert, but at least she didn't need to be sick. That was some consolation. The *only* consolation.

Oh God.

The mere memory was enough to make her want to weep. It usually took a while to recall what had happened the night before, and the details would slowly take shape as the day passed. This was different. She remembered everything so vividly that it was like watching a scene in a film over and over again. The shame was all-consuming.

She had kissed a girl. Even worse, the girl was Caroline. She had done it stupidly, unthinkingly, without the slightest encouragement, and now Caroline would despise her forever. There was always the chance that Caroline would have forgotten, but in this case Grace would feel compelled to admit it anyway.

She pulled the sheets over her head until she became too hot and needed air. She had never felt this terrible about anything in her life. It was as if she had murdered someone. Then she reconsidered, and decided that most murderers were comparatively complacent about their deeds. A murder in cold blood was a conscious, calculated decision, and afterwards there was no regret. Or at least, nothing in comparison to the mortification after an accidental kiss.

The hangover didn't help. She told her mother she was ill, as she couldn't face the prospect of sitting at the dining table with her family.

'This always happens at the end of term,' her mother observed. 'You get run-down. Make sure you get plenty of rest over the holiday. No more late nights.'

'No more late nights,' Grace repeated. Normally she would have argued, but in her present state of mind it was a relief to have someone tell her what to do. If she followed her mother's advice, at least she would be prevented from doing anything stupid.

When her mother had left, Grace got out of bed and turned over the photo of Caroline on her desk. But even then there were a hundred other reminders – books she had borrowed, postcards, presents. Grace simply didn't have the energy to hide them all.

She stayed in her pyjamas the next day, and asked her mother to call Caroline and tell her that she was sick. Grace and Caroline had arranged to meet for an ice cream, but now the mere thought of seeing Caroline again made her feel slightly ill. Their plan to go out for ice cream already seemed dull in its innocence after everything they had experienced over the past few months, and now Grace didn't want to see Caroline anywhere. Maybe she could avoid her for the rest of the holidays. She needed at least a week alone to work out what to say.

Instead, Grace ended up not thinking about it at all. She realised that she felt so much better when she didn't think, although it wasn't easy. She kept having to invent distractions for herself, like watching TV with Barbara or re-reading old magazines.

Grace was in the middle of reading something about boys when there was a knock at her bedroom door.

'Come in,' she said, without looking up.

'You do look rotten.' Caroline was standing in the doorway.

'What are you doing here?' Grace could feel herself turning red.

'I came to see what was wrong. You know, being your best friend and all that.'

Caroline sat at the end of the bed. Grace stared at her, trying to find a clue, some hint of what she was thinking. Her face was usually so expressive, but today there was nothing. Grace bit her lip and tried to find the courage to confess.

'Go on, what's the matter? You can't be hungover still.'

'It's not that.'

'What then? Maybe it's all in your head. An ice cream might make you feel better.'

'I don't think so.'

Grace couldn't bear to look at her any more, and she stared at the sheets as she asked the inevitable question.

'Don't you remember what happened?'

'When?'

'We were with him, on the island.'

'I remember bits and pieces. It's all a bit fuzzy, to be honest.'

'So you really don't remember?'

'Remember what?'

'I – we – we kissed.'

'What?' Caroline laughed disbelievingly.

'I can't believe you don't remember.'

'Are you sure you're not imagining it? Couldn't you – I mean, how did it happen?'

'I kissed you.'

Caroline laughed again, and Grace felt like dying.

'*Well.*' Caroline's smile was painfully hard to interpret.

'You're not angry, are you?'

'Why would I be angry? No, I don't know what to think.' She was silent for a moment, and then she smiled. 'So you've been pretending to be ill for two days because of that?'

'I didn't know what to do.' Grace was aware of how pathetic she must sound.

'Bit of an overreaction, don't you think? Anyway, if you decide to recover, let me know.' Caroline got up and left.

Grace willed herself to be as indifferent as Caroline, to dismiss the incident as a drunken mistake, irrelevant to their friendship. If they could spend some time apart, it might be easier. A distance of a week or two would help Grace to forget, to pretend that everything was normal again. But she had to see the god, which inevitably meant seeing Caroline too. She couldn't avoid both of them.

When they next met, Caroline acted as though nothing had happened. Grace felt pathetically grateful for this small mercy and paid for Caroline's coffee and pastry, not even minding when Caroline made no offer to pay her back.

'I'm so hungry,' said Caroline. 'I could eat ten of these.'

'They're really bad for you, though. Just think of all the sugar.' Grace watched Caroline suck her fingers, one by one.

'What's wrong with sugar?'

'It rots your teeth, everyone knows that. And it's bad for your skin.'

'I never get spots.'

It was true. Caroline had maddeningly perfect skin.

'You ought to get them.'

'Whether or not I ought to get them, I *don't*.'

She smiled and wiped her fingers on the napkin.

'You're disgusting sometimes.'

'What's wrong with you today? You buy me a pastry and then criticise me for enjoying it.'

'Sorry, it's… nothing. It doesn't matter.'

'Well, be like that. I don't care. Tonight's the only thing that matters. What time are we going?'

'Tonight?'

'Of course. It's been three days. He'll be wondering where we are.'

'I suppose you're right.'

'Why, don't you want to go?'

'Of course I do.'

'Well, that settles it. Before we go, buy me another one, please. To apologise for calling me disgusting.'

IX

He lay on the floor beneath the open window, his body divided by the dying sunlight. When they entered the room they could only see his chest, shining like the shelves of the golden reliquaries in the church where they had once worshipped him. His face was turned to the wall, hidden in the shadows.

There was always this moment of awkwardness when they first arrived; the hesitant guests lingering at the threshold, unsure of how to greet their host.

'We brought you something.'

Caroline's voice pierced the silence, forcing him to turn over and look at them.

'Grapes.' Caroline dangled the bunch of black grapes above his face.

'Thank you.'

'We know you don't get hungry, but you must have some pleasure in eating.'

'Sometimes.'

Dionysus plucked one of the grapes and began to chew it slowly, without giving it much attention. His mind was clearly elsewhere.

'What are you thinking about?' asked Grace.

'I know what *you* are thinking about,' replied the god. He looked at her steadily and she turned away out of embarrassment, even though she wasn't sure what he meant. She was hardly aware of her own thoughts, so how could he know?

'You humans are so transparent.' He took another grape, paying no attention to Grace's discomfort.

'What are we going to do tonight?' Caroline kneeled beside him, eyes wide like an eager child.

'That depends, doesn't it?'

'On what?'

'On you. Free will and all that.'

'I'm not sure I have free will any more,' said Grace.

'Oh, you always have a choice.'

161

'Even when I'm really, really drunk?'

'Even then. But the beauty of wine is that it gives us the illusion of not having a choice.'

'It is beautiful,' said Caroline. '*So* beautiful. Let's start now.'

'Very well.' Dionysus presented her with a half-filled glass. 'But there's no rush, you know. We have the whole night ahead of us.'

Grace thought she detected a hint of weariness in those words, as if a night and eternity were one and the same. She glanced at Caroline, whose lips were already at the glass.

Time passed strangely that evening, trickling like sand in an hourglass and then suddenly slipping through their fingers and vanishing. When Grace looked at her watch she could not understand the numbers – it was a mystery, a code she could not break.

'How,' she began, 'how...?'

But she could not finish the question, and neither of them would give her an answer. Caroline would whisper in the god's ear, laughing, and then disappear from Grace's vision. Dionysus said nothing. He stared into the darkness without seeing, moving only to raise the glass to his lips.

Grace suddenly became aware of hands on her waist, Caroline grabbing at her. The room was spinning, and she was moving with the heavy limbs of a deep-sea diver. It took several seconds before she could look Caroline in the eye.

And then, without knowing how or why, she was being kissed with a passion that frightened her. Wine-stained lips pressed hungrily against her own, the kisses becoming more open each time, until she felt Caroline's tongue and with it, a sickening rush of excitement, rising up from her stomach. The heat spread through her and she let it happen again and again, until some nameless instinct told her to stop. She pulled away breathlessly, brushing aside the hair that had fallen over her face.

'Why are you doing this?' She barely recognised the sound of her own voice.

'Does it matter?' Caroline wiped her mouth on the back of her hand. 'I want to do it before we're too far gone to remember. All right?'

'But do you mean it? Do you actually—'

'God, stop talking.'

It was happening again, and Caroline's fingers were in her hair, holding her, pulling her closer.

The god was reclining on the floor just a few feet away; he stared right through them.

When Grace awoke the next morning, she was alone. She knew she was alone even before she opened her eyes. She could sense it, somehow. Perhaps it was because the birdsong was louder, and the room was colder than usual. It was no surprise to see that the god was missing again, but Caroline's absence hurt her. She would have wanted Caroline anyway, but in the circumstances it seemed particularly cruel to be left alone.

She slowly raised herself from the floor and glanced around the room. There was no trace of last night's debauchery except the candles; the red wax had spilled over the edges and oozed across the tiles. Grace ran her finger over the river of wax and tried to remember what she had to do next. She was so used to Caroline being there, giving orders, pulling her off the floor.

At last she summoned all her strength and forced herself to leave. She left the building and emerged into daylight. Despite the shade of the narrow street, it still seemed too bright. She rubbed her eyes and walked in the direction of the nearest bar.

She had intended to drink her coffee standing at the bar like the locals, but it was such an effort to remain upright that she had to sit down at a table. She continued stirring long after the sugar had dissolved. She remembered everything perfectly, but what if Caroline didn't? Or what if Caroline remembered, but regretted? She might even deny the whole thing. The thought made Grace feel nauseous.

She abandoned the dregs of her coffee and went out into the bright square, which was buzzing with groups of tourists and locals gesticulating at each other. She pressed her hand against the tap of the drinking fountain, to make the water burst out of the hole at the top, missing her mouth but drenching her clothes. Normally she would have been embarrassed, but that morning she hardly noticed.

Nothing in the city seemed real to her. She got on a bus without thinking, without even knowing where it was going, and felt like a ghost. After a few stops she realised that she was close to Caroline's flat, so she stumbled off the bus and walked to the faded orange building she knew so well. When she pressed the buzzer the door swung open immediately, as if someone was expecting her.

In the lift she tried to plan what she was going to say to Caroline, but she still couldn't think. She was relieved when the door was opened by Caroline's mother, who still managed to seem impossibly glamorous even in her dressing gown, with no make-up.

'Hello. Is Caroline here?'

'Yeees, she's in her room.' Caroline's mother spoke with an upper-class drawl. 'She came back about an hour ago. I think she's gone to sleep.'

'Can I see her?'

'Weren't you just with her? I thought she was staying with you.'

'Yes, but…' Grace racked her brains for an excuse, and found nothing. Deciding that vagueness was safer than blatant falsehood she said, 'There's something I need to talk to her about. I don't want to bore you with all the details.'

'Fine, I'll see if she's awake. But don't be surprised if she's in a monstrous mood. She's bad-tempered enough anyway, and when she comes back from these sleepovers…'

Grace waited in the hallway for a few minutes, rocking back and forth on her heels. She still didn't have the faintest idea what she wanted to say. Then Caroline's mother returned, eyebrows raised as if to say, 'I told you so.'

Grace tiptoed into Caroline's room, until she realised that the sleeper had already been disturbed. The shutters were closed and Caroline was buried between blankets and teddy bears, but her heavy-lidded eyes were open, only just visible in the gloom.

'What do you want?' Her voice was muffled.

'I don't know,' said Grace. 'I honestly don't know.'

'Is this about last night?'

'I suppose so.'

'Don't tell me you're having another crisis. Even if you are, couldn't you have waited until later? I'll die if I don't sleep.'

Grace sat hesitantly on the edge of the bed.

'So it doesn't matter?'

'What?'

'You don't care about what happened?'

Caroline sighed and sat up, propping herself against the pillows. One of the bears rolled off the bed and fell to the floor, near Grace's feet.

'It matters and it doesn't matter. I mean, life goes on. It doesn't change anything. But at the same time, I'm glad it happened.'

'Really?' Grace felt an unexpected flutter of excitement in her stomach.

'Yes. Aren't you?'

'I – I still don't know what to think.'

'It was fun, wasn't it?'

'But we were both drunk. It couldn't happen normally.'

'What do you mean?'

'Like now, for instance.'

Caroline leaned forward and kissed her, a kiss so soft and fleeting that it might have existed only in Grace's imagination.

'It doesn't have to mean anything,' said Caroline. 'But if it feels good, why not?'

'That sounds like something *he* would say.'

'I know. I'm sure he would approve.'

'Is that why you're doing it? For his approval?'

'Of course not. I'm doing it because I want to. And you want it too.' Caroline smiled – a sleepy, mischievous smile.

'How do you know?'

'You wouldn't be here otherwise.'

Grace felt herself tremble, and didn't know if it was the lack of sleep, the coffee, or some new and more complicated sensation. She took off her shoes and lay beside Caroline, wondering if she would ever understand anything again.

X

Everything was grey. Everything except the grass, which was so brightly and beautifully green, as if to compensate for the dullness of its surroundings. When she looked away from the emerald grass and towards the sky or the strangely stunted buildings – a mere two floors – she felt like Dorothy returned to Kansas. All the colours had gone.

Only this was England, not Kansas, and she was not sure she wanted to be here. She was not like Caroline, who was overwhelmed by patriotic emotion whenever she returned to her country, to such an extent that after a couple of days she was drinking excessive amounts of tea and speaking like a character in an Evelyn Waugh novel. Caroline felt a fanatic loyalty to everything English, but Grace found it disorientating, even alienating at times.

On the Underground with her father, she listened to the conversations of the other passengers and barely understood a word. They were not speaking in words, but making clipped, unmelodic sounds that ran into each other and made no sense.

'Are you all right, Grace?'

She thought he had been reading his newspaper, but he was looking at her.

'Oh, I'm fine.'

How could she explain these feelings of foreignness to her father, who had never been out of the country for more than a week? How could she explain anything she felt?

On the plane, staring uncomprehendingly at the pages of a magazine ('Dear Meredith, I have a problem…') she had tried to think of possible conversation topics for the coming week. She had to stay absolutely silent on the subjects of Dionysus and Caroline, which left very little else to talk about. She could not even complain about her mother. Instead of feeling hard done by when his wife ran off with another man – and a foreigner at that – Grace's father had acted as if it were something inevitable. As it had been bound to happen sooner or later, there was no point in making a fuss. He bore his ex-wife no ill will, and he tutted whenever Grace criticised her mother.

'You oughtn't to,' he said, as they ate dinner together in his cluttered little dining room. 'It's not nice.'

'It's all very well for you to say that. *You* don't have to live with her.'

There was a pause, and Grace shifted uncomfortably in her seat, worried that she had hurt his feelings. But he was only chewing a mouthful of lamb, waiting until he had finished before speaking. This was an old rule of etiquette Grace had almost forgotten; Mauro talked with his mouth full all the time.

'I lived with your mother for nearly twenty years, Grace. I know what she's like. But we all have our faults, and you should try to accept her as she is. Besides, you won't have to live with her forever. You could always come here one day.'

Grace tried to imagine herself living in the tiny house on the hill, with grey skies and no gods.

'I don't know. My life is over there now.'

'I understand. But one day you might feel differently.'

She gave a sceptical little shrug, and they dropped the subject. The future was another topic not to be discussed. It was so far away as to be almost unimaginable.

She thought the week would never end. Walking through the town and catching sight of the clock on the bell-tower, she was horrified to realise that it wasn't even eleven o'clock yet. Only ten to eleven, and only Tuesday. How on earth would she get through the week?

For the first few days it rained lightly but incessantly, so she was stuck in her room – which was not really her room – restlessly turning the pages of books she had no desire to read. She had to find some way to occupy her mind; without a distraction, she would start thinking about the bacchanals she was missing, and if she thought about it for too long, she started to feel sick with jealousy. Forcing herself to concentrate on a Dorothy L. Sayers novel was the only solution, even though the characters and the story and even the language itself all seemed hollow. She tried some of her father's more highbrow books, printed on translucent paper and written by authors with unpronounceable names, but that was even worse. She had to keep re-reading sentences, so she rarely got beyond the first few pages.

When at last the rain stopped, and the sky became a less ominous shade of grey, she spent her afternoons going for long, solitary walks. From the terrace at the back of the grand, red-brick school buildings she could see beyond the sloping lawn, beyond the fields and trees, all the way to the distant rooftops of London: a damp mirage. At the peak of her boredom she briefly contemplated trying to walk there, but as she leaned against the stone balustrades and gazed at the city, unreal beneath the gathering clouds, she decided that there was no point. It was like one of those smudged little towns in the background of a painting, a few brushstrokes added as an afterthought. There was nothing to be gained from looking at it close up.

So she forgot about London and spent the week on the hill, wandering across the vast school grounds – acres of deserted grass, of no use to anyone when there was no cricket to be played – and the fields on the other side of the hill. When she told her father where she'd been, he commented that he was pleased that she had finally learned to appreciate nature. She hadn't. Nature bored her, and she had no real instinct for exploration. The only reason she spent so much time outdoors was that it was preferable to sitting around in a house that did not feel like home, talking when she wanted to think.

She needed to be alone. She needed to think. Winding her way through the almost vertical maze of gravestones on the hillside, she vowed that when she reached the top she would find a place to sit and think, and she would not move until everything was clear.

When she emerged from the gloomy canopy of trees, she was relieved to see a weak ray of sunlight shining through the clouds. Behind the church she found a bench, and she sat down to inspect her shoes. They were filthy, but that didn't matter. One of the advantages of being with her father was that, unlike her mother, he would take absolutely no notice of the state of her clothes.

She stared into the dark cluster of trees and tried to clear her mind. The girl. The god. Both frightened her; both quickened her heartbeats. They were her darkest secrets, but they also made her feel more alive than anything else in the world. What could she do?

She remembered Caroline's smile. Dionysus never smiled. *If it feels good, why not?* Wine and laughter, the electrifying sensation of being loved and desired, wanted and needed. If she closed her eyes she could almost feel it now. Almost, because she could never hope to relive that magic when she was so far away. She tried to remember the exact tone of his voice, the smell of her skin, but it was not enough. It was as inadequate as lovingly tracing the outline of some nineteenth-century silhouette and trying to detect the essence of the body that posed for it. Impossible. They would never come to her here. Dionysus could not live in the dank woods, amongst muddy footpaths and snails. Caroline also seemed too bright for such surroundings. She would be utterly out of place.

But it was pointless to sit here daydreaming about them, thinking of their voices and the way they made her feel. She would never find an answer like this. She might daydream her life away on this little wooden bench, and she would still be no closer to knowing what she was supposed to do. The timid, so often ignored voice of her conscience told her that she couldn't go on like this. Just because she was having fun, it didn't make it right. *It doesn't make it wrong, either* is what he would have said, murmuring between sips of wine.

She wasn't sure where the guilt came from. She wasn't religious in the traditional sense, as her mildly Christian upbringing had left virtually no impression on her. Her parents had given her a vague sense of right and wrong.

Doing well at school: *right*.

Answering back: *wrong*.

Leaving your husband and taking your children to another country so you can live with your lover: …?

Barely protesting when your wife leaves you and takes your children: …?

There were plenty of grey areas. Grace supposed that any strong moral principles she had must be something innate, something she had been born with. Was it the same for other people? Caroline evidently didn't have the same scruples.

Kissing a girl: *wrong*.

Bacchanals: *wrong*.

She didn't know why. They just were. The fact that she got so much pleasure out of the experiences only intensified her guilt.

Which was worse? Could she choose the lesser evil and live with an untroubled conscience? Probably not. In any case, giving up anything was unthinkable. The second she returned she would fall into their arms again, allow herself to be made drunk and kissed, as saying 'No' didn't mean anything.

In a way she quite enjoyed the thought of being weak, powerless to resist. It freed her from the responsibility of making choices, and given that all the choices she made were ignored anyway, it hardly seemed to matter.

A man appeared from behind the trees, startling her out of her trance. A gardener. She resented him being there; she had grown so used to the stillness and silence of the churchyard that this quiet intrusion bothered her.

Perhaps it was a sign to leave. She had been sitting there for long enough, and she had come to a sort of conclusion, hadn't she? To do nothing. That was her decision. Not very satisfying, but nothing ever was, except for the things she was trying to renounce. Evidently without much success. No sooner had she banished them from her mind than they came burning back to her in all their savage, gloating beauty.

Sitting opposite her father on the last evening, she realised, with a pang of guilt, that they had hardly spent any time together. A few meals, a trip to the theatre. It didn't amount to much. She pushed the piece of fish back and forth across her plate, trying to ignore the lump in her throat. At the end of her last visit she had cried; she wouldn't let that happen again.

'Don't play with your food, Grace.'

'I'm not.'

She resumed eating. If her mouth was full, she didn't have to talk.

'So when are you coming back?' He said it brightly, casually, as if she lived just around the corner and could pop over any time.

'Oh, I don't know, Daddy. It depends.'

'You could always come in the summer. You have such a long holiday, and it must get infernally hot over there.'

'It does.'

'The three of you together. Why not?'

'There isn't space.'

'We'd find a way.'

'I suppose.'

She hated herself for not sounding more enthusiastic, for not being able to promise her return. She swallowed.

'It's been awfully nice, though. Thanks a lot.'

He smiled, and then quickly looked down at his plate. A minute later they were talking about the next day. They had to give themselves plenty of time to get to the airport because you never knew, and had she packed yet?

She didn't cry. Not even when she turned and saw him waving at her from the other side of the gate. Once he was out of sight she was seized by that treacherous excitement. Even if they only missed her half as much as she missed them, it was enough.

XI

By Saturday afternoon there had been no appearances or messages, and Grace was beginning to feel hurt. They couldn't have forgotten. Maybe they were waiting until the evening; Grace didn't have that kind of patience. She kept glancing at the telephone as she walked past it in the corridor. She knew Caroline's number by heart, but she didn't have the courage to phone her. So she got out her address book and called Sara instead.

'Hello?'

'Hello. It's Grace. Please may I speak to Sara?'

'One moment.'

Sara's mother didn't sound very friendly, but it was difficult to tell on the phone. Grace waited for what seemed like an interminably long time, twirling the cord around her fingers.

'Hello?'

'Sara, it's me.'

'I know, Mummy said. How was England?'

'All right. What are you doing today?'

'Nothing much. Caroline's here.'

'Oh.'

'Come over if you like.'

'Now?'

'Yes.'

'Fine, I'll be there in about half an hour, I guess.'

'All right, see you then.'

She hung up. Grace put on her shoes and tried to think of reasons why Caroline and Sara had arranged to meet without her. They'd forgotten the date of her return. They were conspiring against her. Which was more likely? The thought of them doing anything together was bad enough, and she couldn't bear to imagine the bacchanals she'd missed.

The city was in the grip of a heatwave. She had expected it to feel warm after England, but nothing like this. It was unnatural. Sweltering on the bus, her hair stuck to the back of her neck, her thighs stuck to the seat, and she briefly made eye contact with the seedy-looking young man standing next to her. In normal circumstances he probably would have tried to touch her, or say something at the very least, but the heat made casual lechery impossible. The man wiped the sweat off his brow and looked away.

Sara's mother was just as icy in person as she had been on the phone. Grace avoided looking her in the eye and lowered her gaze to the delicate golden cross that hung from her neck. She probably blamed Grace for Sara's sudden, inexplicable loss of faith. Grace remembered the rosary beads rolling across the floor and reasoned that this was fair enough. Yet she was not used to being disliked by her friends' parents or perceived as a bad influence, and the way in which she was escorted to Sara's bedroom door made her uncomfortable. Apparently she wasn't trusted to traverse the hallway on her own.

Even before she reached the door she could hear the shrieks of laughter. It gave her a tight, anxious feeling in the pit of her stomach. She couldn't imagine any joke funny enough to cause such mirth, so she assumed that they must be laughing at her.

'Hello,' she said, standing awkwardly in the doorway.

'Oh, there you are!'

Sara and Caroline collapsed into giggles again, and Grace felt her cheeks burn. She wished Caroline would hug her; she hoped she wouldn't. She might give something away. But Caroline was literally rolling on the floor, overdoing it as always, and seemed incapable of making any movement in Grace's direction.

'What's so funny?'

'You tell her, Sara.'

Sara shook her head, still trembling with laughter.

'It's one of those things where you really had to be there,' said Caroline.

'I suppose I should have got here five minutes earlier.'

'Don't be like that. Come over here.'

Grace sat cross-legged on the floor, feeling more self-conscious than she had felt in a long time.

'Are you going to tell us all about England then?' asked Sara.

'There's nothing to tell. I didn't do anything. Have I missed much here?'

'A million things,' said Caroline.

'Like what?'

'We've been shopping lots, and we went boating on the lake in the park – Sara nearly fell in – and—'

'I meant *him*. Have you seen him? What did you do?'

'Goodness, Grace. It's only been a week.'

'Come on, tell me.'

'We've seen him once or twice,' said Sara. 'In the Ghetto.'

'Not outside then?'

'I think he's waiting for you,' said Caroline. 'It'll be better with three of us.'

'Did he say that?'

'He's hardly said anything. He just sits there looking beautiful and terrifying, and pouring out the wine.'

'I hope he's all right.'

'All right?' Caroline repeated mockingly. 'You make it sound like we ought to be taking care of him.'

'In a way...' Grace trailed off.

'He's a god, not some invalid uncle.'

Grace hoped they would continue talking about Dionysus – a week without even uttering his name had been too much – but the conversation suddenly changed. Caroline and Sara said the usual things about the prospect of going back to school (horrible) and Caroline's mother (also horrible), while sprawling inelegantly across the floor and listening to the dreary jazz records Sara was so mysteriously fond of. At one point Sara left the room, and without having planned it or even thought about it for more than a second, Grace asked, 'Did you tell her about us?'

'Tell her what?' asked Caroline, inspecting her fingernails.

'I don't need to spell it out, do I?'

'Keep your voice down. No, of course I didn't.'

'And you're not going to?'

'Why, were you planning on saying something?'

'No.'

'Good.'

Before Grace could say anything else, Sara came back in. It was maddening not being able to talk about it. She should have felt relieved to know that it was still a secret, but there was no relief. Only the frustration of gazing at Caroline, who lay on her stomach with her bare legs crossing and uncrossing in the air, not knowing if it would ever happen again. She might have changed her mind. Caroline was always changing her mind about everything.

The conversation turned to the homework they had neglected over the holidays, and Caroline's resentment of being made to read Dickens.

'I can't believe she expects us to read six hundred pages of that tripe, as if we had nothing better to do. All those unrealistic characters with stupid names. It's torture. I don't see why Miss Harper couldn't have chosen something else.'

Sara began a timid defence of Dickens, and Grace stopped listening. She hadn't read the book, and she had nothing to contribute. Caroline was becoming increasingly animated as she argued with Sara, raising her voice and gesticulating wildly. She could get worked up about a dead writer, and yet she seemed to feel nothing for her best friend. And weren't they more than friends now? It was deeper than that. Grace looked away.

There was an old map of the city on the wall, beautiful but tattered. Grace always enjoyed looking at it when she was in Sara's room, searching for places she knew and noticing the changes. Whole suburbs disappeared, replaced by fields and black smudges which were supposed to represent sheep. The artist had even included ghostly little umbrella pines, the trees that crowned the hills even in the days when Dionysus was first worshipped. There was the orange garden, the pyramid...

As her gaze travelled south she saw something she had never noticed before. There was an illustration of some kind of ancient gate or tower, and it was glowing. She glanced behind her to see if it could be some trick of the sunlight, but when she looked again she was convinced that it was shining with a light of its own. Then there was a voice, at once soft and imperious.

Nine. All of you.

She felt the familiar shiver of excitement and turned to face the others.

'Tonight,' she said, interrupting their conversation. 'He wants to see us tonight.'

'How do you know?'

'It's a message. Look.' She pointed at the map.

'What's that got to do with it?'

'This castle – tower – whatever it is. It was glowing. Then I heard his voice. We have to meet him there tonight, at nine.'

She was pleased to see that Caroline looked a little put out.

'How do we know you're not imagining it?' asked Caroline.

'I wasn't last time. Try to trust me.'

'I don't know.' Sara also looked doubtful. 'I don't really feel like going out tonight, and it's awfully far away. Practically out of the city. How are we going to get there?'

'We could cycle.'

'I don't have a bike.'

'Barbara has one. You could borrow hers.'

'And what are we going to say to our parents?'

'A sleepover,' said Grace. 'Why not? To celebrate my return. They'll never question it. Go and tell your mother now.'

Caroline frowned at the map.

'This had better not be some random whim.'

'Of course it's not a whim. He spoke to me. Why would I want to drag you out of the city at night just for the sake of it? Don't you see? This must be the place he was talking about. Outside. Away from everything.'

'Fine,' said Caroline. 'We can go. But if we end up cycling all the way there and then hanging around outside some old castle for hours, I'm never going to believe you again.'

'There's no need to be horrible.'

'I'm not being horrible.'

She was only being Caroline. Grace told herself to stop being so sensitive. She didn't want Caroline to know that she could hurt her so easily, with just a few careless words.

Past the pyramid, where they were honked at and overtaken on a precarious corner, into the stream of traffic heading south. Caroline led the way, cycling fearlessly into the twilight. Grace tried to ignore her anxiety as a car missed her by a few inches. It was no more dangerous than other things she'd done, and she was bound to be even more reckless in the future. She clutched the handlebars and stared straight ahead. Caroline's hair looked grey in the fading light, and the distance was growing wider and wider.

'Wait!'

Her shout was lost in the wind and the roar of the traffic. She probably ought to check that Sara was still following her, but even a brief glance over her shoulder seemed like a risk on a road like this.

A vast Roman wall rose up beside them, marking the boundaries of the ancient city. Grace was so disorientated that she couldn't work out which side they were on. Had they already left the city? It certainly felt like it. There were hardly any cars now, no buildings, no people. Out of the corner of her eye, Grace caught a glimpse of a woman with long dark hair leaning against the wall, the grass so long that it reached her thighs. A second later and she was convinced she had imagined it. No one would choose to linger there alone, on the edge of the city.

It then occurred to her that she was essentially doing the same thing, and that she might easily have ended up alone. If Caroline and Sara hadn't agreed to join her, she would have come anyway. She wouldn't have missed this for the world.

The tower appeared as rapidly and unexpectedly as the god, cutting into the darkening sky. The street lamps spread pools of light across the road but revealed nothing of the tower. It was just a shape, so dark that it was hard to believe it was only made of stone, and not some mysterious, light-swallowing substance.

'This is it,' said Caroline breathlessly. 'God, what a place. It feels like the end of the world.'

'Not the end. A beginning.' Sara gestured vaguely into the darkness.

'What do you mean?'

'That's the famous road, isn't it? The Roman one. It goes south for hundreds of miles. I read about it once, but I've only just made the connection. This tower is the beginning of the road.'

'Look,' Grace whispered.

They saw a patch of radiance in the darkness, a light taking the form of a man. Dionysus stood on the Roman road and beckoned.

'Watch your step.'

They stumbled over the stones, seeing nothing but him. There were rows of cypresses, headless statues with candles at their feet, but none of it seemed real.

'They used to crucify people here,' said Dionysus. 'All along the road.'

Grace shivered despite the heat and held Caroline's hand tightly.

'Miles and miles and miles...'

His voice faded into a hiss.

'Where are you taking us?' asked Sara. It was a pointless question, as there was only one place they could be going. Out of the city. Further and further away, into the woods and the fields. They would be completely alone.

Dionysus began to walk backwards, eyes blazing. Beyond the fear was the steady pulse of excitement, three hearts beating ever quicker.

XII

That was the night she lost her mind. 'Lost' was the only word that came close to capturing the experience, and even then it felt inadequate. Words always were.

Losing your mind was supposed to be a traumatic, irreversible thing that ruined your life, but in the woods Grace discovered that it was possible to go absolutely, ecstatically out of your mind, and then recover the remnants of your senses and carry on with your life.

In the past she had remembered. Memories of visions, music, Caroline's kisses and Dionysus's transformations. She hadn't remembered everything, and the memories she retained seemed to change colour and shape every time she recalled them, but there was something to hold on to. After the woods, however, there was nothing. The night was a terrifying blank. When she awoke, all she was left with was an inexplicable feeling of violation, and an overwhelming desire to do it again.

There were long, deep scratches running down her arms. She would never know what had caused them. She didn't mind that they were ugly, or that they stung when she brushed her finger over them, but not knowing who or what had done this to her... She shuddered. If only she could shed her skin and become bodiless once again.

'Grace.'

Caroline was crawling through the grass towards her. She had been cut too, and although she was no longer bleeding, the marks were visible even from a distance. The early morning mists were clearing, and all the colours were becoming disturbingly bright. Grace rubbed her eyes.

'I'm scared,' said Caroline. 'I can't remember anything.'

'Neither can I.'

The words felt heavy on her tongue.

'I don't know what he did to us. What we did to him, to each other.'

'If we can't remember, maybe it doesn't matter.'

'Maybe. I guess it must have been fun. We wouldn't have done it otherwise.'

She crawled closer and rested her head on Grace's shoulder. The warm weight helped Grace to feel grounded, to remember where she was. For the first time she noticed that all the birds were singing.

'Do you think it's him?'

'What?'

'The birds. When he vanishes, he has to go somewhere.'

'I used to think he went inside us, but now I feel so strange. Hollow, almost.'

'Maybe he's inside and then he leaves. That's why we feel weird. Something's missing.'

'I'm still too drunk for this conversation.'

Caroline yawned. Even in her current state, tired, hungover and ghostly pale, she was beautiful. For a second Grace contemplated it, but soon she was glad she hadn't. Caroline got up and was violently sick in some bushes, for so long that Grace began to worry. If Caroline was really ill, Grace would have to go and get help, and how could she possibly begin to explain the state they were in?

Grace was in the middle of mentally rehearsing an explanation (*We were camping... We fell in some brambles*) when Caroline returned, half walking, half crawling, and came to sit beside her.

'Are you all right?'

'I think so.'

'When you're feeling better, we should go. It's a long way home.'

'I know. Our bikes are miles away.'

'Where's Sara?'

'In the field over there. Asleep. Or maybe dead.'

'God, what a mess.'

They walked unsteadily to the middle of the field, where Sara was lying face down.

'Sara, wake up.'

'Maybe we killed her,' said Caroline. 'That's why we're all bloody. She was fighting us off.'

'Shut up, Caro.'

When they finally succeeded in waking her up, Grace was relieved to see that she was fairly lucid, and had got through the night without a scratch.

'What happened to you?' asked Sara, eyes widening as she noticed their arms.

'We don't know,' said Grace. 'I guess it'll have to be long sleeves for a while.'

'You mean you can't remember it happening?'

'No, we can't remember anything.'

'That's odd. I can't remember much, but there was definitely a bull.'

'What else?'

'Screaming. How you screamed! Especially you, Caroline. I remember thinking I should have been frightened, but I didn't feel frightened at all. Funny.'

'Hilarious,' said Caroline. Shielding her eyes from the sun, she looked out across the bright field, as if searching for a trace of the night's chaos. The long grass was scattered with red wildflowers, and the tops of the cypresses seemed to bow gently in the breeze, swaying and then rising up towards the cloudless sky, as if they too were awakening from their trance.

'It all looks so peaceful, doesn't it?' Grace slipped her arm through Caroline's.

'It does. If I didn't feel so ill, it might be heaven.'

They began to walk through the grass in search of their bikes. Somewhere in the distance, the jangle of bells and the mournful cries of the sheep floated across the fields. Grace closed her eyes and allowed herself to forget about the long journey ahead. Just for a moment, she could almost pretend that she was already home.

That evening Mauro commented that it had been a while since they had all gone out to a restaurant together. Before Grace could protest, her mother was already suggesting places to go, and Henry was getting overexcited by the prospect of dessert.

Grace could think of nothing worse than sitting in a restaurant for hours, being expected to eat and participate in the conversation. The only excuse she could think of was her unfinished History homework, which also happened to be the second-worst option for the evening. What she really wanted to do was sleep for at least twelve hours.

But as her muttered protestations were ignored, she found herself sitting opposite her sister in a crowded restaurant, slowly sipping water. If she always had a glass at her lips, perhaps no one would notice that she wasn't talking. Then she would inevitably need the toilet, and she could spend at least ten minutes hiding in the bathroom. The meal would have to end eventually.

There was no such thing as a quick meal with Mauro, however. He loved food above all else, and anything less than four courses was a disappointment. When after half an hour the menus were still open on the table, Grace had to restrain herself from grabbing the nearest waiter and ordering on everyone else's behalf.

'Wine, Grace?' Mauro grinned. It was his little joke; when Grace had tried wine for the first time, at his insistence, she had immediately spat it out, declaring it vile.

'No, thank you. I'll stick to water.'

She wished that they had got a table outside. It was infernally hot in the restaurant, a little too close to the wood oven, and much too close to the next table. She could hardly breathe.

'Aren't you hot?' asked Barbara, between mouthfuls of oxtail.

'Of course. It's boiling in here.'

'I meant it's not really the weather for a dress like that.'

Grace tugged self-consciously at her sleeves and said nothing. There was no explanation she could give that would not provoke further comments or questions. She was grateful when Henry changed the subject, asking when it would be hot enough to go to the beach, which beach they would go to, if they would see a shark this time... He rattled off his questions at such high speed that Mauro's English could not cope.

It was already eleven o'clock when the desserts arrived, and Grace was on the verge of reminding her mother that they had school the next morning, when her mother spoke first.

'You've barely said a word all evening.'

'Me? I'm tired, that's all.'

'You're always tired.'

Before Grace could dispute this, her mother continued.

'I don't think these sleepovers are a good idea. Look at you. You're a wreck.'

'I'm not.'

'Yes, you are. Why do you need to have sleepovers all the time anyway? You see enough of each other as it is.'

'You don't understand. It's...'

'What?'

She was so exhausted she felt like weeping. Blinking back the tears, she tried again.

'It's important to me, all right?'

'Barbara doesn't disappear to her friends' houses every weekend.'

'That's because Barbara doesn't have any friends.'

'That's not true,' said Barbara. 'Anyway, leave me out of it.'

'I don't see why it matters to you,' Grace said to her mother. 'What difference does it make if I'm tired or not?'

'I'm worried about you. I don't like seeing you like this.'

'Fine, let me go to bed then. I don't want to be here, anyway.'

'Mauro, ask for the bill, please.'

'But I haven't finished!' Henry was still demolishing his chocolate cake.

'That's all right. We're only asking for the bill. No one's going to take it away.'

'You're so slow,' said Grace, looking resentfully at the mountain of crumbs on Henry's plate. 'You're worse than Mauro.'

'Grace.' There was danger in her mother's voice, and Grace decided it was best not to say anything else for the rest of the evening.

When she got home she was trying very hard not to cry. She had to wait until she was safely inside her bedroom, with the door closed. Crying in front of her family would not only make her look weak, but also encourage them to talk. Whether it was asking questions, criticising or consoling, it was all the same to Grace. She couldn't stand the thought of being talked at. All she wanted to do, more than anything in the world, was sleep.

The two things happened almost simultaneously. She started to cry and she saw Dionysus. She saw Dionysus and she started to cry. One a split second before the other, but it didn't matter. He was lying in her bed with the detached yet possessive air of a cat who has adopted a certain place as his own. She was sobbing, hands clasped to her mouth in a vain attempt to make herself quieter.

The god was unperturbed by her hysterics. Even without smiling he was able to radiate an indescribable energy, a profound sense of fulfilment. A well-fed, satisfied cat, thought Grace. One who felt entitled to appear in her bed any time he liked.

'Not quite the welcome I was expecting,' said Dionysus.

'I'm sorry, it's just…' Grace forced herself to breathe in deeply. 'It's just that I have school tomorrow. I'm tired. So, so tired.'

'You didn't find last night invigorating then? Well, you will get used to it. There's no need to cry.'

He gestured towards the bed, inviting her to lie beside him. Grace was quite incapable of protest, so she lay on her back, the tears still flowing, and listened.

'How you feel now is insignificant compared to how you felt then. You should have seen yourself – how young and wild and full of life you were. Running like the wind, screaming my name while the world around you turned black and gold. *That's* life. It's a richer, deeper life than most mortals could dare to dream of. And you can do it again, and again, and again. You might live forever in one ecstatic second.'

'But I can't remember anything.'

'Better not to. What use are memories? They are only stories we tell ourselves. But when you're with me, you must seize the moment. Let yourself burn. Joy is in living, not remembering.'

'I know.' She couldn't contradict him, not when he was so close that she could feel the warmth of his breath. 'But however petty it seems to you, it's— I've got a lot to deal with. That's all.'

'That's the beauty of wine. You forget everything else. Do you want some?' Grace shook her head and realised that she was not going to receive any advice, let alone a solution to her problems. It was out of curiosity, not expectation of an answer, that she whispered Caroline's name. He understood at once.

'Follow your body.'

'But I thought—'

'Don't think. It will be so much purer, so much simpler, if you listen to your body.'

'I don't know what you mean,' said Grace uneasily.

'You know exactly what I mean. Now, go to sleep.'

It was like the flick of a switch. She slept deeply, dreamlessly, and felt almost human when the alarm went off at seven o'clock.

XIII

There were books to be read, essays to be written and equations to be understood, but none of it mattered to Grace. It was like being at the cinema and looking away from the screen. The pictures kept moving, the orchestra swelled, but in an instant you became aware of its emptiness. It was only a hollow projection, not real at all; the truth lurked in the dark of the back row.

So Grace sailed through the first week of the summer term in blissful indifference. She went to lessons and did her homework, but her gaze was always elsewhere. As she had always been prone to daydreaming, few of her teachers noticed. The only one who detected the deepening of Grace's trances was Miss Seymour. Once, when Grace seemed particularly entranced by the wall, Miss Seymour remarked, '… silent, upon a peak in Darien.'

'Sorry, what?' Grace hadn't heard, and would not have understood the allusion anyway. Caroline smirked.

Grace's distraction reached its peak in a Classics lesson towards the end of the week. She arrived late, which meant that the only free chair was opposite Caroline instead of next to her. Miss Seymour was talking about Aeschylus, an incomprehensible monologue about fate and the Furies that meant nothing to Grace. She mechanically unpacked her bag and then let her hands rest uselessly on her closed books. She couldn't bring herself to take notes, and Miss Seymour, lost in the complexities of her own speech, would surely never notice.

Grace looked at Caroline, who was clearly suffering from the heat. The blinds were broken and the sun blazed through the window behind her. Caroline kept crossing and uncrossing her legs as if she felt herself sticking to the chair, and every now and then she would run her fingers through her damp hair. Grace found it incredible how even the slightest movement stirred her, filling her with a deep, urgent restlessness. She was painfully aware of every time Caroline shifted in her seat or stretched her arms. She was like a boy, thought Grace, just like a boy.

Anyway, she mustn't stare. Furtive, wistful glances were just about all right, but anything more and Caroline would catch her doing it and laugh. Whenever she felt she was coming too close she would quickly lower her eyes until those strange, spidery letters swam into her vision. She hadn't done the homework, and Ancient Greek was, well, Ancient Greek. The words made no sense. Nothing made any sense, except that hot rush of emotion that tore through her whenever Caroline was near.

By Thursday she couldn't stand it any more. She waited until Sara had left and asked, 'Do you want to come over after school?'

'What for?' asked Caroline.

'Nothing,' said Grace, feeling herself flush a little. 'I just thought…'

'All right.' Caroline spoke in an offhand way, as if casually granting a favour.

The sky seemed to sink beneath the weight of swollen blue clouds, and the air was strangely still. Nothing breathed. Then Grace heard the low rumble of thunder in the distance and realised that everything was waiting for the storm.

'I wish it would rain,' said Caroline as they walked to Grace's flat. 'I'm sweating like a pig.'

'Nice.'

'Well, aren't you?'

Grace could feel all her clothes sticking to her skin. She was beginning to regret having invited Caroline. She should have gone home alone to have a cold shower and then lie naked, almost comatose, in her shuttered bedroom. Suddenly she didn't have the energy for Caroline any more.

She half expected to find Dionysus waiting for them, and it was a relief when she opened her bedroom door and found it empty, just as she had left it that morning.

'Your room's a tip,' said Caroline, making herself comfortable on Grace's unmade bed.

'I know.'

Grace went to the window and looked at the darkening sky. The world was still and silent except for a woman singing on the other side of the courtyard. The song was familiar, a melody that rose and fell and finally soared into a screamed vowel that threatened to shatter the windows.

'What a noise.'

Grace couldn't tell if Caroline was being critical or admiring. The Caroline who lay in her bed was not the lively, sharp-tongued girl she knew so well, but a listless, languorous ghost of herself. It didn't matter that they hadn't drunk anything. The humidity was a different kind of drug. They lay beside each other and kissed; long, slow, underwater kisses that seemed to last forever. Grace forgot her discomfort and was aware of nothing but Caroline's lips and the hot, clumsy fingers slipping inside her shirt.

But they wore themselves out and at last fell apart. Caroline let out a deep, contented sigh and closed her eyes.

'This heat is unbelievable. Imagine August.'

'It can't get much hotter than this.'

'You must have forgotten what it was like last summer.'

'I remember. You were hardly here last summer – you were in England the whole time.'

'But when I came back… it was unreal. We went for dinner at this house in the suburbs – some friend of my father's – and even when we left at midnight it must have been something like thirty-five degrees. Humid, too. I had eaten far too much, and I remember walking out into the road where all the walls were overgrown with flowers. It hit you straight away – the smell of all those flowers. I guess that was the first time I felt drunk, and I hadn't even had any wine. It was disturbing, in a way.'

'What do you mean?'

'I didn't feel like myself. I wanted to throw myself into the road, tear off my clothes, scream. I don't know. It only lasted a moment. The heat does strange things to you, that's all I'm saying.'

'Like this?' Grace ran her fingers through Caroline's hair.

'Yeah. We probably wouldn't be doing it if we lived in Sweden, would we? Or even England. Besides, the hot weather suits him. You can tell he's so much happier now he's no longer shivering in that gloomy little church.'

'Are you sure he's happier? It's hard to tell.'

'He doesn't show it like humans do, but in his own way he is. I think so, anyway.'

'And what about your happiness?'

'Me? Oh, I'm quite content.'

Caroline smiled, and Grace kissed her again.

'I wish it didn't have to be a secret,' said Grace, sinking into the pillow. 'One is enough.'

'Please, don't spoil it by talking about it. What is there to discuss, anyway?'

Grace bit her lip. It seemed like there was everything to talk about, and a million questions to ask. But Caroline was not in the mood, and they were both too hot and tired for a serious conversation. Caroline's eyes were closed and Grace could tell from her breathing that she was close to drifting off.

'You'd better put your shirt back on,' said Grace, 'in case someone walks in.'

'It doesn't matter. I can just say that I was hot, which is true, isn't it? Because we're girls we can get away with so much more.'

Yet Grace was never entirely at ease in her bedroom. She felt she had been incredibly lucky to have had all those visits from Dionysus without attracting suspicion, and now it was surely just a matter of time before someone walked in at the wrong moment. Which discovery would be worse? Sometimes she felt Caroline was the more shameful secret, harder to explain and more likely to upset her parents. Either way, she had to be careful. Careful at home, at school, in the streets. There was only one place she could be herself.

She soon grew to love the Roman road, to know it intimately. Hours before nightfall she would wind between the stones and the grass, speeding past faceless statues and monstrous aloes. Caroline was always at the front, leading the way, but even without her Grace would have known exactly where she was going. It was difficult to get lost on a straight road, after all, and there were so many curious little landmarks that she always had a good idea of how far they had gone. There was the hill; the tomb for the Roman noblewoman that resembled a fortress; the tremendous gaps in the stones which meant she had to get off her bike; the aloes; the shell of a church; the sign in Latin which she always cycled past too quickly to read; the headless woman; the faceless men; vast, weird stones that made her think of the beginning of the universe and other planets; the remnants of a villa scattered across the field; the medieval tower.

When they reached the tower they usually stopped. It was a melancholy little pile of stones on a man-made hill, and Grace imagined there were bodies inside. Everything along this road seemed to be a tomb of some sort.

'It's kind of phallic, isn't it?' Caroline remarked when they saw the tower for the first time.

'So are all towers, if you want to look at it that way.'

'No, some towers are more phallic than others. Just look at it – there's the hill at the base…'

'I can't see it,' said Sara.

'You probably wouldn't know an actual phallus if it were right in front of you. Good little Catholic girl.'

Sara frowned but said nothing.

Dionysus had chosen the tower because it was conveniently remote. Even during the day there were very few people who ventured this far down the road, and you were more likely to hear the distant bleats of the sheep than human voices.

The girls developed the habit of coming early, cycling until they were defeated by the sun and then retreating to some shady field where they would sit and talk, drinking warm lemonade and eating crisps. Grace was sure that to any passer-by they must have looked the picture of innocence. Three rosy-cheeked girls having a picnic in the country. There was nothing to give any indication of what was about to happen, unless the passer-by understood English and was skilled at eavesdropping. Caroline in particular saw no point in being discreet.

'We're miles away from civilisation,' she pointed out. 'We can do whatever we like.'

'That's not really true,' said Sara. 'If we did something really bad we could still get in trouble. Arrested, even.'

'Don't be stupid; you can't get arrested if you're under eighteen.'

'Yes, you can.'

'You can't.'

'There were those girls in New Zealand,' said Grace, 'who murdered one of their mothers. They got arrested.'

'All right, but they didn't go to prison, did they?'

'I think they did.'

Caroline looked contemplative.

'I suppose we'd better not get caught then.'

'It's not as though we would ever do anything like that, anyway.'

There was a doubting, questioning tone in Sara's voice that seemed to ask for some reassurance, but both Grace and Caroline remained silent. Grace sipped the warm lemonade while she tried to remember the details of the story.

'Those girls planned the murder. They arranged everything beforehand, and they knew what they were doing. That makes it worse, doesn't it?'

'Whereas we wouldn't have a clue,' said Caroline. 'Is that what you mean?'

'Yes. If – *if* – we did something like that, we wouldn't know at the time. Even afterwards we might not remember. Like these.'

She ran her finger along the fading scratch on her arm and gestured to Caroline's corresponding mark.

'We shouldn't talk like this,' said Sara. 'Acting like we're murderers when we haven't done anything.'

'Ah, but you don't know that.' There was a glint in Caroline's eye. 'We might have done all kinds of things. Taken part in orgies, sacrificed virgins.'

'But *we're* virgins.'

'More or less.'

Caroline often became oddly cheerful when discussing their vices, whether real or imagined. Grace remembered how Caroline had always fiercely supported Lady Macbeth in English lessons, and Medea in Classics. She probably liked to think of herself in that way – a glamorous anti-heroine who had done something terrible without losing all of the audience's sympathy. Grace found Caroline vaguely irritating when she was like this. *You're a schoolgirl,* she wanted to tell her, *you're not infamous yet.*

194

Sara hardly said a word for the rest of the day. She lay in the grass, half-heartedly swatting away mosquitoes and eating the remains of the crisps. Grace could never make up her mind whether Sara was scared or secretly the most zealous of the three. Whenever they talked about Dionysus or the bacchanals Sara was always full of doubts and anxieties. *What if...?* Teachers, the police, parents and priests were always on her mind. Grace remembered how Sara had once tearfully confessed to plagiarising part of a History essay; the teacher had been so taken aback by Sara's tears that he was incapable of punishing her. If Sara became guilt-ridden after copying out a paragraph from an encyclopaedia, how could she cope with this strange new world of sin?

Yet after the night, Sara would awake transformed. Sometimes Grace found it unnerving, how Sara could smile and describe what she had seen so calmly, as if reciting some long-loved poem.

'And then the ivy came up from the ground and grew through us – between our legs, around our necks and bodies. Then there was thunder, the ivy fell away, and we were running, running, running, until I fell into some kind of hole and – I can't remember what happened next. But he was there.'

Sometimes Caroline would push for more details, but Grace wasn't sure that she believed Sara. Even if she was telling the truth, Grace didn't want to hear it. It was disorientating, even upsetting, to hear her friend recount all these divine experiences that she had no memory of.

Sara was at her best the morning after, half asleep and in love with life. With all the birds singing and the memories of the night flooding through her, she was the happiest she'd ever been. When she was completely sober, however, whether at school or in the field, waiting for the night, she was anxious. She became taciturn, responding with a monosyllable or a non-committal 'mmm'. The strain of the wait sometimes seemed to be too much for her.

'It's almost dark,' said Caroline. 'We should go to the tower. He'll be waiting.'

'You're always so impatient,' said Grace.

'I don't understand why patience is supposed to be a good thing. Impatient people get what they want, and sooner. Why wait?'

Dionysus was already there, sitting on a marble ruin that had once been a signpost or tombstone.

'You're early,' he said.

'So are you,' said Caroline. 'Apparently I'm not the only one who's impatient.'

Dionysus seemed not to hear. He stood up, and Grace was struck by how tall he was. There must have been plenty of mortal men who were just as tall, and yet there was something about the size of him that made her nervous. Larger than life, like those statues of emperors with their vast limbs and empty eyes.

But his eyes were different. As she followed him into the tunnel of trees she tried to work out what it was. Something subtle, maybe just a trick of the light. When he handed her the first glass of wine, she dared herself to look him in the eye. It was only a second, but suddenly she understood. Caroline was wrong.

XIV

She had not really expected an answer, and when the door buzzed she could feel the anxious lurch of her heart. After countless visits she still felt like a trespasser. She was torn between the stairs and the lift; just moments after she had pressed the button an old man hurried through the front door and called to her to wait. At least on the stairs she would have been able to rush up ahead of him, but now she was condemned to a minute of awkward silence or small talk.

The old man smiled apologetically as he pressed against her in the lift, which barely had space for two people. He was several inches shorter than her, so she felt as though she were having a conversation with the liver-spotted top of his head. She couldn't understand what he was saying, but she thought there was an interrogative tone in his voice, so she said, 'Yes, yes,' at appropriate intervals. She hoped that 'Yes' was the right answer to the questions, and that she was not inadvertently confirming that she was someone's friend or relation, or accepting an invitation. The old man got out on the third floor, after wishing her a 'good something'. She didn't catch the last word. Morning? Evening? She barely knew what time of day it was.

When she knocked at the door there was no answer, but as he had buzzed her in she decided it was safe to enter.

'Hello?'

He was lying on the floor near the window, not stretched out like the lid of a sarcophagus this time, but curled up in the foetal position. He looked oddly vulnerable, so vulnerable that Grace was on the point of turning back and leaving. He wouldn't want her to see him like this.

And yet, she was glad she had come. Now she knew she understood him better than Caroline. She couldn't claim to understand his misery – probably no mortal could – but she recognised it, which was more than could be said for the others.

She knelt down beside him.

'Are you all right?'

'No.'

She touched his hair and recoiled when she found it wet. Her fingertips were dark red.

'Blood?'

'Of course not.'

It was wine. Whether he was lying in a pool of it or somehow secreting it, she couldn't tell. The drink she loved so much was faintly repulsive now that it was oozing from his body. She remembered that hot afternoon long ago, the milk and honey in the street.

'Squeamish again,' said Dionysus.

'I'm not.'

To prove it, she licked her fingers. The wine tasted strangely hot and metallic, almost bitter. She couldn't imagine getting drunk on it, or at least, not drunk in the usual way. It would have to be a darker, more self-destructive kind of drunkenness. Not the ecstasy of the fields but the squalor of the street.

'It will make you sick.'

'I was only tasting it. It's not that bad, only different.'

'You shouldn't. Wipe your hands.'

Grace hesitantly wiped her fingers on her skirt, which was acquiring an impressive collection of stains. 'Honestly, darling,' her mother had said, with a concerned expression. 'You used to simply grow out of them, now you lose or destroy them. It isn't normal.'

Her hands remained sticky no matter how many times she wiped them. She glanced uneasily at Dionysus, who lay in a slowly blossoming halo of black wine. He was completely still, and as she watched and waited, his stillness gave him a strange kind of dignity. She was reminded of a photograph she had once seen of a wounded lion, covered in gore but still thrillingly alive.

'What's happening?' she asked. 'I want to help you, you know I do, but how can I when I don't understand?'

He raised an eyebrow so slowly that it seemed to be a monumental effort. These slight movements were rare enough to seem significant, but Grace never knew how to interpret them. An eyebrow might indicate amusement, boredom, irritation, surprise or lust, and that was only within the spectrum of human emotion. Who could read that inscrutable face?

'Let me tell you a story,' he said, his voice hoarse. 'No, not a story – a fragment.'

This was what Grace wanted. If she was honest with herself, it was the reason why she had come. To be taken into his confidence, to catch glimpses of a glamorous past and so become closer to him.

'There was a priest in another time, another country. Let's say the north, in an age of kings and Christianity. People worked hard and died young, and there was little laughter in the village until the priest arrived. No one knew where he came from, and at first they were hostile, but they soon grew to love him. He was loved not for himself but for his influence. Do you understand the difference?'

Grace nodded uncertainly. This was not the story she had expected.

'There was sunshine – crops swelling to twice their normal size. In the vineyards it was better still. Fat black grapes close to bursting, which were made into the sweetest, richest wine the villagers had ever tasted. All the women became pregnant, and their children would be golden-skinned and healthy, quite unlike the sickly ones in previous years who left the world just seconds after entering it. The animals were more fertile too, and in just one spring an elderly bull fathered more than fifty calves.

'The villagers had so much to eat and drink – even with the grow-ing population – that they hardly knew what to do with it. So there were parties, in the streets, in the hills, and they all made toasts to the golden age. And although no one said it, they knew it was because of him. The priest.

'He lived among them but apart. I can't tell you what he did – his life was a mystery to himself as well as to others – except that he must have gone to the sea sometimes, because he would bring back exotic silks and spices. There was a harbour with trade ships from the East, and he would buy all kinds of beautiful things for the villagers. Imag-ine a toothless peasant woman parading through the village square in the finest silks, pink and gold, going home to add coriander to her stew.

'Then... I don't know exactly what happened next. I can hear the organ being played by the priest, the barking of dogs and the distant rumble of thunder. There was a party, a festival of some kind. Everyone dancing through the streets, except for the priest. There had been some great change. Perhaps it was the wine – it may well have been the wine, or the child. They found the body of a child buried beneath the stones of the bridge, and they must have seen it as an omen. Do you understand?'

'No,' said Grace.

'Neither do I. But I think in the minds of the villagers there must have been a connection between the priest, the wine and the child. It was only natural that they should cease to love him, or else love him with such a passion that they turned to violence. That night, when the priest was playing the organ and the dogs were barking, they burst into the church and tore him limb from limb. He was ripped to shreds. The women were the most savage – they always are – but I believe it was a man who took a ribbon of flesh and stuck it in his cap.'

He spoke so matter-of-factly that the ending was rendered even more chilling. Grace looked again at his wine-soaked hair and felt a little nauseous.

'It's not a true story, is it?'

'Isn't it? It's vivid enough to me.'

'It's something you saw?'

'Saw, dreamed – I hardly know the difference. But the one thing I am sure of is that the priest was me.'

'What?'

Grace's mind was reeling. She had pictured the priest as a young, good-looking man with a vague resemblance to the god, but that was quite different from them being one and the same. How could Dionysus have lived as a man – worse, a priest – and died at the hands of a peasant mob?

'How do you know it's real? And even if it did happen, how can you be sure that you were the priest?'

'I don't know, but I believe it to be true. I feel it. That's the only kind of knowledge that matters.'

It seemed wiser not to contradict him.

'What does it mean, though?' Grace half whispered the question to herself, but Dionysus heard and betrayed a hint of irritation when he next spoke.

'All these questions. Always asking questions, Grace. Instead of relentlessly asking, you could stop to think for a while.'

'I haven't got your patience. Anyway, I'm curious and my mind's a mess. I can't help it.'

Frustrated, she sat in silence and tried to ignore the burning desire to ask. She couldn't ask questions, she couldn't touch him, she could only sit and wait, watching the wine slowly fill the cracks of the tiles. The room was growing dark, and she would have to return home soon, or else risk missing dinner and being interrogated by her mother.

But she was reluctant to leave him. Maybe it was just a vain delusion, but she believed that her presence was a comfort to him, and she felt a strange, slightly terrifying sense of responsibility. Whenever she entered this room, which could be as spartan and silent as a monk's cell or a den of debauchery, depending on the time of day, she was bound. It was as if they were tied together by some invisible thread; she imagined a golden material as subtle as a spider's web yet stronger than any chain. It encircled her neck, her wrists, and tied her to that part of him that was miserable and everlasting.

'Of course,' said Dionysus after some time had passed, 'it might not be entirely true. At least, not in the way I told it. It came to me in fragments and I put them together, just as you might try to fix an old vase you had discovered in pieces deep in the ground. There are pieces missing, the details are obscured by dirt and time, and you can't be sure of what it looked like originally, but you have the essence of it.'

'That's something. But it doesn't seem to have made you very happy.'

'What does happiness have to do with it?'

'I thought...' Grace hesitated, unsure of how to answer. 'You know I – we – want to help you. When I asked if you were all right you said you weren't, so...'

'Grace, I am not a problem to be fixed. I'm living out of my own time, just like the priest when he roamed the muddy paths of medieval France or Germany, or wherever it was. Melancholy is inevitable. You shouldn't fantasise about cheering me up.'

Grace felt that she was being patronised and resented it.

'I know we can't make you happy. But you could be less unhappy, don't you think?'

'I'm afraid I don't see it like that. But – this may give you comfort – the story of the priest has given *me* comfort.'

'How? It's… gruesome. They loved him – you, I mean – and they tore you apart. What's comforting about that?'

'I died. I can die again.'

She was shocked by the total lack of emotion in his voice.

'But you don't want to die, do you? Not like that.'

The dismemberment that had thrilled her in *The Bacchae* was horrifying now that it was no longer fiction. The wine oozing from his hair was black in the fading light and now seemed even more disgusting to her. When it became clear that he wasn't going to answer her question, she persisted.

'Even if you could die, it wouldn't be forever. You're here now, regardless of what they did to the priest. I mean, you can't die like a human, completely and forever.'

'Thank you for reminding me,' said Dionysus.

'I should go. I can't make any sense of this, and I'm going to be late.'

'Yes, go.'

Even when he was telling her to leave, she felt the pull of that invisible thread.

'I'll be back soon, though. I promise.'

'Oh, I know. I don't need your promises.'

He didn't need anything from her. He was quite changed from the god who had begged her to stay and listen. He wanted her devotion, and yet when she tried to express that devotion he made her feel that it was somehow not good enough. That *she* was not good enough. He was like Caroline, demanding love and attention, and then shrugging when you gave it. Hopefully their supreme selfishness prevented them from noticing how much it hurt her – that was a small consolation.

All that wasted energy, she thought to herself as she walked home through the ruins. *Where does it go?*

XV

'My mistress with a monster is in love.
Near to her close and consecrated bower
While she was in her dull and sleeping hour...'

Caroline stood on the bed, declaiming the lines more or less from memory. Grace was sitting on the other side of the room, prompting only when necessary. Once she had made the mistake of supplying the next line too hastily.

'But she perforce...'

'Withholds the lovèd boy.'

'I knew it, I knew it,' said Caroline indignantly. 'Give me a second to think, will you?'

'Are there supposed to be such long pauses? I thought Puck was meant to be quick, what with being a fairy and everything.'

'I'll be quick once I've had a chance to learn the lines properly. It isn't easy, you know. Let's start from the beginning.'

Grace sighed and flipped back to the first highlighted section of the script. Caroline had been cast as Puck in the school production of *A Midsummer Night's Dream* only yesterday, and after recovering from her disappointment at not being given a more prominent role, she had quickly become obsessed with learning the few lines she had, insisting that Grace help her. It was just as well, thought Grace, that Caroline did not have a part with more lines; she could see herself being trapped in Caroline's room late into the evening, watching her bounce on the bed, chanting incomprehensible words that sounded as though they had been strung together at random.

Still, there was no denying Caroline's passion. Even as she stumbled over the words, she spoke with the same urgency as when she was talking to the god. It might have been a mystery to Grace, but it clearly mattered to Caroline.

'I led them on in this distracted fear, and left sweet— Oh, Mummy, I do wish you'd have the decency to knock.'

Caroline's mother stood in the doorway, looking at her daughter with such a hard expression that it went beyond disapproval, even amounting to distaste.

'I've been on the telephone with Sara's mother. I thanked her for having you to stay on Friday, and she sounded puzzled. She thought you and Sara were here on Friday. I'm quite sure you were not. Shall I call Grace's mother, or would you care to enlighten me first?'

Grace and Caroline exchanged panicked glances. They had all acknowledged to themselves that they would be found out one day, but they had been stupidly complacent, not bothering to talk about it or agree on a lie that would save them. Grace opened her mouth and then closed it again; she had absolutely nothing to say.

'Actually,' said Caroline, who was still standing on the bed, 'it's really all Sara's fault. She asked me to lie about it, in case you said something to her parents.'

'The truth, please, Caroline.'

'We were... camping. It's a sort of school club.'

'Why on earth would you lie about that?'

'I knew you wouldn't mind, but Sara's parents are funny about these things. I think it was something that happened to Sara's father when they were living in Australia. He got bitten by a snake or a spider or something and nearly died. They developed a kind of phobia of nature and told Sara that she could never go camping. She wanted to go and I thought it sounded like fun, so...'

'You're not exactly the outdoorsy type. You were bored after ten minutes in Hyde Park.'

'Oh, well, yes, parks are boring. But this is different. It's real nature, you know.'

'Where?'

'Near that lake beginning with B; I can never remember. Anyway, you needn't worry. It's all perfectly safe and supervised. We go with a couple of teachers.'

'It's just your school?'

'There are no boys, if that's what you're worried about.'

Caroline's mother turned to look at Grace.

'And you, Grace, do you go on these trips?'

'S-sometimes,' Grace stuttered. Why was it harder to lie to Caroline's mother than her own?

'It's terrific fun, isn't it, Grace?'

'Yes.'

'We learned so much about... nature. Birds, you know, that kind of thing.' Caroline was nodding briskly as she spoke, as if this made the lie more convincing.

'If I called the school,' said Caroline's mother, 'would they confirm it?'

'Of course. Ask Mrs Pearson.'

Grace, concerned that Caroline was getting carried away, frowned in the hope of catching her attention. Instead she felt Caroline's mother turn to look at her, and she quickly resumed a neutral expression.

'If you were lying it would be quite easy to find out.'

'I know.' Caroline smiled. *Brazen*, thought Grace.

When her mother had gone, Caroline flopped down on the bed with a sigh.

'That was close.'

'Much too close,' said Grace. 'Why did you make up all that rot about camping?'

'It's not like you were helping, opening and closing your mouth like a useless goldfish.'

'But camping...'

'The way I see it, the closer we are to the truth, the better. We do spend our evenings outdoors. Only instead of roasting marshmallows, we're getting drunk and going out of our minds. Instead of Mrs Pearson, it's Dionysus. Don't give me that look. You must see the funny side.'

'It won't be so funny if we're found out and forbidden from leaving our rooms.'

'We'd find a way. Dionysus is hardly going to let us become prisoners in our own rooms, is he? Now, let's get back to the script.'

'Caroline, I'm serious. I'm running out of excuses for all the clothes I've lost. My mother says if she catches me in a foul mood again she'll ban me from going to sleepovers.'

'It's just an empty threat. You've said it yourself – she's never really cared that much. She gets a bit upset, and then ten minutes later she's drinking with Mauro on the terrace and she's forgotten all about it.'

'But I think she's starting to suspect. Your mother too. Sara's most of all. We can't just keep going on without a real excuse.'

'So it's my responsibility to come up with something?'

'I never said that.'

'Look, next time, we'll ask him. He should have all the answers, shouldn't he? And it's in his interests too.'

'Yes, but…'

'Come on,' said Caroline, running her hands through her hair, 'let's get on with it. The script. Act III. Afterwards… oh, I wish that door locked. Or I wish I had a sweet mother like yours who always knocks. Mine has absolutely no respect for my privacy.'

'The play first?' Caroline's longing look at the door had filled Grace with impatience.

'Yes, the play. Enter Puck…'

At school the next day Grace hardly saw Caroline at all. They were in different classes in the morning, and at lunchtime Caroline was busy with rehearsals. Grace, hating herself for feeling so pathetically needy after such a brief separation, distracted herself by sneaking out at lunchtime to get an ice cream and persuading an initially reluctant Sara to join her. They were not allowed to leave the school grounds during lunchtime until they were in the sixth form.

'Katie and Hannah got caught last week,' said Sara. 'I think they got detention.'

'Well, we'll be more discreet. Anyway, right now I'd risk detention for an ice cream. It's a necessity when it's this hot.'

The temperature had been steadily rising all week, and there were no signs of the long-awaited thunderstorm. Grace and Sara ate their ice creams in a narrow strip of shade just a couple of streets away from the school. It had been difficult to find a spot that was protected from the sun and the erratic streams of traffic; the compromise they made was having to endure the smell, always intensified in the summer heat.

'It's disgusting.' With her free hand Sara waved her hand in front of her nose. 'I don't know why they're incapable of cleaning up after their dogs. In Australia it's so much cleaner. People are more civilised.'

When they had finished their ice creams and could no longer stand the smell, they slowly walked back to school. Grace told Sara the full story of the conversation with Caroline's mother.

'It's ludicrous, of course, but it'll have to do. We'll just have to be even more careful not to make our parents suspicious. What did you tell your mother?'

'I'm normally pretty hopeless at lying, especially to my parents, but this time I thought I was rather good. I implied that Caroline's mother is mentally ill and that she has a tendency to forget or invent things.'

'Did your mother believe it?'

'I think so. She hasn't met Caroline's mother, but she knows Caroline, so…'

'It's better than the camping story, anyway. Well done.'

As they slipped through the back entrance, where they were spotted by some disapproving sixth-formers but thankfully no teachers, Sara said, 'How come you were with Caroline last night?'

'I was helping her learn her lines.'

'You might have invited me.'

'You didn't miss anything. Besides, it's not like the three of us have to be together all the time. You and Caroline have met up without me.'

'I know. It just seems to be happening quite a lot recently, that's all.'

Grace didn't particularly care if Sara felt left out. It was preferable to her being included all the time, and getting in the way of this strange new intimacy with Caroline. Feeling hurt and excluded was something Grace had experienced plenty of times, so she knew it was bearable: one of those inevitable things about teenage friendships. If Sara started getting really sensitive about it, she and Caroline would just have to become even more careful, drawing the circle of secrecy ever closer.

'Friday soon,' said Grace wistfully. 'We'll all be together then. That's what really counts, isn't it? When we're in those fields…'

For a second she was completely taken over by visions of rituals to come – her heart beating like a drum while the trees danced and the wine gushed from the earth.

The bell rang and the trees disappeared. Sara sighed, and Grace could tell that she had also been momentarily transported. They exchanged a look of pained empathy that said more than words ever could, and joined the flow of girls in the corridor. From behind, in their uniforms, you could not tell them apart.

XVI

She was so used to the dew-soaked grass that it was a shock to wake up and feel the hardness of cold stone. It was rough against her cheek – not the smooth marble she often felt in her dreams but time-worn tiles interspersed with fragments of mosaics. She saw a line of tiny red spiders marching across the floor and forced herself to sit up, in case they started crawling into her hair.

Looking up, she saw a vast red wall, thrusting into the sky. Its solitary window was like a blue eye staring right into her. She shivered. The bright blue sky, framed by ancient windows in the mountains of stones that encircled her, meant that it was getting late. The sun must have risen a long time ago, and it would be dangerous to stay for much longer.

'Caro.' It seemed cruel to wake her when she looked so peaceful, but she could feel the return of that familiar, weary desperation. 'Wake up. We've got to wake up.'

'Oh, you're always saying that. Leave me alone.'

'I don't even know where we are. Or where Sara is. And what happened to your shoes?'

'How should I know?'

Caroline sat up and looked at her bare feet, which were filthy.

'Another lie to tell my mother...'

Grace was looking around anxiously, trying to find something she recognised. They seemed to be lost in a desert of stone, a mad ruin that had existed since the beginning of time. There was something profoundly unsettling about the randomness of the walls and columns, and the way the surrounding floors rose high above them on all sides. Her only comfort was the red wildflower rising up from the cracks in the tiles – proof that they were not stranded on some alien planet where everything was stone and sky.

'Caro, where are we?'

'My know-it-all father would be able to tell us. Some ruin. I don't know.'

She stood up and began to pace up and down the room. It *was* a room, Grace now realised, even though the dividing walls had vanished long ago.

'Perhaps it's that villa,' said Caroline. 'Yes, I think it must be. The one the mad emperor stole. There were some brothers living here, and he murdered them and took it for himself.'

'You're making it up.'

'No, really. I bet this is where he had his banquets.'

She pulled Grace to her feet and they slowly circled the room, stepping over odd little geometric patterns and the remnants of a painted dolphin.

'Do you remember anything that happened last night?' asked Grace.

'Not a thing. You?'

Grace shook her head.

'Do you think it's worth looking for Sara?'

'She's probably already left.'

'Rude.' Caroline yawned and rubbed her eyes. She looked at Grace as if she were seeing her for the first time.

'What?'

'You've cut your lip.' Caroline gently touched Grace's lower lip, and then her own. 'I wonder what caused it. Sara might know. I can't believe her, disappearing like that. We're supposed to be in it together.'

'That's what I said. Does it look really bad?'

'It's quite deep, but it's less obvious than some of our other marks. We'll have to ask him to be gentler.'

Even with so many of the walls missing, it was surprisingly difficult to find their way through the villa. There was no obvious route, and as many of the steps had crumbled away, in the deepest rooms they found themselves clambering over the rocks.

'It hurts,' said Caroline.

'You should have thought about that before you so carelessly mislaid your shoes. What's that noise?'

'What noise?'

'Listen.'

There was a deep, droning sound that started in the distance and then came behind them, above them, like some weird primeval vibration. For a moment Caroline looked mystified, even frightened, and then she looked up and laughed.

'It's just a plane.'

As soon as it came into sight, the sound lost its mystery. Grace watched the white line above her and was relieved to feel the sense of dread dissipate. It was odd that she should be unnerved by something so ordinary, but there was something about the villa – some ancient and unknowable influence – that made her reluctant to linger.

'Come on. Quickly.'

Caroline didn't question or protest this time, but silently followed her through the maze of rooms, stumbling over the stones until their feet finally sank into the long grass on the far side. If they ran they would reach the Roman road in no time, but after the night's exertions they didn't have the strength. They could only walk, suddenly pale with exhaustion, and hope that they went unnoticed by all except the god. *Let him see the state we're in.*

Dionysus saw. He saw everything and yawned a great, cavernous yawn, showing his sharp white teeth like the leopards he loved so much. He had seen it all before.

At school the next week they found Sara with her head in her locker, searching for something that was stuck at the back. When Caroline called her name she ignored her and continued rummaging through the locker.

'What's the matter?' asked Caroline. 'You just disappeared.'

'I had to go.'

'I don't see why. It was still early when we woke up.'

Sara finally emerged from the locker. She wouldn't look Caroline in the eye, and she had an odd, pained expression they had never seen before.

'I can't talk to you right now.'

This was not the first time Sara had given Caroline the silent treatment, but it was the first time there had been no obvious cause.

'What's she upset about?' asked Grace, once Sara had left.

'No idea. I suppose it must be something that happened at the... you know. Hopefully she'll have snapped out of it by lunchtime. These moods of hers never last long.'

That morning they were too stressed by lessons they were not prepared for to worry about Sara. When they entered the dining hall and saw that Sara was sitting with a group of less popular girls, squeezed between fat Sophie and a new girl who barely spoke English, they told themselves that they did not care.

By the end of the day, however, Caroline had become indignant.

'How dare she not talk to us? If anything, we should be the ones blanking her.'

They cornered her in a stairwell, waited for some first-formers to leave, and then began their interrogation.

'What's wrong?'

'Why aren't you talking to us?'

'Why wouldn't you sit with us at lunch?'

'Why did you leave?'

Sara looked intensely uncomfortable and unhappy.

'I'm sorry. I just can't cope with everything that's going on, after what happened...'

'*What* happened?'

'On Friday night.'

'You know we never remember.'

'Oh.' Sara stared at her feet as she searched for the right words. 'You were...'

'What?'

'You were all over each other.'

She paused to let the words sink in, and then walked away. Caroline didn't try to stop her.

Without saying anything, it was mutually understood that Caroline would come home with Grace. Returning separately to their own homes and settling down to a couple of hours of homework was impossible after what Sara had said.

'So she knows,' said Caroline.

'I suppose so.'

Grace was experiencing some surreal new emotion, a hot wave of shame and pride. Shame because Sara knew, and a perverse sense of pride because Sara had been shocked into speechlessness by whatever she and Caroline had done. What *had* they done?

Caroline was following a similar train of thought as they crossed the uneven, sloping square that led to Grace's building.

'It can't just have been kissing.'

'No?'

'She was mortified. Absolutely mortified.'

The weight of the word made Grace feel the flush of shame anew. It had a peculiar potency. Even in her more lucid moments she struggled to imagine going much further than a kiss, a tentative touch. Whatever girls did to each other could never be as serious as the things men did to girls. As they climbed, panting, up the dark flight of stairs – the lift was out of order again – Grace feverishly tried to picture the act that had appalled Sara. Each time her imagination failed her.

Grace's mother was not very happy about Caroline being invited to dinner.

'You might have asked me, darling. I don't know if we have enough pasta.'

With the oppressive heat and the unresolved crisis hanging over them, it hardly seemed to matter if they ate or not. They sat in the living room, watching TV with Barbara, only speaking to debate the ideal position for the fan. If anyone had asked her, Grace would not have been able to provide any details about the programme they had been watching. For an hour she was conscious of little else than Caroline's foot pressing lightly against her bare leg. The inane din of the commercials drowned out all thought, but when the programme resumed she could hear Sara's voice, those maddeningly ambiguous yet suggestive words. *All over each other.*

Grace watched enviously as Mauro poured out the wine for himself and Grace's mother. It was white, not the red that she loved so much, but wine was wine and the cool bottle looked particularly tempting on a hot evening. Caroline sipped her water and said very little, until Mauro started asking them questions about their French lessons, and then insisted on speaking to Caroline in French. Mauro's French was better than his English, and he clearly enjoyed having the upper hand in a conversation for once. It was revenge for all the times Grace and Barbara had sneered at his English, but it wasn't fair to take it out on Caroline.

'*Et qu'est-ce que vous pensez de Paris?*'

'Er, *très belle, très jolie.*'

'*Pas aussi beau que cette ville, bien sûr. Mais encore très belle. Qu'avez-vous vu à Paris?*'

'Well, *alors…*'

'Leave her alone,' said Grace.

'Yes,' said Grace's mother, 'let the poor girl eat. Goodness knows she needs it.'

Ordinarily, Grace would have snapped. It was infuriating to hear her mother say that Caroline needed to eat more when Grace was so often told to eat less, repeatedly warned about her impending obesity. Caroline was not that much thinner than Grace.

But tonight she was too distracted to engage in yet another argument with her mother. She and Caroline picked at their vegetables and stayed silent. Caroline seemed reluctant to even look at Grace until Mauro reached for the bottle of wine and poured himself a second glass. Grace saw Caroline glance at the wine and then raise her eyebrow slightly. To any observer it would have appeared so subtle as to be insignificant, but Grace understood at once.

'When the coast is clear…' she whispered to Caroline at the end of the meal. She waited until the others had left the room, and then snatched the bottle and took it to her room.

'Mauro will murder me.'

'Or speak French at you. That's worse.'

In her current state of mind Grace found it difficult to imagine or care about the future consequences of the theft. She poured out the wine into plastic children's cups, which she had taken and kept hidden in her wardrobe because their absence was unlikely to be noticed.

'Cheers,' said Caroline.

With a record playing and the wine slowly going to her head, Grace found it easier to talk.

'It's just so strange. She knows, and she knows more than we do.'

'Damn her memory,' said Caroline. 'I wish we could stop her from seeing, or at least stop her from remembering. There must be something we can do.'

'Like what?'

'I don't know. Drug her? Ask Dionysus for a favour?'

'I doubt he cares. Maybe we shouldn't either. But then... I don't know. What if she tells someone?'

'Who would she tell? And why? I mean, she's kept Dionysus a secret.'

'Yes, but that's because she's involved. She's not a part of... *this*.'

'She still doesn't have a real reason to blab.'

'But if she did...'

'Then we'd be left with no choice but to kill her,' said Caroline with a smile. 'Anyway, I wouldn't worry about it – for now. In a strange way I think I'm bothered less by the fact that she knows, and more by the fact that she knows more than us. Does that make sense?'

'I guess so.'

'There are some things – little things – that I remember so clearly, and yet I have no idea what happened on Friday. Whatever it was, it was enough for Sara to brood all weekend and then not speak to us.'

'It's frustrating.'

'I wonder...'

Caroline took another gulp of the wine, as if to give herself courage for what she was going to say next.

'We could do it again, when we're sober.'

'What do you mean? How can we do it when we don't even know what "it" is?'

Grace was talking rubbish and she knew it. They were both pretending. Grace looked away and caught a glimpse of her shrine, just visible on the lower shelf of the wardrobe. She felt mad just for thinking it, but in a way she wished he were here. Without his presence, and under the influence of only one and a half cups of wine, doing what Caroline suggested was unthinkable.

'Come here.'

Caroline made Grace lie down on the bed and kissed her. Slow and tentative at first, the kisses soon became deeper, almost urgent. When

Grace felt a hand slip between her thighs, her instinct was to push it away.

'We can't.'

'Look,' said Caroline breathlessly, 'it's fine. We've probably done it a hundred times before, and worse. I want to remember it this time. Just give me a little help, will you?'

With trembling fingers, Grace unzipped her skirt and slipped out of her underwear. Fifteen minutes later, feeling the waves ripple through her body, she was sure that neither of them would forget it.

XVII

'Look at you, how happy you are.'

Dionysus stroked her face, as if marvelling at the sight of this foreign emotion. Grace smiled; her skin tingled where he had touched her. They lay side by side in the long grass, watching the sky deepen in the twilight. Caroline was nearby, lying on her stomach and plucking at blades of grass, then scattering them in Sara's hair.

'Stop it,' said Sara, in a placid tone which meant that she wouldn't mind if Caroline carried on forever. Although they had not yet drunk anything, his mere influence was a drug.

Sara had avoided them for a few days, but towards the end of the week she had stood next to Grace in assembly and shared her hymn-book. This small gesture indicated that the awkwardness was over for now, at least. Grace supposed that Sara preferred the risk of mortification to being excluded from the bacchanals. She couldn't worship Dionysus without them. They were all in it together.

There was no more discussion of what Sara had seen. For the sake of their Friday nights they acted as though everything was normal. Grace and Caroline resolved to be as discreet as possible, to prevent Sara from becoming suspicious that anything was going on outside the bacchanals. They took care not to be too obviously affectionate, and even as the wine began to take hold, Grace found herself batting away Caroline's hands as well as the mosquitoes.

'Careful, Caro,' she whispered.

Caroline sulkily withdrew her hands and began to tear up the grass again.

It was not yet completely dark, but the stars were out. The evening was still and silent except for the bleating of the sheep in a neighbouring field. Sometimes it was hard to imagine breaking the peace with their worship, but Dionysus told them to embrace the noise and chaos. They were not disturbing nature but unleashing a wild energy that would otherwise lie dormant. When Grace pressed her palm to the earth she could feel it vibrating, pulsating with the nectars that would add to their ecstasy later in the evening.

They had finished their wine and wanted more. Caroline ran her tongue over his hands and whined like a dog when she found them clean. Dionysus was staring at the stars; one particular patch of sky had caught his attention. They were used to his trances, but not at this stage in the bacchanal, when the consistent flow of wine was so crucial.

'Patience,' Caroline hissed. She crawled towards Grace and they hid their joined hands in the long grass until Dionysus awoke. He blinked, his eyes full of stars.

'Of course, you must have more. Much more. Drink.' He filled their glasses. 'But as you drink, listen. You haven't yet fulfilled your... potential. In order to satisfy me, and yourselves, you must go further.'

'Tell us what to do and we'll do it,' said Grace.

'It doesn't work like that. You will know what to do in the moment. You will feel it in your heart, in your gut, in the deepest, most primal part of yourselves.'

He picked up a slender green snake and dropped it into Caroline's lap.

'Only when you let go of all inhibitions can you be absolutely free.'

Grace could feel herself slipping. She willed time to slow down, to become something she could grasp, but it was no use. The darkness enveloped her, and she was not conscious of anything until she opened her eyes several hours later. Someone was screaming. She looked up and saw the sun. She looked down and saw the blood.

Part III

Dionysus: Then why put off a fate which is inevitable?

—The Bacchae

I

Caroline was hysterical. Her screams were somehow more upsetting than the blood. Grace wanted to beg her to stop, but she could only sit there, mute with shock, and stare at her hands. The blood was bright red and it was everywhere. It was as if she had plunged her arms, right up to the elbow, into a fresh carcass. She gradually became aware of the extent of the mess – how it had stained the front of her dress and splattered down her legs. Caroline was covered in it too, though it was not clear whether she was screaming at the sight of herself or Grace.

'Shut up, shut up, shut up, shut *up*.'

Caroline stopped screaming.

'Just shut up for a minute,' said Grace. 'You're making it worse.'

The girls stared at each other. Caroline looked the worst, but maybe it was only because her dress had been so white. The stain blossomed from her stomach and spread right up to the ribbon on her breast pocket. The ribbon had been white, Grace remembered. Now nothing was white but Caroline's face, transformed by shock into a tight, expressionless mask.

'Are you hurt?' asked Grace. Her voice was so hoarse that she must have been screaming too, though she didn't remember it.

Caroline shook her head.

'Neither am I. At least… I don't think so.'

Grace began to tentatively pat down parts of her body, praying that she wouldn't suddenly stick her finger into an open wound. She was sticky with blood all over, but none of it, thank God, seemed to be hers.

'We've murdered someone,' said Caroline.

'You don't know that.'

'No, we've definitely murdered someone. Where's Sara?'

'Caro, don't be ridiculous.'

'*Where's Sara?*'

Grace stood up, the blood rushing to her head. All around them was grass – endless fields of yellow grass. A brilliant blue sky. No sign of Sara.

'I can't see her,' said Grace. 'Do you remember anything?'

'No.'

'Are you sure?'

'No, really. I can't remember anything. Sara's the one who remembers.'

'We should look for her.'

'I don't want to.' Caroline's voice was little more than a whisper.

'We don't have a choice.'

'I don't think I can stand.'

'Come on.'

Grace helped Caroline to her feet. She didn't want to touch her, but it was impossible for either of them to walk unassisted. They limped through the long grass like lambs taking their first steps, bloody arms intertwined.

It didn't take long. At the other end of the field, beneath a row of cypress trees, were the mutilated bodies of two sheep. The flies had got there first, swarming over the stomachs and settling on the remains of the heads, which were now little more than bloody pulp.

Caroline turned away and retched. Grace forced herself to look, even though she could taste the bile at the back of her throat and feel the tears coming.

'We did this,' said Grace. 'With only our hands.'

'Looks like it.'

'How?'

'Does it matter?'

'Of course it matters.'

'Not right now. Later.' Caroline took a deep breath, as though willing herself to remain conscious. 'Sara?'

'I have no idea. How should I know?'

'I don't want to look for her.'

'Caro, we can't *not* look for her. She's got to be here somewhere.'

'And if she looks… if she looks like that?'

'There's no way,' said Grace.

'You don't know that.'

222

'Neither of us knows anything yet. Let's try to stay calm.'

Caroline was kneeling in the grass, trembling all over. Grace wanted to stroke her hair, to comfort her in some way, but she couldn't. Not while her hands were still caked with blood. They needed water. Water and clean clothes. *But we're in the middle of nowhere.* The hopelessness of their situation suddenly made her feel faint, and for a moment her vision blurred.

'Let's go,' said Grace, trying to sound more decisive than she felt. 'Away from the sheep, that's a start.'

Certain images stuck in her mind like sunspots, nightmarishly bright. Turning their dresses inside out to hide the worst of the stains; frantically washing their hands in a feeble trickle of water from a fountain; stumbling over the ancient stones and freezing with fear when they heard a rustling noise in the bushes. They would have been utterly incapable of explaining themselves to anyone they encountered, for as the initial shock wore off they became tongue-tied. The tears dried on their cheeks and they did not speak.

Sara had disappeared into thin air. If they had hurt her in some way, Grace reasoned, they would have found her, just as they had found the sheep. Her absence absolved them from guilt, at least for the time being.

They passed the faceless statues they knew so well, but no living creatures. When Grace was lying up to her neck in a cold bath later that morning she reflected that the road had felt almost post-apocalyptic in its emptiness, with only the piercing cries of the swallows to remind them that they were not alone. Had the god orchestrated it, clearing the way so they could return home unseen? Even her flat had been empty. She had unlocked the door with trembling fingers, sure that her mother was waiting on the other side, but instead she had entered and discovered, to her immense, swooning relief, that everyone was out.

She reached for a bar of citrus soap and turned it over in her hands, until there was so much lather she could hardly see her skin. She still didn't feel entirely clean, but it was such a relief to be alone in the bath after the nightmare of the morning. She glanced at her blood-soaked dress, lying in a crumpled heap on the bathroom floor, and then closed her eyes. She would worry about the dress later. They would all find lies to save them, in one way or another. Or *he* would save them. It was only right, after what he had put them through.

She was combing her hair mechanically in front of the mirror, looking straight through her reflection, when the phone rang. It was Caroline.

'What is it?' asked Grace, her voice still hoarse.

'Don't you want to know?'

'Want to know what?'

'About Sara, for God's sake.'

'Oh.'

'She's alive, at least.'

'Is she okay?'

'She didn't mention any missing limbs, so I guess so.'

'Please, Caro. Don't talk like that.'

'It's okay, I'm home alone.'

'So am I. It's strange. Call me later?'

'Maybe.' Caroline hung up.

For the rest of the day Grace stayed in her room, emerging only at mealtimes. Not long after the call from Caroline, she heard footsteps in the hallway and Mauro's voice booming, reciting a list of ingredients. He had decided that it was time for one of those extravagant family lunches that went on for hours. The spell had worn off, her luck run out.

In the afternoon she made a few attempts at her homework, but the essay would not write itself, and it was an effort to construct a coherent sentence, let alone explain the causes of the Bolshevik Revolution. So she dropped her pen mid-sentence and returned to bed, where she drifted in and out of sleep. The fan whirred ineffectually on the bedside table, producing only a slight puff of air, but the repetitive mechanical noise soothed her. It clattered on into the night, a distraction turning her mind blank. She felt herself drifting deeper and deeper into a trance, so deep that her dream of a dreamless sleep was almost within reach.

Then, without warning, they came back to her. She saw their steaming, fly-infested entrails spread out across a white bed and felt the tears, long overdue, slide down her cheeks. The memory was awful enough in itself; knowing that she had done it with her own hands was more than she could stand.

As she wept she gradually became aware of the rising heat behind her. It was not the typical heat of the summer but something quite distinct – lighter, and yet a stronger, more defined presence. In a way it was more refreshing than a cold bath, this warmth that spread through and around her, holding her with such tenderness. She could feel his fingers too, stroking her hair, calming her.

'Don't cry,' said Dionysus. 'Don't lose sleep over this.'

'Why not?' Grace wiped her eyes but did not turn to look at him. She allowed herself to be held, finding comfort in the sensation of his fingers running through her hair, and waited for the explanation she so badly needed.

'You're upset,' he said, 'because you think you did something wrong. Society tells you it's wrong. Well, society is not reality. You know reality now. You've had a taste of it. You've enjoyed it. It's only natural.'

'Do you know what happened last night? What really happened? You wouldn't be talking like this if you'd seen it.'

'I know what goes on at my own parties.'

Even without looking at him she could picture his face – the glint in his eye, and a peculiar grimace as a substitute for a smile.

'But what we did... what happened to the sheep. I can't forgive myself.'

He would despise her for being so melodramatic, but she couldn't help it. She took a deep breath and tried to repress a sob.

'Listen, Grace. There's nothing to forgive. The sexual instinct, the instinct for violence – they are as natural and vital as the need to breathe. Only respiration isn't seen as a threat to civilised society, so there's no shame in it. Don't torture yourself by thinking you've committed a crime, when you're only being true to yourself.'

'But I didn't want to do it. I didn't want to hurt the poor creatures, let alone...'

'Not consciously, no, but deep down you desired it.'

'How could I? They must have suffered so much.'

'Yes,' said Dionysus, indifferent to her tears. 'But pain and death are part of life as well as pleasure. Suffering isn't wrong, it just *is*.'

'But it was so pointless, so unnecessary. How can you possibly justify it?'

'What you did last night gave immense pleasure to all of us. You might not believe it now, but it's true. And before you gasp and ask me if our pleasure was worth their pain, I can tell you – it was.'

'I don't believe you. And I don't believe that we're all just bloodthirsty savages who want to tear animals apart.'

'You're in denial.'

'I'm not.'

'Yes, you are. You're like everyone else, blind to the essential truth of humanity. Look at Christ.'

'What about him? What's he got to do with anything?'

'He believed that men were basically good, kind, peaceful. Made in God's image. Well, I would have thought it obvious that the gods are neither good nor kind nor peaceful. Christ was a fool. His idea of humanity was a dream, a lie. How can the world worship a mere mortal who couldn't grasp the fundamental truth about human nature?'

'What do you mean?'

'You know how he died, how they killed him. How would Christians explain his killers?'

Until now he had been speaking calmly, betraying no signs of emotion, but he uttered the word 'Christians' with such undisguised contempt that even Grace, who had shed all her vague Christian beliefs a long time ago, felt afraid.

'I suppose,' she said tentatively, 'they would say those men killed him because they were sinners, or because they were afraid, or because they didn't recognise the truth.'

'Yes, that's probably how they would understand it. But what no one understands – or acknowledges, at least – is that they killed Christ because they wanted to. For the pleasure of it. There was nothing special about Christ; men have crucified men for centuries. Hundreds have died on that road alone.'

Not only the road, thought Grace. *Also in the fields, the woods.* If the crucified ghosts of the Roman Empire ever wandered off the road, they would find the other victims, strewn out across the grass in bloodied fragments.

A shiver ran through her. She swallowed her nausea and willed herself to focus on the conversation. Anything to clear her mind.

'So do you think it was right, then? Crucifixion?'

He sighed, and she felt a hot rush of breath in her ear.

'I neither condone nor condemn. Violence is not good, but neither is it bad. Why is it so difficult for you to understand? I never used to have this problem. The women who danced and destroyed for me in the past mercifully lacked a conscience. No tears, no questions...'

'I'm sorry, but I can't help it. It *is* difficult.'

'It isn't entirely your fault. It's society. Christianity.'

They were silent for a while. Grace finally turned to face him and was struck by the change. His features were only just visible in the moonlight that crept through the shutters, and yet he looked peaceful, somehow... sated. Was that the word? His emotions were unknowable, so far removed from her own feelings that trying to understand him was as futile as looking up in a vast, darkened cathedral and guessing at the patterns on the distant ceiling. She knew it was too simplistic to say that he looked 'happy', but on some level he had to be satisfied.

'It will become easier,' he said, 'I promise.'

She didn't know if he meant that living with her guilt would be easier, or that doing it again would be easier next time. How much blood would have to be spilled before they were all fulfilled?

She sank deeper into his arms. It was like being embraced on the edge of a precipice, yet she had no choice but to trust him.

II

'I can't get rid of it,' said Sara, pale and anxious. They were standing by the sinks in the school toilets, washing their hands. Grace looked in the mirror at Sara's weary, sleep-deprived face, and then down at her fingers. Sara was rubbing the soap into skin that was already red from too much washing.

'Let me see,' said Grace.

Sara rinsed her hands and then raised them for Grace to inspect. She had cut her nails right down to the quick, but there were still tiny traces of red beneath.

'You can hardly see. No one would ever notice, or guess.'

'I know, but—' Sara broke off as another girl entered the room, then continued in a stage whisper that was even more conspicuous. 'It's not about what other people think. It's me. I can't stand it.'

They dried their hands and then went to their lockers to collect their books for Biology, never one of Grace's favourite subjects; it came as an unpleasant surprise to discover they would be dissecting a sheep's eyeball.

'But of course,' said Mr Davidson cheerfully, 'you don't have to. If you're feeling squeamish you can just watch.'

'Squeamish' was a woefully inadequate word for Grace's feelings. She glanced across the room and caught Caroline's eye. Caroline, who was not allowed to sit next to Grace in Biology (or Physics, or French) raised her eyebrow. Caroline's expressive eyebrows could mean many different things, but this gesture was clearly intended to signify *Isn't it ironic?*

Grace was sure she was faking it. Caroline might raise her eyebrow, smile, or – as she was doing now – volunteer to make the first cut, but her pallor betrayed her. It was all an act.

Sara was even whiter, and made no attempt to hide her disgust.

'It's like a horrible joke,' she observed, as they watched another girl in their group plunge the scalpel into the eyeball with the same grim determination she used for tackling school puddings.

'What do you mean, a joke?' asked Claire, who had also chosen not to participate. 'It's not funny.'

'Ha, ha, ha,' said Grace flatly.

'God, you can be so weird sometimes.' Claire's unspoken second sentence was clearly understood – *No wonder you don't have any other friends.*

Once she would have taken offence, but Grace couldn't bring herself to care. Ignoring the queasy, churning sensation in the pit of her stomach, she forced herself to watch the scalpel slice the optic nerve – assuming that was what it was – and imagined it as a lesson from the god.

Look, he would say, *that's all it is, all we are beneath the flesh. Nothing to be afraid of.*

She heard a sudden thump from the other side of the laboratory, and a cry of 'Maria's fainted!' The girls rushed to crowd around her, ignoring Mr Davidson's orders. Sara and Grace remained on their stools, elbows resting on the desk. Heather, who had been doing the dissection in their group, put down the scalpel with a sigh.

'That's the second time she's fainted, isn't it? Last time it was during that disastrous lesson on "the facts of life". Do you remember?'

'Maybe it's just the heat,' Sara suggested.

Maybe it's just because she can't cope with reality, thought Grace. *But then again, I'm not sure that I can either.*

That evening, relaxing on Caroline's terrace, they were all able to laugh about it.

'When you think about what we've been through without fainting…' said Sara.

'All she had to do was look at it, and she was on the floor. *Thud.*' Caroline laughed. 'I swear, she actually made that noise. Like something from a comic.'

Grace's laughs were slightly forced and she was sure that the others' were too, but she reasoned that fake laughter was better than real tears. And one day, after some time had passed, it would be funny. They were just doing the whole 'You'll look back and laugh' thing a little prematurely, for their own sanity.

'Apparently it's not the first time she's fainted,' said Grace.

'No, she's a sensitive soul. Home-educated until she was thirteen, which explains a lot.'

They were lying on sun loungers on Caroline's private rooftop terrace, beneath a glorious orange sky. Although she always felt uncomfortably sticky at the end of a school day in the summer term, especially when she didn't have the chance to immediately change out of her uniform, Grace was glad to be here. A cool breeze stirred the leaves of the potted palm trees that lined the walls, and the large white umbrellas provided welcome pools of shade. In the dog days of summer, a rooftop like this seemed the only sensible place to be.

It was nice, too, to be sitting with friends and talking and laughing about school, as if they were normal sixteen-year-olds. Essentially they *were* normal, it was just that their lives happened to be extraordinary. And even this, Grace reflected, sipping her drink, was only a matter of perspective. A year from now they might be completely used to it, and meeting in a field to get wildly drunk and tear a few animals apart would seem no more unusual than other people's habits of going to the cinema or playing sports.

Now Caroline and Sara were chatting about the play, and how Titania was going to have to be recast if Eleanor didn't sort herself out.

'She's such an amateur. I mean, I know we're technically all amateurs, but there's such a difference between Siobhan O'Neill, for example – she's Oberon – and useless Eleanor stuttering over every line.'

Caroline had sunk right down into the sun lounger and was looking supremely at ease. Not for the first time, Grace found herself wishing that Sara would leave, so that she could be alone with Caroline. If they excluded her there was always the danger that she might start suspecting something was going on, but lately she seemed to have forgotten about that unspeakable incident. No doubt it had been eclipsed in Sara's memory by the events of last Friday.

Grace ignored her lingering guilt and doubt and let her gaze rest on Caroline's face. Her eyes were hidden behind sunglasses, but even at a slight distance her lips were remarkably vivid and pink. It was mesmerising to watch her talk, bright and animated, but it was when her mouth was closed that Grace allowed her imagination to wander, feeling Caroline's teeth and tongue more sharply when she could not see them.

Then she became aware that Sara had changed the subject to more serious matters and she shifted uncomfortably in her chair, as if to detach herself from her daydream.

'Has there been anything about it in the news?' asked Sara.

'How would I know? I don't read the news. Or watch it.'

'Well, don't you think we ought to check?'

Caroline looked contemplative.

'Wait a moment.'

She disappeared downstairs and then returned a few minutes later with a local newspaper.

'Here we are. I wouldn't expect to find anything though.'

'I was just thinking… someone would have found them. They must have had an owner.'

'Yes, but they're only animals.'

'Maybe no one cares,' Grace added hopefully.

Caroline, peering over the top of her sunglasses, began to flick through the newspaper.

'Nothing here. Maybe – no, nothing. It'd be easier if it were in English.'

When she reached the end of the paper she started turning the pages backwards, to skim-read more thoroughly.

'Aha, here it is.'

'Are you sure?' Grace was sweating; sitting in the rooftop breeze, it was unlikely to be an effect of the heat.

'I think so. It's something about sheep… a phrase I don't know, but I bet it translates as something like "grisly discovery".'

'Does it say anything about the cause?' asked Sara.

'No. Wait, yes, it does. Dogs. Dog attack. Then there's a bit about how they're looking for three girls, one blonde, two dark – oh, of course I'm joking, Sara. Here, have a look for yourself if you like, though I doubt you'll understand any more of it than I do.'

Sara attempted to read the article, brow furrowed with concentration, and then passed it to Grace. The article was short, at least, and tucked away on page twenty-three. It was the best they could have hoped for.

Neither Caroline nor Sara seemed particularly shaken by the discovery of the article. Caroline, who was idly fiddling with the straw in her glass, looked as if she didn't have a care in the world, while Sara appeared much less guilt-ridden than Grace would have expected. Grace could only guess that they too had spoken to Dionysus.

'Well, that's it,' said Caroline. 'There's really nothing more to discuss.'

'Until next time,' said Grace.

'Yes,' Sara leaned forward and poured herself another glass. 'I suppose it'll happen again.'

They were remarkably relaxed, even nonchalant, about the whole thing. Who were they trying to fool? Themselves? Perhaps that was the only way to go on. Or perhaps they were all under his influence, his spell. A twitch of the invisible thread and they all relaxed and laughed on cue. Grace sipped her drink thoughtfully.

'Caro, what *is* this stuff?'

'Orange juice.'

'Orange juice and…?'

'Vodka. It's not as good as wine, of course, but I thought my parents were less likely to notice the disappearance of the vodka. I topped up the bottle with water.'

They heard footsteps, and then Caroline's mother's immaculate hair emerged at the top of the stairs.

'Supper's ready, girls.'

'Coming.'

Once Caroline's mother was out of earshot, Grace turned to Caroline and whispered, 'It isn't…?'

'No, don't worry. I told her that Sara's a vegetarian now.'

At the dinner table the girls skilfully fielded questions about camping trips, crushes and Sara's vegetarianism. Nearly everything they said was a lie. To make matters worse, although Sara was used to having to conceal her drunkenness, she was much more giggly than usual. Grace noticed Caroline's parents exchanging glances and panicked. To deflect attention she asked them as many questions as she could think of, interrogating Caroline's father about his job, and Caroline's mother about her childhood in Rhodesia.

'You did a fabulous job of sucking up to them,' said Caroline later, when the meal was over and they were sitting in Caroline's bedroom. Grace was unsure if this was supposed to be a compliment or a criticism.

'I didn't know what else to say. It was excruciating.'

'You need to relax.'

'I didn't have as much of the "orange juice" as you.'

'Good, wasn't it?'

A little while later Caroline's mother came to tell them that Sara's mother had arrived. 'She says it's too late for the tram, and I daresay she's right.'

'Too late for the tram,' said Caroline incredulously, once her mother had left the room. 'If only she knew!'

They all went to the door to say goodbye to Sara; Grace sensed that Caroline's mother was waiting for her to leave as well, but she ignored the hint and went back to Caroline's room to steal ten more minutes.

'I wish I could stay.'

'I wish you could stay too.'

It was strange how the absence of one person changed the whole atmosphere. Now that Sara had gone, Grace felt like she could breathe at last.

'Just think, though,' said Caroline. 'Only a few more weeks till the end of term, and then we've got the whole summer. It'll just be us and him.'

'I hate waiting. I hate hiding.'

'One day we won't have to.'

'How do you know?'

'He promised me. And now I'm promising you.'

Caroline kissed her, with such tenderness that Grace felt herself go weak. It was mad that a mere mortal, as he would have said, could have such a profound physical effect on her.

'Go on,' said Caroline, pushing her playfully. 'Before my mother starts dropping hints about how it's a school night.'

'All right.' Grace stood up unsteadily. 'See you tomorrow.'

'See you.'

III

The summer term crawled towards its end. The afternoons felt longest, sitting in stuffy classrooms and watching the hands of the clock moving so slowly Grace became convinced it was some kind of illusion. Time couldn't *really* be passing that slowly. The nights in the church and the fields had taught her that time was the only thing that always remained outside your control, even under the influence of the god and wine. If she was powerless then, she had little hope of making the clock speed up during French lessons.

She was doing badly in French, but as she was doing almost equally badly in everything else, it didn't particularly bother her. French was the most pointless subject of all. She had no interest in or aptitude for the language, and she hadn't the slightest desire to go to France or communicate with French-speaking people.

When they were given back their mock exams, the girl sitting next to Grace, Alice, gave a small gasp of disappointment. Grace glanced at Alice's paper and saw her mark – 56 per cent. She considered showing Alice her own mark to cheer her up, before deciding that she didn't care enough about Alice to reveal her inferiority. It would be bad enough having to admit her mark to Caroline later.

'*C'est décevant, Grace,*' said Madame Paradis at the end of the lesson. Grace felt tempted to respond with an exaggerated Gallic shrug of indifference, but she was in enough trouble for her low marks without adding 'poor behaviour' to the charges.

'*Oui, Madame.*'

'*Il est pas facile.*'

'*Non, Madame.*'

'*Mais cela ne signifie pas que tu ne peux pas travailler.*'

'*Oui, non… Non, Madame.*'

Forty-three per cent was mildly humiliating, but it was only a mock exam, only French, only school. Knowing that the summer holidays were just a couple of weeks away gave her a feeling of serene detachment, even when she received similarly low marks in Physics and Maths.

Caroline had always feigned indifference, declaring that tests were a joke and that she didn't care what the teachers thought of her. Her mock exam results were mostly in the sixties – a pass, but still the lowest she had ever got. Despite the distractions of Dionysus, Grace and the school play, she suddenly decided that she wanted to do well in her exams, and no amount of persuasion from Grace could make her give up or even shorten her revision sessions in the library. She was there for a minimum of two hours every day after school.

'At least it's cool down there,' said Caroline. 'You should come.'

So Grace came. Not because the library was in the basement, the coolest part of the building, or because she intended to look at any of the books, but because sitting in silence with Caroline was better than not being with her.

After half an hour of pretending to study the diagrams in a Physics textbook, Grace whispered, 'After this we could go to the Ghetto. See if he's there.'

'Later. Maybe.' Caroline was busy making notes on a poem and didn't even bother to look up. Grace wished she could make Caroline see that Physics and poetry didn't really matter, weren't even real. Even outside the meaningless school exams they were a waste of time. Physics was just some made-up rules, poetry a lot of words to say that things were like other things.

How could Caroline, who had experienced the divine truth of existence not just once but over and over and over again, sit there with an expression of intense concentration and take it all so seriously?

An hour later, Grace was feeling so bored and neglected that she thought she might as well leave. Caroline probably wouldn't even notice. As if she had read her thoughts, Caroline pushed a book across the table, her finger pointing to the top of the page.

'Read this.'

'The whole thing?'

'Some of it, at least.'

> *'My life is bitter with thy love; thine eyes*
> *Blind me, thy tresses burn me, thy sharp sighs*

Divide my flesh and spirit with soft sound,
And my blood strengthens, and my veins abound.
I pray thee sigh not, speak not, draw not breath;
Let life burn down, and dream it is not death.'

The poem went on for eight pages, but Grace continued reading until the end. There was something strangely mesmerising about it, in its violence and eroticism.

'That I could drink thy veins as wine, and eat
Thy breasts like honey! That from face to feet
Thy body were abolished and consumed
And in my flesh thy very flesh entombed!'

It was a twisted kind of love poem where Sappho told her lover, Anactoria, how she wanted to hurt her, and then how she wanted to kill God, and then die while remaining immortal through her poetry. At least, that was what Grace understood. Apart from *The Bacchae*, 'Anactoria' was the most disturbing, exciting thing she had ever read, and yet she wasn't sure she completely understood it. It was far too strange to be grasped on first reading, with all those breathless rhyming couplets about comets and oceans and making a lyre out of limbs.

'What does it mean?' asked Grace. The question she really wanted to ask was *Why did you make me read it?* But it was easier to ask the bland, generic question, instead of pushing Caroline to reveal her true motives. Caroline instinctively understood the real question and smiled.

'I don't know. Does it matter? It sounds good and it makes you feel something. That's probably all Swinburne cared about.'

She picked up the book and read the lines in a theatrical whisper.

'I would find grievous ways to have thee slain;
Intense device, and superflux of pain.'

At home that night Grace kept thinking about the poem, about Caroline's smile. She lay in the bath, scrubbing her hands with soap out of habit, far harder and longer than necessary. The reason the poem had struck such a chord, she realised, was not just because it portrayed love between two women, but because it showed pain as something beautiful, even at its most extreme. The gods were cruel, and so were lovers, women – everyone.

Of course it was only a poem, just as *The Bacchae* was only a play, and yet it had stirred something in her. These dead men had stumbled upon the truth, even if they hadn't fully realised it themselves. Or had they? Had Swinburne, that funny-looking Victorian, heard the whispers of the gods as he churned out his couplets? Unlikely, but not impossible. If Dionysus had chosen the companionship of three unremarkable teenage girls, he might well have sought out more talented souls in the past. If not Dionysus, then another god. Apollo over the poet's shoulder, Aphrodite disguised as the artist's model...

'Grace, have you nearly finished in there? Supper in five minutes.'

She was always being interrupted. As she washed the soap off her hands she began to daydream about running away for the summer, sleeping in the fields and living off wine and whatever else the god provided. Caroline would be with her, so she wouldn't need anything else. Just Caroline, reciting Swinburne with a mischievous grin while the sun set and Dionysus filled another cup.

'Grace. Supper, *now*.'

'All right, all *right*.'

Grace's ever longer baths were clearly beginning to get on her family's nerves.

'What do you *do* in there?' asked Barbara.

Grace wished she could explain that it was not just a luxury but a necessity. Even when she was not covered in blood she needed to soak in lukewarm, orange-scented water and feel like she was wholly clean. After the nights with Dionysus she was always convinced that she must be filthy, her hands sticky and smelling of wine and the earth, and some other scent, harder to define. She knew that smell Caroline sometimes had the morning after – a kind of stale, animal smell, subtle enough not to be unpleasant – and she worried that she had it too. What if it clung to her hair, lingering even after an hour-long bath, and someone noticed and became suspicious? There were much more obvious signs that people had missed, but maybe her downfall would start with something small and insignificant – not a shock discovery but suspicion about an inexplicable smell, leading to unanswerable questions and the final disgrace of the truth. No, it would be more than disgrace. It would be... the end of the world.

Grace sniffed her wet hair and was reassured to find it smelled of nothing more sinister than coconut shampoo. Then, ignoring the warning of 'supper *now*', she got out of the bath and began her routine of carefully inspecting her body in the mirror. She had to be so careful, not just because of the scratches on her arms, but also the marks on other parts of her body, which were easy to miss if they did not hurt. Recently she had found bite marks on the side of her neck, only they did not look like they had come from human teeth.

'A vampire!' Caroline had exclaimed with delight, when Grace showed her. Grace had made Caroline bite her gently on the arm to compare the two bites and concluded that Caroline was not her attacker, but that was all she knew. She kept her hair down for a week.

The bite marks had faded, and now there were only a few scratches across her thighs, marks that only Caroline would see. Grace remembered standing in front of this same mirror a year ago and finding fault with everything. Her thighs were too thick and had stretch marks; there was hair where there shouldn't be; her breasts were uneven. She had examined herself from every angle, frowning to see that her stomach was still not flat, no matter how little she ate or how much she exercised. At one point she had felt so miserable that she had written in her diary – long since abandoned – *If you hate your body, what's the point of existing?*

The things that had bothered her then were still there, but now they seemed irrelevant. Instead of dividing up her body into satisfactory and unsatisfactory parts, she saw herself for the first time as a whole. However imperfect, everything was connected, everything worked to make her mad life possible. She was young and healthy, and more alive than she had ever been. She was beautiful. Not in a conventional sense, not in a way that would ever be recognised by others, but there was something about him, about being in his presence, that made her aware of her femininity. She had never thought about it before meeting him, but now she understood why the majority of his followers had been female. Men were always subjugating women, making them powerless even as they claimed to love them. But Dionysus understood what women were capable of; he knew they could be stronger, more fearless than any man. He freed them and asked for nothing in return but devotion.

'Grace?' Barbara's voice floated through the bathroom door. 'I've been sent to see if you've drowned.'

'I'll be one minute.'

'It's going cold.'

Grace quickly got dressed and made a half-hearted attempt to dry her hair, even though she knew it would soon dry in the heat. Regardless of the temperature, Mauro would always shake his head disapprovingly whenever he saw her or Barbara with wet hair, convinced that they would catch their death of cold.

'Where's Mummy?' asked Grace, surprised to see only Barbara and Mauro sitting at the dining table. Henry often ate earlier, so he would probably be in his bedroom, but she could think of no reason for her mother's absence.

'Out,' said Mauro, pouring himself a glass of wine. 'Her friends from the tennis club.'

'Tennis club?'

'Mummy's been playing tennis for months,' said Barbara. 'Don't pretend it's news to you.'

'Sorry, I'd forgotten.'

As Grace began to eat her pasta – an impenetrable tangle of congealed lumps of cheese and undercooked spaghetti – she tried to remember a moment when someone had mentioned tennis, even in passing. Nothing came to mind. Not that it mattered; it was just another reminder of how they led entirely separate lives. They were like strangers on the metro, occupying the same space but hardly registering each other's presence.

It was odd having dinner without her mother. She was usually taken for granted, but now that she was Out, it somehow didn't seem right without her. Barbara was drinking wine, which was quite unlike her. Grace was almost tempted to comment on it, or to demand that Mauro pour her a glass too, but then something held her back. It was better to wait, to watch, to try to identify this change in the atmosphere.

Mauro was telling stories about his childhood, reminiscing about the time his father brought an eel home and his mother, horrified, made him flush it down the toilet.

'For a week,' said Mauro solemnly, 'I did not use the toilet.'

Barbara laughed loudly, and for at least a couple of seconds too long.

'Of course, in these days no one eats the eel any more.'

'I'd like to try it sometime,' said Barbara.

'Ugh.' Grace pulled a face.

'I will take you,' said Mauro. 'I know a place in the country.'

'I don't want to eat eel,' said Grace.

'Then don't come.' Barbara was looking at her strangely, as though she were looking not at her but through her. Was it possible that she was drunk? Grace had never seen her sister drunk before, but she ought to be able to recognise the signs by now.

Mauro and Barbara continued talking, while Grace pushed the pasta around on her plate. She had no appetite, and she wanted to prolong the meal in order to work out what was wrong. All she knew was it was something in the atmosphere, like the electrical charge before a thunderstorm. The air was heavy. Perhaps it was too humid, that was all. They were all sweating, hair plastered to the backs of their necks.

Barbara laughed again at something Mauro had said, something that wasn't remotely funny. The humidity had made her brain go soft. Grace was feeling sleepy and stupid too, as well as some other emotion she couldn't quite name.

'Grace?'

'What?'

'You're going out tonight, aren't you?' Barbara looked serious all of a sudden.

'No.'

'But you usually go out.'

'Well, tonight I'm not. Is that all right?'

'Of course.'

Barbara and Mauro exchanged glances. Grace got up, considered helping to clear the table, and then thought better of it. Her mother wasn't there to make her do it, and if she did it without asking, Mauro would think he had some kind of authority over her. He wasn't even her stepfather. He was just a man who inhabited the same space as her and sometimes gave her food. Food which she didn't even like.

'Grace?'

'Yes?' Grace paused in the doorway and waited to be rebuked.

'Goodnight,' said Mauro.

Even in her bedroom with the door closed, she still seemed to hear them. Mauro's voice droning, Barbara's inexplicable bursts of laughter. For the first time in weeks, and for no apparent reason, Grace found herself thinking of Pippin and resisting the urge to cry.

She had to drown it all out. Anything would do. She dragged herself out of bed, rummaged through the tattered covers of her record collection, and put on a song. It was an old one – that song she had played to death even as she pretended not to like it. 'Everybody Loves Somebody'. His voice was somehow comforting and unsettling at the same time, making her nostalgic for something she couldn't even name. Music to brood to. She blinked back the tears, and when the record finished, she lifted the needle and played it again.

IV

Dionysus put a segment of the orange in his mouth. He was only eating it because she had brought it to him, Grace knew. He never seemed to experience hunger. She watched him eat the whole thing in silence, his head resting against the wall. On the other side of the window above him, an apocalyptic display of thunder and lightning raged. She was glad they were safe and dry in his room in the Ghetto, and not exposed to the elements in a field. Mauro overestimated the dangers of wet hair, but a bacchanal in a downpour like this was another thing altogether. She imagined herself running through the trees, slipping in the mud and getting soaked to the skin. In a way it might be better, more appropriate to dance in a wild storm, but she shuddered to think of the aftermath. They would probably all get pneumonia and die. *He* didn't have to think of practicalities, but that was because he didn't have to live with the consequences.

'What if,' said Grace, thinking out loud, 'we lived here all the time?'

Dionysus swallowed and wiped the juice from his lips.

'A nice idea. Why don't you?'

'Sometimes I think my family wouldn't even notice. Or they'd notice, but they wouldn't care.'

'You know that isn't true.'

'It is.'

'They love you. They're your family, after all.'

This idea seemed to bore him immensely. He picked up another orange and began to peel it.

'You don't know what they're like. They're all completely self-absorbed.'

'All the more reason why they would miss you.'

'What do you mean?'

'They don't see you as a separate, independent person. You're just another facet of their own identity. So if you were to leave – to run away in the night and come to live with me – I'm quite sure that they would come looking for you. Or for that part of themselves that they're suddenly missing.'

'What about Caroline's family?'

Caroline was lying with her head in Grace's lap. She was in the depths of a wine-induced sleep, dead to the world.

'All families are exactly the same,' said Dionysus.

He closed his eyes, as if he also wished to sleep. Perhaps it was a sign that he wanted to be left alone, but he had called them here in the first place. Sometimes Grace came to see him because she wanted to; there were other times when she sensed instinctively that he wanted her. She would feel a pull of that invisible thread, something tearing at her chest, and she would have no choice but to come to the Ghetto and ring the bell with no name.

'Have you had any more dreams?' she asked. 'You know, like the one about the priest.'

For a moment his eyes were glazed, and he stared across the room as if he hadn't heard her. Then he turned to look at her and said, 'You want a story.'

'Well...' She hesitated. 'Only if you want to tell me.'

His eyes glazed over again, and she imagined him unwinding the webs of his memory, searching through thousands of years of myths and dreams. To him everything was real, regardless of whether it had happened or not.

'I'm in the desert.' He spoke so quietly that it was difficult to hear him above the downpour. Grace edged closer, taking care not to let Caroline's head slip. 'I'm in the desert, and all I can see around me are miles and miles of white sand. A burning blue sky – quite different to the skies here. I'm kneeling in the sand, my hands tied behind my back, and I suffer from an unbelievable thirst. It is as if all the blood in my body has dried up. The last thing I see is a veiled woman weeping and a tall, dark man striding across the sand towards me. I am blind-folded. Then the whipping begins. One, two, three... Never-ending. A pain you can't imagine.'

Grace waited for him to continue, and was disappointed when she realised he had finished.

'Is that it?'

'What more do you want me to say? Shall I describe the pain? Do you want the gory details?'

'No, no, I didn't mean that. I meant… don't you know where you were, who the man was, or why you were being whipped?'

'I can guess. Arabia or Africa. The man was someone I had wronged, or perhaps a jealous tyrant like Pentheus. He whipped me because I had made love to his wife, or stolen his people, or revealed myself as a god, or simply because he enjoyed it and found a man to flagellate every Tuesday.'

'So you don't know.'

'I told you, Grace. I am not omniscient.'

For a while they sat in silence, listening to the rain. Grace stroked Caroline's hair absent-mindedly, trying to work out why the story bothered her so much. She looked at his arms and legs, what was visible of his chest, and was struck once more by the perfection of his skin. Despite centuries of suffering, having been tortured and torn apart and put back together again like a divine Frankenstein's monster, his body was remarkably smooth and unmarked. She remembered how unnerved she'd been by his hands, noticing that his palms were unlined.

There was no reason why a god should be expected to scar and carry his wounds with him. She had heard of visions of Jesus where the marks of the nails were still clearly visible in his hands, but then Jesus, as Dionysus would have delighted in reminding her, was only a man, not a god at all.

'How does all this fit in with your philosophy of pain?' she asked.

'What do you mean?'

'You said that pain was a natural thing – not evil – and something everyone had to suffer. Even you?'

'Even me.'

'But surely there's a difference between the pain you get when you trip over a stone and that kind of sadistic pain.'

'You could draw the distinction that a stone receives no pleasure from tripping someone up, whereas my torturer probably thoroughly enjoyed himself. But I don't think that is what you are really asking.

You want to know how I, a god, can give such an unemotional account of my suffering, and not talk of revenge or punishment.'

'Well, I would have expected something. Literature and mythology is full of it.'

'You have to understand that the gods are not equally powerful in all places and all times. The golden ages are few and far between. There were times when I was weak, and if I was captured, imprisoned, tortured, there was little I could do but accept it. When you have experienced pain in all its forms, you learn to be a little more… stoic.'

'I never thought of you as being stoic.'

'Oh, it doesn't last. In another life I'm sure I must have hunted down that man and made him pay, made him suffer unspeakable things. That is how the world works. It's like a great circle.'

He drew a circle in the air, an innocent shape that was supposed to represent an endless cycle of revenge and suffering. Grace glanced down at Caroline, who had slept peacefully throughout the conversation, quite oblivious to the horrors that the god had hinted at.

'We should go soon,' said Grace. 'But I'll have to wait for Caroline to wake up and the rain to stop.'

'Yes. You wouldn't want to get wet.'

Behind that soft, almost neutral voice lurked a cutting sarcasm. Grace consoled herself with the thought that it was better to be on the sharp edge of his tongue than whatever weapons he had used in the past.

V

The torrential rain lasted all week. The Embassy party, which Caroline was obliged to attend every summer, had to be moved inside. The gardens were practically flooded.

'Such a shame,' said Caroline. 'I wanted to show you the statues, and the maze, of course. When I was younger I used to play hide and seek with the other children – it's one of those games where it doesn't matter if you don't speak the same language – and then when I grew out of that, Anna and I used to spy on people. Anna's father was a Vatican emissary or something like that. I think they've left now. Anyway, we saw people getting up to all kinds of things when they thought they were hidden by the hedges. It just won't be the same indoors.'

Caroline had been allowed to invite Grace to the party, on the strict condition that they both behaved themselves and did not do anything that might embarrass Caroline's father.

'He gets very sensitive about these things. According to him, a misuse of cutlery might lead to a diplomatic incident.'

Grace felt quite nervous beforehand. Caroline's parents always made her anxious anyway, and she was not used to attending formal events. When she arrived at Caroline's flat and saw her dress and her make-up, she immediately regretted not having made more of an effort.

'I would have got a new dress,' she explained, 'but I'd have had to ask my mother to take me shopping, and at the moment all she does is argue with Barbara.'

'What about?'

'Stupid things. Barbara answering back. Some situation with Mauro I don't understand.'

'You ought to exploit the situation,' said Caroline, putting on more blusher. 'Now that Barbara's the black sheep, make your mother see you as the good daughter and she'll buy you all kinds of things.'

'Henry's her favourite.'

'Didn't you say that your father likes Barbara best? Poor middle child.'

Grace had never thought of it like that before, and it stung.

'Never mind,' she said, turning away from the mirror. 'There's more to life than family, thank God.'

The Embassy was the grandest building Grace had ever been in without having to pay an entrance fee. From the outside it was blandly elegant in the way that so many buildings in the city centre were, but when Caroline's father led them up the marble staircase and into a vast room with a high frescoed ceiling, Grace realised that it was something special. It was four or five hundred years old, but her experiences over the past year had given her a strange sense of history, so that the Renaissance now seemed relatively recent. There were statues and paintings that looked as though they were probably worth millions, though that was only a guess, as Grace knew nothing about art. The paintings didn't really interest her, and nor did the crowds of well-dressed diplomats and their wives. All she wanted to do was stare at the ceiling, which was covered with swirling clouds and half-naked gods leaping from chariots or embracing each other. She was sure Dionysus must be among them.

Caroline was craning her neck to see.

'We'd get a much better view if we could lie on the floor.'

'Don't even think about it,' said her father. 'I want you to act like adults.'

'Does that mean we can have wine?'

'If you can find a waiter to serve you.'

'Come on, Grace.'

They linked arms and made their way to the nearest waiter who was holding a tray of wine glasses.

'Not the quality I'm used to,' said Caroline, within earshot of the waiter, 'but it'll do.'

They slowly circled the room, looking out of the windows at the storm raging above the umbrella pines, and watching the guests pass by in twos and threes; despite the mix of nationalities, somehow everyone looked the same. A few of them greeted Caroline or gave her a nod or a smile of recognition. Grace felt invisible, but it was better to feel invisible than conspicuous, and besides, she didn't care about anyone except Caroline. After a while she grew hopeful that no one would talk to them, and that she would have Caroline to herself all evening.

'How many of these people do you know?'

'A few of the old ones – friends of my father. But a lot of people we used to know have left. It's always like that with expats anyway, and then a lot of people have been leaving because of the economy and the country being on the verge of collapse.'

'What kind of collapse?' This was the first Grace had heard of it.

'How should I know? Ask my father, he'll give you a whole lecture.' She turned around and gave a little sigh of impatience. 'Isn't there any proper food here? I'm sure we had more than some measly canapés last year.'

At Caroline's insistence they went in search of more wine and canapés, in the fear that supplies might run out, leaving them hungry and sober. Every now and then Grace would look up again and search for Dionysus among the clouds. She thought she could detect a wreath of ivy leaves, and some kind of stick that might be a thyrsus.

'Found him,' she said.

Caroline wasn't listening. In the few seconds it had taken Grace to look up at the ceiling, a boy had appeared out of nowhere and started talking to Caroline.

He was about their age, English, and utterly nondescript. His name was something like James or George or David or John, and Grace forgot it the second after he introduced himself. He and Caroline vaguely knew each other from the party the year before, and their fathers worked together.

Grace distrusted him from the start. She would have resented anyone who talked to Caroline that night, but she could see the way the boy looked at Caroline, the way he smiled and – what was worse – the way Caroline smiled at him. They were making small talk, pretending to be grown-ups as they commented on the other guests and asked each other dull questions.

For the first time, Grace disliked feeling invisible. The boy wasn't bothering to ask her anything, though she wouldn't have wanted to answer even if he had. His attention was focused solely on Caroline.

Grace wondered how Caroline could bear to talk about school with this boy, whose name and face were equally forgettable. Perhaps she was just being polite, and she would find a way to end it soon so she and Grace could escape to another room to drink wine and talk of secret things.

But after a while she had to admit to herself that it was unlike Caroline to do anything just for the sake of politeness, and it was becoming clear that the boy wasn't going to leave her alone. Caroline kept encouraging him by asking questions and smiling. Grace loved Caroline's smiles, but not when they were directed at strangers.

'I'll be back in a minute,' said Grace, even though she had no idea where she was going. Caroline didn't hear her.

Grace walked off into the crowd, adrift, looking for someone to talk to until she remembered that she didn't know anyone else, except for Caroline's parents. Talking to them would be even worse than remaining alone. She found a chair at the side of the room, next to a marble bust of a man who was just as bland as the English boy. From here she could see almost everyone in the room, and keep an eye on Caroline from a distance. Grace knew that she probably looked pathetic, sitting there by herself, but at least she had a glass of wine. If she sipped it slowly it would give her something to do, making her look less lonely, and if she gulped it down and then had another she would get drunk, making her feel less lonely.

These days it took a lot to get her drunk. She wished she were drunk right now. Leaning back in her chair, she imagined that she was in one of her ecstasies, tearing everyone apart. People were not that much bigger than sheep. The woman in the turquoise dress was dismembered in an instant, her insides spilling across the marble floor. The man next to her disintegrated into a pile of torn flesh and blood, while James or George or David or John screamed as he was torn limb from limb, his blood spraying across the walls and windows, right up to the painted clouds.

Grace was almost beginning to enjoy herself when she saw Caroline and the boy, disappointingly intact, leave the room together. There was a chance that they were looking for her, but she very much doubted it. Watching Caroline disappear gave her a horrible burning feeling, intensely physical yet impossible to place. She set down her half-empty glass and went to find the toilets, vowing to stay there until Caroline came to find her.

There was not much to do in the toilets, except glower at her reflection in the mirror and lather her hands in the hand cream she found by the sink. Whenever a woman came in and gave her a questioning look, she would shake her head and gesture towards the empty cubicle. She was only waiting for Caroline.

Some inestimable amount of time later, she appeared.

'Oh, here you are.'

Caroline went to the toilet and came out to find Grace staring at her, waiting for her to say something.

'What?'

'Have you finished talking to that boy?'

'So that's why you're in a huff. What have you got against him?'

'Nothing. I just don't understand why you want to spend the whole evening talking to a boring boy. I thought we were supposed to be here together.'

'I'm allowed to talk to other people.'

'It's more than talking. Flirting.'

'I am *not* flirting. I'm just being friendly.'

'Stop being friendly then.'

'You feel threatened because I smile at people who aren't you. Is that it? It's not like you own me.'

'I never said that.'

One of the women Grace had been mentally dismembering entered the room, and Caroline, sensing that the conversation was going to become too private for a public toilet, walked out. Grace followed her to a deserted balcony overlooking the garden. If they stayed close to the walls they were just about sheltered from the rain.

'What can I do without you sulking?' asked Caroline. 'Is eye contact acceptable?'

'You're making me sound like I'm paranoid. I'm not. I just don't like you spending all night talking to some… some *boy* who clearly likes you. If you cared about my feelings at all, you wouldn't.'

'God, it's not like we're married.'

'Well, what *are* we?'

Caroline folded her arms and looked out across the windswept maze; the outlines of the hedges were only just visible in the dark.

'I don't know,' she said at last. 'I'm sure people at school would find some creative ways to define us if they knew.'

'You care about what they think.'

'Of course. So do you.'

'Yes, in a way, but it doesn't really matter. What matters…' Grace struggled to find an ending that Caroline would not laugh at for sounding sentimental. She took a deep breath and tried again. 'We're in so deep. With each other, with him. Do you know what I mean? There's no going back.'

Caroline looked puzzled, as if she didn't understand how this was relevant.

'We've got to be able to trust each other,' said Grace. 'I wish you would promise not to—'

'I'm not promising anything. If you're jealous, that's your problem. We're together practically all the time and you're coming home with me tonight, so I think you'll survive if I talk to Brian.'

'Who's Brian?'

Caroline went indoors, leaving Grace alone on the balcony, watching the rain. *He* was probably watching it too, alone in his room in the Ghetto. They could all be there together, lost in the ecstasy of divine wine, and instead Caroline had chosen this stultifying party and someone called Brian. It was incomprehensible.

Grace went inside, pulling at her shawl to stop it from slipping; she had to take care not to expose her shoulders. She could either hide in the toilets or spy on Caroline. Both options were pathetic, but that was what she was reduced to in Caroline's absence. Holding the edges of her shawl, she returned to the frescoed hall and looked for the blondest head in the crowd.

VI

The girls lined up on stage to take a bow, beaming as their parents and classmates applauded dutifully. Puck stood near the centre of the stage between Oberon and Titania. Smeared in green face paint and wearing a costume that had been left over from a production of *Robin Hood*, she was almost unrecognisable. Some leaves had been hastily stuck on at the last minute, to make her look wilder. As Grace clapped she reflected that she had seen Caroline looking much more wild and ethereal than this, and that Shakespeare didn't have a clue about what it really meant to lose your mind in the woods. She tried to catch Caroline's eye, but she was still a triumphant Puck, blinded by the stage lights and grinning at no one in particular.

Grace rushed backstage to see Caroline, hoping to be the first to congratulate her.

'You were brilliant,' she said, flinging her arms around her. Caroline hugged her back but pulled away after a few seconds, conscious of all the people swarming around them.

'Careful, this green stuff gets everywhere, and I'm shedding leaves. I feel like some kind of diseased tree. Did you like it?'

'Of course.'

'It was fun, but I'm glad it's over. Can you believe they made me wear tights in this weather?'

Then Sara was there, earnestly complimenting her performance, and then Caroline went off to find her parents. Grace started to feel abandoned again, until she told herself to stop being so sensitive. It was ridiculous to fall apart every time Caroline looked the other way. Besides, it was the end of term – the end of the school year – and they would have the whole summer together.

Grace had been longing for the summer holidays for months. It was the closest thing to freedom. Now she no longer had to pretend to care about her exams – she was quite sure she had failed all of them – she could do as she liked. When she overheard her classmates discussing their plans for the summer, ranging from weekends in Paris to cruises in the Caribbean, she smiled to herself. She had already fought and won the battle to be excluded from the family holiday. She could not dream of wanting to be anywhere else, not when she had been promised a long, enchanted summer of bacchanals in the fields. Yet if Dionysus had suddenly announced that he was leaving the city and beginning a journey across Europe, Asia, wherever, she would happily have followed him to the ends of the earth.

Sara had not been so lucky. Her parents' friends owned a villa on a Greek island, and Sara had been sentenced to spend two whole weeks there.

'I couldn't think of a good enough reason not to go,' said Sara, sighing heavily. They were sitting on the steps of the fountain in the square, shifting every now and then to chase the shade.

'You should have just said, "I'm not going. You can't make me," and left it at that. What could they do? They're not going to physically pick you up and put you on the plane.'

'I know, but they're already so suspicious about everything. You don't know what my parents are like.'

'They're lovely,' said Caroline. 'Much nicer than mine.'

'That makes it harder to argue with them. Anyway, we're not going until next weekend, so until then I'll just have to make the most of being here.'

They sat in silence, each reflecting on what 'making the most of being here' meant. A pigeon hobbled towards them and began pecking at some crumbs on the step.

'Oh, look,' said Sara. 'Poor thing. It's missing a couple of toes. I wonder if it feels pain in the same way that we would?'

Caroline gazed at the pigeon, unmoved, and then looked at Sara.

'After what we've done, don't you think it's just a tiny bit hypocritical to get upset about a crippled pigeon?'

'No.'

'You can't do things like that every week and then—'

'Not *every* week, Caro. Don't exaggerate.'

'All right,' Caroline conceded. 'Not every week. But it wasn't a one-off either.'

After they killed the sheep, there had been an unspoken acknowledgement that something similar would probably happen again. Whichever way you looked at it – as the price to be paid for the pleasures of the bacchanals, or as a sick kind of pleasure in itself – it was inevitable. Once you crossed a line, there was no going back.

Grace had predicted that Dionysus would encourage them in his usual, chillingly matter-of-fact way ('The more blood spilled, the more you enjoyed yourselves'), and she was right. She had also predicted that they would get used to the violence, although she could not have guessed how quickly.

In the aftermath of the second incident there had been no screaming, and she remembered Caroline humming as she washed her bloody hands in the drinking fountain. It was frightening how quickly something could become normal. But Grace had lost all sense of normality the moment the god walked into her life, and she knew it was easier not to fight it. If she accepted her life, however strange and violent it became, she was more likely to retain whatever was left of her sanity.

Before, she had survived by not thinking about it, but as the bacchanals grew wilder, avoidance became impossible. It was like seeing something burst into flames right in front of you and closing your eyes, or looking the other way. The bigger the fire, the more unnatural it was not to accept its existence. Grace had noticed that of the three of them it was Caroline, who quickly overcame any initial qualms to embrace every aspect of the bacchanals, who seemed the happiest. *Be like Caroline*, Grace told herself. *Don't just look at the fire – throw yourself into it.*

The last bacchanal before Sara's departure was messy, even by their usual standards. There had been a violent storm in the night, and although Grace only had the faintest memories the next morning – drums, lightning, slipping in the mud as she chased or was chased – the evidence was there. They had dirt and leaves in their hair, and their bare legs were streaked with mud and gore. Grace looked down at her dress and realised with dismay that it was beyond repair.

'A cow this time,' said Caroline, rubbing her head with the cleaner part of her arm. 'A bloody *cow*.'

'Where?'

'Over there, near that ruin.'

'Just the one?'

'Come and see for yourself.'

They stood near the carcass and tried not to breathe too deeply.

'We can't just leave it,' Sara said at last.

'We can't move it. Are you out of your mind?'

'Maybe she's right.' Caroline looked thoughtful. 'Do either of you know how to start a fire?'

'No.'

'No.'

'Well, how hard can it be? You take two sticks...'

Caroline began rubbing the wood together, while Grace and Sara watched, becoming increasingly impatient.

'It's too damp, Caro. Give up.'

'I think I read somewhere,' said Sara, 'that cows have dangerously high levels of methane in their stomachs. If you did start a fire, mightn't it explode?'

'I don't know.' Caroline dropped the sticks. 'I'm not a scientist. Do you want to have a go?'

'Forget it,' said Grace. 'It's getting late.'

Sara took a couple of tentative steps closer to the cow and muttered something under her breath.

'What's she doing?' Grace asked Caroline.

'Praying.'

'To who? Dionysus?'

'It had better not be any other god.'

At home Grace hid her filthy dress beneath a loose floorboard in the bathroom. She hoped that she was the only one in the family who had noticed the floorboard, because it would be very difficult to explain the collection of bloodied rags. When the coast was clear she would find a way of disposing of them properly – perhaps in a neighbour's bin – but she was still waiting for the right moment.

After soaking in cold water for an hour or so she wrapped herself in a towel and walked down the hallway towards her bedroom.

'Grace.'

She turned and saw Barbara standing behind her.

'What?'

'Come into my room for a minute.'

'Wait, let me get dressed first.'

'No, come now.'

Barbara rarely initiated a conversation with her, and it was especially out of character to invite someone into her room. In the past Grace had been strictly forbidden from entering Barbara's room, and now she was obediently following her into that dark, cluttered space, curious about what Barbara could possibly want.

'Sit down,' said Barbara.

'I'll get your bed all wet.'

'That doesn't matter. No, sit over here. Closer to the window.'

'What's going on?'

'You tell me.'

Barbara closed the door and turned towards Grace. She looked concerned, even upset. Barbara was usually so calm and indifferent to everything that Grace was unsettled to see her like this. She came to sit beside Grace and made her turn slightly, to get a better view of her back.

'How did this happen?'

'How did *what* happen?'

'There's a massive scratch – more like a cut – all the way down your back.'

'Oh.' She turned to look, but it was out of her range of vision. She needed a mirror.

'Hang on, have you only just realised? Were you not aware of it until…' Barbara trailed off, and cautiously placed a fingertip on the edge of the cut. 'Does it hurt?'

'Not really.'

Grace felt oddly calm. She didn't know how she was going to answer any of Barbara's questions, but somehow she trusted her not to be unreasonable about it. She was grateful that it had been Barbara who noticed, and not their mother.

'It looks really bad. I mean, I can't imagine what caused it. You have to tell me.'

'I can't.'

'Why not?'

'I…'

'Don't you know?'

Barbara was sounding increasingly horrified, and Grace decided that the best approach was to be as honest as she could.

'Yes and no. I have some idea. It's really difficult to explain.'

'Try.'

'No, I can't.'

'It's all right to have secrets, but not when it involves you getting hurt like this. Go and look in the mirror.'

Grace stood up and turned her back to the mirror above the dressing table. It was unfortunate that out of all the cuts, bites and claw marks she had received over the last few months, this had to be the one that Barbara noticed. Though not particularly deep it was long, and so fresh that it was still a vivid shade of red, blossoming into purple at the edges. It looked worse than it felt, and she wished that, for once, it were the other way round.

'You're not going to tell Mummy about this, are you?'

'Grace, I have to. She has to know.'

'No, she doesn't. Promise you won't tell her.'

'I can't promise you anything.'

'If you tell her…' Grace willed herself not to panic. There had to be a solution.

'What?'

'I'll tell her about…'

'*What?*'

'Mauro.'

A pause.

'I'll tell her,' said Grace slowly, 'about you and Mauro.'

Until that moment she hadn't even put her suspicion into words in her own head. To be saying it out loud seemed ludicrous, blasphemous. But she had said it. Out of sheer desperation, she had played a card without even knowing what it was.

'You wouldn't,' said Barbara. She had gone pale.

I was right, thought Grace, her heart racing. *My God, I was right.*

There was another, longer pause, as she calculated what to say. She had won, but she had to be careful.

'I will,' said Grace. 'I'll tell her everything. She ought to know, after all.'

'I'm going to tell her. *We're* going to tell her. But not yet. It can't come from you.'

'How long has it been going on?' Grace didn't want to give away how little she knew, but she couldn't resist asking.

'Not that long. I mean… depending on how you define it. A few months, I suppose.'

'How awful,' said Grace, who was not yet able to comprehend the scale of the awfulness. Unlike Barbara, she hadn't had time to think about the repercussions.

'I really don't want to talk about it.'

'Good, because I don't want to know about it.'

'So you won't say anything?'

'Well, no. Not for the time being at least. But only if you keep this quiet.' Grace gestured to the scar. Barbara nodded.

'Do you…' She cleared her throat. 'Do you want me to put some cream on it?'

'If you've got some.'

As Barbara rubbed the antiseptic cream into her back, Grace watched herself in the mirror. She always looked different in different mirrors. Unrecognisable sometimes.

'That'll do, thanks.'

Grace looked at her reflection, at the reflection of Barbara's pale, anguished face behind her. Two strangers stared back at her.

VII

'You've got a terrific scab. Ugh. If it were me, I'd probably be picking at it.'

Having finished her inspection of Grace's back, Caroline zipped up her dress.

'I seem to have so many more of these marks than you,' said Grace. 'Maybe you do this to me. Ever thought of that?'

'It's possible.' Caroline ran her fingernails over Grace's arm. 'Maybe I transform into a leopard or something and maul you. That would explain a lot. It'd help us to come to terms with the killings, too.'

'You mean you'd rather think of yourself turning into some kind of wild animal than staying human and doing... that.'

'Exactly. Even if we don't metamorphose – is that the word? – metamorphose into a beast, there must be some kind of transformation. We can't remain completely ourselves the whole time. Otherwise we wouldn't feel so strange. Don't you think?'

'We could ask him.'

'We could, but we wouldn't get an answer.'

'By the way,' said Grace, 'I had a very awkward conversation with my sister.'

Part of her would have preferred not to talk about it – talking about it meant thinking about it – but it was too shocking not to share. Caroline was usually the first one to know all the gossip, and it was perversely satisfying to be the one breaking the news for a change.

'I can't believe it,' said Caroline, when Grace had finished. It seemed she was still shockable in spite of everything. 'That's repulsive. *Mauro?*'

'I know.'

'I mean, aside from the fact that it's practically incest, what on earth does she see in him? He's so fat and beardy and *old*.'

'He's forty-five.'

'Exactly.' Caroline shuddered. 'Still, what luck, right? She can't blab. You're safe.'

'For now. I know I should be relieved, but I keep thinking about it. It's so wrong.'

'If only your mother knew. Her deviant daughters…'

'I'd rather not think of myself as a deviant.'

'You are, though. You deviate from normal standards of behaviour, what with your lesbianism and your violent tendencies.'

'Well, so do you.'

'I know,' Caroline smiled. 'I'm a deviant too. Speaking of which…'

Caroline went to the drawer where she kept her stolen treasures and pulled out a crumpled newspaper article. Grace's heart sank.

'Oh God, what is it?'

'An obituary for our cow.'

'Be serious, Caro. What does it say?'

Grace grabbed the bit of paper, but the words swam before her eyes and she couldn't make sense of a single sentence.

'Nothing much,' said Caroline. 'More speculation about dogs, but of course they haven't a clue. The only thing that worried me is that the first article was on page twenty-three, and this one is on page fifteen. We're moving closer to the front. We'll be headlining soon.'

'It's not funny.'

'No, but it's interesting, isn't it? Imagine if this becomes a proper news story and they actually start to investigate it. This amazing, unsolved mystery captivating the whole country.'

'Why are you fantasising about it? It would be an absolute nightmare.'

'Oh, but they'd never suspect us. They'd accuse a million men before they ever got to us. We're girls. We could *never* do a thing like that.'

'There are lots of female criminals who have been caught. Murderers, even.'

'It's only a few animals. We're not murderers.'

'Yet.'

'Yet!' Caroline giggled.

Grace looked at Caroline and saw that her gaze was slightly unfocused. Was she drunk? It was three o'clock in the afternoon and they hadn't seen Dionysus for more than a day, but stranger things had happened.

'You know, Caro,' she said, stroking Caroline's hair, 'having all these secrets means we have to be more careful – discreet. You don't take unnecessary risks that might make people suspicious.'

'I'm *so* discreet.'

'You're really not.'

'I'm discreet and my parents are stupid,' said Caroline softly.

One night it was raining, so they went to his room in the Ghetto instead of the fields. Grace was secretly relieved, as the ritual of cycling down the Roman road, drinking, tearing an animal to pieces and doing God knows what else, and then cycling home the next morning was becoming exhausting. The bacchanals in his room would never be quite as intense or pleasurable, but there was the consolation of knowing that home was a fifteen-minute walk away.

As soon as they arrived, soaked in spite of umbrellas, she knew that something was wrong. He was sitting cross-legged on the floor, staring at them, and the wine was dripping from his hair. A thin stream trickled down his forehead and into the corner of his eye, but he made no move to wipe it away.

For a moment Grace stared back at him, while Caroline started to drink one of the cups of wine he had set out for them.

'Caro, wait.'

'What for?'

Grace could not find the words to articulate her unease. Even if she had been able to, she could hardly have spoken right in front of him. He wasn't speaking, but he was surely listening.

She took slow, reluctant sips of the wine, trying to ignore how similar it tasted to the strange, bitter wine she had once licked from her fingers. It didn't taste bad, just different. It had a peculiar density; if she had spilled it, it would not have sprayed but oozed.

'Mmm...' Caroline was lying on the floor making low, almost carnal sounds of pleasure. Grace had only drunk half as much and the room was already changing shape. As she slipped she gazed at Caroline, as if those vacant blue eyes held the key to all the mysteries of the universe.

Outside a dog was barking, and under the spell of the wine the bark multiplied, surrounding them on all sides, trapping them in a chamber of mirrors and echoes. The last she saw of Dionysus was his face floating somewhere above her, his eyes rolled back so that there was nothing but white.

She was stranded on the bank of a river beneath a black sky. The water was black too, the waves crested with silver. There was no light, not even a moon, and yet she could see everything with horrible clarity. She stared into the river and saw that it was full of bodies – some human, some animal. Some of them were only limbs, random arms that reached out for her. Even though they didn't belong to a body they were horribly alive, writhing in the water, pale and rotting fingers beckoning her to join them.

The river was so wide it might have been an ocean, and it was too dark to see to the other side. She knew that the only way to safety was across that terrible expanse of water, yet crossing it was unthinkable. There was no boat, and if she tried to swim the bodies would drown her. Even as she stood on land they were trying to grasp her, a severed hand or an animal's head straining out of the water.

Then the screaming began, faint at first but increasingly piercing. Some dark, feverish instinct surged through her and she knew it was Caroline, screaming for her on the other side of the river. They were both in imminent danger; she understood that now. She began to run, in an awful kind of slow motion as if she were running on the moon. The faster she tried to run, the slower she moved. Her heart was pounding and she was delirious with fear, knowing that she was running not just to save Caroline, but to save herself too. Someone was chasing her. *He* was chasing her. Even without looking behind, she knew. One moment he was a hunting dog, then a bull, then a leopard and then, infinitely more terrifying, formless.

She was running out of breath and he was getting ever closer. She could hear his footsteps thundering behind her and feel his burning breath. When he caught her, she knew what he would do to her, and the mere thought of it made her weep with fear.

The terror was all-consuming. He was right behind her now and he could grab her at any moment, but he knew he had all the time in the universe. They could play this game forever. Caroline's screams were fading in the distance.

Sobbing, Grace realised what she had to do. The second he touched her she threw herself into the ground with all her strength and felt herself sinking as the earth grew over her. It happened so quickly that he was left clawing impotently at the ground, bellowing with rage and frustration.

I'm going to live forever in the black earth beside the black river beneath the black sky but at least I'm safe from him and no one can touch me any more because I'm dead dead dead.

The soil was in her eyes and then she woke up, her whole body damp with sweat. She could hear Caroline retching, and as she sat up, trembling, she realised that she needed to be sick too. She waited until Caroline had finished and then crawled to the dirty, windowless little bathroom, where she was sick again and again. They took it in turns, and when there was finally nothing left they lay side by side on the hard floor, shaking, and waited for the light.

Dionysus was still there, or at least his body was. He was slumped over on the floor, resembling nothing more than an empty shell. The wine was still dripping from his lips, the only sign that he had not been dead for centuries. While the wine flowed there was some life left in him.

Eventually it became lighter, and they could hear the dog barking again. Somewhere nearby, a TV was wishing the viewers good morning, then trailing off into a stream of incomprehensible vowels. Grace walked unsteadily to the window and saw that the rain had stopped. The garden below was almost eerie in its stillness, empty but for the solitary bird singing in the orange tree.

'I want to go home.' Caroline's voice was hoarse, her hair so damp it was plastered to her scalp.

'Can we leave him like this?' Grace gestured towards the god.

'I think he's already left us. It doesn't matter. I need to go home.'

Grace went with her. She was too scared to be alone after what they had just gone through, and Caroline said there was a good chance that her parents would be out. When they reached Caroline's room they stopped only to take off their shoes and turn on the fan, and then collapsed on the bed. The open shutters were letting all the heat and light in, but after a night running through endless darkness, the sunshine was comforting.

Despite the heat Grace felt the need to touch someone, to remember that she belonged to the world above, not the underworld of her vision. When Caroline felt Grace's fingers on her arm she flinched.

'Get off. It's too hot.'

They slept for a while, drifting between light and shadow, and then found themselves talking to each other. Grace had no memory of the beginning of the conversation; perhaps she had been talking in her sleep.

'I don't want to talk about it. It was too awful.'

'But was it the same as mine? The black sky, the river…'

'Yes, yes, it was the same. I remember everything.'

'How could he let it happen to us?'

'*Let*? What if he *made* it happen?'

'Why?'

'He's sick.'

'We're sick.'

'Not as sick as him.'

'It wasn't *him* chasing us, though, by the river – it was—'

'*Don't.*'

'I was so scared.'

'I've never been more terrified in my entire life.'

'I can't believe he did that to us.'

'He was probably suffering even more.'

'Even so.'

'Even so *what?*'

'I can't really think straight right now, but I think, I think – we're in really deep.'

'I know.'

'Too deep. Maybe we have to end it.'

'You don't mean that. We couldn't.'

'I don't think I can take another night like that.'

'It might not happen again.'

'You can't be sure.'

'I know, that's why I said *might*.'

'He'll explain. When he's better, he'll explain.'

'I don't want explanations. I want to feel human.'

Grace put her arm around Caroline, and this time she stayed still.

VIII

The clock was out of sight, but the half-light that slipped through the gaps in the shutters made her think that it must be close to dawn. It didn't matter when or even if she slept, now that school was over, but it was disorientating sometimes, waking up with no idea of what time it was.

She raised her head and saw him; she was surprised by how little surprise she felt. He was slowly spinning on the swivel chair next to her desk. Although it was too dark to be sure, his hair looked clean and his eyes had colour once more; they no longer rolled back in his head, white and terrifying.

When he noticed that she was staring, he stopped spinning.

'I'm sorry,' he said, not sounding the least bit sorry. Grace was too tired to mind, and besides, you couldn't expect the same level of sincerity from gods as you could from humans.

'Are you better now?'

'I think so. The... *sickness* has passed. It was terrible but it passed.'

'Will it happen again?'

'Yes.'

'What does that mean for us?'

'You cannot have faith – true faith – without some element of danger.'

'So we're going to go through it all again. The river and the chase. That's what you're saying.'

'It's a possibility. When you worship someone as unstable as myself...'

'Unstable?'

He stared at her for a minute, as if waiting for her to work it out for herself. When she remained silent he sighed; she had never heard anything quite like it. It was a haunting, gasping sound that seemed to fill the room.

'I shouldn't expect you to understand. How could you? It's too much to ask of a girl.'

'And if I were a boy?'

'Or a boy, or any other gender. You're all the same.'

'I still don't understand what you want from me. Nothing I do ever seems to be good enough for you.'

'No, it never will be.'

'Then why do you come here in the middle of the night and sit there and look at me, when there's absolutely nothing I can do to help you?'

They had come full circle. She had a sudden flashback to one of those early conversations in her bedroom, when she had asked him, 'What do you want from me?' He was stronger now, and she was changed in ways she could not begin to understand, yet the dynamic of their relationship had, in some sense, always been the same.

'You wish I hadn't come.'

'No, it's not that. It just seems like… it's like you're always here.'

'Yes, I am always here,' said Dionysus. 'Still here. Still *here*.'

His final word was uttered with such menace that it chilled her. He disappeared, leaving no trace of his presence apart from a strange, almost metallic scent. It took her a few seconds to recognise it – the bad wine. She shivered and pulled the sheet up to her neck, relieved to be alone again. If only he would save his visitations for daylight, when she was awake and dressed and more able to cope with his fits of melancholy. Despite her tiredness it was not until a couple of hours later that she was finally able to fall asleep again, dreamless in the daylight.

One afternoon, bored of lying in bed, she went to a museum. Grace avoided museums and art galleries wherever possible, as they made her tired; she associated them with Mauro attempting to explain everything in an embarrassingly loud voice, and her father lagging several rooms behind in his eagerness to read everything, making the visit last hours.

The museum she had in mind was housed in a palace near the train station and was ignored by tourists and locals alike. In a city full of museums and art that you could see for free, in churches or in the middle of the street, it was easy to overlook a lesser-known museum with only a few statues and mosaics to recommend it.

Mauro had dragged them around there once, and Grace remembered very little about it except the horror of the mummified child, upsetting unsuspecting visitors who had only entered the room to look at the coin collection. Although she didn't have a specific memory of seeing one, she was sure that there must be at least one statue of Dionysus in the museum, and she was curious to see if those marble bodies looked any different once you had seen the real thing.

She had the museum to herself, just as she'd expected. She walked through silent galleries of columns and tombstones and fragmented torsos, paying no attention unless she caught a glimpse of a face. She was sure she would recognise the statue by its face, even if all the sculptures depicting male beauty or divinity looked more or less the same.

When she finally found him, in a room on the second floor, it was because of the ivy. She was disappointed to realise that the face told her nothing – it was only the ivy wreath in his hair and the frozen wine cup that made her recognise him. His arm was outstretched, the cup suspended in mid-air as if he were just about to offer it to her. She followed the lines of marble, from the outlines of his thigh muscles to the curls of his hair, and searched in vain for a familiar feature. This god was a stranger. The body was too small, too fixed, with no sense of the wild blood that pulsed through him. He was just a boy, so obviously based on a mortal model. She could not find the man she knew, let alone the god.

The eyes came closest. She took a step forward and looked up, into the empty eyes of the statue. Marble was not always so cold and unfeeling. She remembered Mauro showing her the figures by Bernini, the spectrum of emotion in those white faces. A talented sculptor could make marble express an infinite variety of passion, and yet the gods were all eerily alike. Apollo, Dionysus and Aphrodite gazed across the galleries with a chilling indifference. This serenity masked an eternity of unknowable suffering, yet Grace knew those eyes. She had followed them down that dark road; they had watched over her in the night, in woods, ruins and bedrooms. She gave the sign next to the statue a cursory glance and then walked away.

On the top floor there were mosaics of ships and sea monsters, which were beautiful, but they didn't really interest her. Then she walked into a room within a room, walls that transported her to a Roman garden. There were trees drooping with the weight of their fruit – fat pomegranates and great globed oranges – while painted birds perched in the branches. The blue sky was cracked, threatening to flake away.

Admiring this artificial garden was a woman with dyed red hair. When Grace walked around the bench she realised who it was, and spent a few seconds debating whether it was too late to retreat.

It was too late. Miss Seymour turned and saw her.

'Grace, what a surprise! I didn't expect to see you here.'

'I just came to see… you know.'

There were few things more embarrassing than encountering a teacher outside school, and Miss Seymour was the worst. She would probably keep talking, trapping Grace in the garden room with a monologue on Roman art.

'Isn't it extraordinary?' Miss Seymour's heavily ringed fingers gestured towards the fruit trees. 'This was a room in a villa belonging to the wife of Augustus. We think of emperors and royalty living in rooms of gold and marble, but for her the ultimate luxury was the simple beauty of the natural world. The colours would have changed depending on the time of day, and they've tried to replicate that with the lights. Look.'

Grace looked, and saw that the walls were slowly, magically changing under lights that dimmed and brightened, mimicking the effects of the moving sun. She sat on the bench beside Miss Seymour and watched the sky transform, grateful for the silence. Perhaps after a few minutes it would be acceptable to tiptoe out of the room, leaving Miss Seymour transfixed by the trees.

'Are you having a good summer, Grace?'

'It's been all right. I'm not looking forward to results coming out, though.'

'Oh, yes. I marked your paper. Yes…'

Miss Seymour trailed off, as if mildly embarrassed by the subject.

'What about your summer, Miss?'

'It's been quite pleasant, apart from the heat. I can't stand the heat. I come here for the air conditioning as much as the exhibitions.'

There was a pause while Grace tried to think of some polite phrase that would allow her to escape.

'I hope you don't mind me asking,' said Miss Seymour, 'but... is everything all right?'

'Yes. Why wouldn't it be?'

Grace suddenly became conscious of her bare arms and the marks that were visible even in the artificial twilight of the garden.

'Sometimes I thought I should have said something,' said Miss Seymour.

'I don't know what you mean.'

'Not everyone would notice, but if you've been through that kind of unhappiness, you know.'

'I'm fine. Really, I am.'

'Let me see.'

Miss Seymour peered through her glasses at the long, thin marks that ran down the inside of Grace's forearm.

'Scissors, I suppose?'

Grace tugged at her sleeves, mortified. But then the mist of panic and confusion suddenly cleared, and she realised that there was only one response that would save her.

'Yes.'

'I knew it,' said Miss Seymour, with a forced flatness to disguise her sense of triumph. 'I've seen it too many times. You know, the others thought I should mind my own business, but I was quite sure...'

'The others?' Grace was startled.

'I'm sorry, I shouldn't have said that. But I'm afraid we speak quite candidly in the staff room, just as you girls do when we're not around. I wasn't the only one with concerns.'

'You don't need to be concerned,' said Grace. 'It's just... a phase. Look, these are old. I won't do it again.'

'Ah, I wish I could believe you.'

Another visitor entered the room. The man didn't look like an

English-speaker, but it was safer not to take the risk. Grace waited for an agonising twenty seconds as the man glanced around the room before leaving, and then asked, 'What do you mean?'

'Some habits are hard to break, even with the best of intentions. And you know that I have a duty of care…'

Grace's mind reeled.

'But you wouldn't tell anyone.'

'I have a duty of care,' Miss Seymour repeated. 'If I had a daughter, I would want to know.'

'*No.*' It came out as a gasp. 'You can't tell my mother.'

'I don't really have a choice, Grace. Not to act would be… well, irresponsible. Quite aside from the forms they make us sign, I feel I have a responsibility.'

'*Please* don't say anything. I promise, I won't do it again.'

'If your parents know, they can get you the help you need.'

'If my parents knew, I would…' Grace hesitated, summoning up the courage. 'I would hurt myself. I mean *really* hurt myself.'

Until now, Miss Seymour had retained her composure. But with four words, it was as if Grace had knocked all the air out of her. Miss Seymour took off her glasses and started cleaning them on the sleeve of her cardigan as she tried to think of what to say.

'You know,' she said at last, still compulsively cleaning, 'you're putting me in a very difficult position.'

'I know,' said Grace.

'I have no way of knowing if you – if you *meant* what you said just now.'

'I did. I do.'

'I'm only trying to help.'

Now that the panic was beginning to subside, Grace couldn't help but feel a little sorry for her teacher. She looked so pitiful without her glasses, small blue eyes blinking. She was only trying to be nice, in her own misguided way.

'The most helpful thing you could do,' said Grace slowly, 'is leave me alone. I don't mean to be rude. But I have to deal with this on my own.'

'Mmm.' Miss Seymour put her glasses back on and then looked

pointedly away from Grace, turning her attention to the painted garden.

'I'll be fine. I *am* fine.'

'Mmm,' said Miss Seymour again.

Grace glanced at her watch.

'I really ought to go.'

Miss Seymour sighed and turned back to look at her.

'Please take care of yourself.'

'I will.'

'And maybe we can have a little chat when you come back in September.'

'All right.'

'Goodbye.'

'Thanks, Miss. Goodbye.'

Grace stood up and walked away, out of the garden. It was incredible, she reflected, that a chance encounter with her teacher in a museum had almost exposed her. All the risks she had taken, all the adults who might have so easily stumbled upon her secret, and it had been Miss Seymour who had tried to save her.

Caroline would laugh. Even the god might be amused. But they didn't know. They hadn't been there, so they would never know how stressful the conversation had been. In an alternate universe with a more persistent Miss Seymour, Grace could almost see herself breaking down and confessing the truth, right there on the bench. *Almost.*

Her hair stuck to the back of her neck, and her damp clothes clung to her. Only her throat was dry. Grace took the stairs two at a time, and came out into the sunlight.

IX

'It's disappointing, Grace. Very disappointing. What have you been doing all year?'

Her mother put the piece of paper on the table and then looked at her expectantly, waiting for an answer. Grace wished she would at least put the paper back in the envelope. From where she was standing she could still see the black columns of ink, those shaming numbers.

'I tried my best and it wasn't good enough. What do you want me to say?'

'*This* is your best? Forty per cent in Maths?'

'You know I've never been any good at Maths. I can't help it.'

'But even in the subjects that are supposedly your stronger ones – English, fifty per cent, Classics, fifty-eight per cent.'

'It doesn't matter. They still let you back next year, whatever you get. It's not like I'm going to get kicked out.'

'What's the point of you going to school – of us paying for you to go to school – when you're not willing to make the slightest bit of effort?'

'She can't help it if she's not academic,' said Barbara, who had been listening from the other side of the kitchen.

'Shut up, Barbara,' said Grace.

'Barbara, leave us, please. It's not helpful.'

Barbara left. Grace couldn't remember her mother looking this upset since the separation. She wasn't angry, just deeply disappointed. Grace was used to being made to feel inadequate, but not quite like this. She felt a sudden flash of anger.

'All you care about is my marks.'

'It's not all I care about, but I do care. Of course I care. Any parent would.'

'You think I'm stupid, or that I don't try.'

'I don't think you're stupid, but I do think—'

'You just judge me, and you never even bother to wonder why I'm like this. You don't care.'

'Of course I care.'

'You don't care about *me*.'

'Grace, you're getting a little hysterical now. Why don't we leave this conversation for another time?'

'Even my teachers care more than you do. When was the last time you asked me if everything was all right and meant it?'

'Fine. Is everything all right?'

Grace had a vision that lasted a split second, where she revealed her scratched arms and slipped out of her dress to reveal the scar on her back. She took a deep breath.

'Everything's wonderful. Thanks for asking.'

She needed that escape more than ever. She drank the wine as if it were water in the desert, as if she feared it would run out even while knowing that it would last forever. He would flow until the end of time. He raised the bottomless cup to her lips, and then to Caroline's, and watched them descend.

When Grace opened her eyes the next day she had forgotten everything. The night was a blank; the day was a blank. She had been crawling through the grass for minutes or hours, head spinning, when she realised that Caroline had been there too. She couldn't remember Caroline's presence the previous evening, and in the haze of the morning she could barely even picture her face, but a faint, whispering voice of reason told her that Caroline must have been there.

Now there were no signs of her. There were only trees, so many that they hid the sky. The fallen pine needles stabbed her hands and knees, and she forced herself to stand.

'Caro? Caro, where are you?'

No response. She stumbled on through the woods, oblivious to the fresh cuts on her arms and shoulders. She had to find Caroline. Nothing else mattered.

She walked with a new sense of urgency, calling Caroline's name. At last she came to a clearing where birds were singing, and saw

Caroline sitting in the middle. She was dreamily going through the motions of putting on her torn stockings.

'Didn't you hear me? I was looking for you.'

'I heard someone calling my name, but I didn't know it was you.'

'Who else would it be?'

Caroline looked up and smiled – a smile that made Grace come to a halt and stay where she was, on the edge of the circle.

'Grace, the most exquisite thing has happened. You won't believe it.'

Caroline went on to tell the story in such detail that Grace was forced to believe it. How the god had taken her by the hand, taken her here, kissed her with a mouth that burned, filled her completely, doing it again and again until she thought she couldn't take it any more, until she cried out and there were bats and strange birds, a leopard at her back, the feeling rising up within her and then bursting, while he was pulsating, transforming, turning the moon into the sun.

'I can still feel him now,' said Caroline. 'It's like he's still inside me. It's like...'

Grace didn't stay to listen. Her world collapsing, she ran back the way she had come.

Because she was running, she tripped. She tripped over a time-worn stone in the road and fell on her knees, adding another cut to her collection. For a moment she stayed where she had fallen, breathing hard, until she became suddenly, inexplicably convinced that someone was watching her. Raising her head, she saw a man staring at her through iron railings. For one mad second she thought that he was in prison, or else *she* was in prison and he was on the other side of the bars.

Then she forced herself to look up, to look round, and saw that he was standing behind the gates of an enormous villa. She could just about see a fountain in front of the house, and a profusion of potted plants. She hadn't realised until now that there were any houses on this road, and it was surreal to think of families living among the ruins and the cypresses, perhaps dismissing the screams they heard in the night as the cries of birds.

The man was talking at her, but his words were noises. He looked too shabbily dressed to live in a house that grand. A gardener, perhaps.

Grace shook her head, hoping to communicate the correct response to whatever he had said. *No, I don't understand you. No, I don't need help. No, I can't tell you why.*

The man was becoming more agitated, reaching through the bars towards her. Still shaking her head, Grace got to her feet and walked on, back to the city. She wanted her bedroom more than anything in the world, even though she knew that as soon as the door was closed, the tears would come. She couldn't cry now, while she was out in the daylight and so focused on putting one foot in front of the other, but later she could give in, and perhaps even find some relief in her tears.

Her family didn't question why she locked herself in her bedroom all day. Her mother assumed she was still sulking about her marks, and thought it better to leave her alone. Grace kept mechanically getting up to change the record, hoping that the music would drown out the sound of her crying. She deliberately chose the most tortured-sounding singers she could think of, melancholy women whose voices seemed to strain to breaking point.

Turning over the record for the fourth or fifth time, Grace crept back into bed. It was a double betrayal; that was what really destroyed her. If Caroline had slept with anyone else in the world it would have broken her heart, but *him*? She knew that they all lost control and could not be held entirely responsible for their actions, but she was convinced that Caroline would have done it sober. Heartless, fickle, horrible Caroline, who knew what men wanted and would give it willingly, without sparing a thought for anyone else's feelings.

She might have eventually come to terms with a conventional infidelity, even forgiven Caroline one day. But the strangeness of the situation overwhelmed her, making her feel stupid and helpless. It was something that was not supposed to exist outside Ovid. Worst of all, buried somewhere deep beneath the hurt and anger was the squirming jealousy. Although she would not fully admit it to herself, she envied Caroline's pleasure – an experience that nothing else could compare to. She thought of that radiant smile in the woods and felt sick.

She hated Caroline. She would have hated him too, if it were possible to hate a god, but instead she focused all her energy on hating Caroline. The next time the record stopped she didn't bother to turn it over again, as she was no longer crying. Instead she lay there quietly, imagining kissing Caroline and then tearing her body apart with her bare hands. She tore her limb from limb, watching the blood run down the walls, and when it was over she did it again.

She must have slept a while, and when she opened her eyes he was there, as she knew he would be. He sat at the end of her bed, so close she could feel the warmth of his body.

'Go away,' she said. 'Please.'

'What's wrong?'

'You know.'

'I can't read minds, Grace.'

That was a lie, she knew. He wanted to make her say it.

'What you did to Caroline.'

'What did I do to Caroline?'

Grace sat up and stared at him, incredulous.

'You can remember things that happened two thousand years ago, but you can't remember sleeping with Caroline?'

Dionysus frowned and was silent for a moment, as if he were trying to search the vast and cluttered expanse of his memory.

'How strange,' he said at last. 'I should remember that.'

'It doesn't matter. I don't want to talk about it. Leave, please.'

'Ah, I see. Jealous again. Poor Grace.'

He stroked her arm and she felt some kind of charge, like an electric current, rush through her. She moved away and told him to leave again, sounding considerably less assertive this time. She hated it when he was miserable, but now that he was happy – or temporarily satisfied, at least – it was somehow worse.

'It's only sex,' he said. 'Nobody died.'

'I wish Caroline were dead.'

'She will be one day. So will you. For now, try to enjoy life.'

She closed her eyes to make him go away. When she opened them again, there was a full glass of wine on her bedside table, ruby red and smelling of the south.

X

The sleeves were long enough, but the neckline was just a little too low, revealing the edge of a wound. Better not to risk it. As the dress was discarded on the changing-room floor her mother, who was waiting on the other side of the door, asked her if it fitted.

'It fits, but I'm not sure I like it that much.'

'Why don't you let me come in and have a look?'

Grace heard the doorknob rattle and panicked.

'Don't, I'm in the middle of changing.'

'You shouldn't be so self-conscious. It wouldn't be the end of the world if I saw you in your underwear, would it?'

Not the end of the world, but pretty bad. Grace turned to look at herself in the mirror and inspected the damage. Her back was healing well, but there were so many marks that would be difficult to explain, and everything looked worse under the harsh changing-room lights.

Her mother had promised her shopping and afternoon tea. It was as if she was being rewarded for her poor exam results. Pushing through the crowds in the city centre and trying on clothes was not exactly enjoyable, especially in the July heat, but she appreciated that her mother was trying to make her feel better. Grace suspected her mother was trying to make herself feel better as well, stung by the accusation that she didn't care about her daughter. But Grace was prepared to make the most of it, and she was grateful for any distraction. Lying in bed, listening to records and ignoring Caroline's phone calls, was becoming boring.

In the end Grace chose one of the long-sleeved dresses, insisting that she preferred it to the more summery ones. Then they went to the English tearooms by the steps, a strange little time-warped place that had been designed to intensify expatriates' homesickness. Grace's mother had never gone there in the early days, but after a couple of years she had become a regular.

It was too hot for scones, but they ordered them anyway and spent half an hour picking at them between sips of tea.

'Perhaps it would help,' said her mother, buttering the remains of her scone, 'if you told me what was going on with you and Caroline.'

'You don't need to know. *She* knows what she did. I'm waiting for her to apologise.'

'She can't apologise unless you give her a chance to talk.'

Grace shrugged and looked out of the window, watching the rose-sellers and the sun-drunk tourists staggering down the steps. She was glad to be inside where it was cool and tasted like England, but she wished she could extract herself from the conversation.

'I know I've never been Caroline's greatest fan, but I do think you should talk to her. All problems can be resolved through talking.'

'That's really not true.'

'I know how horrible it is to be upset with a friend, but if you talk to her I think you'll feel much better. And however upset you are… well, that passes with time.'

'Not everything can be fixed with a conversation, and not every feeling passes. You don't understand. I hate her. I never want to see her again.'

'This is the problem with these intense attachments.'

'What do you mean?'

'I know she's your best friend, but I've always thought you were a little bit *too* close. You know it isn't healthy. At your age you should have lots of friends.'

'I've got Sara.'

'Lots, not two.'

'Well, it's one now. And you're right about me and Caroline. It isn't healthy.'

Eventually Caroline grew tired of having her phone calls ignored, so she decided to turn up at Grace's flat. From her bedroom Grace could hear the muffled voices of Caroline and her mother in the hallway. Caroline was talking in that mature, self-possessed voice she used for conversations with adults. Grace hated it. She hated Caroline. She even hated her mother a little, for letting Caroline into the building even though Grace had made it quite clear that she never wanted to see her again.

'Can I come in?' Caroline was knocking on the door.

'I didn't even want you in the building, so why would I let you into my bedroom?'

Caroline came in anyway and sat down on the chair by the desk. It had only been four days, but the hours of tears and fury Grace had spent thinking of Caroline made her look different. She was almost a stranger.

'If you've come to apologise…' Grace began.

'I haven't come to apologise.'

Grace had been so convinced that the conversation would begin with Caroline saying sorry that she didn't know what to do next. She stared at Caroline and tried to detect a trace of a motive in her steady gaze.

'Why are you here then?'

'To see what's the matter with you. To get you to come back. You can't really have a *bacchae* of one. It's a bit absurd.'

'You're not going to say sorry?'

'What for? Because I enjoyed myself in a way that didn't involve you? Is that it?'

'You cheated and then sat there looking all smug, as if I should congratulate you.'

'It wasn't cheating.'

'How can you say that? It was the exact definition of cheating. Sleeping with another person – well, not a person… but that's beside the point.'

'It's like I told you before, Grace – we're not married.'

'No, but we're something, aren't we?'

'For God's sake, don't cry.'

'I'm not.'

'I never made any promises. Neither did you. Our… friendship, whatever you want to call it, has absolutely nothing to do with anything else. I'm not going to be made to feel guilty for something perfectly natural—'

'There it is again, *natural*.'

'—that I did when I was out of my mind anyway. To claim that we have no responsibility for our actions when we kill and then to give me a hard time for this… It's hypocritical.'

Grace was wiping away the tears, and for a while she could not speak. Caroline came to sit beside her and handed her a tissue.

'Look, I'm sorry that you're upset, but I'm not sorry that I did it. I'd do it again. *You* would do it.'

Grace shook her head.

'You don't say "no" to him,' said Caroline. 'When have we ever said "no"?'

'I just can't believe...' Grace took a deep, shuddering breath and tried again. 'I just can't believe that the only reason you're here is because you can't do the bacchanals without me. You don't care about my feelings at all, do you?'

'God, I said I was sorry. What more do you want?'

Caroline was becoming visibly impatient, and the look in her eyes had hardened.

'You're so un – *dis*loyal,' said Grace shakily.

'That's not true. I'm devoted to him, and after all we've been through together...' Caroline stood up. 'When you're ready to stop crying about it, call me, okay? You don't have any idea how much he needs us. He's wasting away while you're crying about nothing. Where's *your* loyalty?'

'Just shut up, Caro. Leave me alone.'

Caroline left, and Grace's repressed sobs came out at last. She had forgotten to put on a record, and after a while she heard some taps on the wall, from Barbara's bedroom.

Tap, tap, tap.

The wall was asking if she was all right. Grace didn't feel like moving to respond, and she wasn't sure how many taps signified 'No'. She was getting a headache. All she wanted was to be left alone, and she had Caroline appearing and Barbara tapping. Dionysus would probably arrive next, uninvited as always.

The tapping ceased, and a moment later she heard the distant swell of the song from Barbara's room, in mockery or sympathy. Everybody loved somebody, but what Dean Martin failed to mention was that not everybody was loved in return. Grace put the pillow over her head and waited for the song to end.

XI

She hated Caroline, but she loved her more. She loved *this*.

The world was shining, spinning, and she could taste it again. The wine flowed like a divine river, sweet and rich and so strong that a single cup was enough to send them reeling through the fields, hands outstretched. Even when they worshipped it was a game, a race, with the god hovering tantalisingly close and then vanishing. Sometimes she thought she could see him floating into space bit by bit, his body dissolving into stars and nothingness.

'I've missed this,' said Sara, gasping for breath, clutching at Grace's arm. 'So, so much.'

Sara had returned from her holiday so pale and withdrawn that her parents had sent her to see a doctor. The official diagnosis was anaemia – 'I might be anaemic as well,' Sara conceded – but the real cause of her illness had been the two-week separation from Dionysus. The god stroked her hair and told her that the cure was wine and a night in the fields. She would be back to her usual self in no time.

But despite his reassurances, murmured seductively into Sara's ear as they walked arm in arm down the Roman road, she seemed to have a new kind of fervour and desperation. Two weeks' separation had seemed like a lifetime to Sara, and she was convinced that she had missed out. She had to make up for it somehow, to prove to herself and to them that she was more devoted than ever. Grace, who remained lucid for a little longer, watched Sara tear frantically at her clothes and sprint screaming into the trees. It was not a scream of terror but of triumph, calling to the god and the awakening earth that she was giving herself to Dionysus, body and soul.

Caroline was already far ahead, lost in the night. In a brief interlude of awareness, before she slipped into the dark sea of wine and oblivion, Grace felt the insidious little pangs of jealousy, twisting around her heart like slender vines. Caroline should have been here with her, holding her hand, whispering and kissing her before the wine took over. Instead she was lost, somewhere on the other side of the trees, while Grace was left alone. Not truly alone, of course – the god was with her – but sometimes she needed Caroline's touch to guide her, to give her the courage to go through with it.

They had not talked about the argument again. Grace had neither forgotten nor forgiven, but she knew that Caroline was right. They all needed each other too badly to let one night come between them. When Sara returned, it became even more necessary to pretend that everything was normal. Grace could not seek Sara's sympathy without revealing the nature of her relationship with Caroline; however hurt she felt, she had to keep it hidden. Pretending that nothing had happened was much easier for Caroline, who fancied herself an actress, after all, but for Grace it was a strain. She tried to limit the time she spent in Caroline's company to the bacchanals, as she could forget her anger more easily under the numbing influence of wine.

One time when she was not as far gone as the others, she awoke early, when it was still dark. Sara and Caroline were nowhere to be seen, but she was shocked to see Dionysus lying in the grass, his chest heaving. Crawling closer, she saw that he was completely naked, his body covered in cuts and claw marks. Even in the dark she could tell the difference between blood and wine, and she was shocked by the depth of some of the wounds. One was so gaping she could have inserted several fingers into it.

'Oh my God,' she whispered, hardly able to form the words. 'What happened? What…'

'Don't touch me.' His voice was remarkably steady, given the state of his body. There was no humanity in his face, and for a moment she drew back, afraid. Somewhere in the half-light of her stupor it occurred to her that maybe this was what he wanted. It was the same masochistic instinct that had driven Christ to go willingly to the cross. Stupid, blasphemous thought. Grace laughed until she cried, and then crept closer to him. She wouldn't touch him, but she would lie near him, listening to his tortured breaths until the sun rose.

Sara's return coincided with the departure of Grace's mother, Mauro and Henry. Grace and Barbara had both been excused from the family holiday. Once, the thought of escaping to the beach and swimming in cold water would have been tempting, but now there were other temptations.

Grace dreaded the prospect of being alone with Barbara. If only her sister had gone to the beach too. She could have had the flat to herself, instead of having to endure stilted conversation over dinner – usually a clumsy concoction of Barbara's, or a takeaway pizza when they wanted to treat themselves. When one of them felt it was absolutely necessary to talk, it was usually heat-related ('God, I'm melting'; 'It must be getting close to forty'; 'When are we going to get air conditioning like the rest of civilised society?'). Mauro's name was never mentioned, and both made a pointed effort to avoid any question that might be perceived as personal.

'It's too hot to eat,' said Barbara, wiping the pizza grease from her fingers. 'Maybe now's the time to go on a diet. You know, I read in a magazine that there's something called an ice cream diet. You only eat ice cream – nothing else.'

'Really?' said Grace, without a trace of interest in her voice.

'But I think you must get sick of it pretty quickly. I mean, even if you change flavours, it's still always ice cream, isn't it?'

They were really plumbing the depths of banality now. Grace sighed heavily and took a sip of Coca-Cola, which was so warm as to be almost undrinkable.

'By the way,' said Barbara, 'where were you last night?'

'At Caroline's. Obviously.'

'And what are you doing tonight?'

'Maybe going to Caroline's again. Or Sara's, now she's back.'

'You could invite them here. Now that Mummy's away, you could have sleepovers here every night. I don't mind.'

'What does it matter to you if I'm here or at Caroline's house?'

'I'm just saying. Also, I feel sort of responsible for you.'

'You're just looking for an excuse to spy on me. Either that, or you're lonely.'

'That's not true.'

Her remark had had the intended effect; Barbara looked at once ashamed and a little hurt. Then she swallowed and said, 'I've been worrying about you, you know. I know you think I should just mind my own business, but I can't. I can't stop thinking about your scar. How did you get it?'

She asked with flat, timid intonation, hardly daring to make it a question.

'I told you, I'm not telling you. Not unless you want your thing with Mauro to—'

'Never mind Mauro. Please, can we talk about it?'

'No.'

'It's not just the scar. You've changed. I hardly recognise you sometimes.'

'You're imagining things.'

'I'm not. The only explanation I can think of is drugs, though that wouldn't explain the scar. But when I see you in the morning sometimes, it's like you're not even here. You're just... *absent*.'

'I'm tired. I haven't been sleeping well.'

'It's not the same thing, and you know it.' Barbara was speaking with that superior tone Grace hated.

'Just because you're older than me doesn't mean you get to act like Mummy.'

'Well, if Mummy can't know then someone has to look after you.'

'I don't need looking after. I need to be left alone.'

'You're left alone *all the time*. You're never here. You could be using drugs for all I know. Going out with Caroline to take God knows what and then engaging in – I don't know – some weird self-harm ritual.'

Grace laughed.

'You're not far off.'

There was a long silence as Barbara stared at her. Stared and stared, as though she had just encountered an intruder in the middle of the night. Grace should have felt mortified, or at the very least uncomfortable, but instead she found that she didn't really care. Her half-confession had been liberating. What could Barbara do, anyway? She was only family. After the conversation with Miss Seymour, Grace felt that she could fight them all.

'I have to tell Mummy,' said Barbara quietly. She said it as though it embarrassed her; this was the absolute last resort.

'Are you going to call her?'

They glanced at the phone on the wall, at the scrap of paper with the hotel number.

'Yes.'

'But you know that I'd call her afterwards and tell her all about you.'

'Yes,' said Barbara. It came out as a whisper.

'If I were you, I'd wait.'

'For what?'

'Till they come back, at least. We've got a week.'

'What difference does it make?'

'Not a lot. It saves the awkwardness of the phone call, though. Some things ought to be said face to face. Also, it gives you time to think of an explanation.'

'Me?'

'For Mauro.'

'Grace, you're being so unreasonable.'

'You're making me be unreasonable.'

Barbara was still looking at the phone. Then she watched Grace cross the kitchen, take the paper from the counter, and tear the hotel number into shreds.

'This way you won't be tempted to call her. Or *him*. I know it must be hard.'

If Grace had slapped her, her expression would have been much the same.

'I think I will go to Caroline's tonight,' said Grace decisively. 'Don't wait up for me.'

This time it wasn't a lie. Instead of cycling out of the city, which was what she usually did when she claimed to be going to Caroline's, she walked through the city centre in the humid dusk, oblivious to car horns and swallows and all the noise and colour that surrounded her. She reached Caroline's flat just as the street lights were coming on, illuminating her bedroom window. Sara was already there, trying to keep her hands steady as she painted Caroline's fingernails.

'What's the point?' Grace sat on the bed and watched. 'One night out there and it'll all be ruined.'

'Yes, but it looks nice for now,' said Caroline, admiring the hand that had been finished.

'And it feels good to do something normal,' said Sara. 'Doesn't it?'

They spent an innocent evening together, talking and watching TV, and eating the cake Caroline's mother had made in a rare burst of domestic productivity. Grace watched Sara closely – it was easier when she was not drinking – and tried to see what was different about her. There was a slight tremor in her voice, and an air of anxiety that was definitely new, even if Sara had sometimes seemed nervous in the past. Whenever Dionysus or the bacchanals came up in conversation she quickly changed the subject, which was hardly necessary in the privacy of Caroline's bedroom.

Caroline was cheerful – almost *too* at ease, considering everything that was happening. If she noticed Sara's nervousness it didn't seem to bother her, and from the way she talked you might have thought her life was perfectly ordinary. Grace found it almost offensive, the way Caroline talked about shopping and other trivial things as if these were the most interesting aspects of their lives. But as she watched Caroline change into her nightdress, Grace had to admit to herself that the main reason she was annoyed was that since the argument, Caroline had practically been shunning her. Even when they were alone together, Caroline behaved as though they had only ever had a platonic friendship, nothing more. Grace liked to think that it was different during the bacchanals, but there was no way of knowing. Each night was a black hole that spat them out and left them with bruised bodies and empty minds. She would never have a single, solid memory, let alone any definite proof. That night, lying in bed next to Caroline and listening to the unmistakable soft breaths of sleep, she wondered if it would ever happen again while at least one of them was fully conscious.

She had been lying awake for some time, her thoughts too confused and chaotic to drift into sleep, when she became aware of Sara tossing and turning on the mattress by the foot of the bed.

'Sara,' she whispered. 'Are you still awake?'

There was a pause, and then Sara whispered back, 'Yes, I can't sleep.'

Grace got out of bed, taking care not to disturb Caroline, and crouched down on the floor beside Sara.

'Are you all right?'

'Why?'

'You don't seem all right. You seem... I don't know how to describe it. Scared, almost.'

'I suppose I am.'

'Scared of what?'

'I don't know exactly.'

She couldn't see Sara's face, but the tremor in her voice was even more striking in the darkness.

'You must have some idea.'

'It's just this feeling... and a dream. I know it sounds stupid.'

'What dream?'

'I'm in confession. Normally you can't see the priest, of course, but in my dream we're face to face. I'm telling him everything – literally everything – that I've seen and done. All my sins. Even the things that aren't sins. Little details, like the tears in my dresses or the colour of the sky after it happens. Then, all of a sudden, he's covered in blood. It's like this great waterfall – like someone's pouring it all over him, only I don't know where it's coming from. It's this steady stream, so thick that soon I can only see his outline. I wish I could explain. It's just so awful.'

'It's just a dream. It doesn't mean anything.'

'I know, but it's still horrible.'

'You're not going to confess, are you?'

'Of course not.'

Caroline stirred in her sleep, and they were silent for a moment, holding their breath without knowing why. Then Sara continued, 'I haven't been to church for months.'

'Good.'

'It's so hard though.'

She let out a shaky little sigh. Grace said nothing. This time the silence lasted so long that she thought Sara might have fallen asleep. She was just about to get into bed when she heard Sara whisper,

'Sometimes I get this feeling. It's like the most awful thing's about to happen.'

'What thing?'

Sara didn't answer.

'What thing?' Grace asked again, louder. She waited until she was sure that Sara was either asleep, or pretending to be asleep, and then crawled into bed beside Caroline again. Maybe Sara was finally going mad. Not the ecstatic madness that they knew so well, but the irreversible, unhappy madness that got you sent to rooms with white walls and bars on the windows. If it was happening, she supposed there was no way of stopping it now. Some things were inevitable.

XII

Grace walked into the kitchen, still half asleep. It was only the sight of Barbara attempting to cook that gave her some idea of what time it was. She had come home early in the morning, her hands smeared with blood and her head still spinning, and gone straight to bed. Sometimes the after-effect lingered, and even now, having slept for several hours, she could feel that weird energy pulsing through her. She seemed to inhabit her body more fully, with a deeper awareness that made her sensitive to even the subtlest sensations. The sunlight blinded her, the smell of the coffee was overwhelming, and the churning, familiar ache in her stomach was so intense that she could distinguish each individual pinprick of pain, yet somehow the combined effect gave her a sense of peace. She was living on a higher plane of existence, while Barbara bustled around with pots and pans, oblivious.

'Grace, do you know how to boil an egg?'

'Of course.'

'Can you show me how? I've made a mess of it.'

'Oh, in that case... no, I don't know.'

'Never mind, I suppose I'll just have to have a sandwich instead. Do you want one?'

'Yes, please.'

Grace sat at the table, dreamily running her fingers over the rings in the wood, while Barbara prepared their meal. Grace wasn't sure if it was technically breakfast or lunch, but it didn't matter.

'They'll be back in a few days,' said Barbara. 'I can't wait.'

'Are you sure about that?'

'I meant for the cooking.'

'I'm looking forward to our family meeting.'

Grace hadn't meant to laugh, but it came out before she could stop herself – a shrill, hysterical laugh.

'What's the matter with you?'

'What?' She was still laughing.

'Just look at yourself. You've got that awful, empty look in your eyes again, and now you're laughing at something that isn't even funny.'

'But it *is* funny.'

Barbara's seriousness was making it even funnier. Grace would never be able to make her understand that none of it mattered. Their secrets were only powerful because they called them secrets, but neither of them had anything to fear. Tears, scandal, disgrace, so what? Dionysus would laugh too. It was like fearing the rain.

'It doesn't matter, you see,' said Grace. 'If we get wet.'

'What?'

Grace thought, *It's only rain. It's only water. The god will give us shelter, or give us wine to make us forget. Drown our sorrows. Drown ourselves. Or is it burning? For him, I'd do it all.*

Grace said, 'Nothing.'

Poor Barbara. She didn't understand, and she was practically squirming with guilt and discomfort. Her inability to boil an egg paled in comparison to her other failures.

'I should have said something earlier,' said Barbara. 'I feel like the worst person in the world.'

'You're not that bad. Comparatively.'

'God, it's like you're talking in riddles. Please can you tell me what's going on?'

'I'm fine,' said Grace. 'Absolutely fine.'

Grace smiled a spaced-out smile which was less than reassuring, then got up and left the room, still feeling quite serene. She hadn't even been lying, after all. She *was* fine. The god was having some kind of crisis and Caroline no longer cared about her, but as long as the influence of the wine lasted, she was happy.

These days the wine was much more powerful, so that they felt drunk for hours afterwards. She usually savoured the sensation, loving the slow shift from drunken daze to heightened awareness and back again. It gave her a sense of divine indifference, and she imagined it was the closest a human could come to feeling like a god – the glorious feeling of being above the world while belonging to it wholly, truly, with your flesh indistinguishable from the atmosphere surrounding it. Most of all, she loved how the wine made everything beyond the shimmering confines of her body beautiful yet utterly unreal. She treasured these hours when she could think of Caroline, even look her in the eye, without the slightest pain.

Yet it wore off. It always did, sooner or later, and the memory of the pleasure was not enough to protect her. One afternoon she lay in bed remembering Caroline's smile as she described what she had done, and the mere thought of it made her feel ill. She had to do something. She couldn't just lie here in stale sheets and let Caroline slip away, drifting into realms where she could not follow.

She chose her moment carefully. In the aftermath of the violence, Caroline was often at her softest, her most affectionate. The blood that had horrified them the first time now seemed entirely right and natural, and even though they were both covered in it, Grace hardly noticed. The bodies were far away, Sara was nowhere to be seen, and while Dionysus's presence lingered on, there was no sign of him in the woods that morning. They were alone.

Grace began it, but there was no resistance from Caroline, not even a momentary hesitation. She was so used to it that her body responded before her mind was fully conscious. It seemed to happen in slow motion – clumsy lips kissing and licking away the bloodstains, fingers crawling and slipping, their bodies pressed together as she desperately tried to keep the feeling. If only they could do this forever, nothing would ever come between them again. Not even a god.

Then, without warning, Caroline pulled away. It was over too soon. Grace was left with empty arms and the sudden, stark realisation that there was nothing she could do to keep her. The wine had dulled some of her senses, and she didn't realise she was crying until the tears turned into sobs. She cried until she could no longer see clearly and the branches above her were transformed into a green haze.

'You're never satisfied,' said Caroline. 'What do you want now?'

'It's not what I want, it's what I – I *need*.'

'What do you need?'

'Something that stays still. Something to hold on to. I don't even know. Sometimes it feels like one of these nights, I'm not going to come out on the other side.'

'Wouldn't that be wonderful.' Caroline slowly, ineffectually wiped her fingers on a handkerchief. Grace had a sudden fantasy of someone finding them there. She imagined the shock, the disbelief, the police and the ambulance, their parents in tears, psychiatrists and rooms with white walls. For a moment it didn't seem so bad. Then she looked up and saw that he had found them. He stood among the trees, appearing all the whiter in contrast to their bloodied clothes. Grace was reminded of paintings she had seen of Christ, only this man was not good and had never pretended to be.

'I want you to do something for me,' said Dionysus.

The world was dark and quiet and empty. There was only him, shining by his own light, eyes wide as they gazed into his past and future – the eternal circle.

'I want you to do something for me.'

They looked up at him, solemn and silent, their devotion burning through them.

Anything.

Their faces, lit up by the god's light, were no longer their own, but the faces of all the women who had loved him and followed him through the centuries of light and darkness.

'I've been waiting so long for this moment to come, and now it is finally time. I knew from the moment I awoke beneath the pyramid. From the moment Ariadne breathed her last. When I first licked the wine from my lips, when I burst from my father's thigh, I knew, I knew. My girls cannot save me, but they can do something so much greater, so much braver.

'I have given you pleasure and freedom. What will you give me? You have laughed, wept, killed and loved for me, but it is not enough. Not while I am still here, lingering on the threshold.

'You think you are free. Yes, you are – compared to the others. But you do not know *absolute* freedom. The complete liberty of the senses, the final bonds severed. Tonight you will feel it. All of you. I will feel it most of all.

'The road is not enough. The fields are not enough. Tonight I will take you to the heart of the city, that sacred hill. The shrines and temples have gone, the fires burned out long ago, but the energy remains.

This time your sisters will be there to guide you, to feed the flame. You will give yourselves absolutely. Only then will we be free. Are you ready?'

They were trembling with fear and eagerness, their eyes so wide they seemed to contain his whole reflection. It was almost enough to make him smile. He filled a cup of wine and raised it above his head, into the dark air.

'To life.'

XIII

They crawl beneath the orange trees, oblivious to the moon and the white dome shining in the distance. The only light they see is his, terrible and golden, so bright it burns their eyes. Their lips are black with wine, but it is only just beginning. They cling to one another and make low, guttural moans, wanting more, wanting him.

Bodiless fingers claw at them, covering their eyes and slipping into their mouths, while strange winged creatures flutter above them, eclipsing the moon. One moment he is there, the next he is gone, vanished into the trees. They need his light, his warmth. Above all, they need his wine. The snake she was caressing is suddenly twisted in two, crushed by impatient fingers. Where is he?

The singing starts, rising up from the earth, filling the air like the golden echo of a drum. Only women could sing like that, women long dead who know what it is to love and be loved by a god. A beautiful thing. There are no men here.

She is in the grass. She feels the mouth, the tongue, but despite the pleasure riding through her, so strong that at times it makes her blind, she will not be satisfied. She sighs and pulls at the girl's hair, making her stop. They are craving something else now, and though they know the throb of that dark impulse, how it steals through you and casts a red cloud over your vision, it has never been this strong before, this urgent.

The drum beats quicken.

They hold hands, nails cutting into each other's palms. The hill is a whirlwind of sound and movement, animal cries and strange dancers that stamp their feet, making the earth shake. He is above and around them, but they want him inside them, filling them with ecstasy, cutting mind from body and freeing them at last. They are so thirsty, so desperately hungry, that nothing on earth will satisfy them.

They see a deer, alone. She is almost hidden by the trees, but he shines his light and makes her visible. Still holding hands, they creep closer, their breaths so loud that they cannot hear the drums. They want her. One step closer, then something shrieks and they are on her, tearing into her skin, pulling at her hair and limbs with all their god-given strength. Her screams only excite them. Fingers are twisted off one by one, scattered across the grass. Her dark hair is torn from the roots and now hangs from the branches of the trees. The screaming seems to go on forever, until her body ceases to be a whole, a single, unified thing, and is transformed into bloody fragments.

Walking across the wet grass, they look for him. They are still shaking, hearts racing. The blood is in their eyes, soaking their hair and the tattered remnants of their clothes, and still it is not enough. They want him. He wants them to find him, and they will.

The gravel crunches beneath their bare feet. They follow the path to the edge of the hill, to the place where the dome hovers on the horizon like the setting sun. He is there, waiting for them, beautiful as only gods and the dead can be.

Someone must be following, someone leading the way into the trees, but what happens next is not clear. The night is so dark, the music so wild and loud. When they do it to him, he makes no sound, no resistance. The last thing he sees – and it is his dying wish, that it should be the last – is the silver moon. Then he is in pieces, falling where the oranges once fell.

Even though he is gone, the music goes on and on, louder and louder. They stand still and feel the slow return of something they cannot yet name.

'I – I –' she stutters, and touches the other girl's face as if it is her own.

Then they are screaming, running into the hot night. They run out of the garden, away from the blood and the orange trees, and into the silent, lamp-lit streets where people sleep behind high walls and shuttered windows. They run down the hill, screaming until they wake up the city, screaming so that he might hear them.

If he hears, they never know.

Acknowledgements

First and foremost I want to thank every person who pledged for *In Exile*. The book you're holding right now quite literally wouldn't exist without you. Whether you're a friend, a relative, or a generous stranger, I'm so grateful for the faith you had in this book. Thank you.

A huge thanks to the team at Unbound (Xander, Josephine, Sara), and to Kwaku for being there at the very beginning and guiding me through the process. My amazing editors, Eleanor Rees and Claire Gatzen, made *In Exile* an infinitely better book – thank you!

Thank you to my English and Classics teachers at Surbiton High (Mrs Ditchfield, Mrs Henry, Ms Huntley, Mrs Hay, Mrs Spooner). I appreciated your support and encouragement at the time, but perhaps even more so in hindsight. Everything's connected – without you I wouldn't have gone to Oxford, or ended up in Rome, and I might never have read *The Bacchae*, in which case *In Exile* wouldn't exist, and my life would be very different...

From excellent teachers to excellent tutors. I'm grateful to everyone who taught me at Oxford, no matter how briefly, but especially to Bart Van Es, Jeremy Dimmick and Ben Burton at St Catz, and Stefano Evangelista, who introduced me to the 'Greek gods in exile' genre and the Walter Pater short story that inspired this novel ('Denys L'Auxerrois'). You can't be a writer without being a reader first, and you all gave me the best education in reading that anyone could wish for.

To all my friends across the world – thank you so much. Thank you for pledging, for asking 'How's it going?' and for being excited on my behalf. I'm lucky to have you. The same goes for my wonderful colleagues at the British School, Montesacro. And my students – if you're reading this, it means I've done my job.

To my family – Liz, Dean and Harry Turney – I can never say thank you enough. Thank you for your endless support, but thank you for your criticism too, for your feedback on early drafts and suggested plot changes. (No thanks from Pippin!) Thank you Auntie Barbara for reading and caring from the beginning. All of your encouragement made me feel that becoming a published author wasn't just a dream but something I could actually achieve.

And finally, Valeriano, *amore mio. Sono troppo inglese per farti i complimenti che meriti – soprattutto qua – ma rendi la mia vita romana molto più bella. Grazie di tutto.*

Patrons

Gabriella Aberbach
Eli Allison
Katya Balen
Laure Belotti
Alberto BG
Rachel Blackford
Beatrice Blythe
Nathalie Boisard-Beudin
Davide Bolognesi
Jonathan Bray
Roma Brennan
Will Burgess
Tara Burton
Eleonora Capretti
Sophia Cauteruccio
Andrea Cirilli
Sue Clark
Emily Corbett
Catie Costa
Viona Deconinck
Natalya Din-Kariuki
Alys Earl
Sian Eastwood
Gemma Eglinton
Yenni Fabres
Georgia Farley
Maurizio Fascitiello
Robert Ferri
Fiona Finch
Anne Louise Fisher
Cat Flynn
Caroline Gale

Martina Gannon
Miranda George
Grace Gillies
Lindsay Gillies
Charlotte Goff
Katy Gowland
Harriet Green
Rosie Hans
Sophie Harris
Maximilian Hawker
Anwen Hayward
Johnny Herbin
Ross Herbin
Rebecca Hindle
Vanessa Ianni
Martina John
Christian Jorgensen
Lara Julia
Nataliya Kazantseva
Emma Kendall
Patrick Kincaid
Jan Knight
Khalid Kurji
Roland Lasius
Elizabeth Laval
Claudio Leporati
Julia Lewis
Elizabeth Li
Amy Lord
Olivia Madin
Gregory Mahdesian
Anna Marshall
Joanna Maskens
Alessandra Mattei
Steph McPaul
Martha McPherson